MORE INTIMATE
A LOVER'S KISS

A catalogue record for this book is available from the National Library of Australia

NATIONAL LIBRARY OF AUSTRALIA

Published 2022

ISBN: 978-0-6455595-5-2 (epub)
ISBN: 978-0-6455595-6-9 (paperback)

9 780645 559569

Published with the aid of Jumble Publishing and Editing (https://jumblepublishing.com)

More Intimate a Lover's Kiss

by

Brigid Morrigan

More Intimate a Lover's Kiss

Here is the tale of one soul's journey, the terrible story of a man who would presume so much and place himself so high, to fall for many, many lives and find himself, Vampire Lord and Slave of Satan. In a cycle of damned existence that spanned the world and many hundreds of years, Fate played her fickle hand and one lowly destiny was set on a stage, far off in time and space.

Does the story have a setting? Well, the barren waste of a vampire's heart is the place most travelled, the anguish of the soul of one so accursed. This tale has journeyed the Trade Winds, seeking peace and finding naught but pain in the world, each step along the way an awful lesson in the fate of the soul of man; a path to understanding and awakening, out of the Dark.

I am Julian… This is my Tale.

I have scribed these words
in knowing the creature that I am
and knowing the paths I choose to tread.

On my search for eternal light,
        I accept my Fate.

Contents

Chapter 1

I had not been aware as a child, why my place in society was never fixed, but staying alive and growing up in the times of my youth, did not allow me the luxury of examining the misfortune of my miserable beginnings. How I survived at all to this day is a mystery, since my mother had conceived me after being raped and left for dead on the side of mighty Rome's public *freeway*. She, a gypsy woman, had been rescued at the point of death by my first guardians as they travelled from Pompeii to Gaul, and in their Samaritan hour had taken her to work beholden as a servant. She never recovered from the malaise that had taken her mind when she was found, but her body and womb were rescued by her saviours' meagre generosity in the first weeks of my embryonic life, and she was put to simple tasks in their southern provincial vineyard. My association with that woman was, sadly, brief and my infancy spent in part, fostered with these stern and callous farmers. The matriarch had, somewhat hesitantly, taken me on when I was born, but it soon became clear to them that the malady of my birth damaged foot was a permanent feature, and by the time I had reached my seventh year they cast me from my home.

My youth certainly was that of a vagabond and bastard. I remember most of it sitting at the curb side of a dirty little town square, begging for alms from the ruddy hard women who wore at the pavement with their heels. And yet later, after watching the "lifters" who worked the markets, I took from these same women what they denied me.

I was thin and tired in those innocent days, I had thought it malnutrition, a thought which could amuse me now but as a young boy, caused me great anguish. Always craving to feel the vibrant heat I sensed from those around me, each time my hand would slip close enough to pick a pocket, I would thrill at the fire it would stir in me - the bigger the person the greater the fire, so of course I targeted only the largest and most affluent ladies. The most vivid of memories, were those times when fate allowed me to stand close enough to one of these giant mothers, to take the heat from her very bosom. But I could never say this was healing, since a cuff to the ground was always their response.

Occasionally I would be beaten by the mate of one of my victims, but I soon learned how to cast my eye on the softest and most innocent of targets and somehow, I survived. Even so, my existence was poor, as poor as the place that gave me grim shelter and after years of hiding in alleys, stealing from people who could never give me what I needed, I was caught in the dark like a ship's rat.

A squad of Roman Legionnaires stole through the small coastal village under nightfall, looking to replace oarsmen that had mutinied and been put to death on their barge. My captors laughed when they got me into the hold of my daytime prison, making bets on how long I would live. The bitter edge of their laughter stung me awake from the blow that had seen me abducted, their practised amusement taunted my scrawny frame and the deformity of my withered leg. Yet for all their callous banter, they saw me shackled, manacled and wedged between two barbarians, on a seat behind an oar. Instantly I was warm, the savage pounding in my head abated, I bathed in the infinite and endless heat radiating from the warriors around me, and for all the horror

I'd seen in my brief life, I blessed Rome for keeping its slaves so healthy.

My incarceration in the barge was, to this point in my life, the best home I had known. Two good meals in each day and enough body heat to keep me warm all the time. It was the intimate closeness of human life that saw me grow through my teenage years and saw me grow, almost, to match the size of my bench mates. But as my childish form bloomed into the stature of a young man, in that awful moment when I became beautiful enough to attract the eye of my keepers' master, I was initiated into the hideous truth of servitude to the Roman Empire. Not quite the blustering brawn of my fellow oarsmen, I was no match for the attention given to me in the barracks where we were locked at night.

Out of sleep I was stirred with a large and dreadful hand over my mouth, "Make a sound and I'll kill yer!" A rough, ale smelling shadow came over me and pinned me to my cot. A laugh and a rotten cough followed the stench and a statement that made me cold, "Spread 'm, beauty, or you'll be oarsman no more." There was a pressure on my legs and my thin blanket was ripped away. In his voice, the echo of a viscous bark took me back to the prison barge, and I knew my attacker to be the Legion Sergeant. But this knowing was not to save me, I was much smaller than he and chained to the foot of my cot and so, shuddering with fear, I surrendered.

He chuckled over me as he felt my body go limp and in an instant he was on the bed, reeking with ale, demanding in lustful power and I felt myself tense as he began to roughly work against me. I could see his filthy eyes widen in disbelief as my body inadvertently rejected his advances, and so he

3

took to slapping my face with a closed fist. The pain in my head overwhelmed the pain in my arse and brutally he forced his way into me. I let out a cry of agony as he cracked open my virginity and for that I received another barrage of beating. Blood stung behind my eyes as he used me, lying hard and heavy, pinning me securely, and for hours I cringed beneath him as he worked to spend himself. In his throws he called me "darling" and "sweet" and even played gently with my hair, but I had no ears to hear him. I was minutely aware of each moment of violation and the searing pain of being torn apart by this vile intruder.

When finally he left me, I rolled weak onto the floor and vomited, collapsing pathetically next to the bed. I lay there that night, shivering with cold and pain, and by morning my sleepless gaze was fixed and bitter with hate.

I took my place at the oars, watching for the sergeant under leaden eyes, and when he appeared to drill the oar guards he was smiling. Rage boiled in my mind and impotent fury burst from every pore. Fury of pain stung at my soul and somehow, from some infinite well within me, heat drew from all things living. Life sucked even from the very air, fuelled the very core of my hate and around me the slaves turned suddenly blue and frigid with cold. A few of the smaller men slumped dead behind their oars and a guard, ashen faced, urgently called the sergeant's attention. At the moment he turned to face me, I let boiling hate pour out like licking fire. It roared across the gloomy hold to consume him.

Instantly the vile Roman burst into flames and panic ensued, the screaming inferno fell in a blaze onto the deck before the rows of oarsmen and quickly set the barge alight. The Legionnaires,

4

gripped by fear at the sight of their leader burning beneath them, flocked like startled sheep from the hold, away from the fire and up onto the deck. But we who were tethered into our positions, could only watch as the fire took hold and eagerly devoured the boat.

Within minutes the blaze had greedily consumed the rows of men and was upon me, licking at my club and foot, working its way in searing pain up towards my body. The crisp smell of scorched hair filled my lungs in one last breath, and then I was on fire. In a moment of torment, before my skin with my nerves roasted off my body, I felt as great a pain as any human could bear. And then death, that sweet saviour, held out to me its skeletal hand. Release and freedom from pain was absolute, a sense that overwhelmed the feelings of mortal flesh, I sat transfixed amid the burning pyre, watched the barge tip easily into the water and quietly sink.

Sitting at the bottom of the harbour in a smouldering and waterlogged wreck, I reviewed my life in much the same manner as I have done many times, and finally came to such a conclusion as "What next?" I had been consumed in flames and drowned in the water and still I sat behind my oar, chained in a tomb with the other dead slaves, reflecting on a short and unfulfilled life. The frustration of such justice blossomed within me, and after some time I allowed that to be my first stirring to self-preservation. I was still manacled to my scorched bench mates, their rotting bodies already bloated and covered with a writhing ecstasy of carrion eaters feasting, but though I had burned the same as the other memories of flesh, no meat eater had yet come for me. I scanned myself in the deep water and saw myself whole, but how could this be? I had watched the searing fire consume my eyes before they had shrivelled from their sockets, yet now I could see quite clearly and more, I could see all of me! My foot, the whole left leg that had once been a wasted club had been restored. My form was normal, smooth, perfect and even so, the pain I had been dealt at the mercy of my captors was gone! My eyes, which observed the movements of transient shoals darting in frenzy around the corpses, saw their fleeting dance in torrents of rainbows. They flashed through golden streams of the current, their colours, flow and iridescent beauty, gaudily captured my stunned attention. My gaze danced with their gory play and at last came to fall upon the shackles which held me in this curious tomb. I reached, with an odd knowing, into the metal heart of my chains and seared apart the very fabric of their structure, rupturing the water in an explosive wave, and the fish darted away, helter skelter through the drowned boat.

I vaulted from the bench and swam purposefully, following the direction the shoal had taken, and pushing my way through the charcoal debris of a hole burnt in the side of the barge, let the current take me out into deeper water. I floated along with the sea's movements, my eyes filled with vivid illumination from the captured rays of the sun, dancing in a fury of brilliant life and soft, high song, whispered in an eternal memory of sound. The captured ocean steered my course until I was caught upon a rock at the base of a pier, I had come at last to the mouth of the harbour. Drawing myself up, lizard like on my hands, I was caught dreadfully by a shaft of late sunlight glinting from the water's surface. I flinched from the searing pain of its touch on my newly sensitive eyes and the scorch of awful heat that caressed my naked skin.

Hiding on the evening side of that shallow pier, cowering from the gaze of sunset, I waited in searing misery until the sun's flaming orb had left the sky and wiping streaming tears from my eyes, knew I could not face such merciless heat again. Now dead and newly resurrected, I was to be, by choice, a dweller in the protective shroud of night.

I sat on the edge of the pier for many hours of that first night, reliving the strange and cruel events that had led me to my place in the dark, and cold anger filled my soul. I could plan a journey, any journey that would take me far from this place and the awful memory of my last day in the sun, but as time crawled, a sensation crept into my spine, gnawing and clawing at my innermost places. It spasmed through me awfully as hunger and a freezing need to consume mortal life heat. My need was conscious now, unlike it had been in my ignorant life, to take the essence that had always been denied me, to take until I was burning, filled eternally! And so I ran. Indeed, I was so consumed, I could have been flying even then.

Desolation in my soul raged its need for life heat, guiding me to where I could find people. I sensed a rush of knowing, turned fixated on a small wharf-side hut and drew it to me so it might have been transported. In an instant I was beside the rough window, a blazing wound in the wall, watching around the piercing glow of firelight. The three occupants sat in camaraderie, a pint of ale each to see them through the night. Their mute companionship reflected harsh under the bruising heat of the fire, and flares of life essence danced burning, around and through each human form. Now I could see what had drawn me to their presence, what called to the ice that gathered in my soul, and what marked them so well for me in a world with no light. Had I been less consumed in my hunger, and had I known more of my own being, I may have held some strategy for my approach, but I cared not for diversions then and burst forth into the room, stirring the three soldiers into alarm.

"Slave from the barracks!" shouted one, a hand on the sword by his side, and his gaze burned on my exposed skin.

But my need was greater and faster than his attack. I rushed across the room, knocked the blade from him and in a long slow motion, I gripped his throat in one hand and lifted him easily from the floor. My forefinger edged now with a wicked talon, pierced casually a delicate hole in the neck of the legionnaire, and a pulsating drop of liquid life ran down onto my hand. The touch of mortal heat ran blazing over my skin, calling to the very depths of my hunger and sparked my soul in a yearning that covered all my senses. Drawing the hapless man down to me, my eyes were fixed to the glow of life blood oozing from his neck and bringing him to rest at the end of my nose, I breathed deep of the aroma of his essence. Like the innocence of a new rose, a fragrance that filled my core, my lips parted curious for the pleasure of this essence and my tongue like a viper, darted out to savour its first taste.

Warm. Sensual. Eternal.

A growing pleasure spread gloriously from my tongue. A taste known since before I was born, what I had always needed for my survival, and though in life I had imagined that need was beyond me, now it was mine to take. I ran my tongue along my finger in a yearning lap and let my lips come to rest on the soldier's bulging throat. One strong bite and the flesh came apart under my teeth. A long flood of fresh blood gushed its way to the back of my mouth, and down until my whole body was afloat with glory in the essence of life. I was fixed in my rapture, infinite in its pleasure, warming me, taking me closer to home than I had ever been. Lost in awe of the sweet mercy of human fire, I missed the last beat of the legionnaire's heart.

When the flow of blood came to a startling halt, I drew myself away from his throat, disgusted at the drained corpse, threw the carcass to the ground and turned to face the others. They seemed not to have moved at all, only now stirring and rising to their feet, but I did not dwell on that in my lust for life blood, and I was all too soon to learn of my dreadful talents.

Reaching out, I snared both of them in a grip that had been fuelled by the life of a man and held them for my pleasure. When they realised they had been caught, both men struggled and tried to break free, but my head connected with the temple of one and he fell to the ground unconscious. Struggling and aggressive, I took the other in iron fingers and worked his neck, virgin smooth, up to my mouth. Hysterically the soldier thrashed against my advance, screaming and shouting for help, but I silenced him in an instant. My eager teeth sank into the succulent flesh that clothed a great river of blood, and once again, the floodgate that I opened burst forth with an intoxicating sea of life. The heat of human fire twice thrilled my senses, but too soon the sublime flow had run out, the body that had sustained it hung limp in my hands. Again I was greeted with frustration and disgust for the empty corpse. I shook my head briefly, picked up the unconscious soldier who had fallen in an obscene pile by my feet and raised him before my desperate mouth. My bloodied lips ached for his vital fire, my soul needed to be filled with the pure and living power of humankind. The Roman came suddenly conscious before my voracious lips and panic erupted in his eyes. He thrashed and screamed impotently in my embrace, struggling against his fatal predicament and his life fire flamed across my skin as he begged for me to release him.

I smiled cruelly in the face of his pitiful plea, the strength of my will silencing him, "No," I said softly, "you are mine now and so too the life that you hold. What would make you think that I would ever let you go?" I took hold of his stubbled chin when he moved to turn away, holding his face close to mine and in his mind, terror took hold. I opened my mouth, advanced on his neck and bit right through the beginning of a scream. As an ecstasy of life blood flowed from him, the struggle subsided. I was aware when his end came and held myself from draining the flow that came from his dead heart and so, with this last kill there was no hint of sour carrion blood, I was left intoxicated and in love with the piercing sweet essence of living mortal fire.

Now I would not say I was a callous man, but my wits in the days just after my awakening and my need for vengeance, for the brutal crime that dammed me to existence in the night, would not do me the honour of allowing me morals. The need of my body, for the life blood of mortals, was stronger in me than any thoughts of right and wrong as I rampaged my way across Gaul.

Finding shallow caves and corners by day, I hid in agonising misery from the cruel harsh light of the sun, letting my life take its meaning from the darkness of night, stealing and killing where I would to fill the needs of my new nature. Neither concealing my crimes nor my path, I made my way steadily along the country of Rome's fine freeways, moving northeast out of Gaul, picking easily on the regular garrison posts that fell in my way. Travellers on the road, to their fortune, were immune to my attentions these first nights, my vengeful need for Roman blood blinkered my sight, casting its own protection on their bright flames in the dark.

Growing a trust for the talents that were flowering within me, I learned how to fly through the will of quick movement, and how to hold myself shadow like in the dark and more terribly, I discovered my ability to subvert the will of mortals. I raped the blood from their dying bodies, holding their small and fragile minds, cloaked, frozen under this new knowing of my will. So I made my way by night and grew to know the creature that I had become.

I flew high over the freeway, the full moon bright on its stone face and was drawn, a firefly to the next Roman post on the road. I had made two kills earlier in this night and was ready for a third. Landing silent in the darkness at the edge of the fort, I scanned the perimeter for a victim and was arrested by the sound of a woman sighing in the night. Turning my attention, I could see into the room where the whore lay abed with her Roman lover, their heat in the night reaching out to me. I was taken in awe by the blaze that came from their sexual union and let it carry me into the room.

I stood yearning in the light of a single lamp, its tallow glow no match for the writhing couple, and watched the flames of their passion rise until I was pulled towards them. Transfixed on the blazing heat of union I moved close to their aethereal flames and was dangerously caressed by the billowing energy. Like a moth I hesitated on the edge of this writhing creation, the woman's soft cries filled the empty night as her passion filled my eyes. I watched in hard fought for silence, reaching into the energy, feeding from the surfeit, but her gaze came sharply to focus on me and in a fateful instant, they knew I was there.

The whore screamed and the soldier, with more energy than I would have credited, threw his woman thrashing into my arms. I wrestled with her lithe form and in that moment, the soldier was off the bed and in possession of his short sword.

The Roman quickly moved before me, dragged the whore away with his free hand and poked at me with his blade. "Get out cur!" he barked roughly and darted the sword out to split my skin with the metal tip.

Maybe I would have moved to obey, but my eyes were drawn to the wound I had been delivered on my forearm. I knew he was speaking to me, but I could hear nothing over the gushing roar in my ears and my eyes held fixed to the trail of slow black fluid that oozed on my skin. In my malaise, I received another delicate stripe to match the first, and then a primal rage came over my mind.

…I remember nothing then but a great mist of night and void until, at last, the sour taste of carrion blood filled my mouth…

I threw the empty corpse from me in disgust, the haze and roaring in my mind dispersed, the meagre room restored to my senses. I was greeted by the awful sound of screaming and turned to see the terrified whore cowering in a shadowed corner. Quickly I moved to her, crouching down, breathing a deep lung full of her exquisite life heat and abruptly her scream stopped. I brushed my lips across her cheek and breathed like ice by her ear.

"Would you like my love?" I asked, letting my fingers lightly caress this new aura of terror that danced in waves across her skin. Although panic still clung to her, I could feel her press into my hand and I was moved to sigh. My voice stilled to a breeze, her sobs grew soft under my touch and the sight she had witnessed, whatever that may have been, flowed like water from her mind. I ran a hand smooth over the supple mound of her breast and my fingertips came to rest lightly on the arch of her neck. "I have never tasted a woman," I said simply and saw the innocence of my gaze reflected in her cow brown orbs. My sight slipped from their reflections and dropped onto her throat, watching minutely a tiny pulse throb under her kid smooth skin.

"Will you hurt me?" Delicate speech stirred the muscles of her slender neck.

Looking back into her gaze I knew I could answer in truth and I said, "No, oh beautiful whore, I will kill you but you will have little pain." Compassion rang in my voice and stirred tears in those earth-coloured eyes, she nodded imperceptibly at the deal.

Savouring the moment of drinking from that flawless and feminine neck, I was gentle with my touch, stroking and caressing her tenderly as I sat close beside her, nuzzling my face softly to her throat. Her woman's feel and smell flowed over me and schooled my bite, arrested my teeth upon the delicate skin, intoxicated by the sublime pleasure that female flesh could hold. Lightly her throat pulsed under my sensitive lips and as she held on to me with a gasp, I let my teeth shear through her skin and into the blood-filled vein inside. Life gushed from the woman into me, I could feel the flow burst into my body, a sensation so intense I could hear the roar of its tidal wave in my soul, and eagerly I drowned in this ocean of female life. I heard soft cries of sweet agony as I drained her body and all too soon she died.

I pulled free of her throat as her heartbeat stopped and closed my eyes in bliss, the ruby sight of her life essence filled my mind. I held the dead woman against me with reverence.

…Horribly, a vision flashed into my memory…

The memory of a time and place that was not my own came around me and the lamplit scene of another death. A woman was naked, shrinking in the corner, dying in the same carnal manner of this whore. But in the instant I saw, I knew intimately, awfully, that the woman was me! In the last heartbeat, I saw her murder with her own eyes. Her attacker sat before her, the cool, blood smeared face of a pale and beautiful angel.

My eyes flashed open in horror; the kill's fresh calm pushed cruelly away by what I had seen. What was the meaning of the vision in my mind? Why should it suddenly come to haunt me in this moment? I pushed the whore from me shocked, and recoiled from the scene. I could not look at the carnage around me with such an awful spectre bright in my mind and turning, I fled from the room.

I took to the air and pushed my way out into the night, rushing blindly as fast and far as I could go, being chased by my memory from the Roman post. Out over the road and high above the meadows, I flew recklessly away from that terrible vision. Fields gave way to rough hills, jagged and barren, reaching for me in the glow of false dawn, their cruel spires gave up haunting shadows of damnation. Anguish spurred my flight, ranging on through the hills, their great expanse a moment in my passing and high over the rapidly approaching forest. Lost in a torment of confusion, I was blind to the advance of the sun, its passage hastened by my headlong rush east, and before I could prevent its assault on my senses, the universal blaze had penetrated the horizon. Like arrows lanced from the sun's very soul, fire exploded in my eyes, and caught frozen in the sky, I thralled in the ecstatic pain of growing day. In that moment of torture and bliss, the sun had caught my heart and consumed my body with its promise of light and heat, trapped me like a moth burning in a candle flame. Its awful love seared my eyes from their sockets and pierced deep into my mind. I broke into a torrent of sweat, my body racked by the heat of pain that spasmed in great floods from my tormented brain and in that exquisite moment, my senses went blank.

I awoke briefly as my fall carried me into the high canopy, the crashing foliage whipped painfully to bring me back to consciousness. Then, another cradle of leaves and a collision with an ancient stone hard branch sent my mind once again into oblivion.

Cool gloom greeted my swollen eyes when I first opened them to the deep green that surrounded me. The dark and quiet place was soothing to my sun loved pain. Careful against my aching head, I rose to the magnificence of the chill forest. Haunting and ghost like, the ancient trees watched me in protective eternal night and although I could still feel the pull of sunlight, the depth of green was rampart against the day. Still and cool, these mighty sentinels gave off no flames to offend my sight, their solid and eternal forms soothed away my pain. I was caught by the sound of whispers held on the air, the heart of magic. And I reached for the sound, an echo calling, holding for me the promise of shelter from eternal damnation.

"You are home now," there was a whisper carried on the light breeze and an imagined voice caught my ear. Assaulted by a tempestuous wind, I was blown off balance, "Imagine nothing vampire. See us, don't see us, hear us or not, this is our place."

Peering intensely into the gloom, I was greeted with a vision of unearthly heat, dancing before me. "Dryad," I murmured under my breath, the recognition of these creatures came from some deep corner of my mind.

"The trees have given to you the knowing of us." One of the forms danced inches from my face, its glowing essence forming briefly into a reflection of my eyes which blinked once and then disappeared. "We will care for you until the end of time."

Muffled peace stirred and found me in the gloom as the dryads spoke and I carelessly allowed myself to be taken by their promise.

"We hold peace for you, oh beautiful one. The forest has told us of the creature that you are, and what beauty to have in the first of your kind. Stay and be loved by us and we will show you who you are." The whispering voices caressed me like love. "Rest with us and we will tell you of your unique incarnation."

Beguiled, I lay on the soft forest floor and on a breeze, dryads whispered to me of my fate.

"In the days before humans walked the soft green carpet of our mother, our bright creator gave forth love, the glory of life. In sublime wisdom, our creator gave all things the gift of its own great essence, so all might live within the union of heavenly light. All things echoed the presence of the Word of Spirit and lived in the grace of that Word.

"Loving all and knowing deeply of its own being, our creator begat its own sun in glorious union with the universe and so too, our mother, whose beauty resounds the Word, far into the Cosmos. When grace stretched out its wonder into the realms, then came forth on the face of our mother, all manner of the creator's presence and the spirit of all that is mystical was born. Like the sun in the sky are the powers bestowed upon creatures of spirit, tied in the magical creation dance between the sun and our mother, and we the creators on earth. All manner of things came from our blessed oneness, and with our mother we filled the void.

"Without discrimination and where creation was needed, we spirits poured out the reflected love of the sun and took our place eternally joined to our mother. Great mountains, vast forests, deserts of hot blowing sands, oceans consumed of life, all things we created and bound ourselves to, our devotion to the vastness of creation itself. Mighty gorgons we loomed cycle after cycle, caring for our supplication and our creator wept for the grace of our reflected love.

"In wisdom born of the divine Word, humans were brought forth onto the face of our mother, their powers, a blessing for all creatures. Within the soul of their clay forms, the light of the sun shone forth clear, these unique beings were created in the image of their father and unlike the beautiful reflection of the creatures of spirit, were separate. Born each time with a new and clear knowing of the creator and our blessed mother, each life came forth with choice. A choice to be born and a choice to die, with the blessed gift of resting in death, laying down life and taking up that mantle as they chose. But much more than this was the creator's gift of the choice of his knowing. To live eternally a beacon of light or to turn from the sun and forget. Forget the source of the beginning of life, forget grace and the Word of creation and live alone, to die alone without seeing the light of grace flowing from all things.

"And there were those who forgot, humans who lived without seeing the light of the sun, hiding in the darkness even from the essence of that which created them. Committing the only sin against the universe itself, humans fostered a knowing of only their small and immediate selves, denying the existence of all else in their separation of form. They spawned cycle after cycle, each encouraging the next to forget what all are born knowing and in isolation, fell from grace. And when so far from the vision of All are humans, that an act of creation can be committed in the gravest atrocities against the Word, a creature is born.

"Half returned to the realm of the spirit and half in the realm of flesh, held to the world of mortals by his need to gather the heat of the sun that burns within them, the vampire hides his face from all beings. His sight in the power of the eternal sun is so great that his eyes will burn from their sockets, should he turn upon its infinite gaze. So lost is the fallen soul of vampire kind, that condemned forever to walk in the dark is this pitiful creature, even the blessed release of death no solace, for the cruellest fate is to be awoken as even the taste of rest is held just beyond reach.

"But we will give you rest, blessed vampire first of your kind. Sleep, for your walk in this realm is just beginning and reaches for aeons before you. We will care for you and give you a dream, and teach you what you need to begin."

In the twilight still of the watching trees, I slept cradled gently on the forest floor, and I dreamed a dream of becoming.

I flew over the dark forest a free being, the full face of the moon shining on me with its radiance, reflecting iridescent fire in my sight. Cool and silent, the white beacon lit my way as I rose high into the clear night and took the knowing of the atmosphere. In my mind's eye the shift of flesh and bone crystallised into an element of air, the sensation of a mist came around me and my human frame dispersed into a cloud. Floating lightly on the currents, I took on substance, bittersweet and given up by the sky, and taken by the mournful rush of the wind, I let my thoughts scatter like mist trails in the cool air. Dryad song reached for me, high and soft, and their tale of my damnation echoed my place in the dark.

I pushed my will out over creation in an agony of injustice, feeding the heart of my storm self from a well of cold longing, and grew to boil with the fury of a storm. I filled the sky, raging at the crime of my existence in the dark, boiling over the spectre of the dryads' tale and rained lightning and thunder from fury in my soul. My fate had been sealed by a trick of human vanity in which I could not fathom my place, and now I was trapped to walk eternally, so far from the sight of God. Pouring forth torrents of sheeting rain and hail to the land below me, the violent storm purged the edge from my anger and when the rage was spent, I shackled the cold burden of my fate. Racing thunderheads slowed, melting in the face of my bitter will, congealing, rolling inwards, and the fury that I had been regained human form.

Down I travelled, coming to rest upon the earth once more, taken by the path of my dreaming, and I was nursing with a noisy pack of cubs at the breast of a she-wolf. The mother had neither noticed my arrival, nor did she stir as I was accepted to suckle with her active brood, and in the milk that flowed from this gentle mother was instinct; instinct to vanish in the night, the will to fade into shadow and the four-leggeds' cunning mastery over the dark. Wisdom of instinct and strength to control its savage counsel was given to me at the breast of the wolf, the knowing of when and how to kill, and the resources to sense the approach of others while taken in that rapture. Clever keys of survival, false trails and deception, flowed with the luxury of milk, all instincts to carry me and more, indeed, an intimate and eternal knowing of the mind of an unrivalled predator.

And then, with she-wolf leading, we were running silently through the dark forest. Our passing whipped a dance of branches swaying in our wake and with my new sight watchful of movement, we ranged through the trees. Racing lightly with the cool wind, we ran, knowing the presence of life, smelling and hearing the small forest creatures scatter fear-scented from our path. I breathed deeply the air around me, caught a smell so fine, a delicious aroma of powerful essence and I knew the intimate draw of life. In the darkness, the she-wolf slowed her pace and came carefully, to stand watching a small clearing in the trees. Upwind and glorious in the moonlight, the shadowy form of a stag was scraping its antlers on the rough edge of a rock, sharpening away velvet in preparation to fight for a mate. Silently the wolf touched her nose to my naked flesh. Then she was off, stalking in a wide circle one way and I knew I was expected to copy her in the other direction. In a union of unspoken law we attacked the deer.

The unwitting creature stood basking in the moonlight and scenting us too late, we were upon it. The wolf flung herself in a feint at the head of the stag and deftly avoided the long tines it lowered in its own protection. But in that defensive moment, the deer exposed a shoulder and I flew at him, teeth and talons bared. The creature screamed, my long fangs anchored easily in the soft hide as I worked my jaw closed through straining muscles, and he wrenched me from the ground, thrashing in an attempt to dislodge me from my hold. But the she-wolf used the distraction to her great advantage and besieged the throat of the beast. In a single, expert bite she brought our victim crashing to the ground.

Still alive though brutally sedated, the stag lay panting before us, the smell of his fear hanging an aphrodisiac on the crisp air and the she-wolf pawed the ground, my tacit order to finish the kill. A dangerous glint in the eye of my accomplice betrayed the thin line drawn by control over instinct, the justice of a social hunt was the need for social rules and in the game of kill or be killed, that code

21

was judged by life and death. So, with a movement of submission not natural to my human form, I leaned cautiously over the injured beast and tore a living muscle from its heaving neck, the succulent blood gorged meat oozed in my hands as I laid it at the feet of the wolf. In display of her position as leader, she sniffed my offering disdainfully and raising a bloodied lip to snarl, lifted the piece of deer and stalked off into the darkness. I watched silently as she left, knowing there would be no more recognition of the moment we had shared and when she disappeared, I turned on the fallen stag before me. Stirred by its death scent in my nostrils, I attacked the beast with a passion and a need to drink, sinking long canines deep into the quivering flesh of its neck and I gorged on the river of life that pulsed thickly from the open vein.

And in that enchanted moment, I was flying.

High again in the night, I let the breeze hold me hovering in the sky, small and dark, a shadow against the heavens. What had been my body as an element of nature, now cradled my sensitive form of bat in flight, and I had a deep knowing of my place in relation to all things around. My voice and hearing worked as one to hold my position above the landscape and though my eyes could see little, the shrill of my high song echoed clear in my sensitive ears. Clever and efficient, bat's augmented senses gave me intimate understanding of my surroundings and the small, quivering nose guided my flight on an airborne trail of blood. Sounds and the searing aroma of mortal life laid an impeccable path for my descent from the sky and I dropped toward the dark earth on its trail, eager to reach the scent that drew me on. I hovered beyond the deep orange glow of a campfire standing sentinel against the dark, and I looked down to watch the bright fires of two humans sitting close together before the small blaze.

In an exquisite moment of knowing the key to changing shape, my aerial form exploded and dropped, a hundred vermin, scattering around the boundary of light. Through a veil of fragmented consciousness, I approached my victims and in an instant was upon them, their screams ringing clear through the dark forest. I thralled in the lust of a double attack, tearing, renting flesh and sinew with a hundred hungry mouths, eager to cleave the very life from their horror-stricken bones. With vision clouded in blood, my vermin form gnawed in short time, through to the dead hearts of my victims and in the ecstasy of the kill, was transformed again into the now familiar form of a cloud.

Rolling, a mist carried lightly by my will along a track, I came across another small camp in the deep forest. A brightly painted wagon sat beside the crude road that crossed my path and fog-like and still, I settled around it.

A woman as brightly painted as her carriage, was tending the small hot fire and started at the sudden mist. I cast my will to strike the mortal witless, a cloak as dense as the haze surrounding the camp, but to my surprise she resisted my touch with a cry.

"Papa, papa come here." She turned slightly, calling urgently to the doorway behind her, but the older man had already come to the stairs.

"I know, Margueritte," he replied in a stifled voice, "come by me now" and beckoned her to him.

They knew I was here. In their minds I saw the vision of my face behind the mist as they penetrated my shroud, and together they radiated an unconscious heat that consumed me in fire. My will shivered under their defence, pain of dissolution recoiled from their flames and wounded, I was forced once again into my human form.

"Quickly, Margueritte, while the creature is vulnerable," I heard the old man call as I fell into a naked crouch on the ground and turned to his shadow on me, a dagger raised to strike me down. In an agonising moment, the delicate fire of metal erupted a tidal wave in my head, as the blade stabbed mercilessly through an eye and lodge to the hilt in my brain. Roaring exploded in my ears and blossomed from my mouth in a cry that echoed thunderously in the heavens. Black blood oozed from my tortured socket, and I rose before the mortals. The old man gasped and fell away to stand cowering beside his gypsy daughter and I raised a hand to touch the knife handle thrust obscenely into my face. The young woman glanced horror stricken at my injury and turned away, but the old man was struck dumb by his foolish actions, so I held his gaze and in deadly calm, withdrew the knife from my head.

I was greeted again with an overwhelming roar of the ocean and staggered a little with the pain of the freshly flowing wound. I cast the savage blade into the fire and screaming, attacked the gypsy. In his dread, he took a step backwards and I used his momentum, flying at him and knocked him to the ground.

Slow, black blood, dripped onto his face as I held him easily beneath me. "You think to kill one such as me, old man," I spat, my voice coming from somewhere beyond the dream. "I am a creature of the darkness, foolish mortal, I am not bound by your existence of life and death. But if you wound me then see what I become." In an awful moment my form shifted and I was gorged with a terrible lust for blood, a hideous new yearning for the essence of mortal life that stirred a brimstone growl from deep within. Under me, the gypsy's eyes bulged wide from his head, and in their reflection I saw my hideous form. A creature with the face of a demon, fangs bristling in my wide evil grin, no lips to conceal their vile cruel points. But in an instant the mirror faded and he was lifeless beneath me. Shocked at being cheated from the taste of life blood, I became aware of the woman behind me, and turned my attention, drooling, to the strain of her screaming throat. With a speed that defied even my cloud form I flew at her, caught her in my long-clawed arms, and suddenly she was still.

"Have you more strength than your father?" My question was a deep growl, stirring air that turned rancid in her nostrils and she looked at my hideous face in rebellion.

"My father was old and stupid," she replied, an edge of old hate in her voice, "but I am not so foolish, I know I am to die."

I threw back my gorgon head and shrieked a laugh at her defiance, even in the clawed arms of my most evil nature, gypsy arrogance flashed in her eyes.

Her voice was sly and quiet as she spoke, and I came close to hear her. "But if I am to die, then I would take from you what you take from me."

Recoiling I pushed her away, suddenly lucid in the midst of dream spawned thrall, her proposal seared my heart like a flame and shocked me from my intent on blood. Terrible isolation and damnation in the dark stirred at the thought of her deal, shocking my form to congeal, once again, into the naked body of a man. I looked into her eyes in the instant of my transformation and in amazement of her gaze, I understood her request. The image of my face had captured the attention of the gypsy and I could feel a small and pitiful tide of love coursing through her heart.

Cold rage welled within me, rebuffing such shallow emotions in the condemnation of eternal life and a bitter laugh rose to my lips. "Love is not something you will find in my realm, mortal!" I spat at her and her eyes grew cold and hard under my derision.

The gypsy looked away, her mind shrouded from me and I could feel cheated hunger growing to take me once more. Indeed, she had not asked for love and even so, freely offered satiation from my terrible appetite. And so, the need for her essence to fill my cold soul shattered my moment of dilemma and again the dream carried me on.

"But for a taste of your blood I agree to your request," and my arms reached out to hold her once again. In a flash, I sank four long canines into the supple surface of her neck and gorged on the exquisite taste of her essence. The long flow of blood slowed as her heartbeat began to fail and within moments of her death I pulled away from her. With my eyes fixed to the punctures in her throat still oozing sweet life I spoke, "And now, daughter of my dreaming, I will keep my bargain." I raked a taloned claw through the skin of one palm and in the roaring of my wound, offered the black liquid for her to drink.

With strength born of a death throe, the gypsy bit into the gash I had opened and the quick draw of blood numbed all sensation about the wound in my flesh. She suckled from my essence until I could feel blood flow from me in great rhythmic throbs of ecstasy and I groaned. The sense of her draining my life fluid caught me in a transported moment. But as she fell from consciousness and that cup of pleasure was snatched wickedly from my grasp, I began to see the awful possibilities of my vile passion. Disgusted at the evil this nightmare could commit, I pushed her from me and fell weak to the ground. The dream had indeed shown me of my existence as a creature of the night, creating others of my kind, damming all around me forever to die and fall from my eternal walk in the dark. Lying wasted by my experience of evil creation, I saw the mortal death of Margueritte. A smile played across her black stained lips, as I watched the last of her rich life blood ooze in a steady flow from her throat, and with a small sigh she was gone.

The soothing sense of fog came about me and I was lifted from the earth once more, to sail out high into the night

…Suddenly I awoke from the dream, dancing forms of dryads flamed all about me and their excitement stirred me from sleep, but when I opened my eyes they came close, beguiling. "Oh beautiful vampire, your dream song fills our forest with light. Do not wake, oh fallen one, you have an eternity to live, and we will fill it for you in your dream."

The whispers of the dryads' sweet voices lulled and caressed me, but my stirring brought forth a seed, a waking hunger for blood and it shattered their spell. Slow growing instinct overcame my need to rest and I rose, shaking their enchantments from my mind.

I called out to the forest, cutting through soft pleas to lay down and rest, breaking the silence that weighed upon me. "I have heard your words, dryads, and I have seen the things of which I am

27

able. But rest with you can only lengthen my eternity, your dreams can only cause me pain. You have twice damned me now, lost in night, both awake and asleep. I condemn you as evil, more evil than I, oh sisters, and I shall not be fooled by your ways again!"

The soft whispers around me changed to cries and shrieks while I spoke, and visions of aether danced in fury before me as the dryads heard my mutiny. In a tornado of vicious winds, they came for me, whipping the forest in their rage to strike me down, and I catapulted myself up into the trees above. Screeching like harpies, the dryads chased me through the high canopy, encircling me in a trap to hold me in their realm, but as I saw the forest roof approaching, I congealed into the airy form of a cloud and slipped past their impotent rage.

High in the atmosphere, I flowed with the currents of air, rushing far from the dark forest and boiling through the night, unseen, silent and following the need that had stirred within me. Below, I watched the hills fall away to long fields, and the ragged silhouette of a small village came before me. The flares of mortal life drew me down.

I crept naked along the outskirts of the village, tasting the air for heat of mortal kind, and drawn to the brilliant light of a farmhouse, I paused before the open door. The sound of an angel called melancholy to me in the dark, the cry of song at a mortal's hand as sweet as the draw of blood, and the sound of heaven's music held me transfixed in the doorway. In the house was a man with his back toward the night, a dulcimer alive in his hands, and I was caught while his life flare burned vibrant in my gaze and his genius of love thrilled my soul. I closed my eyes away from the distraction of his mortal heat and the immaculate sound suspended time. My senses were taken by him and his angel song, and lifted me from persecution in the dark.

In an agony that wrenched open my eyes, the music vanished. The musician had turned and was caught in his movements, staring dazed at my rapture. In defence from his innocent judgement, I threw my hands out and turned to flee from the avenging angel, but his words arrested me.

"Don't be afraid," he spoke, his voice soft and as beguiling as the dryads' touch, "I am pleased you like my music," and I turned back to his gaze. "Come into my house and I will play for you." He held up an inviting hand and his skilful essence reached for me.

I was caught in a war between the need for blood and my craving for the beauty of his music. In my hesitation he began to play again, sending imploring fingers of ecstasy to lull me into the room. I moved unconsciously, far from the light of the room's small fire and collapsed heavily against the wall; tears of melancholy flowed unhindered from my eyes. His song spoke to me of all the mortal pleasures I would never know and an eternal place in the sun and when he had finished, cold depression settled on me in a shadow that found a home around my soul.

"You need clothes," his voice broke my silent contemplation and I raised my gaze, stricken and empty, to look at him.

"I will kill you," I replied blunt, but he was shaking his head.

"No, I don't think that you will, vampire. I know of your kind and you have no defence from the magic of my music," and his clear eyes smiled at me. "You look hungry." His statement was simple but true enough to make me realise that he had some knowledge of me. "How long has it been since you fed last?"

My head swam in confusion, the dryads had told me I was the first of my kind, and I remembered no evil acts of creation outside the spirit's dream, so how could the youth know of my existence? Growing suspicion rose in my mind and slowly I shook my head, framing a question from my scattered thoughts. "How do you know of me... of my needs?"

"You are not the first vampire seen in these parts, my friend, although I'll wager you are the most unusual I have encountered. Your vile kind had raped this country for hundreds of years." He shrugged in a light defence of his explanation, "if you are found you will be killed."

I laughed bitterly, mocking his assumption and my voice was hollow, "I died in a Roman barge with fifty slaves, I am undead. I walk the earth eternally, I cannot die!" The end to my statement took me back into melancholy and the torture of my reality. I pushed my damming thoughts away so hunger took me once more, and with a sob I rose from the darkened corner. "If I stay you will die, so I must go."

But he barred my way, gently taking me by the arm and I flinched against the caress of his vital fire. "I will give you clothes and then you can leave." His soft eyes encouraged me and I allowed him to lead me into the small sleeping room beyond. He reached onto a shelf and retrieved a neat bundle. "So you died in Rome?" he asked, casually tossing the folded clothes to me.

As I dressed in the rough-hewn fabric, I briefly told him of the end of my mortal life beneath that harbour in Gaul, and when my tale was finished he was staring, awe filled, into my eyes.

"You are Julian," he whispered.

"No," I replied. "I have no name."

The young bard shook his head in growing excitement, "You *are* Julian. I have heard the tales of vampires in these parts, through all of my journeys to these lands, and the stories of how you came like a thief in the night, to begin that evil race with Margueritte. That tale is legend now, the tale of a gypsy's liaison with the devil and it was she who named you Julian, and she who made your story legend. But that was over five hundred years ago," he paused amazed. Then, "Since you had never again been seen, you had been taken as a fantasy of her making, though Margueritte has been loose in the world ever since."

My face grew grave as he spoke, his words stirring my memory of that insidious sleep, and in that brutal moment I realised the deception, the lie and the callous use of my power to toy with the lives of mortals. Cold fingers touched my soul, bitter resignation to the birth of vampire kind, the chains of eternal life and hunger flooded in. "Then it has been five hundred years and more since I have seen the world and tasted the blood of a mortal," and my lips ached for the swirling heat of his essence. I saw horror growing in the eyes of the beautiful musician and turned my gaze from its pain. "Now let me leave!" and I fled the house.

Out of the darkness of ages of need, instinct led my path away from the calm of the bard's small house and I flew through the quiet village, scanning the streets for life to ease my ancient lust. On the outskirts of the sleeping town, flickers of vibrant heat flared, catching my attention, and I descended upon a lonely horseman in the night. I exploded from the sky, my momentum carrying the rider cleanly from the back of his mount and behind me, I heard the beast whiny and bolt away in panic. I rammed the traveller hard against the high trunk of a tree in my lust, blowing the air from his lungs. Without a thought, I sank eager canines into his pulse. Thrashing and screaming, high off the ground, I held my victim in an iron embrace and gorged my ancient hunger on the power of his life. Cleansed in the sweet release of mortal life, I was aware when the heart came to its last faint beat. I withdrew my deadly kiss and dropped the empty corpse to the ground.

Bliss held me locked in its reverent embrace as piercing heat filled me to the core and I landed, the soles of my feet gently cushioned on the soft earth.

Strength flowed through my form and I was washed clean of the haze of my insane beginnings, created anew in the world, my mind's eye clear sighted and the path of my existence laid out eternally. Free suddenly was I, of the malaise I had endured since my watery grave, indeed even to the crazed beginnings of my mortal life, free to see my life ahead, reaching forward into infinity and damnation. My lust for the life blood of innocent mortals, the insanity of needing its awful touch to restore the knowing of what I am, poured before me in visions of crimes I would commit, if only to survive. Howling with the cry of a wolf, I mourned my doom to the night sky and the endless stars flashed back in tiny mocking flames. A knowing within stirred me suddenly from my indulgence and I flashed a glance at the Eastern horizon. False dawn had stirred on its boundaries and was pushing me to flee. That awful reminder of my prison in the dark, gave forth its warning then to my instinct, I set my sight far from the infinite blaze of morning lights and flew off into the dark sky.

Far away from the approach of dawn I ranged, over fields and hills, villages and towns and eventually to the sea. I slowed my flight and stood on a wind beaten cliff, overlooking this monster before me. The crashing of waves hard against the cliff lifted spume high into the air, embracing me in the cooling sting of salt. Firing my skin from her icy heart, this most holy of water from the primordial mother poured over me, and I plunged from the high cliff into the chill sea below. Swiftly, in imitation of the very denizens themselves, I moved my way through the ocean giant and knew the sirens in their watery home. Their voices called to me in the same lulling sweetness of their sisters in the forest, but I was immune to their foul spells and toyed with them as I passed through their realm. And when the beauty of their song became vile with their true nature, I swiftly rose from their evil clutches and burst forth into the sky. The naked glow of the coast beyond the sea beckoned me, and skipping lightly over the fuming waves, I flew ashore.

Over land I began my search for a den, I could outwit and outrun any creature of spirit, but I could not run forever from the face of the sun, and so, I made my way over the rolling countryside. Soaring above a forest, I came upon a cave, set deep into the harsh face of a cliff side above the trees, and in its haunting twilight, I endured hell's nightmare.

I kept record of that time, cringing under the suffering heat of the sun, flinching from its maddening touch and survived, the lowest of animals, cowering into the darkest corners of the cave. Sitting beside the open maw by night, watching the turning of the stars as they flamed their radiance into the cosmos, I soothed the pain of each hellish day and slowly the rhythm of my need became clear to me. Within the passing of one cycle of the moon, from when it gazed its full face upon me, I could feel clarity slowly leaving me and rising in its place, the pull to kill once more. I marked the times of the moon's blazing glory with a stone on the wall, and watched the crude scratches grow as the hours of sunlight took my mind. By the time I had absently marked twelve of these wandering lines I could see instinct only, my agony in the cave by day and by night consumed my failing senses into a wrenching lust for blood. When the full moon sent her strongest tide toward me once more, the sun had destroyed my reason. Bloodlust had me forget even that the marks had seen a year go by and drowning in freezing hunger, I flew out into the night.

The mortal heat of a village in the forest drew me to its bright fires and I dropped to the ground, an army of rats seeking for prey. I scurried up to the wooden corner of a building and writhed in vermin ecstasy up the stairs. The draw of life blood spurred me on, flames of human union reached out to me through the wall, and I congealed to stand before the door, insane and lusting for their mortal essence. I reached for the handle and silently let myself into the room, their lovemaking blossomed in flaming life around me, and I was caught by the raw blaze flowing from the couple. I stood entranced by their vibrant light, drowning in the flood of human coalescence, easily seduced in my lunacy, until I was alerted sharply by the high scream of the woman on the bed. Her young lover rose immediately to her defence and snatched up a long slim blade that rested idly against the wall. With a cry of rage the pale young man crashed naked across the room toward me, brandishing the sword close to my face.

"Get out, dog!" he barked, his position behind the weapon giving him courage.

But his essence had come perilously close, my hair reached for its vibrant waves and smiling, I bathed in his living fire. I would not be thwarted so easily by this small human; his presence had deeply stirred my hunger and my eyes glinted a dangerous warning to him. "Do not harm me, mortal. You have neither the wits nor the strength to keep me from taking your life and my need is greater than any of your passions."

The young lover trembled lightly at my words, the tip of his sword wavering dangerously close to my skin and in a horrifying accident, the blade fell forward and cut a long gash in my cheek. In pain and rage, black blood from my dead heart flowed in a gushing roar, pulsing down my face and in a convulsing wave of berserk madness, I blacked out…

…Carrion and the stench of a corpse brought me reeling back to my senses, my blood lust inflamed by the bitter taste in my mouth—a terrible knowing of something deeper—and I heard the woman screaming. I turned to see her crouched in the corner of the room and in an instant I came by her, kneeling like her own lover beside her frozen form.

"I have killed others like you."

I caressed her flaming hair, the vibrant heat of its own life snaking along my arm, and I was touched again by the knowing of something haunting, deep in the eyes of this woman. In my lust for the quenching fire of her life, I pushed a gnawing whisper away from my mind and reached my hand around her throat. Drawing her up to my lips, I fixed my deadly fangs into her tender neck.

Long and drowning, a moment of rapture in the taking of life filled my senses with the flow of blood, and in the serenity of her heart's last surrender, I collapsed in ecstasy by the dead woman's side. But even so, in that moment of peace, my gaze became suddenly filled with the memory of a woman dying by my hand and I knew I had seen this vision before. To my horror, the memory gave up more, this time, of its awful truth and I saw through her eyes, the approach of death. The beautiful and terrible angel toyed cruelly with long red locks that framed my feminine sight, and I knew that the blood-stained face in my vision was my own. I was both predator and prey in some awful trick of fate and yet even that moment of truth was no solace, the cruel angel descended terribly upon me, a piercing sweet pain erupted amid my fear and drained away life until I was dead.

My eyes flew open and fixed to the blank face of the woman before me, I had seen her dying twice and knew somehow, that I had been destined to take this path tonight. Fate again had damned me, in this frail human and my vision of another life, that fickle mistress had so casually condemned my soul. In anguish and melancholy pain, I held the lifeless body to me, crying out to the heavens to show me why? Why was I condemned to see the fate of this woman, why was I so condemned to know her to be myself born of another existence, predator and prey equally in fate's game? Why? Why?! Painful questions of my eternal sentence flowed in torrents from my imprisoned soul and dropped like silent echoes into the stillness of the night.

Chapter 2

"Mann'ah, you have been chosen to walk the great road to the city of Pompeii, your skill with Roman law will take you far." The Archdeacon's gold flashed as he drew breath. A light of pride flashed across his familiar face, "On your journey you will be under the mastery of Merlin and will carry all His title and respect. Go well, my son." The ancient High Druid smiled broadly as he clasped my arm and turned in a long moment to present me with the traditional sachel of my new position.

He moved along the line of year-mates onto the next posting, the next fresh journeyman, but I did not hear what positions they had gained. A rush of excitement washed the ceremony from my mind and I was caught in a roaring of my powers that filled my ears and stirred glee to the pit of my gut. I had been assigned to go to the country of Rome's finest civilisation, after nineteen years of study and with only boys for company, I was to go with the blessing of the Archdeacon and with the title and magic of Merlin!

Lord Tiwas stood with the Masters at the grand gates of the College, their full robes stirring gently in the morning breeze. My Master, the Archdeacon stood proud as a peacock as we journeymen passed before him. Raising his hand high into the air my Lord blessed our journey with his magic, "Your path will always shine bright and show your way in the world, go with the blessing of the gods." And from the tips of his fingers gold rain showered around we thirteen journeyman Druids.

The journey across Briton was not of itself uneventful, our small group had wandered many miles together before our paths separated. We three Province bound men travelled slightly south leaving the main group within the first day of our journey. We passed through Dun Cowen and our bard Nathis under Taliesin had sung for our supper in the small tavern. I as Merlin, had passed judgement on the ownership of six cows. To my chagrin we spent a week in Cornwall in the home village of Nathis as he lay abed with a broken ankle. We were visiting his home on our way through and in his enthusiasm, he had fallen out of his favourite tree.

I paced at the foot of his bed straining at the inconvenience and fuming with the yearning to leave without him. "You'll just have to follow when you recover and catch up with us at Bethynium!" I spat at him, not looking at the expression of pain on his young face as I cut at him with my words.

"But you can't just leave me, please, Mann'ah, I'll be able to travel in a week, even sooner if you help Raido care for my foot. Just don't leave me."

Raido put his hand on my arm and he stopped me as I tried to pass him. "You owe him that much, Mann'ah, we have been together for a long time, at least see us onto the road to Rome."

I pulled myself free with a sneer, "What care I for your company? Our roads will part when I reach Pompeii and you will not see me again. Why should I waste my time now?" Pain flashed into the eyes of my lifelong friend and caught me in guilt. "Very well, to the bitter end then, sweet Raido," and I stalked fuming from the room.

I snatched a dun pony from the stalls and rode bitterly into the woods, flanking the beast any time the canter slackened. The rhythm of the race fuelled my anger at the delay in my journey and I rode the animal even harder. I had taken myself to the crest of a hill and there the sweating pony came to a standstill. I turned him for home and stood out, watching the little village far below, my fury bellowing around me. I raged as I dwelled on how much my path could be ruled by the futile need of those insignificant remnants of accursed childhood and I cracked the sky with anger. I called up all the rage of the winds of Manannan and the fury of the storms of the Morrigan to wage war on this place for the time of our incarceration, and in that moment the sky darkened and the storm began.

In sheer and evil pleasure at releasing such a torrent, I rode all the way down to the village laughing like a mad man, letting the pony walk nervously, its ears twitching with every one of my lunatic chuckles. I set it to convulsing once as my laugh echoed through the rain drenched forest, but I took its mind with a thought formed hand, squeezing its brain with my power, until it was reduced to stillness through pain. I released my will and it walked on numbly, a trickle of blood lining its way down the pony's left nostril. Leaning forward on the animal's neck, it stumbled under the weight shift, I locked my knees and it grunted. I reached out and ran my finger down the small red trail, picking up its essence and raised it to my lips. I could smell the tangy odour of iron against the warm scent of hide in the rain and as I licked my finger clean, I could feel the warmth of the fresh blood ease the savage pull of my desires. I laughed and scooped up another finger full, and giggled in the ear of the numb pony as it stupidly walked me home in the rain.

It was late night by the time I came into our room, Nathis lay snoring, his foot sitting proud on the bed. I could not see if Raido was asleep, his back was to the doorway, but I was set in my intent to punish him for holding me in this place and asleep or no, I would take out my shallow revenge. I threw two cloaks as I stood in the doorway, one for Nathis to keep his sleep from interruption, and one for Raido for the dream of his life. I had him rise in his sleep and become a dog for me and I came up behind him, using my anger and frustration like Hades in the storm. I raped the unconscious youth, tearing at his skin until blood flowed and released my tension in vengeful pleasure.

In the morning Raido took himself off into the forest, he would not look at me as he rose, wrapping his robe painfully around him. And neither did I want him to, for I was still in fury and his silence gave me fuel to rage.

Each day I worked silently beside the Healer Druid caring for Nathis' ankle as I had promised, but such close contact did nothing to heal the pain I had caused my pathetic companions. I waited out my sentence, easily avoiding the attentions of my fellows and as the week passed, I spent time dreaming of my lust for my new life and how much I would enjoy my first taste of a female. I sat before our door watching the village women go about their day and cursed the Brehon creed of common law.

We reached Gaul from the village in three days, I wanted nothing more than a quick journey after my incarceration but the crossing by ferry had been rough and I, never a very good seaman, arrived on the beach of Bethynium, feeling sicker than a night on the ale and bitter at the betrayal of my stomach. As the boat was pulled up on the shore, I threw myself from the confines of the stinking deck and lying on the sands, I puked one last time. Gasping around my own retching, I cursed the gods for their lack of love in giving me such a weak gut.

My companions gathered around me and raised me to my feet.

"Can you walk, Mann'ah?" Raido enquired, leaning around me to brush off my robe.

"My legs are more suited to land," I snapped in return, pulling my arm from him.

Neither of my companions would walk by my side as we made our way inland, which was as well since my mood did not improve as we travelled. My anger followed me in a gathering storm and from the corner of my eye, I could see the lightning flashes reaching down to destroy the path I had left behind.

The road through Gaul was smooth and paved, an architectural trademark of the Roman Empire, the heavy taxes imposed by Caesar had been used well to ensure my journey was smooth. Once setting my feet in the right direction and knowing now it was only time that separated me from the place of my fantasies, my mood improved enough to retain a civil air. After many miles, I found the others had come around and as is the nature of old friends, our conversation became easier and forgetful of what had gone before.

Roman roads are easy to follow and for the most part free from highway thieves; Caesar built his towns around garrisons that were stationed every few miles along its length, so for three Druids schooled in the arts that had led us here, a safe passage and lodgings at night were never a problem.

42

In each place we stayed, the surroundings were the same—Rome's over use of a town plan that worked well but lacked imagination. Even so the women were all beautiful and not once did I see a feminine form without feeling all the desires of my young hormonal body. But my education in common law held my patience, and in Pompeii I knew my long-awaited plans would flower.

The days got hotter and our attire changed from the robes of our cold Druid home to the light skirts of the Romans, and as we journeyed purposefully on, we attracted less and less attention from the people we passed on the road. We spoke no Gaelic now, careful only to use Rome's tongue as we moved into the stronghold of the world's dominant nation. I made it my business to listen carefully to local gossip each time we stopped to rest. I at least, intended to be knowledgeable in subterfuge of the Romans before I arrived at my destination.

Our voyage continued onward, seemingly endless as we travelled, and in the distance arose mountains that the road would guide us through, growing nearer day by day. Gossip had a band of gypsies ranging the foothills, that attacked small groups of travellers, taking them as easy prey, and I smiled more than once at the warnings delivered to us in the taverns we frequented. Although I know of no mortal who could take a Druid by surprise, I heeded the warnings enough to discipline my thoughts with protection and defence spells, always scanning the roadside for herbs to complement my sachel. The distraction was enough to allow me a measure of peace as we travelled by day, although night-time was still painful for all of us. Within a short time we were heading upwards along the road and into the Southern Alps at the mouth of the Empire itself. The pace of our journey was slowed as we made our way through the hills and for the first time as darkness approached, we had no roof to sleep beneath.

"The stars will make excellent companions tonight, my friends," I said with much bravado, gathering dry wood for a fire.

Nathis sat watching me in the gathering night. "We should have a watch though," he commented nervously, "and I really do not like the thought of a fire with a smoke trail for bandits to follow."

I laughed lightly mocking him, "Dear Nathis, I have some bloodroot and mouse-tail root in my sachel, enough to start the fire without smoke." My laugh grew louder and I threw my arms out toward the towering mountains, shouting my challenge. "And who would dare attack us? There are none with our powers here, let the insignificant hoard come if they dare, I will crush them like twigs in the fire." In the rising energy of my display, I showered the pile of tinder with my powders and set it to blaze with a spark from my eye. Raido had already turned away and disappeared into the cloak of night, but Nathis just sighed and warmed his hands.

We sat feeding the small blaze for maybe an hour before Raido returned, a brown hare and a fat wild pigeon slung over his shoulder for our meal. He tossed them down before the fire and without a word disappeared once more. I cared not, he had supplied our food, let him sulk in darkness if he so chose. But dressing and cooking our meal took from my mind memories of that boy that I had known for years and who I knew, had held a deep love for me. But even activity could not stop those thoughts for long and when he returned, drawn by the odour of the cooked meat, we sat in silence brooding.

44

There was not a word spoken for hours, although Nathis had taken out his harp and was strumming a soft ballad, but when a breeze stirred though our camp and brought with it the scent of another man, I felt my guts tense. Raido too had been brought sharply out of his malaise and with finger speech warned the young bard. I was aware that his melody had faltered a little, but to the untrained ear the hesitation sounded like a change in the song and with deliberate intent, Nathis began to weave spells into the notes. Aural magic is powerful when used by a Bard, under Taliesin no layman could resist its call and slowly from the dark emerged six men, drawn to stand just within the pool of firelight. I scanned their minds quickly as each one stepped into the light, casting them under a cloak of stillness to keep them captive. Raido was signing a message to Nathis as I slowly lowered my eyes, aware that there were still more just beyond the camp. It had occurred to us all that whoever was resisting the harp's pull would have to have had some schooling in the Arts, so Nathis continued with his lullaby, skilfully gathering energy from the song and focusing the will of surrender through the night. Off behind my right shoulder I heard a groan, then the rumble of a war cry being born, and from the sound of a scraping hoof echoing from all around the camp, came a roaring warrior.

Quickly I turned on my heel and spread my hands. Sucking power from the fire and the earth all around me, I threw a solar disk between the camp and the night, the dark sky brightened to the blue of day and our attackers were exposed in the light. Five riders in a milieu of horses sat stunned at the side of the road, the advancing warrior was checked by his horse as it baulked at the brilliance of the disk and bolting, threw the rider to the ground.

As the sky darkened once more I focused on the riders I had for a brief instant seen and taking their minds, I trapped them with the same stillness I had cast over the others. I drew them unwittingly forward, but felt a mind slip through my mental fingers, its movement sinewy, like the dance of a woman.

"Ah, a gypsy witch," I hissed sensing the darkness around me, amused by the resilience of her mind. But once I cast a cloak of terror to chase and consume her, I knew she was mine. I could feel energy rising from the back of my balls as I reached out and seized her and when I felt my touch penetrate her mind, I probed tentacle-like, deep into her own powers and wrenched them forth to strike at her own men. A scream tore from the darkness and the whole gypsy band fell dead. The horses sensed the deaths and added their screams and whinnies, drowning the sound of the woman, bolting, cantering off in the confusion and all I could be surely aware of, was the current running between me and her. I could feel her resistance to my touch and although I could easily have killed her with the irritation she arose in me, I sensed her deep from within my manhood and that saved her life.

I reached out toward where I held her in the darkness, throwing my arms wide and cast from each fingertip a tentacle, and as she struggled against my touch, I wrapped each of them round her and pulled her in to me. I watched her form congeal out of the night and loosened my skirt to fall softly from my waist. There was a look of beautiful frozen terror on the mask of her face and her lithesome form moved an erection to consume me.

Feeding her terror with the seat of her own power I brought her before me, her fine light blouse stirring gently over her fearful breaths and at the height of each terrified lung full, the pout of her nipple pressed darkly into the fabric, an angle to interrupt the smooth beauty of each orb. I would soon know of the taste of these things and my tongue darted out to moisten my parched lips. I reached out with a hand and took the fine material, tearing it from her perfect breasts. Hardly could I hold my attention when I first beheld them and I moved very close to her, rubbing the frozen points across my belly. I reached down and tasted for the first time, the fruits of the breast of woman and was fixed, I could have stayed attached, suckling like a babe forever. But in my youthful lust, I needed to know more of her fruits, how was the kiss of a woman, especially of one so beautiful? I held her face, her jaw slack with terror, I could not kiss that. But what of that secret hole I had heard so much of, and but for my initiation into life, had never experienced? I raised her to my urgent phallus, using her own withering supply of life to lift her off the ground, and I found and entered her sex. Fire stirred deep within me, erupting from my throat in a blossom of ecstasy as I took her whole weight on my greedy erection, and in my glee I slashed at her breasts, opening long wounds and moved to drink the blood that oozed down onto her nipples. What release, I could sense my ejaculation leave its mark in the infinite moments of eternity! Looking down from my rapture, I let my sex urge spend itself and slowly the gypsy witch sank into a small pile beside the glowing fire. The dying embers of her mind reflected in the night air as I released her from my will.

In the aftermath Raido and Nathis moved quietly from their concealed place, back to the glow of firelight, but as they looked from one dead gypsy to the next in silence, I could see the horrific fear of what they had seen me do scarred forever within their eyes. In silence they retrieved their sachels from beside the fire and in silence returned to the road. In the gloom of false dawn I gathered my things and followed behind.

We did not speak at all on the road for the next few days, our passage through the beautiful countryside of the northern province spreading before us as we came down out of the mountains. The paved way flowed from us along the landscape and after many miles a naked crossroad stabbed its impression across our path. With a mental sigh and a smile that almost parted my lips, I approached the signpost sitting starkly, offensively interrupting the road's horizontal flow and saw the end to my sullen companions.

Expressionless I turned to them as they walked slowly up behind me, "It seems here is where our paths diverge, my friends." I smiled a flat, dead smile, "I wish you well, brothers. I will not forget either of you."

But Raido spat before me with more vehemence than I had seen in him since Nathis had broken his ankle. "I don't want you to remember me, Mann'ah, I cannot forgive either your crimes nor my weakness for allowing you to use me so, and neither will I condemn myself to keep you in my thoughts. You have shamed even our gods, *brother!*" His final word, a viper, spewed before me.

Nathis turned and cowered from us both and continued slowly on the road to Rome. Raido regarded me for one final time and shaking his head, parted my company. With a snort of disgust at their departure I turned and made down the road to Pompeii.

Within the span of two years I had entered the highest echelons of the architectural masterpiece that was Pompeii's centre of the worship of Venus. I was so involved in the exquisite game I had woven around myself as I climbed hierarchical steps, that I was having the best time of my life. Oh, how I loved my post, I had used all the learning I had accumulated to see me into a position of great power and influence in the temple. I had manipulated easily the weak-minded fools around me, and today I had planned my greatest gambit yet.

The dawn was beautiful, the morning air crisp and the sun rose swiftly into the magenta sunrise. I drew back the heavy drapes from my window and breathed deeply of the sweet fragrance of the city.

"My lord Merlin." A soft voice came from behind me on the bed and I turned to see a temple virgin still laying where I had used her the night before. "Do you still need me?" she asked tentatively, a silk sheet held thinly to her breast, ready to escape at my command.

It rose my ire that she would want to leave me so soon so I denied her the release. "You will open for me now," I replied and approached her on the bed. Her eyes were flat with hate when I looked into them but what cared I, I took her heart casually with my mind and squeezed tightly until gasping she fell back with a shudder. "Much better," I mused and opened my robe. This was indeed my favourite slut, no one could give me the feel that she had, ah, I could have wallowed in it all day. I bent my head to her breast and licked the stiff nipple, but the bitch still lay flat and unmoving, so without feeling, I took the erection between my teeth and bit it off. At last I had a reaction from her as she lashed out at me cursing and screaming, and I smiled as I held her at arm's length.

"It's a good thing I like you, Rose-Marie, your looks won't last forever." I laughed, rolling the nipple end around in my mouth and then spat it at her face.

"You evil bastard," she screamed tearing herself from my grasp. "British fiend, you will burn in hell for this."

Laughing over her curse, I let her foil my grip and run sobbing from the room. Ah, what a life.

The temple of Venus had suited me well, as my introduction letter from my Lord Tiwas himself had given me instant power in the priesthood who ruled this mighty establishment. As Merlin, keeper of Law, it took very little time for my plans to come to fruit. Today was to be the first in a long tradition of rituals, honouring *my* gods in *my* way. For months I had sought augurs, being shown again and again how powerful this day was to be. I had cast my magic in subversive ways and the fruits were the rites I had set at the very core of the faith of the temple.

I rose calling my attendants and dressed for the ritual, I would look fine on this day. I could smell the scent of god-driven force coming in on the breeze and knew the time of my power was at hand. As I took the weight of my beautiful formal robe, heavy with the fine gold work commissioned in the design of my fore bearers, I could feel sublime power growing within me that would make me the absolute master of this place.

Gaily I marched through the corridors of the temple, chuckling low to myself as I played out, for the hundredth time, my ritual takeover of power in this place. Hard though it was to keep my own counsel in such a grand scheme, I had isolated my thoughts from all, keeping my plans pure, until I had woven the essence of the gods around me in a barrier no one would dare penetrate. The rich tapestry lined walkway soon ended at the grand entrance to the inner shrine and I paused on the threshold, watching the activity within. I scanned the faces of the crowd assembled and then on to the ritual dais at the high point of the hall, all were ready for my presence. Orthos, my most favoured young priest, was already in his place beside a mighty gong, peering through a high window for the sun to be framed in its conjunction in the sky. The little priest watched intently, a growing excitement on his rosebud face, a look that caught in my heart, distractingly reminding me of early days in love and lust with my lamentable Raido. But the piercing sound of three loud cracks from the young priest's hand, shook away my memories and my rite was begun.

Standing in the doorway, I cast forth my powers in a blanket over the congregated hoard, suppressing any thoughts of their own and imposing on their small lives, my will. I reached like a conductor into each consciousness and began to play my great manuscript. As I walked regally to my place on the dais, I put each person to the floor in supplicating worship and travelled as a god through their midst. Groans of pleasure issued all around me as I let sexuality leak into the atmosphere—better than any aphrodisiac—and I rose to my waiting throne. A smile played across my face as I observed from my high vantage point. The orgy like a slumbering beast, stirred from its innocent dream. Temple virgins and priests came before me in staged precision, disrobing under my will and moving out into the crowd, my favourites bending to sit, thrall-like by my feet. I watched the orgy stepping up in power as the virgins and priests added their impetus, and in short time I could see energy flaming over the mass of writhing flesh. In the corner of my eye, I caught a glimpse of movement and Orthos came into my view, holding the tethers of three white goats. I was distracted momentarily by his beautiful face, another vision of Raido marring my perfect orchestration. But as I fixed my gaze on him, the spectre of Raido's pain disappeared in the passion of my magic.

At my signal, two of the goats were released and driven bleating into the orgy. I gave out more of my will and within moments the animals were caught by the crowd, forced down and taken in ecstatic madness. The delicious vision before me was inspiring, I took the power generated by the scene below and sent it back threefold, sparking the writhing mass into greater lust, and the energy in the vaulted temple filled me with zealous pride. A wicked blade found its way into my hand as the third beast was held before me and I, in a bliss that cracked the sky with thunder, reached out and slashed the throat of my sacrifice. As red life from the dying goat sprayed forth, pumping in great gouts like bloody sperm over the writhing orgy, the rumbling from without came stronger on the air, and the temple became dark as power gathered.

"The time of the gods is at hand," I bellowed righteously into the room holding the bloody knife aloft like a sentinel. "Bow and behold me, Merlin, for I have been taken into the realms of the gods. For now and evermore, bow to me for I too am a god!" A peal of thunder broke in answer to my affirmation and I writhed, orgasmic in my own power.

But within moments I could feel a change, a movement in the air that brought me back to focus and I felt the floor shudder under my feet. In an instant the temple was full of the choking sediment of black dust, the incensed orgy fostering a scream that was growing in the back of my mind. The very temple itself began to shiver and within the turning of my eye, the roof was sheared from the walls that held it. Huge blocks of stone and volumes of thick black ash fell murderously onto the hapless crowd below, and screams of death rose from the blood-stained floor. A great section of the wall behind me was torn from the crumbling temple and in horror, I turned to face the gaping hole. Through the haze of black dust I could make out the silhouette of the great mountain that shadowed the city, its summit sheared off, the raped hole of an unwitting virgin, gouting clouds of hellish dust out and over the sky. In thunderous explosions the mountain gave forth great rocks and boulders, ejaculating their massive forms high above the gaping peak, and in that frozen instant I saw Raido and his beautiful face, staring mournfully at me from the raging scene.

"Your acts have not gone unnoticed, Mann'ah." I could feel his whisper in my brain. "The gods have always seen what you have done with your power."

"But why..." I struggled with this vision. "I have had omens and signs confirming my place," I poured forth my explanation in rising anger. "I have been shown. I have the right!"

Sadly the spectre smiled and shook his head, "You have abused the gift of your being, foolish mortal. You have pushed yourself far from the love of your gods. What a waste this life has been for you, with all your powers and position. You have sentenced your soul forever to walk in the dark." Insensibly I watched as the ghost faded from my sight, each of the selfish acts that condemned me, flashing across my mind's eye.

I stood choking in the clouds of dust, the scene of reality and that of my life playing before me, and when finally each of my abuses had embedded deeply in the fabric of my soul, I watched mutely as the mountain sent out its loudest roar. A score of avenging boulders flew across the sky and in that awful moment, death claimed me.

Chapter 3

I returned to my twilight protection from the sun, with the lingering nightmare of a dead woman's face and saw, clear sighted, my eternal walk in the dark. The heavens rolled by in night-time splendour and stars flashed their mocking brilliance upon the reflection of my fate. Why had that merciless ruler of man's fortunes played such an awful part in my existence? I had been condemned with the desire to take life, even as far as taking the life of a being that shared my fragile soul. Why? I was damned forever into a hunger for blood, the gravest crime against God's law, and had indeed, sealed my hideous fate. I raged against such justice, imploring those callous stars as they turned flaming before my grim shelter, desperate to fathom a way to be free of the chains that bound my soul.

Sunrise came and I hid from the blistering reach of its unceasing stroke, holding my arm pressed hard against my streaming eyes, crying, wailing, screaming; anything to hold onto sanity in the face of day. If I hoped to keep the fragile strings of my reason and perhaps, make some sense of the damnation of my life, then I would need to make a place for myself somewhere in the world of mortals. A deep place to hide from the sun by day, to protect me from the brutal call of its fiery heart, a place of permanence that would carry me through the centuries, hiding me from human eyes and the pain that I would cause them. So, when twilight came and night blossomed before my retreat, the still cool of a darkened sky released me from my awful purgatory and I set out to find a home.

I ranged far over the land I had come to, a silent cloud rolling across the starlit sky and came upon an isolated castle, magnificent and brooding above the stark land, its high spires called alluringly to my sorrow and I descended to settle around its mighty form. I tasted the cold stones of the fortress with a mist of awareness and finding my way to the grand entrance, I flowed into the heart of the castle. A courtyard opened out before me as I gathered beyond the gate, a mighty ziggurat guarded by the outer walls sitting shrouded in its midst, and I knew there was a place beneath the cool dark stone that would be enough to protect me from the sun. The sounds of mortals sleeping broke my contemplation and dropping into my vermin form, I scurried about the grand structure to seek out their heat in the night.

I ran around the courtyard walls and moved like a writhing ocean across the cobbled floor, stopping here and there to run up the wall and peer into the castle depths. A great hall opened before my vermin eyes, as I sat in narrow windows that ranged its length and beyond the inner wall, flames blazed from an open door. A hundred strong, I poured into the hall, skittered quickly under the open vault and gathered to peer into the room. A bed of skins and animal furs greeted my splintered sight, a roaring monster slumbering in its depths and I knew I had found the master of this stronghold.

I congealed with a delicate touch of shape change and stood naked by the doorway watching the flames of sleep rise from the covers. The vitality of life held my gaze and I was caught transfixed by the beauty of mortal fire. A sigh from beside the snoring hump of furs held explanation for my fascination, and I watched the master's bed mate roll over into my sight. With an imperceptible groan, I realised the fire of their lives were still high from lovemaking, that passion captured me more than any other lights of humankind. I would have turned to leave, but the slumbering giant rolled in the bed, his arm connected sharply with the woman's face and startled her suddenly awake. Crying out, she twisted under the veil of furs, thrashing against the blow, I heard a string of curses and the barbarian awoke with a loud grunt and rage filled eyes. He reached out with a fist to strike the woman, but she had already rolled off the bed and away from him, crossing the floor as she scrambled to her feet. I took the quiet knowing of the shadows and stood unmoving as the woman, naked and flaming in the dark, moved toward the doorway. She paused, her hand light on the cold wall, so close to me that her essence flowed onto my skin.

"Where are ye, bitch?" the growling barbarian spluttered. "Get back here!"

"I have no need to share my bed with you, Saxon oaf." Her breath floated out, iridescent on the still air and a sigh came unbidden to my lips. The woman's eyes darted toward my hiding place, shock dampening her vital fire. "Who's there?" she whispered and reached for me.

On the bed the Saxon crashed around, damning the woman and a blinding flash set aglow a tallow lamp. The shadows revealed me as I flinched from the sudden light and the woman gave a startled cry. I peered carefully around the viscous illumination and my gaze was caught by a sudden smile, a moment of bliss amid chaos.

There was silence as the giant registered my presence and then, with a mighty roar, he rushed from the furs to tackle me. Naked he charged across the room, a great hairy lumbering bear, yelling as he

57

advanced and I stepped easily around his foolish flight, aiding his crash as he careened into the wall. Curses erupted from the Saxon as he turned holding his head in pain. I reached an arm into his flaming rage and pinned his bulk to the wall. The captured man struggled under my tenacious grip, thrashing against his predicament, igniting the flames of his essence and I was caught by the weaving of his life fire around my hand, drawn unerringly down into primal need. My soul craved for his mortal heat and I leaned close to his throat, but behind me I heard the woman laugh, a satisfied sound that arrested me, and I turned to meet her clear eyes.

"Are you so willing to see him die?" I asked and her gaze challenged me.

"Indeed," her soft voice was defiant, "I have no love for that brute, since I am his slave!" She tossed an arrogant curl from her shoulder and smiled low, "I have worked for many months to see his end."

The woman's flame grew bright with lingering hate, calling to old memories in my soul and I tasted her revenge, "You know that I will kill you too."

She shrugged, "Yes, but rather that, than another night with him."

The indignant bear growled around my restraining hand and his arm flashed out, reaching for the woman, but his power was no match for my immortal strength and I held him fast against the wall. His face was blue from the pressure of my hand on his throat, his gaze rolled up into his head, spittle foamed from his lips, and before my eyes the life fire dulled and left a corpse in its place.

I dropped the body to the floor and turned to the woman who was studying my naked form intently. "I have been waiting for you," she said and her life fire rose to an inner excitement.

"Are you so eager to court death?"

A laugh rose easily to her lips and she crossed the room to clothe herself loosely in one of the sleeping furs. "To know my magic is enough to draw you here is worth the price you ask." Her voice was soft and full of her wiles, drawing me slowly toward the harsh pool of tallow light. "But I know enough of you to know that I am safe, at least for now."

Her words drew chill into my core and I turned away from her alluring voice, "What right do you have to know me?"

She gathered the fur against the night chill and sat facing me on the bed, beckoning for me to sit beside her, but the lamp glow stung at me and I stood mute. Her eyes sighed under smooth lashes and with a graceful shrug, she began to speak.

"There is a tale told by bards of old, about the coming of vampire kind. Their story is ancient and tells of how a gypsy queen, alone in the darkest forest, fell into the path of a demon whose beauty was so great, that she fell under his spell. So taken was she, by that angel of darkness, that she made a bargain with him. She thought to walk with him along his dark path but to her woe, he abandoned her in the night. She roamed the land in search of the angel that had stolen her heart and her life, but never again found that grail and in her pain, created others of her kind." She smiled and shifted slightly, but the horror of her simple tale turned my face from her gaze. Anguish born of my evil deed welled from my eyes and I heard her through pain of damnation.

"Legends of vampires are popular on cold winter nights and never more so was the legend of Julian, since in times past he was seen again. A bard of great power had been caught in the path of this dark angel and by the magic of his music, had turned the vampire away. But the beauty of this creature was so great that the bard was inspired, and to this day tells his tale. And so, in every house of the land, on the darkest night, songs of the vampire Lord are played and his legend is told to give comfort and keep his evil kin at bay.

"I have listened well to the tales of your kind; I know the songs and I have planned long for your coming. I have been calling out to you, I have used my magic and waited, through all my suffering for you to come to me. Oh yes, I know you, my beloved Julian." Her words stabbed me, drawing me to look at her through tear-stained eyes, and her gaze flamed as she watched my sorrow.

Her tender beauty seized my soul and I flinched away from a deeper yearning, "How could you know of my torment, mortal?"

A long smile came over her lips and the promise of love flowed liquid in her life fire. "I listened well at my stepmother's knee, my fallen angel, and I know many things, and this also I know, dark prince, you will take my life this night, it is your nature and something I cannot change. But before I die, I would make a bargain with you to give me something in return."

I raised an eyebrow to the lilt in her voice, I had heard such a sound before and I guessed the contract even before she spoke. "I cannot bargain with what I cannot give." My voice was flat as I responded slowly and her tender essence caressed me again.

"Oh, beautiful Julian, I would be yours forever. Make me of your kind and I will stay with you for eternity." Her voice reached deep into my soul and set me aflame with hope, drowning me, catching me in a spell of love deeper than any of my magic. She rose from the bed, the fur slipping from her blazing form and stepped away from the savage tallow light to come to me in the shadows. "For eternity," she whispered and reached to bathe me in her life flame.

What moment in a lifetime of pain had I fallen upon, in the form of this one small human? In the still between the space of my cold heartbeat, she had offered her love and come to me without reservation. Her essence caressed me, warming my heart and calling to the hunger in my soul, my infinite cold lust for life. But her shining eyes were upon mine and the heat of her sweet breath on my face. "I cannot condemn you to a life such as this," I whispered, trying to push away the yearning that threatened to engulf me.

Irritation flared around the shining flames of her life and her eyes sparked but she smiled softly and said, "I am doomed to slavery if I stay here, and even so I would be killed if I am found in this place with him." She cast a quick glance to the corpse by the door, then looked back at me with soft defiance, "I know of your nature well enough, Julian, to know that you are bound to take a life tonight. Take me into your realm and we will be together for the rest of time."

Smooth and elegant, she offered to me her silken throat, holding onto my icy skin as I raged against the need she stirred, holding me fast as my appetite consumed me in waves of her vital heat, and I came close to her smooth, pale and flawless neck. I rested my cool lips on her vibrant skin and with reverence and restraint, began to drink.

Ecstasy and soft cries of triumph filled my senses as I drained the life from her lithe being, her willing cries fading as heat flowed searing into my soul, and when her heartbeat faded to an imperceptible throb, I forced control over my quick passion. In blood heightened agony, I knew the hand of fate had once again toyed with me, that fickle mistress once more, had drawn me into the taking of life, and in knowing my evil deed, I raised my face up to the night and howled a mournful cry.

In that moment I could feel the presence of another being just beyond the door and I turned, shocked from my woe, to see the flaming essence of a mortal watching me. With a cry the man spun around, calling loud into the night, fleeing noisily back through the great hall. I was caught suddenly between my need for love and the threat of discovery by the other occupants of the castle. Sobbing, I stood confused by this awful predicament but the last curling essence of the woman in my arms rose with its promise, and so I cut my breast with a long and deadly nail. Roaring filled my mind, the sound of my own escaping energy, and I held the beautiful woman close to the oozing wound. For a moment I felt nothing from her, aware only of the maddening rush of threatening oblivion and thinking that I had already killed my chance of love, I held her tightly, mourning for her loss. But my essence was in her mouth, instinct had taken her and sweet damnation rose from my cold core. Within moments I had been drained, but her suck tempered the roaring void that threatened hell and suspended oblivion in frozen relief. I felt the sickening loss of my life force and at the end of my strength, pulled myself from the dying woman. Black blood stained her perfect face, the failing heat of her body held my sorrowful gaze and as I watched, she died.

I laid her gently on the floor and retreated to the shadows in horror at my actions and sat against the frozen wall, staring into the dead eyes of hope. Time passed and all was still, the expectation of what was to happen next held me, and I wondered at her awakening into my dark realm of eternity. I waited, anxious as the vision of the woman's living beauty was mysteriously restored upon her dead body, growing until she herself was an angel to behold, and when at last the transition was complete, her form began to glow with its own cool light. Life came suddenly to her face and she opened her eyes.

Slowly, as if in some pain, my beautiful companion rose and came to sit before me in the dark shadows. "I am Niamh," she introduced herself, but I was caught in the sight of her. Neither the empty void of a corpse nor the blazing sun of mortal life, she sat before me glowing with the soothing light of the moon. In her eyes I could see all my existence in pain and I was filled with aching for her angelic grace. Within the cool silent flame of her newly created being, love wove a spell through its moonlight essence, I felt her catch my thoughts and she smiled at me speaking from some silent place deep within my mind.

And so we are together, my love, for eternity. I started as I heard her voice and she reached out a cool hand to mine. *Surely you know that a vampire can hear the thoughts of others?* Her voice echoed in new memory and in the instant of her deep touch, I found cool peace, a vampire charade to mock the clear-sighted vision of pure love. I had created a goddess, a torch of immortal flame to walk by me on this hell spawned path, eternally damned by all my vain needs and arrogant stupidity. Tears flowed relentlessly for the sentence I had given to my beautiful Niamh, now by my hand those endless sapphire eyes were condemned to the surface of the earth, forever chained in the dark.

"No, Julian!" she cried softly, raising her hand to my face. "I knew it would be like this, but I have seen Margueritte and I know that her beauty was from you." I recoiled from her exquisite touch and again she reached for me, "and I have seen the beauty in you too, my love." She caressed my cheek in her lovely hand and I yearned to her cool touch, drowning me with sweet love and peace. For the first time in my life I experienced joy in the arms of another.

The flare of life essence suddenly dragged my gaze from Niamh's eyes, a writhing blaze that betrayed the presence of many humans, flamed just beyond the wall. A volley of arrows loosed through the open doorway fanning through and around the pool of tallow light.

We have been found, I heard Niamh's thought, and beside me she pressed hard against the wall. A second round of arrows shot wider than the first, whistling through the shadows, a couple passed dangerously close to where we hid without cover. But then an arrow clipped the rim of the tallow lamp, splashing flaming liquid onto the bed and quickly the furs caught alight. A cheer from beyond the door erupted as flames took hold in the chamber and a couple of the Saxons entered carrying dangerous, mocking weapons. I seized Niamh and held her behind me, pushing away from the wall as the barbarians marked my presence and they turned to face me. Flames writhed from the blazing bed and their aggressive life fire burned in the room, the air danced under the chaos of heat and tortured my being.

"Stay behind and follow me out," I spoke quickly and moved cautiously forward.

Both men gave a savage roar and moved toward me, I flinched from their onslaught and suddenly, I was caught with a sickening sense of danger that far outweighed the presence of these small mortals. The lights of false dawn reached in from the great hall and called to my stricken soul. Caught between the blaze that grew behind me and the threatening imminence of dawn, caution succumbed to raw panic and I rushed at my assailants in screaming urgency. I knocked the first sword away and raked one quick claw through the soft flesh of the barbarian's throat and he, with a startled sigh, sank to the floor. The other had missed my lightning attack and, even before he knew I had moved, I took him in an iron grip and broke his neck in two.

Other Saxons were entering the room and I turned to see their advance, but before I could move, a blazing fur flew by me to land on the front guard. He fell into the midst of his comrades, shocked and burning and they retreated beyond the doorway. I glanced to where Niamh stood by the fire, she had donned her rescued dress and encouraged the blaze to spread around the room. A smile rose on my cold lips for her quick and clever action.

"We must find a place to hide from the sun," I said, summoning her away from her task. "Come, we must escape while they are confused."

Niamh came to me and took my cool hand in hers. "There are so many of them, Julian. Surely we cannot get by."

"We must. I can feel the approach of dawn, we have no time." My fear infected Niamh and her eyes became grave. Sounds beyond our perilous shelter proved that the barbarians had recovered from Niamh's attack. "Stay close to the wall, I will settle this." Quickly I moved from her side and into the writhing monster of flaming life that filled the great hall.

A great mass of human life flowed in the deep twilight air and I rose to fly quickly across the vaulted roof, high above the caressing flames of the Saxon hoard. Like a great wave they registered my flight above them, their focus followed me as I came to land by the great entrance, and I turned to face them with my back to a fierce itch that warned of day. I drew power from the threatening sun and cast my will over the trapped army, stunning their rage silent and spoke deep into each fragile mind, "This is my place now, leave before night fall, or I will take you for my own." I released my hold on the stunned men and panic erupted in my wake. Turning from them, I saw Niamh across the courtyard standing by the corner of the looming ziggurat, beckoning me to her side.

"Follow me," she called and moved quickly along the dark wall.

Under the shadows, she led me through a squeaking doorway that sat, pinched in the corner of a grand iron portcullis, entry to the temple's inner vault. I swung the gate shut behind us and took the smooth catch between my fingers, twisting the metal to lock the entrance way and cast my gaze fearfully through the bars to see the first piercing rays of the sun. Urgently I took Niamh by the hand and rushed with her through the twilight hall. Smooth century worn walls gave way to a narrow walkway and down into a crypt that had been carved into the living rock, far below the church. We fell into the dark space and I turned, a hand raised to face the corridor, anxious should any of those vicious rays penetrate the depth of our haven and I stood for a moment reassuring myself of safety away from the touch of day. A smile played on my lips, I could feel the sun rising above, though naught but the dark reflection of stone greeted my gaze and cool, damp air stirred lightly through my hair.

"We should be safe here, until tonight at least," I said. My sight returned to the small chamber and I saw Niamh, lying in a pool of her own light, unconscious on the bitter floor. "Niamh!" I called and rushed to her side, lifting her, like a jewel into my arms. "So you sleep by day, my love." Gently, I brushed my lips across her alabaster cheek and carried her still form to where a stone crypt stood silent in the middle of the vault.

I sat by Niamh's side as she lay on the tomb, watching her midnight flames give off glowing light into the dark chamber, the passing sun carried the hours away and I waited for my love to wake. For the better part of the morning I could hear humans scurrying around elsewhere in the castle, and the scent of smoke grew thick in the air. The sound of bowstrings, flinging arrows into the temple proper, echoed down the corridor into our sanctuary and fire had taken hold above. Smoke and faint light from the burning church took the place of human voices and by the time that its blaze had died, there was silence.

Niamh lay quiet and unaffected by the furore of the Saxon army, remaining asleep as daylight reigned, her delicate face an island of peace amid deep russet curls, holding my gaze as the world raged beyond our haven. I reached into her dreams trying to touch her mind, but found only the knowing of flight and life in the dark, and I withdrew as she learned of her being through the blessed release of sleep. I sat watching her, not daring to think of an eternity with her by my side and yet gently daydreaming of our meeting and the way she had laid such a promise of eternal companionship in my cold heart.

As dusk approached, Niamh became restless in her dream and I touched her mind again to find blood lust rising within her, I recoiled in fear of its hideous touch and pulled away from her. I remembered well that awful drag on my being, and knowing how that madness would transform my gentle companion, I wept for her. Damned into lusting for life each night, how long would it be before she could control the demon within her? Or would she be cursed this way until the end of time? I stepped from the stone dais and made for the corridor that led upwards into the setting sun.

Fire still smouldered here and there in the mighty ziggurat, smoke and ash hung thick in the air, and though the blaze had destroyed its trappings, the structure remained impenetrable, blocking the last light of the sun. Cautiously I crossed to the entry, iron bars that still flamed with the essence of day, and shielding my fragile eyes, flinching against its touch on my exposed skin, I approached the writhing maw.

Beyond the gate, quiet voices betrayed the presence of humans. "I don't think I can be here when they wake up, Cedric," one spoke uncertain.

Another grunted in derision, "Then you'll be a coward, Randalf the White. There are ten of us, we'll lop of their heads as soon as they try to come out."

"If they didn't perish in the fire."

"Fire can't harm the likes of them."

Voices in argument rose until the leader roared and turned their attention to the sun, "We don't need to be arguing now, do we, lads," he bellowed.

"They'll be awake soon enough, so stand on your guard."

I looked to take advantage of their ignorance of my nature. They did not expect to be attacked in the day, so even though it would cause me great discomfort under the maddening light of the sun, I would do just that. I crossed quietly to the mechanism that raised the great gate and took the lever of a wheel, lax against the chain that worked the portcullis. I steeled myself against the sun's death rage, opened the door amid a tyranny of metal noise, and when it was high enough to let me pass, I secured it and rushed to stand before the startled men.

"You think to mock my warning, mortals," I spoke with authority that I did not feel, peering at them through streaming eyes and cast a blanket of void to hold them witless. I stood in agonising defiance under the last curling flames of sunlight. "Listen well, foolish creatures. I am master of this place. To come here will bring only death to you. Be gone and let any who can hear be warned, I will kill all who come to find me here." I loosed all but two of the humans and with my words ringing clear in their minds, I chased them away with shadows of night. Screaming with the nightmare I had planted in their sight, the Saxons fled across the courtyard and beyond the castle wall. But the two I had held in the void stood mute and insensible before me.

"Come," I said shortly and retreated into the ruined church.

The barbarians walked slowly, moving puppets that followed my direction and in the dying rays of sunlight, I restored the iron barrier against the world of mortals. I led the hapless couple through the twilight chamber and down into the soothing dark

69

haven where my love lay in the last of her sleep, bidding them to wait as I returned to her side.

In the cool tomb, Niamh was responding to the coming of night, her undead essence raged around her, tinted with a hunger that was drawing her from sleep, and she moaned softly and twitched against the restraining hand of her dreams. I reached out to sense that fiery master of day, its flaming orb sinking quickly below the horizon and as the last of its rays left the sky, she was awake.

Demon eyes flashed open, forgetful of the love that had been promised and the vampire raged within her. Scent of human essence caught her attention and with lightning speed that defied the grace of her sleeping form, she crossed the darkened crypt and fell upon the first of her victims. Power of hunger and the savage need of her new nature sent the insensible barbarian sprawling to the floor under her, shocking the malaise from his fragile mind and I watched as his face turned stricken, his vibrant aura flooded with panic and he thrashed against his awful predicament. But Niamh's strength was more than that of any mortal and she pinned him beneath her, descended quickly to silence his dread and feast on his life blood.

"Do not drink from his dead heart." I moved to crouch beside her, revolted by the beast that she had become and yet knowing, unless she learned this restraint she would remain in the grip of her vile nature. But she was taken by the moment of her passion, evil lust flared around her and made me recoil, she had become a monster, a monster such as I, vile and condemned forever. In the vision of the creature feeding, writhing in the mortal heat of life, hunger stirred deep inside and trapped me in its desire, taunting me as I strained to control its wicked

70

touch. I waited in brutal agony for the moments to pass, and when she lifted her head triumphant from the drained corpse, I hid my face from the compelling evil in her eyes.

"No, Julian," she whispered, "please do not turn from me. Of all the things I have survived through my life, that I could not bear." Her sensitive fingers touched my face and she raised my gaze to meet hers. Those lapis pools were suddenly washed clean of the beast I had seen when she woke and love flecked, silver and gold in their depths, drawing me to ignore that I had ever seen such a creature. She leaned into me and kissed me then, energy sparked between us and warmth flowed over my cold soul, her cool lips washed me lightly in rivers of love and I lingered in her soothing essence, forgetful almost of the memory of my own sinful nature.

"Show me the wonder of your realm." My beloved moved to face me and her hand swept down to take mine.

I could still feel the pangs of hunger flowing in her, even though she buried her pain deep within.

"You need more," I said simply.

But she shook her head with a smile and her long curls stirred under the casual movement. "Not in our home." A spark flamed into her vampire glow. "Not where love will dwell."

My eyes strayed from her and to the slow mortal fire that burned witless around the other man and Niamh turned to see.

"Let him go," she whispered, "there will be many others, we need not take him too. But," she looked into my eyes and smiled, "you have no clothes and he has plenty and, besides, what a tale he will have to tell when he is found by his fellows, naked and fleeing with demons on his heels."

I took the Saxon's clothes, releasing him to run, screaming into the night and my beautiful Niamh gently teased my absurd appearance in barbarian skins. And so, smiling in love and laughing with newfound freedom, I took my angelic companion by the hand and we flew out into the night.

We rose above the dark stone walls of the castle that had so dramatically become our home, ranging high into the starlight sky and over the sleeping land. Niamh hummed a light melody as we flew, and together we explored the realm of our eternity. Shimmering fields of human care gave way before us to a mighty forest and we descended to skim its edge, coming to rest where a small river flowed down from within.

Tall oaks stranded with mistletoe loomed dark behind us, around moss covered rocks the brook laughed under sweeping fronds of willow trees. Niamh sat, her back to a graceful moonlit trunk and watched the water smiling quietly, concentration in her eyes. "I see so much clearer, better than I did before," she whispered reverently, "and I am sure I can hear every sound, even to the subtle breeze in the treetops."

I laughed lightly but she put a delicate finger to my lips and bade me listen with her and above the cackle of water bound spirits, other demon song echoed in the forest depths. "The songs of dryads hold no interest for me," I said, breaking the spell they wove around the tree lined edge and dismissing the poisonous allure. "I have been trapped by them before."

Niamh gazed at me curious, "Where is the song you hear, Julian? I hear as far as the distant field and the owl as it flies through the wood but I hear no music."

"Ah, my love," I replied "I have been seduced by the spirits of earth and caught for centuries, entranced by their vile song. I will be forever haunted by the nightmare of what they have given to me."

Sweet Niamh came close to me and bade me tell her of my life, taking my arm around her, resting her soft deep curls on my shoulder, and I told her all I had been dealt by the hand of fate. She wept when she heard of the cause of my mortal death, indeed she cried for all of my time as an outcast human, and when I recounted that first sunset, I too wept for the crime of my existence. But for all those times had been unjust, she wept all the more for my time alone in the dark. I told her of the dryads and their evil games, how they had given to me the dreadful knowing of glory in the kill, instinct for self-preservation and power over the shape my form could take and how, through their twisted manipulation, I had unwittingly brought about the birth of vampire kind. I told her of my meeting with the bard and she smiled curiously as I spoke but said nothing, and when I came to the auburn-haired reflection of myself I had seen in the vision, she held me as I cried for understanding.

All was silent for a while and I lay cradled in her lap, her hand on my brow and then in a whisper, Niamh told me her own story. In her mortal life she too had been an orphan brat but not as wretched as I. To her fortune she had been blessed with the happiness and love of a family to nurture her in her growing years, hearing tales at her stepmother's knee of the realms of spirit and magic, firing her young imagination with tales of the creatures of the night. Seeing potential in the growing child, her stepmother had quickly initiated her into the circle of the village coven and over the years, passed on all its secrets and lore. But even the power of witchcraft could not save her family when marauders attacked their small village, and she was taken for the pleasure of the rampaging horde. Forced to watch the hamlet as it burned and was razed to the ground, her family were flogged, raped and thrown into the consuming flames and Niamh was taken by the leader, a slave to his bed. For months she had been held prisoner, as the Saxon invaders used the castle for a base, and at night when the barbarian slept, she had worked many spells for my coming. "So you see, my love," she said at last, "I too know a little of the magic that hides in this world and I know secrets of my own.

"My mother told me of my soul, a perfect reflection of its maker, always learning, growing and the journey it takes through each incarnation. She would speak of the choice that each person made to be created anew, returning each time to the world of mortals and a life they decided upon from beyond the womb. In her tales of vampires, she would tell me of their immortal souls, and how that breed cheated themselves from growth into heaven by their choice to stay bound on earth. Even I have made that decision, to be by your side," and she raised a hand as I protested. "To be with you, my love, is worth the price I have paid. But, my beloved Julian, you have had no choice in this life, and I believe that fate is showing you why. Pay heed when your soul shows you of its journey and one day you may find peace."

I pulled away, her words innocently mocked my eternal torture. "What peace can one such as I expect? Even my tormented soul has shown me that

I am a monster, damned and accursed by my vile nature forever."

Gently Niamh touched my cheek and I gazed into her cool eyes. "I do not believe that, Julian. There is salvation for all who seek it, even for you and me," and those endless depths flamed with conviction. "You will see, my love.

"Still, come with me and I will give you a gift." She stepped from her mossy seat and crossed the stream to where it babbled into a rock formed pool. "Sit by me and look deep into the water," she drew me down beside her and gazed into the pond. "Mother called this scrying, she always said you should do it under the light of the full moon, although I'll hazard that you would see whether or not. So try, my love, stare into the pool and let it take your thoughts, and you will see."

I gazed into my reflection on the water's face, long white hair stirred moving softly on a cloud of subtle energy, a being of its own consciousness around the glow of ivory skin, the proud strong line of a nose, high fine cheek bones and a beguiling mouth masked the evil within. But, oh, to my sorrow, I raised my sight and looked deep into those perfect and fathomless eyes, pain of centuries and anguish of living in the dark welled within their depths and I was drawn into the agony of seeing my own pain. Drowning in an ecstasy of damnation, I was caught by those searing orbs, held by the beautiful mask of the demon that returned my gaze and in that frozen instant, I was taken into the seeing of another life.

I saw, with other's eyes, an angel before me in the twilight and his alabaster face was again, my own. In the vision I had become a young man in easy conversation with friends, standing on a harbour side dock, watching the sun as it blazed dusk's glory, and I revelled in the easy sight of its warm glow. But a voice disturbed my contemplation, Julian was speaking and I could feel innocent and trusting devotion in my mortal heart. He wore two sleek, deep tinted disks sitting in some unusual frame high on his face and in the growing darkness, he removed the strange contraption and the eyes cut into my soul. With a pain that lanced into the young man's heart, I felt the melancholy touch of forsaken devotion and hopelessness, and turned in anguish from the vampire's gaze.

Awful waves of desperation rose to consume me and I recoiled from the vision, tearing my sight painfully from the weight of emotion and then I was released. I recoiled from the pool, tears rising quickly to stain my face and blazed an accursed look at my innocent companion.

"How could you show me such a thing?" I accused, the truth of her shattered by crystal tears.

She reached for me and held me though I would have pulled away. "Oh, my most beloved fallen angel," she whispered and sudden panic quickened her words. "Do not judge me so harshly. Let me walk beside you, Julian, and together we may fathom this mystery yet." She caressed me with whispers of sweet love, soothing the edge from my pain.

I stared into her cool vampire flame and felt hope reach for me on the wings of Niamh's words. With her exquisite guidance and wisdom, perhaps we could fathom a solution to my dreadful existence. With her help, perhaps one day I would be free.

Chapter 4

All my life, I have *known*. I'm not quite sure what or how it was that I knew, but something would whisper in my heart at night as I lay abed and I would know of things; flying and rolling free in the sky, seeing all too clearly into the hearts and minds of men, passing through time and space as surely as if it were a dream. My ma said it *was* only a dream and not to bother about it, so I kept my visions locked deep inside and pretended a normal childhood. But even so there were things that came to me, warnings of life and the people around me. So on the day my family life ended I had already been pricked awake by the dread of what was to come.

"What's the matter, Jeremy?" My young sister stirred beside me as I was woken from my sleep with a terror of consuming dread.

"I don't know but I think we have to leave." I sat bolt upright in the bed, an awful weight on me. Only Rachael had been favoured with the secret of my gift, she was quite familiar with the power of my knowing and quite readily followed me from her bed.

"What is it, Jeremy, what's happening?" Her voice was picking up in excitement of fear as we left the bedroom and made our way through the small farmhouse. But I was busy trying to think of a way to persuade my inflexible parents to follow my premonition and as we rounded their doorway. I was already fathoming quicksilver thoughts to convince them to leave their bed at this dark hour of the day.

My father's snores rose in swirling heat from his sleeping face and I stepped up to him calling for him to wake. "Please, father, I have a terrible feeling, wake up."

He raised one stern and blood shot eyelid, and grunted at me to leave him alone. "It's the rest day of our Lord, Jeremy, go back to bed."

"But please, father, you must listen to me, I have had an awful feeling."

"Just a dream," he murmured, snorting a yawn. "Back to bed with you," and he turned away from me, his snore growing back into sleep.

I reached over to my mother and called for her but her sleep was deep and she would not rouse, and anyway, I was caught in the middle of a cry by the growing sensation of something coming up to the farm. In a terrified moment, I stood frozen with horror and seething with frustration over my sleeping parents. With a defeated sigh I turned and dragged my pensive sister from the house.

In the chill predawn air I could see dark shapes flowing steadily out over the fields below the house, wolf-like and silent the shadowed forms moved quickly towards us. I grabbed Rachael urgently and made for the near edge of the wood, hiding scared in the dark and watched as the invaders came upon our home. Within moments I could hear the frozen scream of my mother and turned in slack horror to see my sister's wide eyes peering at me through the gloom.

"I'm going back," I whispered and she gave a startled cry. "You stay here and keep quiet. I won't be long." What I, a scrawny youth of fourteen, could do to save my parents I did not know, but I was certain that I had to try. So I set off around the tree line in the direction of my mother's cry.

Crouching into the shadows I came around the corner of the small house and was greeted by the bright flames of a fire taking hold of the barn. I moved behind a bush and watched the barbarians drag my screaming mother into the light of the burning building, my father stumbling behind, a vicious gash in his forehead flowing openly with blood. Two of the marauders roughly beat my father to the ground and held his head wrenched back by the hair. Four of the others took my mother's arms and legs, and pinned her cruelly over the railing. More of the invaders came from out of the dark and I could hear them speaking in a harsh bark, arguing over the spread-eagled form of my whimpering mother. In a final grunt, one large man reached out and cuffed his fellow savagely before he turned on my mother and tore away her nightdress.

In the flickering light of the growing blaze, I watched as he released the string of his trous and a brutal look of pleasure reflected in his eyes. The barbarian's member was so large that I quailed in horror at the sight of its engorged length. I had seen the erect size of my father by accident once, but it was well proportioned compared to this monster and my heart stopped as I watched the marauder force it full length into my screaming mother. In fixated horror I sat dumb, my eyes held by the sight of the barbarian's hideous assault on the trembling body of my mother, but my malaise was cut short by the high wail of my sister and she was dragged forward by a newcomer. Rachael was pinned next to my mother, the high bar of the railing hard under her chin. I heard the blood rush through my head as another barbarian opened his trous and displayed himself, and shrinking from the sound of my sister's penetrated scream, I turned retching and fled from the scene.

With my eyes stinging in the painful tears of
what I had witnessed, I ran through the woods,
instinctively following an old woodcutting track that
led through its dark heart and beyond. For hours the
end of my home and family chased me hauntingly
through the silent trees and I hardly noticed the
sunrise in my headlong plunge away from all I had
known. My flight took me rushing down the
indistinct track, giving way suddenly to the wide
span of a river and in the blinding flash of reflected
sunlight on its fast-moving depths, the loamy bank
gave way beneath my feet. I was pitched
unmercifully into the cool water, falling hard and
seeing stars as a submerged rock collided with my
head. Water choked my lungs as I sank beneath the
flowing current and I gasped my way painfully to
the surface of the river. My will to survive stung me
into shallow awareness.

Hazy with the roar in my brain, I watched as the
sky moved above me, the soothing cool touch of the
rambling stream easing the screams of Rachael and
my mother from my tormented mind. The sweet
noises of the running water lulled me into stillness
and I lay supported in its nurturing embrace for an
aeon until I came to rest. Weeds, driftwood and the
refuse of moving water checked my path and I came
to the corner of a pier. The current swirled in eddies
as it caught in the dead end and I lay dazed, half in
and out of the stream. The decaying stench of rotting
fish finally brought me back into my head, I crawled
heavily out on to the muddy bank coughing, and
puked water from my bloated gut. Numbly and after
long minutes had passed, I gathered my strength to
drag myself from the riverside and fell unconscious
concealed just inside the wood.

When I finally awoke the sun was blazing its way into the mid-morning sky and casting its reflection blindly from the flowing river. I turned my throbbing head from the piercing light and groaned in the pain of concussion. Hearing the sound of voices coming nearer and still hidden just within the shadows of the trees, I rose cautiously to watch their approach. The lilting sounds of laughter floated gently around the water's edge as four brightly dressed women came to the riverside, shedding their clothes as they prepared to bathe. I cast my gaze over their faces as they moved past my hiding place and out onto the pier. When the last woman fell into my sight, I was caught in eternity by her face, the polished ivory of her perfect skin framed in a blazing sun of her deep flaming curls. The glory of her vivid beauty reached deep into my soul and rendered my heart ablaze with longing, a deep and unfathomable need for her fire to touch me. I knew we had been together for eternity, two halves of the same whole, fire and ice drawn together forever. My gaze wandered around her perfect form as she stood naked on the edge of the pier, my eyes knowing every supple curve on her intoxicating body and felt the sting of lust in my groin. My breathtaking lady dived slick as a fish into the water and splashed in its cool depths, in play with her friends. Guiltily I watched the women bathe taking cold comfort from the attention of my hand until they climbed noisily from the water, collecting the clothes they had left waiting on the pier. I gathered my senses, rose from my place in the mud and followed them as they wandered back up the path they had first walked down.

Behind them and out of view, I struggled along the path through the woods, the beacon of flaming red hair guiding me to the edge of a small town and out of the trees. I followed the vision of my love through the alleys and back ways until they disappeared into the doorway of a noisy and well patronised inn. My heart flew apart in torment as she vanished from my sight and I slumped down to sit dejected by the alley, lost without the vital heat of her beauty to light my way. I sat within the dark shadows, lost even to the passage of day.

In the evening twilight I stirred out of a waking dream by the sound of my lady's beautiful laugh as it drifted on the breeze from the other side of the building, and in alarm I rushed after the angelic noise. I ran blindly down a lane behind the house and turned into another, imagining I would reach the street and the retreating music of my lady's sweet voice. But instead the way led me into the shadows of a dead end and in a moment of panic, I was filled with dread. In my mind's eye flashed the faces of three insidious men and as I turned to flee, they were standing before me.

Blocking my escape from the blind alley, the ugliest of the three men laughed rough with the sound of too much ale. "Well now, well now," he mused, the stale stench of his breath floating across the air between us. "Look at this tender morsel now, will you, Fredrick," and he turned his head dangerously to his companion, his eyes never leaving my tattered form. "It seems we'll be having a party ourselves tonight after all," and in a movement that seemed too quick for his massive bulk, his arm snaked out and anchored roughly on my arm. I cried out and tried to pull myself free but the brute had me securely, his mates came in to lift me from the ground and carried my thrashing form into the corner of the alley. Expertly they threw me down over a hard wooden crate and exposed my shuddering body in the same evil way I had seen forced on my mother and Rachael. My face was pressed cruelly into the splintering face of wood and my trous were torn from my slim legs. Virginity was stripped from my young backside and I, a whore at the mercy of my captors, surrendered to the ecstasy of rape. All three took their turn, the last so incensed by watching his mates that he lay into me with closed fists, beating me about my head until I cried out and he laughed roughly, adding his orgasm to the crime.

Lying mute and alone in the night, I could hear the demon laughs and hard footsteps of the rapists as they disappeared into the dark. I lay very still until I could not hear even the echo of their evil presence, then rose and held up my trous in unconscious shame. Shuffling and awkward I made my way back around the inn, to the road at the end of the alley and stood to watch in a confusion of senses, a bright and writhing scene.

Half closing my eyes against the light, I could make out a marketplace, a carnival set against the night in the heart of the little town, a gay and colourful parody of my plight and yearning. I cast my gaze out into the crowd for a touch of my lady. Frantically my eyes searched under heavy lids, the pain in my body consuming me in the steady crawl of its fall into oblivion and suddenly I was fixed on the long red locks of her burning hair. I stood in a long moment, the sight of her angel face intoxicating me, soothing me to forget the suffering of my circumstances and as she turned, I was transported. Her face in all its ivory beauty turned softly toward me and I caught her gaze in mine, the moment of our contact lifted me from all what had gone before and washed me with love. Staring into those ocean depths I saw the essence of my soul reflected back and thralled in the promise of love held in those universal pools. But in my bliss the terrified pain of my body reached up to take me back into its shock, and before I could even look away from this vision of beauty, my mind had been taken into a mist of anguish and I fell unconscious to the floor.

Chapter 5

Time flowed like the easy current of a stream, when love burned its place into my well of sorrow, my deepest places of darkness filled and shone with ever new hope. Niamh showed me peace in easy friendship and a comfort of belonging that I had never tasted, she laid me on the hearth of love and I warmed myself by her fire. I was lost in joy of living, just living; busying my mind with the smallest and most mundane tasks, bathing in the light that washed over me in waves of open love and letting my sweet Niamh guide my existence.

Our den beneath the castle became a cool haven from the ravages of day, my love and I made a place for us in the deep crypt, bringing furniture and flowers to mask the rot of old death and for all I could still smell the decaying remains that shared our sweet prison, with Niamh's love, our retreat became a home. She brought books to keep me company in my hours of exile from the sun, the times that her sleep separated me from love's devotion and we acquired a modest library. My lovely companion sat for many hours patiently showing me the elegant form of the written word and encouraging me to read with her, Niamh guided me through the books we collected. So during the day while my love slept, I would read of the realm of man, learning reverence for the mortal spirit that expressed itself so eloquently through flowing words and fired my imagination with its brilliance.

At night we flew together to the lilt of Niamh's sweet song, rising in the deep twilight time and ranging over our domain with naught to beat but the sun. Hunger would be strong within her as she woke and, although I could sense the awful gnawing of vampire nature within her, she controlled her savage instinct and selected her hunting grounds with care. At first she chose the invading colonies of Saxon marauders as I had reeked my vengeance on Romans in Gaul, but her lust for revenge was short and within a week she revealed to me the extent to which she had planned her descent into my realm. Niamh knew of mortal misery in this land, that which she called Briton; beggar colonies and outbreaks of disease, bands of outcasts that would not miss life and indeed seemed almost pleased at times to see our spectre of death. In morbid fascination I watched her feed, the creature that overcame her in the thrall of blood revolted me as much as the refreshed flames of her essence trapped me in their sight. She would come to me after, to hold me and wash me in stolen rivers of love and the edge of my hunger subsided.

On currents of vampire essence and, oh, so slowly, I pushed away the presence of hunger in my soul, soothing my pain in the sweet company of my lovely Niamh, gaining from our love solace from the call of instinct. In those years, I found such a peace in love with my simple existence that eventually, I rejected the whole world in favour of peace and learning in our castle hide away and the search for an answer to my soul's awful path. Niamh teased me unmercifully about my hermit ways, but never once did she question my retreat and always, when she had fed well, she came to me, bathing me in love and mortal essence, showering me in radiant light and keeping cold silence at bay.

I studied the world of the mortals beyond my exile, treasuring the unavowed beauty of their world in the sun. I learned of the tradition that had built around vampire kind, stories and myths of great adventure, thinly disguising the horror that these creatures had made legend. I learned, through a wonderful book of maps, to place myself anywhere in the land and from heavy carved leather-bound volumes, I learned the secrets of hidden realms. Niamh took on the mantle of my education in much the same manner as her stepmother, taking me through an endless time of freedom from my nature and deeper into love of her kind heart. She introduced me to her world slowly through intoxicating tales written to read at night, the logic of science and the beauty of art, engaging me in long hours of study until she gauged me ready to be shown the secrets of the Great Art. In the cool evening of the end of a difficult volume Niamh placed a small book in my hands.

"In here is my stepmother's knowing," she said, her hand lingering over the work. "It tells of what is hidden deep in the consciousness of mortals and waits beneath their primitive fears. As you gave me your eternal gift, so do I give you mine, read it while I am gone and when I return, I will share with you something else." She caressed my face and kissed me with an excitement of patience and left me to my study.

The little book fell open in my palm, as if the secrets that it held had given the power of life under my hands, opening magically to the first sheet of handwritten script.

"*Here is the book of my shadows. I have looked deep into eternity and see what is in the hearts of man. From the beginning of time we have had power over earth and air, fire and water, the connecting of the spirit of man is the great pivot of the laws of the universe. And here in my book I will show you, the way we move the world and create the cosmos, the way we are bound by the Word as we cycle from life to life."*

In a breath the leaf lifted from my fingers, turning as I ended the page in a knowing of my gaze, and in the words that followed I was to learn of the Art of Earth Magic. From the book flowed spells and charms, enchantments to know and command all elements and spirit creatures of the world and incantations to create in their realms, using their powers in every imaginable way. I learned that my gift of shape change had been more than an accident of falling into the dryad's realm, but a way for those creatures of spirit to control human destiny, so I recognised their awful part in my existence and gained the knowledge to survive in their world. I flew through the pages eagerly drinking the wisdom that they held and learned the greatest curse of a mortal who chooses the hidden path of the gods. Held upon a path of judgement, in cycles of many lives, a witch would return into flesh and pay retribution for the awful choices made in the growth to light, and as the cover closed under my touch, I imagined the atrocities that would have had to occur to take me so far from the light and into darkness.

As if the book's closing marked a signal, I could feel the rush of fresh essence filling me with its warmth and Niamh was at the entrance of the hall, her eyes bright with excitement. "I see you have finished." She crossed the floor and sat beside me taking the book from my hands, "My stepmother had the gift of foresight and so did I, until I met you, my love, I had the knowing of your coming long before the Saxons invaded our home. Your pain reached out to my senses and I fell in love with your melancholy beauty, and when my stepmother died, I used my magic to draw you here. But when you came, my sweet Julian, your kiss took that human gift from me and I trapped you, unwittingly, into a one-sided bargain."

I began to protest but she lifted one hand and shook her head delicately, "I did, my love, I had the gift to tell you of things unknown to you and yet in my selfish need, I denied you the benefit of that knowledge. I should have known my death would mean an end to the powers I had as a mortal." She paused for a moment and then her clouded face changed. "But I have brought you a surprise that will take up my duty," and she rose suddenly excited. "I have brought my stepmother's cousin, who has the sight as she did. Some say he can see even further than she could, but that will be for him to prove." She had crossed to the entranceway and turned to face me. "Will you see him?" she asked quietly, her gaze apprehensive in the face of her petition.

I weighed the question, knowing that I had not been taken by instinct since I had cloistered myself with my books, nor had I been close to the essence of a mortal, I would have no defence from the truth of my nature. Niamh must have known of the peril this human would face in my presence. "I cannot," I replied in fear.

"You have met before," she said, casually lulling me with the calm in her voice, "and he survived that meeting with you, my love. Let me bring him to you, he knows well the risk." She disappeared for a moment and I sat staring into the cool shadows.

I could feel her return and the flames that reached out to me from the human beside her, and I pulled myself free from the scent of life blood that filled my senses, trying to overwhelm me.

"Julian," I could hear Niamh speak over the roaring of my need and I rose, my gaze fixed to the vibrant heat of the mortal, "this is Terrin, my mother's cousin, he is a man of great wisdom."

I hardly noticed the words she spoke as I looked into the eyes of her companion, the memory of music I had heard from his hand flooded into my mind. I sank down into the chair held by the magic woven in my soul from ages past.

"Ah, what a difference there is in you now, Julian," he said conversationally, walking carefully across the vault to my chair. He sat in the other, an odd counterfeit of my beautiful companion, and his easy smile was betrayed by curiosity as his glance touched me. He had aged since I had seen him last, little wonder, that brief meeting was a lifetime away for him, and now he had the stature of a much older man. My gaze rested on the deep lines of crow's feet by his clear laughing eyes.

"It has been a long time, old friend." His voice was as soft and sweet as Niamh's and I could see how her life had been formed by a woman of this blood.

"Yes," I sighed in the regret of a life that had moved on without my knowing, how many years had I lived since I had seen Terrin as a younger man? My eyes wandered from the intoxication of his gaze and came to rest on the iridescent pulse of his neck as he spoke to me.

"I have made a very good living from my meeting with you and so, I see you have improved your position too. I am pleased to see you again, Julian." His conversation dropped to a hush and he reached out to touch my shoulder.

I tensed, anticipating the waves of his life essence flowing out from his hand onto the jacket, but the heavy leather shielded me a little from the caress of his human blaze and in dawning relief, my anxiety subsided. I sighed and leaned my bare face closer to him, blinking involuntarily as I was caressed by his flames and a stab of hunger flashed savage through me. "I would have killed you," I whispered and pulled away, and smiled faintly as the horror of consuming need came under my control. I relaxed back into the chair and accepted his mild scrutiny with a sigh.

The old man was instantly aware of my change of heart and with an odd look returned my gaze. "Many things have happened since those days, Julian. I have learned much since our first meeting. If you let me, I can help you gain wisdom in knowing the soul that you carry." The flaming essence of his mortal lights danced as he spoke.

I gave a short and hollow laugh. "What of your knowledge would help one dammed as I, bard? I am cursed far beyond your mortal understanding."

The old man brought his fine hands together before his mouth and mused over the examination of my eternal being. "I can see many things in you, my friend, even as I did that night. I see the torment of the damned glowing in your eyes." His words were spoken softly but they chilled my soul. "I can see all of the devil's minions repent in your wake, condemned from the light for eternity in your living nightmare. The tortured fragments of your cursed soul are caught in the rapture of your being. The evil that you have become shields them eternally from salvation, condemned to walk with you, forever in the dark."

Horror took me as his words froze in the void and I could feel the writhing presence of these demons all around me, wailing into infinity, giving me their pain. "Julian, I am not the one who can give salvation from your past, but I can give you understanding and perhaps a clearer path."

I turned my eyes away from him, seething in new agony, "Your knowledge can only bring me pain, bard. I care little for lives gone by, even this one, now leave me."

I heard a sigh from across the room, Niamh had been holding her breath and waves of frustration radiated from her mind, but the old man had reached into his sachel and pulling out a small lap harp, began to softly caress its glistening stings. Poignant and heavenly, music poured forth and captured my soul, renting its fragile heart from the monsters that lurked within and out to the anguish of the melody he wove. Yet again I was caught and held by the powerful skill of this master magician and I gave myself to the holy chorus of harmony, weeping in the beauty of sorrow that it held. Tears flowed and filled my sight and under the spell that he cast around me, Terrin gave me a vision of my beginning.

I saw a lonely road that cut through dark mountains and a campfire put up against the night, three friends sat cosy round its modest blaze and kept watch on the break in their journey. Under the cover of darkness I saw a band of gypsy thieves come upon them and prepare for attack. But in the melee that followed I was blinded by the use of great magic and when my sight returned, one traveller was standing in a torrent of fury, his power ranging out into the night in an arrow of flame. A savage scream answered that arrow and in an instant the gypsy band fell dead to the floor. I watched in horror as a woman came stumbling into the camp light and stop, like a marionette, before the traveller.

He abused her violently and when spent, he cast her lifeless by the road. I roared in the pain of knowing this to be the moment of my conception, a crime of the like to create an evil such as me, my anguish took me blissfully from the vision and I rose from my chair.

"Go, bard, or I will kill you," I hissed, the torture of his beautiful music stopped and I retreated into the shadows.

"Thank you, Terrin," I could hear Niamh whispering "I feel the sun is coming, you must leave now, I will let you out."

"Go with God," he replied loud enough so I would hear. "Both of you." The sound of footsteps withdrew into the corridor and above, groaning iron of the closing gate and then, still.

In a silent moment Niamh returned, crossed the floor lightly and reached out to me. But my torment held me from her, my breaths coming ragged with sorrow. "I will have no more of your ways, I have already had an eternity of pain, I need no more, leave me alone with the pieces of what I have left."

"Forgive me, my beloved Julian." I could feel her overpowering urge to hold me and she folded sobbing to the floor. After an eternal moment of hearing Niamh cry beside me, I took her in my arms and she held me in the cool of our home. Small caresses and sighs of vampire love gave my soul peace from pain that boiled within.

The sun travelled steadily through the day and I sat with the small book that Niamh had shown me, the pages made little sense as I struggled against the demon that had been stirred by the awful closeness of a mortal. When the sun with its baleful glare, descended below the horizon, gnawing hunger rose suddenly in me. Niamh woke as twilight gave its sweet peace from the ravages of day and in the gloom, a flash of knowing consumed me and I was ready for the kill. She came to where I sat distracted and I pulled sharply from her, rising to pace the room.

"What is it, Julian?"

I turned and looked into her deep eyes, the passions of my need clouded my sight. "Your cousin's visit has stirred an old longing," I said sharply, my instincts growing to consume me. "I will return soon."

I flew up the dark passageway, swiftly through the ruined church and cloaking myself in a shadow of night, I soared out into the sky. Mortal flames of life called me from the lonely castle and down into the land below me, I ranged far across windswept fields and high over the brooding depths of a forest, the well-worn track leading me on to the essence of human life. In the relative shelter of the forest's edge, a small village burned with the fires of mortal kind and flying above its bright glow, I saw a human taking a lonely path into the trees. I descended upon the flaming life and attacked, knocking my victim to the ground in the fury of my instinct to kill. Suddenly I was on top of the screaming mortal, my desperate teeth reminding me of ancient rapture in the kill and the ecstasy of first blood. My body contorted, writhing in the pleasure of vital essence flowing into my dead core, the taking of life my only instinct and infinite in my moment of bliss. And when the spasming strength of my victim failed, I extracted my cruel fangs and a sigh flowed, enchanted from my lips.

"So quick," I heard a woman's light voice and felt her presence the instant that my rapture faded and in the amazing clarity of stolen life, I gazed up to see her sitting in a tree. In the moment of my recognition she pushed herself agile from the branch and landed softly before me, the rich folds of her elegant cape flowing in rivers around her intoxicating beauty and dark mystery, alluring in the blaze of her vampire glow.

"Greetings, Margueritte, I see we too meet again." My welcome was as cool as the ice in my soul.

I could see jealous fire in her boundless eyes as she spoke, "I searched the world for you, my Julian, and thought I had found you many times, but no, you took yourself from me and never returned. I have looked for you through centuries, I have been alone through time, how could you abandon me?" Her voice grew very still in the passion of hate, her slight form shivering in control.

"I have not hidden from you," I replied levelly, oozing sensual calm into her mind.

But her anger broke my spell and she hissed, "I will not be got by you again, demon!" Her eyes maddened beyond control and she flew into me.

I was roughly knocked to the ground amid the fuming cloud of her magnificent cape and Margueritte screamed thrashing out, clawing at me with her long talons. She rent long gashes in my hide jerkin and bared her savage fangs to slash into my flesh, but before I could react to her attack she had been knocked from me and was taken full force into a tree. I rose slightly to see the violent storm of vampire fury crashing into the mighty trunk as Niamh flew to my defence. But Margueritte recovered the shock of her blow too quickly and

95

shot upwards into the forest heights. Screaming, Niamh launched after her following like a harpy, I could hear the pursuit echo through the trees and I chased them, following their sound into the woods. The thrashing of branches high in the canopy told me that Niamh had caught the gypsy vampire and screams of battle greeted my senses as I came upon the scene. Hanging poised in the air, the two assailants moved to round each other and as Niamh circled to find a break, I could see a long and wicked branch held malevolently in the hands of Margueritte. I called out to Niamh, an insidious fear rising from my guts, but as I watched, the dark gypsy lunged forward and gorged the branch deep into the heart of my only love. I felt the sting of death take my beloved as she dropped through the treetops, down to the dark forest below and a roar of anguish blossomed from my dread-stricken throat. I made ground between myself and Margueritte, but she had seen me coming and flew off quickly, fleeing through the camouflage of the trees. Incensed, I hunted her through the deep forest, driving hard on her glowing trail and then out across the dark landscape in the ageing night sky. Faster than the wind, mile by agonising mile I neared her and at the end of the race, within my grasp, I clutched frantically at the billowing wing of her cloak. Gaining an iron handful of the smooth fabric, I wrenched our flight to a brutal end. She screamed with fury as she turned on me and the slow warning rumble of wolf nature caught low in my throat as we faced each other in the air. Without hesitation Margueritte attacked, her vicious talons lashing out to wound as I held her from me, but even as she thrashed berserk in my grip, I could feel the gnawing presence of the sun growing on the horizon. I gasped and Margueritte was arrested by the same instinct, coming to a sudden halt in realisation of the dawn. The first sharp ray of light flooded over the rim of the world and laid its blazing finger on me and I was thralled by its heat. The magnificent flames of its searing hell bored deep into my eyes and I turned to hide my face in the deep soft folds of Margueritte's cape, escaping into the peace of its dark barrier against the light. I heard a curdled scream escape from the trembling body that I held against me and in a horrific moment the solid flesh of the vampire had turned to chalk under my grip, falling in clouds of dust from the rich fabric in my hands.

Alone in the sky, under the shroud of the limp cloak, I was caught by the momentum of Margueritte's disappearance and fell to the naked landscape beneath me. The ground caught me, ungiving and rocky as I collapsed terrified in the shelter of my dark mantle, and I lay exposed to the fierce rays of the morning sun. Each time I tried to move, a shaft of vicious light would peer into my awful tomb and I was caught in agony of its fire. Hour after gruelling hour, I waited for the sun to release me, a dark and wailing beast fixed immobile to the earth and I endured its crawl, from horizon to horizon, in eternity. I lay still and bleak, my mind filled with the unimaginable horror of the vision of Niamh as she fell forever from my sight and I wept an ocean of sorrow for the loss of my love.

At last the wretched gaze of the sun's light sat just beneath the horizon and I threw off my prison to stand defiantly, staring at the flames of sunset, casting my rebellion at the seething crimson sky. I had discovered the secret to endure, however humble, the seething power of the sun! I lifted

Margueritte's cape from the bundle of clothes that were her only remains and fixed it like a saviour about my shoulder, smiling faintly at the irony of my discovery in the face of her dissolution. But the vision of my sweet Niamh returned quickly to haunt my sight and I turned to follow my flight back to source of that terrible scene.

I flew through the twilight sky and into the heart of the trees, the screams of the vampire's battle still echoing in the lofty heights, but to my dismay, when I came to rest on the ground where my love had fallen, I was greeted only by a pool of dark blood staining the forest floor. Quickly I followed the easy spoor of vampire essence along an overgrown path and on to the village beyond, the black and lifeless trail led to the forest edge by the grove where I had killed the night before. I heard the roaring of many angry voices and made my way silently to the edge of fire light.

My beautiful Niamh and the unfortunate mortal who had been my prey were propped meat like on a dais in the town square. All around a crowd of humans reacted to the violent fire of their preaching leader. I retreated a little into the shadows, the sight of the barren corpse that I had loved, burned its memory into my sorrowful heart and I could feel the chill of my lonely and lost soul rising to consume me in pain.

I stood beyond the sting of torch light, villagers raged over the crimes of vampire kind, their mortal flames bright with righteous condemnation and from the woods, men brought dry branches to pile before the dais in a space ringed by the angry mob. The body of my beloved Niamh was pushed casually from the dais by the boot of one man and tumbled, in an obscene parody of her grace, onto the dusty hard worn ground. All eyes followed the movement and two men dragged her by the arms onto the crude bonfire, a black and broken trail of blood stained the ground behind her. I knew she was gone, the corpse before me held nothing of what had been my beautiful Niamh, but I could not let the memory of her be so violated by these insensible mortals. I would take her earthly shell from these weak and simple sheep and lay with her, deep in the sanctuary of my memories of love. A sob rose in my chest and sorrow sucked at the vital heat of all around me, taking even the light of those blinding torches and I turned it on the crowd.

"Still!" I commanded, letting my will cast from my outspread hand, a net to capture mortal minds and all noise ceased.

I stepped from my place in the shadows, extinguishing each muted light as I passed and made my way through the silent hoard to the frail bundle, lying like a broken bird in a nest of scattered branches. The scent of decay had already taken the corpse and I hesitated, the odour clawed at my senses and the savage black maw of her chest pierced an ache of isolation heavy into my heart. Gagging against a shudder of nausea, I took the cape from my shoulders and covered the corpse, lifting the bundle gently into my arms, and in the midst of all those still human lives, cried my loss to the heavens.

Danger! A warning flashed through sorrow. I looked out to see a small group of mortals emerging from the forest and as I saw them, so they saw me. Fear came first into their eyes and then as one, they cried a barbaric sound and charged for me. A short mirthless laugh came to my lips, I rose from the ground cradling the body close as I broke into free air, the thwarted humans shouted curses after me, and I flew away, releasing the crowd back into chaos and leaving the riot behind.

Under the dark walls of the mighty castle, what I had vainly made a home returned to the crypt it had been from ages past, and I laid the corpse of my love gently on the cold stone floor. I moved the heavy slab that marked the tomb and its weight grated a mournful sigh that echoed into the air, taking the place of love's sweet laughter and bringing ice into my core. A cloud of ash blew lightly from the broken seal and eddied up, settling with a sigh of the long dead across the furs of Niamh's bed, a shroud to mark the last sleep of my lovely companion, and I interred her body in the dust of centuries. The crypt closed and a light sigh flew up to linger with other echoes and kept me company through the bitter night. And after that eternity, the sun rose and brought with it humans.

Lonely echoes and sighs of the dead were chased away by shouting above and the sharp crack of stressed metal. I lay on the bed of my lost love, letting the noise wash over me, attentive only to the sun rising above until iron screaming told me that the mortals had gained entrance to the church. Under the weight of isolation, I dragged myself from the soft furs.

I stumbled through the dark chamber and into the corridor where already, the flames of human essence and harsh torchlight flared along its length, and I flinched from the sudden illumination. A roar and a scrape of metal issued from the front guard and the lights jerked and moved quickly down toward where I stood flinching.

"No! Come no further!" I cried, instinctively willing my command into their minds. "This is my place and you will die if you dare enter, be warned!" and I retreated back into the cool dark of the crypt.

Startled voices fled back into the church and I sank against the wall listening to the fear of a vampire that walked in the light of day, and then an awful boom drowned the conversation. Clouds of dust billowed into the vault and another deep hammer echoed to the sound of falling rocks above me, I heard a prayer being spoken in the language of the church, and then all was quiet. In the peace, I climbed the corridor until I came to the rocks that had fallen from above, the passage was blocked, sealed effectively against my escape and I had been entombed. Better it was, for a soul like mine, to be locked forever away from the sight of man, better to exist in company of the dead and sleep far from the reach of the sun. I would lay on the bed of vanquished love and keep my cold heart until the end of time. So I returned to the cold tomb and rested, listening to the sounds of peace disturbed as memories and voices hung, caught in the crypt.

I lay mesmerised, unknowing of time, only the rise and fall of the sun and whispered echoes. And then song came to take the place of echoed voices. Niamh sang a ballad into the still air, and slowly her vision appeared in the darkness. She flew on the wings of an unseen breeze, shimmering with an unearthly haze, watching me through her melancholy tune and beckoning gently with a transparent hand. I tried to reach for her but my leaden flesh resisted the attempt and only my mind flew to embrace my love.

"Julian," she whispered and the air took up the sigh forcing us to part, making her form indistinct and away from my heart, and her eyes became full of tears. "There can be peace for you in this life, beloved vampire, remember this always for it will lend you strength to walk your path. I cannot take this journey with you; it is for your soul only. But I will come to you and help, my love, when you have need, for I promised you I would be with you for eternity. Know that I will keep my bargain with you, I love you and one day, in eternity, know that we will be together again. You have lived through much but take heart, there is an answer for you somewhere in this life, sweet angel, and there will be an ending to your quest, if you are strong. I will give you a gift before parting to give you strength and courage, learn well from the sorrow of this life, Julian, and one day you will see, by the strength of your own acts, I promise we will be together again." She blew gently a kiss to me and my sight faded into void.

Night, eternal darkness and peace from the cruelty of life, solace from nature, the sun and the moon. No mind. No body. No soul.

Memory, a flash to stir a dream.

No memories. No feelings, no visions of spirit... *Please, I cannot.*

Tall spires, bleak grey skies, melancholy contrast to the depth of stone, I was taken absolutely into a vision and dreamed the dream of another wretched and wasted life.

Chapter 6

Above me towered the dark heights of the monastery, the cold grey stone of its ancient covenant with God brooding with the approach of night. I, an eleven-year-old boy had been sent by my large family, in their duty to the schooling of our clan and absolution in the eyes of our Lord, and walked innocently under the maw of the giant entrance into this most horrific of prisons. My Lord Bishop was standing by the pinched stairs of his office waiting to greet a long line of boys that had been recruited from my district.

"Ah, welcome, boys, welcome." He smiled out of small eyes and rubbed his fat hand together at our arrival and then turned to our keepers. "Go with God, my brothers, you have done a great service this day," and we were led into the dark corridors of the monastery proper.

Our dormitory was a long room, deep within the bowels of the mighty structure, its cold and cave like walls gave no promise of sun and the only light I ever saw in that filthy prison, was the smoky haze of a tallow lamp. It was there that I endured the first years of my time in learning of the ways of God's service.

The routine of our days was a drudge of cleaning and tending the habits of the monks, painful lessons in the wrath of our Lord and the law of the Church. A code of sin was instilled within each of us boys even before the end of our first year in the monastery; terrible screams that echoed at night struck us obedient in fear. The thrashings that I endured at the hands of my masters were constant and no sooner had one set of wounds healed, than a brother would take to beating me again and cow me to his will. I was underfed and malnourished by the priests, they kept us weak and sickly in the name of God. I was so ill in those days that even at night when the boys disappeared from our dormitory for hours on end, I would lie like a corpse not caring and not hearing the screams in the darkness. When at last it came my turn, I hardly saw the dark shadow forming over me in the night and when large arms reached down to me, I lay still and let him lift me from my cot.

I was taken into the luxury of a private room that I had never seen since coming to the monastery and the hooded monk lowered me gently onto a soft bed. I revelled in the smooth blanket beneath me, the figure above groaned lightly and a drip of liquid fell onto my face. I looked up starkly and the monk fled from the room. Within moment of his leaving, the door opened again and a richly dressed man walked through, his eyes on me greedily.

"Take off your clothes," he said briefly to me and began himself, to undress.

I watched him as I slowly took off my patched habit and trous, his gaudy jewellery rattled on the table as he took off his boot, leaning heavily on the wooden top for support. He puffed and panted until he had extracted his large flaccid body from the clothing that he wore and finally he turned to face me.

His eyes wandered minutely over my skin and a slow smile began to play on his lips. "This one's the best yet," he muttered to himself and heaved his enormous form onto the bed beside me. As I watched, too weak to care or defend myself, he ran a pudgy hand over the length of my body, all the while murmuring, "Yes, quite the best yet, quite the best. Hmm, yes the best." He turned me over and ran his fingers over my back, his caress lulling me with its gentle feel, and when I closed my eyes I cared not whose touch it was. Long and loving, the hands stroked my back and down onto my buttocks, kneading my muscles with expert precision, relaxing me and loosening my whole body. A clever finger pressed against my shameful hole and moistly worked its way into my body, I could feel my guilt thrill to the movement of his finger and I sighed under the touch. Without speed or hesitation, the finger was replaced by the savage thrusting of the monster on my back, its greedy pushing accepted painfully into my bowel. I writhed in virgin agony under the weight of sex, an awful sense of excitement perversely rising within me. But all too soon the flabby giant had spent his seed and he rolled panting in sweat onto the bed. Within moments of his pleasure I could hear screams echoing in the night and it was to the sound of those awful screams that I fell asleep on that soft bed and dreamed a beautiful and terrible dream of flying.

Free from the bonds of the world I fly, a part of the boiling landscape as I stretch my way across the sky. I am the storm and the creatures that ride in its wake, I am the essence of the dark. No vaster creature dwells than I, for in my true nature, I am the all from which nature flows and the storm is mine. On I ride in this knowing and quite naturally, for I have known this element for an age and then...
...down I come to land and then...
...what is this I see as I dream? Help me, Lord, I cannot watch...

"Brother Martin," the vestry boy burst through my cell door, "you… you told me to let you know, they have arrived."

I started and the blood drained away from my skin as the brash youth shocked me from a doze. My dream already descended to older places as I came awake and guilty for my tardiness in falling asleep while studying, I rose from my desk.

"Good, good," I replied, nervously cleared my throat and laid aside the gospel I had been reading. Absently tying the cord of my habit, I slipped on my sandals and followed the boy down into the great hall where the holy party waited.

"My Lord Inquisitor," I held open my arms as I approached the entourage and directed my gaze toward the sombre figure in its midst. When he turned, I could feel his hawk-like eyes reaching into my soul, weighing my life by his righteous scales, "I am Brother Martin. My Lord Bishop has been taken ill and asks that you allow me to offer my assistance while you stay with us." My carefully rehearsed speech dropped like copper coins into the void of the Inquisitor's sight and in the silence I coughed lightly. "Please follow me and I will take you to your rooms."

I shuffled uncertain by the group and walked before the Inquisitor across the hall. The Holy Emissary followed at my elbow and I took him to an apartment that was concealed at the end of a long corridor.

"We are honoured to have your Holiness in our modest cloister," I spoke conversationally as we neared the door. "I surely hope that you will be comfortable here." I pushed open the door and smiled as I turned to admit the Inquisitor.

He gave a brief nod at the rich interior of the large living room. "This will be adequate," he said, his voice cloaked in ice. "Now show me the judgement chamber."

Shocked a little at his request I stammered, "Of course my Lord. B...but I would have thought you would like to refresh yourself first." He brushed my words away casually, his eyebrow jerking as I stuttered my speech.

"Show me the chamber, monk." he replied curt and brushed past me out of the room.

Hastily I walked back down the passage with the royal entourage and came before a heavy wooden door set in the wall. The lock's key was hanging from the cord about my robe and I fumbled with the folds of rough cloth in my attempt to find it.

"Come, brother, we cannot wait 'til Judgement Day." There was mocking laughter behind the Inquisitor's words and his group tittered at his wit.

I cringed from his appraisal of me and tore the damnable key from my cord, but allowed myself to regain some composure before giving it to him. I moved eagerly out of the way and he unlocked the door, stepping through to the room beyond. The flow of his entourage poured in behind him and I followed, red faced and angry at my foolishness.

"Ah, yes," he was saying as I stepped into the room. "This is just fine." He rounded the vaulted space, gazing up into the gallery and came to stand by the inquisitor's seat that stood high on the central dais. He eased into the grand chair and rested his hand easily on the lavish desk before him. "We will begin the trial upon the morrow!" his voice boomed out, echoing high into the empty public gallery.

"Have the witch brought before me by morning, brother, and we shall see the game unfold." He looked down to hold me in his gaze and I shrank back at the sight, the power of his voice forced me to obey and I left the chamber.

I rushed through the corridors and down into the monastery's dungeon and came to where Brother James kept watch on his prisoner. I walked through the dungeon's outer door, the monk was kneeling by his small desk naked and shivering in the cave-like underground chamber, long slick cords of a well-used scourge snaked red spider trails across his back as he prayed for salvation. I was arrested by the image etched in his flesh, the beauty of his tormented repentance painted an exquisite picture of agony and I could feel the excitement of guilt building in my loins. I watched his rocking prayer, he was too lost in the rapture of retribution to know of my presence and I let my eyes feast on his pain. My hand strayed under my robe and I brutalised myself in an ecstasy of guilt and shame until, in waves of cooling release, I gave the terrible seed of my sin against God into my hand. Quickly and with long practised deception, I raised the disgusting liquid to my mouth and sucked my fingers clean of their all too damming evidence.

Brother James was crouched low to the ground now and I spoke softly from behind, "The Inquisitor has come, brother, the trial is set for the morning."

My words jerked him upright and he shrugged painfully back into his robe. "B…brother Martin, thank you," he stammered and turned to me. "None too soon, I think. The witch has been an evil presence, ever since she's been here. I will be glad when this is over." He struggled into the meagre chair at the desk and picked up a quill, hovering over a manuscript. "I will bring her on the morrow then," he said shakily and dismissed me.

Leaving the dungeon, I was drawn back to the hall and the Inquisitor's party, returning with them to their apartment.

"We will dine in our rooms," the Inquisitor directed me from the comfort of a chair, giving me a long list of the requirements of his group.

I smiled affably and raised my hand, checking him in the midst of his flow. "My Lord, we have received instructions from Rome with your requirements and have carried them out to the letter. Be assured that your needs have been well taken care of." I shrugged slightly in defence of my words, and my smile fell mute as he fixed me with an icy glare.

"I am not a man who likes interruptions, Brother Martin, be sure you are aware of that," and his eyes became narrow with distaste.

I fled the frozen ice of his eyes, aware of my horrible error and to quell an awful fear that sat heavy in my heart, I made myself busy with my charge, bustling around the kitchens and preparing meals for the monastery's guests. I delivered their food in silence amid the whispered taunts and dreadful stares of the holy party, and then retreated to my cell to pray. As night darkened the sky through my tiny window, I prayed before the crucified image of our Lord and Saviour. But even as I whispered my litany, thoughts of the Inquisitor and his party intruded like a sin in my mind. I gave up my attempt at prayer to sit on the edge of my cot, wondering about these messengers of the Church.

I slipped from my cell and through the dark monastery, and came before a carved panel in the wall. With a small push on one of the carved roses, the panel gave way under my hand and I stepped into the hidden passage behind the wall. I walked quietly through the small corridor and came eventually to the peephole behind the wall of the Inquisitor's rooms. I pulled back the cover and put my eyes up to the wall to look beyond, and I saw the royal Inquisitor lying naked on his large bed amid the writhing flesh of his escort and surely, I could feel the sin of lust stir from the sight. I watched the orgy in fascination, oh, shame in human weakness, oh, pitiful in the sight of God, I stood engorged with the rapture of the writhing scene. In sin, I gave sweet shame into the warming folds of my robe and eternally damned by guilt, I fled back to my cell.

"Dearest, oh, dearest Saviour," I called to my statue of Christ the Lord as I knelt before its condemning carved eyes. "Do not cast me from your sight, save me from my damnable lust." Reverently I snaked one arm under the meagre cot and brought out my scourge. Oiled and well worn, the long tails moved under my fingers with their own life and I took my robe from my shoulders, bearing my back for purifying repentance. "Christ, most powerful Lord, Lord God and all your heavenly hosts, save me from my sin," I wailed and flicked my scourge so eloquently over my shoulder, striking out at the cursed flesh on my back, the expert snap of each tail cutting deeply into my skin and searing sweet redemption into my soul. "Save me, Lord, save me, Lord, save me, Lord..." I cried under the ecstasy of my pain and finally, when my mind was black from the roaring of blood, I collapsed blissfully on the floor.

The next morning I stood at the back of the judgement chamber, my hands covering my head against the deafening roar of the crowd assembled.

The Inquisitor in his wisdom had given this trial as a public proceeding and folk from all around the city had quickly gotten word. The witch was brought in by my Brother James and the crowd erupted, shouting abuse and hurling rubbish at the manacled wretch. She was taken and chained in the stocks at the foot of the inquisitor's bench, and then the royal Inquisitor stepped imposingly up to the dais. He gazed around, up into the gallery and immediately the chamber was taken in hush. With a hint of a smile the Inquisitor moved to the grand chair that was his place and sat facing the captivated audience.

"We have before us a witch," he began, skilfully holding the crowd in silent awe. "Self-confessed in the eyes of God and the Church, with a marked confession from her very lips, condemning her as a bride of Satan." With a quick snap he sent a large piece of parchment spinning across the desk. The crowd erupted at his action, but as he spoke again, the mob was silenced by his chilling words. "But this trial is not as simple as that, as this confession proves. There is the work of the Devil in this place and my inquisition will root out all his minions."

The Holy Judge sent the spectators into another frenzy and with catlike grace pushed out of his chair, the condemning note raised before him and he rang out the confession, cutting through the roaring crowd like a knife. "This is the sworn statement of Judith May Smith, dated this seventh day of September in the year of our Lord twelve hundred and sixty-seven:

I, Judith May Smith, do confess, of my own free will and in the mercy of the judgement of our Lord God, of my liaison and pact with the Devil. I, on the night of July the thirty first on this year of twelve hundred and sixty-seven, did take the life of a

*chicken in bargain with the will of Satan and
became a black cat. In this form I came to the
monastery of St. Justinian and did have carnal
pleasures with the monks. I bewitched many of the
brothers and took sacred into my pact, two monks,
signing their bargain with their own blood, and they
did give their souls to Satan and join my witch's
coven. In my plea for the mercy of God I give their
names that they too can be saved from eternal
damnation in hell."*

The crowd roared as the Inquisitor paused in his
speech and his word struck deep into my soul, two
of my brothers had been involved in witchcraft right
under my nose and to my horror I hadn't seen, but
my thoughts froze as the inquisitor began to speak
again.

*"Forgive me, Lord, and let my repentance be a
consuming fire, for I have defiled two men. Oh, let
Brother Daniel and Brother Martin be consumed
also for they are heretics such as I."*

I felt the blood come to a standstill in my veins as
the sound of my name fell into the cavern of the
hall. Before I could move I was held by two of the
prosecutors and drawn inexorably up to the
Inquisitors dais. Daniel was brought forth just as I
and we stood facing the High Judge behind his
towering desk.

"I see the Devil in your eyes," he said examining
each of us in piercing detail. "What have you to say
to this sworn statement?" He cast the confession
down toward us.

I gave a startled cry and fell to my knees, and
from the corner of my eye I could see that Daniel
had done the same. "My Lord Inquisitor," I begged
pitifully. "I have done nothing, I am innocent, I have

never seen this woman before." I heard the monk beside me, begging and pleading his case as I.

"So you would call the Holy Inquisition a lie, would you?" The Inquisitor was on us in a flash, holding the confession out over the bench, shaking the parchment in my face. "This document is taken under the oath of our Lord God and cannot lie. You prove yourselves to be heretic by your own words."

"No, no, my Lord, please!" I called out, throwing up my hands in defence, sealing my fate with each word I spoke. "Please, my Lord Inquisitor, I beg you, I am a reverent man, an honest man, I would never..."

"Enough!" shouted the judge quelling my fevered pleas. "My Lord Prosecutors will take these heretics and extract a confession from them. May God go with you." Among the eruption of noise and airborne rubbish, Daniel and I were led from the hall.

Shackled and manacled, we were taken into the dark dungeon of the monastery and chained against the wall, the agents of the inquisition ranged themselves comfortably around the cold dank chamber. One of the men, the High Prosecutor, held in each hand a heavy piece of parchment. "Brothers, these are your confessions," he said holding the sheets before us. "They are each the same, explaining your liaison with Judith May Smith, your pact with the Devil and your heresy against the Holy Roman Catholic Church. In bewitching others of your order, they each accuse two of your fellow monks to join you at the stake. Now, who would like to sign first?"

Weakly I stared bemused into his eyes, "I have done nothing," I whispered still holding to my innocence.

The Prosecutor laughed briefly. "Stupid bastard," he said shaking his head and gestured to one of his fellows. A small and older assistant came from the fire grate, a glowing red brand held carefully in a ragged cloth and with a nod from his leader, approached us. The wizened man moved close to Daniel and touched the molten tip of the brand to his arm where the robe had fallen away and I could smell the scent of roasting hair floating on the monk's tormented groan. The Prosecutor moved to me and used the brand to cut away my cord. The heat of the metal soon burnt through the rope, my robe and delicately touched my skin beneath. Pain flared on my body and I began to pray. The robe hung loose about me, my naked flesh exposed cruelly to the searing heat of the brand, ribbons of agony flowed through the pale skin of my chest, blissfully cleansing, more insistent than even my scourge could be in its call of retribution. I groaned in the ecstasy of holy purification and whispered my litany of prayer.

"Christ, most powerful Lord. Lord God and... all your heavenly hosts... save me from my sin," I gasped with ragged breaths as the burning poker gouged deep into my breast and sent blood exploding into my brain.

I woke to the splash of fresh water on my face and the dull throb of long supplication and found I had been tied, seated in a chair, with my hands clamped onto a table. The High Prosecutor was sitting opposite me, absently sipping from a frothy mug of ale. He toyed with the corner of that awful parchment and looked deep into my aching soul. "You will sign this confession with your own hand, Brother Martin," he said quietly, a spark of malevolence flashing in his dark eyes. "For only this can save you from prosecution by the Inquisition."

I recoiled from his word and turned away. "I am innocent," I whispered hoarsely, a bright vision of God in his wrath, dancing in my mind.

"Be that so then," and his tone was callous with merciless pleasure.

Two more chairs were drawn to the table and a Prosecutor sat either side of me holding my hands. Bent to their task they studied each one of my fingers minutely and I could feel smooth metal under the nail of each of my thumbs. Agony jumped up my arms and caressed me as the cold tip of metal thrust slowly between my thumbs and the quick that carried each nail, and then the ecstatic separation of flesh from flesh. I cried out in agony and as those digits went numb, they moved on to the next. In precise co-operation the two prosecutors tore casually at my forefingers and screaming, I could feel the nail bending, tearing from my finger under their touch. The torture moved onto another finger on each hand and then the blessed release of darkness took me.

The second time I returned to consciousness, I was chained, freezing and naked in the dark with my face against the wall. The vile stench of ale behind me lingered rotting in my nostrils, my distended and swollen hands sang in frozen lethargy. The warm heat of another body pressed hard up against my back and I heard a voice speak into my ear. "Confess, fool," came the whisper and another wave of rotting air passed over me.

"But I am innocent," I replied feebly, my voice raw from screaming.

I heard the click of a sadistic tongue and then the hard rod of a prick against me. Callously the tool was shoved hard up into my shivering body and the Prosecutor rammed me against the wall. His rhythm was merciless with lust, but I had much practice with cruel lovers. Willing my muscles to relax around his motion, my breath became soft with the scent of this pleasure amid all my pain. But as suddenly as he woke me, the warmth of his rutting body was gone and I was left alone with my thoughts in the cold night. I began a small, hushed prayer in the darkness, crying for my God to release me, wailing my innocence to the freezing wall and finally, in a haze of exhaustion and dreadful pain, I fell asleep.

I came out of oblivion lying, chained spread eagle on a smooth wooden bench, I looked up into the blank gaze of the High Prosecutor. "Do you confess?" he asked mildly, his tone betraying savage humour and deadly intent. "For if you do not, the rack will loosen your tongue."

My hands throbbed against the chains that bound me, a fresh agony of torture in my horizontal position. I did not know if I could bear this new torment, but I still protested my innocence in their eyes and in the sight of God. The Prosecutor looked up from me, his lips curling slightly as he nodded to someone beyond my gaze and in that moment the strain of slack was taken against me. Each of my limbs groaned under the pressure of being torn slowly away from my body.

I screamed out in agony, begging for them to stop. "I will confess, please!" I cried frantically, "I am guilty, I will confess," and the tension on my limbs disappeared.

I was untied and forced to stand, but my legs gave way painfully beneath me and I had to be aided across the room. I was placed in a chair by the small desk and the confession paper was slipped before me.

"Read it, Brother Martin, the Inquisitor will be here soon to see you sign."

I picked up the parchment with trembling numb fingers and read its dreadful account:

I, Brother Martin of the Holy Order of Justinian, do confess, on this thirteenth day of September in the year twelve hundred and sixty-seven of our Lord, of my own free will and in the mercy of the judgement of almighty God, of my crimes of heresy in the Holy Roman Catholic Church. I have been, in the years of my cloisters, in deep and secret consultation with my vile lord Satan, Prince of Darkness. I have given my soul to the Devil in a pact signed in my own blood and have drunk the blood of others to cement that pact. I have taken witches into my most holy places and defiled God's shrine with carnal lust. In my crimes I was aided by my brothers _____ *and* _____ *and I pray that they will be purified with fire as I. Forgive me, Lord, in this hour of my repentance and take me in the blessed fire of your righteous exculpation,*

Have mercy on my soul

witness to the confession

_____ _____

Brother Martin *Brother Pious Tiberius*
High Inquisitor

The empty spaces on the page filled my mind with chill horror, I could not implicate my fellows when I had seen them do no wrong. "I cannot sign this."

But the Prosecutor just smiled over the knife he was using to par his nails. "Oh, but you can, dear monk, and you will, or I will return you to the rack." He slid a long quill across the table. "Oh, and you need not worry about the empty spaces, we have names to fill them," and his smile was long and slow. I shivered against the ache in my joints and picked up the quill. "Wait for the Inquisitor," he said softly.

I didn't have to wait for long though and when the Holy Judge came into the dungeon, he watched as I signed the confession with my small, cramped signature.

"Good, good, the morrow will be a good day to burn, eh, Brother Martin!" with a conspiring cuff on my shoulder, the Inquisitor snatched the parchment from under my hands and stalked off, an evil laugh ringing through the torture chamber.

I was taken, put into a cell and locked in the darkness to mourn my fate. I knelt on the cold damp floor and wrung my swollen hands in prayer for salvation. Rats and crawling insects answered my frozen cries in the cell's perpetual dark and I endured the infinity of my prison. I had neither food nor drink to comfort me and spent that day breathing the foul smell of defecation piercing its rancid way through the agony of my tortured senses until I lay, frozen in my surrender to God.

From somewhere beyond time, a cold grey light cracked harshly into my eyes and the shadow of the Inquisitor fell upon me. I felt rough hands and was pulled from the oblivion of my position on the floor. A sack was tied mercifully around my waist and I was dragged whimpering from the chamber. I was thrown onto the back of a stinking wagon, oxen driven from the sombre monastery and out into the city below.

In the crowded town square, I was roughly assisted from the wagon and turned to the onslaught of rubbish being dumped on me from the pressing crowd. The noise was terrific and I cowed away from the ugly faces around me, their spitting curses showering over me as I was dragged forward. The robed forms of the Inquisitor's men broke a path through the rioting crowd and even though I was knocked more than once to the ground as I was taken against the flow, I was roughly led a nightmare path to the stake.

On a raised dais atop an enormous bonfire of snap dry twigs, I was bound, hung by my wrists against the solid face of the pole that kept the whole structure erect, and watched as the High Inquisitor sprang lightly to the platform before me. The barrage of rotting vegetables stopped immediately and the crowd silenced in the presence of the High Judge.

He cast his eye over the crowd. "You have heard, in the trial of these most loathsome creatures, of their heresy and crimes under the vengeful eye of God. In the mercy of the most Holy Roman Catholic Church, the witch queen, Judith May Smith, and the Brothers Daniel, James, Peter, Julius and Martin, are all to be sentenced to the cleansing fires of God's most righteous mercy and will be forthwith burned at the stake until dead!"

The throng erupted at the Inquisitor's bellow; his words chosen for the impact he knew they would have on the madding crowd. He turned and smiled with malevolent glee at my pathetic position, before he jumped from the dais and walked away. The smell of burning tallow greeted my abused senses as the Lord Prosecutor came into my sight holding a flaming torch, and in the wild ecstasy of the assembled riot, touched its wicked light to the tinder below me. In a frozen moment the fire caught hold and was licking its deadly way towards me. As the blaze caressed my feet and legs, I was caught in the rapture of a vision of an angel, his beautiful flaming white hair and sorrowful eyes entreating me to be still. In the blinding light of incineration, I held out my hand to him and he mercifully took me from this life.

Chapter 7

Pulse.... Beating.....

Life, stirring.....
Memories. Ahh!

Pain......
Anguish, of the heart.....

Choking dreams and visions of souls lost, giving up lifetimes in the dark. The sudden throb of dead blood stirring in the agony of my heart's first beat. Pain echoing in skin unused to the movement of cold essence, rapture in the hell of waking and the knowing of my incarnations in suffering. Slowly I woke from the long draw of deep sleep. Memories of lives flashed before me, placing their knowing deep within my mind, every name and circumstance burned a firebrand in the eternity of my soul. Air stirred in my nostrils and I drank a long draught of something old and familiar, but the smell had turned rancid under the press of centuries of dust and giving a startled cough, I opened my eyes. Lovely Niamh still glowed in the air above, the spectre of her last moments a ghost, frozen in my sight and alluringly out of reach. I yearned, raising a hand to her beauty but that tiny movement raised a lashing curl of dust to shatter the illusion above me and in pain I was awakened once more to the world.

Gnawing hunger, the need for heat in the shivering darkness and the instinct of my tormented soul blossomed, tortured from my rigid form. Joints curled that had been immobile for an aeon, tearing cold ligaments and muscles into agonising fire, lifting a woeful, primal scream from a voice that had been laid to rest lifetimes ago. My body stretched, sinews of a viper and the hunger had me, drawing me from my ancient bed, luring me across the chamber and stirring dust in my wake. I darted up the corridor and came to a rockfall created in ages past, the mortal rejection of my soul. In fury I tore at the stones with bared claws, time proved to be my ally and breaking through to ground level took less than I imagined. Centuries had worn the barrier thin and indeed, when I emerged into the soothing glow of star light, I saw that the castle itself had been eroded, taken away until only a pile of rocks here and there on the brow of a windy hill marked its passing.

Up into the night I sailed on the currents of mortal fire, scanning the landscape for life essence. My vision was so powerful now that I could easily make out the smallest of forms around me. Into my sight came a writhing pool of human light camped against the night. I was drawn in seething pain to the piercing brilliance of life blood and descended with a passion born in the hell of my instinct to kill.

There were four or five sitting around a fire and I attacked, undiscriminating but for the distance between my victim and I. Latching my long talons around his neck, I dragged the mortal shocked from his seat and lifted him high into the night. In that most exquisite moment, my fangs pierced his yielding throat and an eruption of life heat gushed into my frozen soul. A long sigh of immortal pleasure held me as I drew my bite lovingly from the deep oozing punctures on the neck of the new corpse and contorting against the burning passion of blood, I released the body to drop to the camp below. Cries and screams from the panicking humans caught my terrible attention, calling to my newly resurrected need for mortal heat, and I swooped out of the sky to snatch another unwitting victim from around the fire. The man in my hands stared frantic into my eyes, his legs and arms thrashing, his scream curdling under my grip. I brought him to my lips, quickly ending his voice with a deadly kiss, and I drowned in a river of blood that consumed my senses in the heat of human fire. This corpse too, fell like a sack to the ground and I followed it down to where three humans remained. The fresh surge of blood deep in my soul spurred instinct to kill again. I landed upon the sweet earth and shrouded the mortals in calm, holding them witless and without fear. I took each one in lightning speed, eagerly taking from them the flames of their blazing lives.

Rage of blood haze subsided, the maddening desire of life essence receded into a dark corner to brood in the well of my soul, and in its place came the clear and awful remembrance of my true nature. With no one to walk beside me along my path, so I was condemned in the cycle of taking life, knowing the madness would control me and I would be forced to kill without thought again and yet again. Could one such as I find peace, destined to forever stumble alone on my eternally damned walk on earth, a creature so devoid of the heat of the sun and damned to lust after mortal life forever? My beautiful lost companion had said there was a way, or was that just a foolish hope held against the looming endless cycle of my immortal state?

I stood on the edge of firelight reflecting on the dead bodies before me. I did not care for who they were or dispose myself to think of their origins, but I needed to know more of the world I had come into, so without remorse I ransacked the lifeless remains. I came up with little more than a purse full of shining coins, a kerchief and a wicked little blade that was concealed, sheath and all, on the forearm of one of the group. The whinny of a frightened horse caught my ear and I turned from the fire to see tethered mounts steaming in the night beyond me. I gathered up my cache and slowly moved beside the blackest of the beasts, only flames of its vital fire gave away its presence in the darkness. With delicate whispers, gentle touch and the magic of my will, I came close to the creature's face.

"You will carry me, oh, dark one," I nuzzled lightly against the strong warm flesh of its neck, the soft caressing fire of horse essence played duet in the reacting field of my long white hair. My words and soothing thoughts tamed wild fears of death and masked from the animal, the scent that I carried.

I had never been on the back of one of these creatures and pulled myself awkwardly to straddle the large heaving body, but when I lifted my presence slightly, the horse whinnied and my seat found itself easily. My mount snorted out clouds of steaming heat into the night air, catching a foot impatiently against the cold earth and I was caught in the iridescence of muscles moving fluid under his black hide. The animal sighed feeling the long fingers of my hold and in a moment of surrender under my will, gave its mind to my frozen soul. As dark as the abyss of my being and dancing in the fire of mortal existence, I named the beast Demon in my mind, anguished in memories that stirred of other lives and I set my heel into the shimmering flank.

The horse exploded through the night, carrying me swiftly across the cool landscape, long strides sure under the magic of my touch, his path guided instantly at my command and rushed, mane flaring in the tornado of our passing. The dull thud of horse hooves turned to clatter as the landscape gave way to a neat, well-worn roadway and at the end of my sight, human flames burned, a sprawling mortal engine of life undulating on the horizon. I set my mount to a windblown canter and made my way to the edge of the city.

Sounds of laughter and the glow of life assailed my senses as I came to the foot of this giant of writhing heat, and slowed to a walk before moving into the throat of the beast. In the darkened street, long walls of human life towered, casting their own eerie shadows out into the night, the flimsy barrier of stone walls melted from view as I yearned toward the mortal flames all around me. I rounded a corner, into the pool of warmth flowing from a lit building and came to rest Demon before its noisy entrance. My mount laid back his ears, moving skittishly as discordant laughter replaced the soundless rush of the wind and I reached to his neck, casting his mind silent before the inn doors. Sliding lightly from his back, I tied him to a stout railing, he snorted as I moved away in greeting to the horse tethered near, and I stepped under the low doorway into the harsh light of the room beyond.

Glowing fire and smoking lamps filled the tavern with needless light and my eyes set to watering under the blaze of mortal flames before me. But squinting and straining my sight, I made my anxious way through the fury of life. I stumbled blindly against a chair, the naked flesh of my hand was drawn dangerously to the essence of the human that caught my fall, and I recoiled from the heat and piercing voices that lanced my senses so keenly. Laughter rose into the smoky air as I retreated from the pull of these mortals, and made my way carefully across to a long, high counter at the head of the room.

The innkeeper stood flaming behind its well-polished surface and as I reached a corner, he turned and walked across the stone floor. "Will it be ale, sir?" he said as I watched him with tear-stained eyes.

"I need a room," I said flinching from the proximity of his fire and tossed four coins from my purse onto the table.

The innkeeper's eyes flashed wide as the gold pieces came to rest under his gaze. "You'll not be needing all that," he glanced nervously at the patrons nearby and put his hand quickly over the coins. His face moved close to mine in furtive conspiracy and I recoiled from his reaching life heat, "I'll see to it myself."

"I have a horse to stable and I would prefer an inner room if you have one," I spoke quietly but let the innkeeper be taken by the strength of my need.

With a brief nod the vibrant mortal closed his hand over the coins I had given up and gestured towards a door beside the long counter. "There is a private lounge in there where you can wait. I'll have an ale brought to you," he smiled openly and drew back, pocketing the money.

"I cannot bear the stench of ale," I said arresting him. "Bring me something else." He looked about to speak again but I cut him off, walked the length of the counter and into the room beyond.

The door closed on the melee of the throng outside, I was taken by the muffled quiet of this soothing and more comfortable room, the sounds of life behind me lowered to a dull roar and silence engulfed me. The piercing gaze of too many eyes touched me as I entered, but I cast them away sharply, sending the few occupants back to their quiet conversations and swilling of ale. I found a nook to rest in, shrouded from the roaring blaze of fire in the hearth, and the lights of mortal kind that flamed in the scant tallow light.

In short time a buxom young woman came into the room, a tray in her expert hands and crossing to the table before me, she made herself busy with the arrangement of my drink. An enormous transparent cup floated deep golden liquid in an eternal ocean as it swirled in a life of its own.

"My master won't be long with your room, sir," she said, her small hand lingering on the drink. "This is Benedictine, do you know of it?" I shook my head, lingering on the delicate skin of her wrist, iridescent and vibrant with the glow of coursing life blood. "Well, be advised then, sir, it is by far better when you warm it up in the glass." She lifted the vessel to rest between her fingers and swirled it around lightly, "Like this. The warmth of your hand heats the alcohol through the glass and strengthens the brew."

She offered the vessel to me slowly and I cradled the warm drink in my hand, a smile toyed with the corners of my mouth as my frozen touch drained mortal heat from the molten amber liquid. "Thank you," I whispered, the quick rush of stolen essence sparked light in my cold eyes. A timid look overcame the serving girl, a flare of life heat radiated from her form and clutching her tray tightly to her breast, she turned and rushed from the room.

Alone, I lifted the glass before my face and inhaled the rich deep aroma, its scent reminded me of love lost long ago, and pushing seducing pain from my mind, I took a sip of the amber liquid. The searing spirit of human creation burned over my tongue, warming my aching soul against the ravages of its immortal journey and slid like acid into my stomach. I could feel intimately as the foreign liquid invaded my flesh and gripped my body in an agony of heat as rich as the draw of life. I was caught in ecstatic pain, held as the fibres of my being were ripped by its blazing fire, scorching my soul in its flow. A long slow sigh escaped from my thrall and I raised the drink, heavy before my molten eyes, staring out into the room through the clear vessel. I had heard of glass once before, ages ago when I had been mortal and a slave to the Roman Empire, yet never had I experienced a cup made of such a substance firsthand. Within the clear frame captured by the vessel's edge, the seething cloud of human heat was cut suddenly dead, and I saw the room, flat and lifeless. The furniture held mercifully still under my gaze, a tallow lamp sat mute on an even plane of dead wood. A shadow came over my startled discovery and above me stood the innkeeper. My gaze was drawn to his bright aura, and I lowered the glass to the table.

"You like the Benedictine?" he said with a deep earthy voice and smiled, mopping his fleshy neck with a large wad of cloth. "I have your room, sir, bring your drink and I'll take you up." He moved to cross the room and beckoned for me to follow.

I flinched as the door opened on the lighted tavern beyond my quiet isolation, defensively raising an arm as we walked through the blazing heat of life caught seething among the rafters. We reached a corridor leading within and I groaned mutely, breathing in the sudden peace. By the cool light of the inner walls, the innkeeper led me to the stairwell and up to the rooms above.

"Are you afflicted?" he asked casually, I could feel his reserve.

"My eyes are sensitive to light," I replied, and thought to fathom a mortal explanation for my vampire sight as we climbed the stairs. But he easily nodded his head and paused in his effort, to look over me in a brief appraisal, "Ah, yes," he puffed. "I knew another like that once, all white like you and pale, but he had pink eyes not blue as yours. I wouldn't be letting too many people know of your problem, these days, though," he cautioned and held his kerchief high on his brow. With a deep apologetic sigh, he led me onto a broad landing and to a small door set unobtrusive and shadowed in the corner. "Now you would be very fortunate, my friend. I have a room on the inside of the inn that has not been occupied for some time, so I am pleased I can meet with your requirements. I have had your horse put in the stable out back, magnificent animal that one, I might say."

He reached out with a large iron key, unlocked the solid barrier and let me into the room. Small and comfortable, the apartment was illuminated by a fire blazing in the small hearth and he dropped the heavy key onto a table by the door.

"Do not disturb me tomorrow," I turned on him before he could leave. "I do not take the sun too well." I made sure the round innkeeper was aware of my need for solitude and he nodded amiably under my gaze.

"Indeed, sir," he smiled. "I am Thomas by the by, just ask for me if you should need anything. Is there a name I could call you by, sir?"

His casual question stirred an old longing in my soul, a name called softly on the lips of love and I closed my eyes against the pain of a vision of

Niamh. "Julian," I whispered and stepped from him into the room.

I felt a subtle wave of recognition come from the mortal and a sharp intake of breath. "Well, er... I... I wouldn't think you would be wanting to use that name, sir," he stammered from the doorway, and I looked up at him sharply as he cleared his fleshy throat. "I mean, these days, the Inquisition, well. sir, it's everywhere."

But I could see in his shocked face that there was more behind his words, old drawn fear, immortalised in legend stirred knowing in the innkeeper's mind and so I replied, "You choose then, it matters little from life to life the names we choose."

"I have a cousin, Jack is his name, it is simple but do you think it would fit?" I could hear him rush over the words, eager to steer away from the small but growing fear that nagged at his mortal core.

"Greetings. Thomas, I am Jack," I said slowly, a smile taking my mouth as I offered up a formal greeting. "It is good to meet with you. I am in your debt for taking me into your house with such trust." I cast my will to blanket fear from the innkeeper's mind and his face transformed as my spell held him. Taking out his kerchief once more he closed the door and left me to the still quiet of my room.

I hoisted a large armchair easily from the pool of fire light and dragged it across the wooden floor to the darkest corner of the room, sitting heavily into its cushioned depths and cradled the frozen pool of my drink. In the mute glow of firelight, the glass was a window of freedom from pain, its thin veneer causing a barrier between my fragile eyes and the vibrant blaze of the fireplace. From my place in the dark, I stared into the hearth's blazing heart and thanks to this unlikely shield, I was able to look upon heat; oh, yes, there was still pain, but a sweet agony that lulled and caressed, and held me transfixed. Coals formed and disappeared as I watched flames licking over their fuel and the madness of my first day began with the coming of false dawn.

Even looking through the glass, my eye was trapped by the pre-dawn glow, sharp and offensive in my vision, cutting through my mind and I was caught with the horror of being above ground at dawn. In the dark inner room, I could feel the gnawing of sunlight piercing its way into my mind, searing into my eyes unmercifully and I groaned with its coming. The Benedictine glass slipped eternally from my trembling grip and shattered like liquid fire to the floor. I raised my hands and urgently covered my tortured sight, their light barrier no match for the sight that I could see through the walls and in panic I took to the bed to cover my aching gaze.

Soft and luxurious, the sheets had a feel that reminded me of a battle in flight, I had known this touch in a hand full of a billowing cape. When I put my head beneath the soft fabric it covered me as I had been on the open ground in the shelter of Margueritte's remains, protected surely from the sun's maddening rays. In the soft cave of the luxurious bed, I lay in the hours of sunlight, considering the glass I had broken. What good fortune had led me to this place, my delicate prison under the fury of the day? In the calm of my unlikely haven, I was given strength and disconcerting freedom from the curse of sunlight. With a rising hope that was tainted by the hand of fate, I determined to take advantage of my discoveries.

Thoughts of the glass stirred my sight in a memory of a vision from beyond sleep. I saw the angelic bare face of myself captured in the last rays of a dying sun, sleek disks of deep blue glass sitting fixed before my eyes. I could feel the soft hand of hope lulling me as that merciless light crawled across my skin in its journey through the sky above, and I set my thoughts to puzzle how to darken the colour of glass and fix it to my face. Straining with the impatience of waiting for day's end, I eagerly engineered my return to the human race, and when I could feel the last ray of the sun's baleful stare take its touch from the face of the earth, I rose, a phoenix in the flaming ashes of dusk.

I left my room swiftly, taking the stairs in bounding strides, but I was checked at the entrance to the tavern proper by the noise of activity within, and so I lingered at the open doorway until a young woman with a tray walked by me. I hailed her dazzling form, flinching slightly as she brought her life fire within my reach. "Fetch me Thomas," I said curtly, holding up my hand in defence of her writhing heat.

But before she could move, the innkeeper joined her and he broadly gestured with careful hands. "Ah, good evening, sir. Alison, this is Jack," he said by way of an introduction to the serving girl and she bobbed a wide-eyed curtsy before disappearing into the crowd.

I beckoned the landlord impatiently and drew him into the calmer atmosphere of the corridor, resisting the pull of his light as I came close to his mortal warmth. "I need new clothes; can you find me a tailor?"

"Oh, of course," the innkeeper raised his voice in a throaty laugh. "I happen to know an excellent tailor and cloth man. I gather the silk sheets are to your favour?" he asked with a wink and carried on before I could reply, "My establishment boasts the finest exotic sheets in the whole of the south country. M' man goes regularly to the orient, gets the finest fabrics in the world. He's a Moor, y'know."

I shook my head at the unfamiliar name and cut him off, "I also need someone that can work with glass and metal."

"Indeed, sir," he replied quizzical, but I impressed on his mind the command of my will and he nodded in consent.

"Bring these people to me here tonight. I will be in my room." I released his arm from my hand and turned to the stair, "Have some Benedictine sent up, Thomas," I said and returned to my upstairs sanctuary.

I paced the floor impatiently until there was a timid scratching at the door.

"Come," I commanded with strained anticipation and the young serving girl let herself in the room, a tray in her arms balancing a bottle and glasses as she manoeuvred the catch.

"Your Benedictine, sir," her voice was a little breathless as she avoided my gaze, setting the tray on the small oval table beside the hearth. "I'll leave it here to warm," she said pouring a long drink in the silence and turned to the fire to cheer its sullen grate. I watched her breast rise and fall as she took short, excited breaths, the iridescence of her vibrant skin flushed with rising blood and she rose to face me. "I've heard tell that you're Julian come back from the grave," she said, an innocent challenge in her eyes.

I raised an eyebrow, my sight held by her blazing essence. "And if I am, lovely Alison, what would you do then?"

I let her excitement be taken a little into the thrill of apprehension. "I don't know," she whispered timidly, but curiosity drowned her girlish fears. "And besides, I told Gwen that you couldn't be that old, those tales have been told for centuries." But her prattle fell short as her gaze roved over my ancient clothes and up into my eyes.

"I have been called many things in my life, but for now I am Jack," and my sight narrowed slightly in warning. "So know me as that, sweet child, for my other names have much more terrible faces." I smiled faintly and the young woman was beguiled. "You would have me kiss you," I stated seeing innocent desire in her mind and I crossed the room to stand before her, even before she had seen me move. I pushed my face into her seething fire, bringing my lips close to her ear. "Would you have me like this?" I breathed, slowly circling my arms around her and bringing her warmth close to my body, the ache of life blood tormented me in delicate waves, caressing with more skill than any lover's touch and I could feel the soft feminine form move, supple to fit against me. *Ah, mortal*, I thought and let her catch the refrain, *would you be so willing if I were not Julian? And would you let me taste of your sweet blood, if I were?* She looked startled into my eyes as she heard my thought. My voice became soft and alluring as I rose to catch the fright growing within her, "And would you let me love you, forever?"

134

I brought my lips close to hers and warm air of her essence flowed over my skin to dance lightly with my hair, a sigh parted their ruby perfection and I touched my naked skin to hers. Fire danced from her soul, raw and searing against my lips and I recoiled from its touch, a serpent stinging in my ancient isolation and I released the girl, pulling free from her caressing fire.

"I cannot!" I said turning away, lonely tears stirred in sympathy with old pain of love's memories.

I could feel her watching me as I stood embroiled in grief, confusion softened her voice, "What have I done?" she whispered.

Raising my eyes to meet hers, I showed this innocent the raging pain of hundreds of years lost in the dark and she drew back in fear. "I have done enough for both of us, Alison, be thankful I am Jack."

A knock from without fell sharp into the silence, breaking the mortal's wide-eyed gaze from mine. In alarm she ran to the door, threw it open on the men waiting beyond, and with a gasp before the landlord and his companion, the maid ran quickly to the stair.

"Ah, Jack," suppressing a quizzical glance toward the fleeing girl, the innkeeper smiled broadly and entered with over eager bravado. "I have brought the tailor as you have asked. The glass and blacksmith, I have sent for and will be here within the hour." He bristled efficiently under rolls of fabric and crossed the room to throw his load onto the bed, and as he mopped his brow, I recovered from my stinging memories. "This fine gentleman, my friend, is Leon." He waved his kerchief at the massive structure of his companion as another heap of rolls were tossed on the bed. The dark man turned and I was caught by the startling white eyes of a giant, whose skin was as black as the coat of Demon and from whom life essence bloomed coloured in violet and indigo swirls. "He is a Moor and speaks little English, so I would say you won't have to talk much. Just show him which fabric you prefer," he waved a disdainful hand at his burden. "He will do the rest. I'll be back later."

Crossing the floor, the corpulent innkeeper puffed and moaned as he fumbled with the heavy latch and when the door closed, I returned my gaze to the enormous opalescent being. In the veil of his jet skin, his human fire had a deep cast, soothing and cool to my eye, and the vivid colours of his rich dress flowed in complement to his writhing life flame. His eyes caught me with their startling contrast of white and the void of his pupils, and I could sense the careful and knowing veil that was drawn behind their endless depths. The giant was studying me, as intently as I he, and slowly he extended one hand in invitation to examine his wares. I crossed the room and came to stand before him and he pulled away a little as I leaned down to feel the rich cloth, but I could sense nothing from his mind, and so I toyed with the beautiful textiles. The flow of carmine silk ran softly through my hands and I chose the roll from the pile, the fabric's deep luminous glow held still in my sight. And too, I found a roll of corpse heavy plush, blacker than the eyes of the tailor, cool against my skin and I lifted it to join its unwavering partner.

"I know silk," I said slowly rising to face him, "but I have never seen this other one, it is very lovely."

The dark mortal was watching me with suspicion though as he spoke, his strange deep accent betrayed no emotion, "What is this charade, vampire? I know your kind too well to be taken by this act." His brow creased slightly as he took another step backwards. "Am I to be next for the kill?"

"I have called you here only to make me clothes, tailor," I replied weary of the reminder of my sorrow, his suspecting stare changed into surprise at my words.

"You speak Moorish," he said, shocked into showing the fear of me in his heart.

I returned his gaze levelly, "I speak as I choose, as I always have." I cared not to create any illusion around my presence in the face of his accusations. Would there be a time where I could live free of the legacy of Margueritte?

"I will not work for one of your kind," his dark voice held a bitter edge. "I have seen the evil that your breed have done."

Remembrance flowed with his accusation and Niamh came with her beautiful eyes into my mind. I turned from his gaze in suffering of ages past, my voice rough with sorrow, "Then you condemn me back to the hell I had sought to escape."

We stood for a long moment as the tailor measured my words against his knowing of vampire kind, the room cold from his accusations, and when his voice came again, I was caught by the breaking of silence.

"I have heard of one of your kind, a prince of darkness centuries old, talked about since the coming of the Vampire Queen."

The soft echo in his voice drew my sight back into the present and into his gaze once more. "I am Julian," I whispered and his dark face grew soft with understanding.

"Yes, I would have thought it so." The reply floated from him on a cloud of essence.

"Will you work for me?"

I could see thoughts of old tales flicker though his mind as he weighed my question, but his mind betrayed little more. "Will I be safe in your company?"

"You have my word."

Vibrant eyes moved their piercing touch from my skin and the tailor reached into the folds of his brilliant jacket to remove a long cloth measure. And without a word, in surety of my bond, the dark giant approached, arranged me like a marionette and took stock of my frame.

Each time his life fire caressed my exposed skin, I flinched against its searing desire. "Make haste with your work tailor, I care not for your touch." My words were softly spoken though I could feel hesitation for a moment in his contact. But his hands worked quickly over me then and in short time he stepped back to examine my choice of fabric.

"I will make you a bliaut of the silk and hose of the black," he mused over his design. "I have just returned from the orient with this cloth," he spoke absently fingering the rich pile. "It is known as velvet," and turned to smile briefly at me.

I had seen the fashion of the day through tortured eyes and cared not for the tight leggings and long skirts favoured by the mortals of this time, so we talked a little and settled on a design. Long straight velvet trousers would flow low over silk hose and velvet lined boots, a shirt of the carmine silk and a jacket of the plush, fitted into my waist with long folds of cloth hanging to my knee, it would be a simpler and more fundamental version of the Moor's own dress. I insisted both jacket and trous be lined with silk and when he had finished taking my instruction, I offered him a Benedictine.

"I will have these made up on the morrow and bring them to you when the sun is gone," he saluted me with the large glass.

I retrieved my drink from the low table and moved out of the presence of mortal heat, turning my head from the bright lights of fire and human together.

"You are not like the others I have seen," the tailor spoke quietly, his voice low and rich as dark velvet.

I met his gaze. "There are none such as I. I have been damned and lost for a thousand years or more, what could you know of my existence?" I stared at him for a long moment, but any answer he might have given was cut short by a knock at the door and Thomas came bustling into the room, chatting in light conversation with the other human behind him.

"Ah, Jack, I see you have finished with Leon's tender ministrations." A smile echoed across his broad face. "This gentleman is skilled in both glass and smithcraft, so I thought I would seal both your needs in one." The innkeeper slapped his companion affectionately on the shoulder. "I will pour you a drink, Richardson."

Briefly I told the smith of the affliction of my vision as he warmed and sipped his Benedictine, and the solace I needed from the severity of light. Our conversation ranged across the spectrum of colours in glass and the delicate frame that would be needed to hold the concave disks in place, finally settling on the design that my protection would take, and the wiry smith left with Thomas, clucking and muttering over his challenge.

Alone with the silent Moor drinking quietly before the hearth, I retreated to my chair beyond the fire's reach and sat watching the flaming essence of his life float on the pleasure of the spirit he consumed. Long moments passed, I let my vision be held by the curling flames that rose above his dark form and hardly noticed when he began to speak.

"In Granada we have tales of the undead that have come, in legend though our history. A Gypsy Queen and an immortal prince parenting the race of vampires that came to our land. I have seen and heard of the creatures that range the world in the night, but not for many years have their awful forebears been seen."

A smile played with the corners of my mouth as he fell silent. "Margueritte died by my hand," I said softly, remembering her ill-fated end.

"You would kill one of your own?" His eyes were wide with disbelief.

"I have told you there are none like me in this world. I have been alone for a millennium. Margueritte chose her fate, she was my creation, mine to decide upon her existence." I leaned forward slightly in the chair and cast my gaze close to his veiled mind. "Know this, friend Leon, that if I could I would take back the life I gave to all my vile offspring. Had I known of the evil of my acts in those days, even Margueritte would not have been born. But I have been tricked into this life by my own cruel destiny." My words dropped clear into the air between us, "I walk eternally in the dark, far from communion with all that lives; alone, immortal and empty, forever." Speech stilled, I retreated into the shadows of my chair, away from the allure of his flaming light and pain of remembered suffering reached over me.

For long hours, the human watched me from by the fire, his dark eyes flashed occasionally as his thoughts ranged over our brief conversation, I sat sipping at the flaming essence of alcohol and brooded in the dark.

"Do you intend to be here when the sun rises?" I questioned him, I could feel the tug of false dawn stirring my aching need for asylum from the cruel light of day.

The tailor rose as my words pricked his realisation of the time and hastily, lowering his glass to the small table, he crossed the room to the pile of fabric. "No, certainly no," he spoke and gathered the rolls into his giant embrace, leaving the deep red cloth alone on the bed. "The silk is a gift, do with it as you please. I will be back tonight with your clothes." He briefly turned to me under the weight of his burden and then quickly left the room.

Dawn with all its torments came screaming with the fury of the sun's new rays and I launched myself to the bed, the deep red sanctuary of rolled fabric holding spear still in my agonising sight. I cringed in the darkness of my inner room, flinching from the awful piercing stare of sunlight and fumbled with the long bolt, unrolling it tent like, to hide from the day. Inside the ruby cave of silk I sat under sentence and waited, a void of peace from the searing heat of the sun to soothe my accursed soul. And even when I would move a little and there was a parting in the fabric, the shafts of light invading my prison caused me no pain. Indeed, I had to be shown this perhaps five or six times before I realised I felt no pain from the sun at all, and slowly I moved to peer tentatively from my shelter into the empty room beyond.

First with one eye gingerly peeping from under a crack and then more adventurously with all my sight, I looked into the seething flames of the sun above, its writhing rays dancing with infinite fire through the small room, threatening and caressing with its light. But even though I could see nothing past the flaming air, I felt no pain and moved to push my head, inch by inch out into the light. I realised that I had seen myself standing in the sun, in that memory of a life gone by, but still could not credit the relief I was given by the flimsy dark red material. I laughed an age old and tormented laugh, driven high by my hallucination of heat from the sun. By the time daylight began to wane, I had been forced back into darkness by the probing light, its cruel illumination consumed my senses in madness and I hid my eyes from its demonic allure, clearing my sight in the steady rich folds of silk.

As darkness approached and the sun touched its molten orb to the rim of the world, I emerged from my strange safe haven to see the last vibrant rays shafting their way into my dark room. The retreat of daylight restored my sanity, and I rose from my cave on the bed to a timid scratching from outside. I crossed the room to open the door on Thomas and the dark tailor who stood behind the innkeeper with folded velvet in his arms. I stepped back and allowed them entrance to my den, moving out of their intoxicating rays of life.

Leon smiled lightly and offered up his burden to me. "See if they fit," he said casually and dipped his hand into a fold of his clothes.

I took the pile and retreated into the darkness, away from the fire and human heat and tore the cracked leather that I had worn for centuries from my frozen skin. I slipped into the silk lined clothing, revelling in the chill refuge, the high collar of coat and blouse floated beneath my reacting hair, soothing the fire of life from its lashing dance. Cool velvet sat smooth beneath my fingers, fine and heavy, tailored well to my shape and I let the fine clothes mould into my form.

I turned smiling at the humans before me, their fires bright with my elegance and I saw Leon holding a small flat box in his hand. "I went to see Richardson on my way here and he gave me this to give to you."

I crossed the room quickly and took the case from him. Within sat a simple frame of light silver, two oval concave disks of glass sat held by the fine metal. When I took them from the case I was surprised to see the long arms attached to position it on my face were neatly tucked behind, connected to the frame with modest hinges. I hadn't thought of that clever trick. The deep blue bowls peered at me as I took the small machine from its box.

"Very good," I whispered opening the arms carefully, sliding the frame onto my face. The room darkened before my eyes, a barrier of soothing blue between me and the heat of mortal kind, all light and movement suddenly disappeared from my sight and I could look upon humans without being painfully drawn to their fires. Albeit that they now looked like dead flesh without their flaming auras, but this I could bear better than the sight of their burning heat. A sigh flowed slowly through my smiling lips.

"I gather these are to your liking then, Jack," said Thomas with wide appreciation.

I cast my sight around the dim apartment all things were still. "So this is how mortal sight is, I had forgotten," I whispered moving toward the men. As I reached out to touch the innkeeper's face, I could feel the pull of fire on my exposed hand, betraying life essence in the flat dead flesh but all else was cut from my senses and I was free to stand beside the mortals without the urge of my awful instinct. I gave a small chuckle, "Ah so now I am civilised, hey, my friend?"

A flat bead of sweat broke on the stout innkeeper's forehead, the drop glinting dead light onto my eyes, and my hand fell to lightly stroke his fleshy neck.

Beside me Leon shifted uneasily, clearing his throat, "Ah, yes. More human, eh, Julian?"

Thomas pulled back from my touch, the spell broken, and with a swift and nervous laugh turned on the black giant "Stop ye talking that gibberish, Leon," and then too quickly to me, "Don't mind him, Jack, 'tis that Moorish language. But I have work to do so, I'll leave you gentlemen to settle up," and with an uneasy mop of his brow, Thomas fled from the room.

I had forgotten payment for my clothes, "How much do I owe you?"

The tailor gave an admonishing wave and shook his dark locked head. "I have a proposition for you," his bass voice plucked at my curiosity. "Bring your money and come gambling with me and then I will set a price." I was caught as surely as prey. Leon's words fell into my mind like ice. To go out into mortal life and be among their vibrant lights without suffering, beguiled I let him lead me from my room and down to the street below.

We took the back streets, away from the torch light that illuminated the more public road and ranged through the city until I could smell the essence of the sea, down into dark alleys until we arrived at a tall narrow house slotted into a row of many of the same. Leon gave a sharp knock on the plain door, preceded me into the tallow and ale rancid air of a card game and we stood to one side observing the play. My companion whispered the scant rules of this game he called Brag, and when a defeated opponent left the table, I slid easily into the chair.

"That'll be the seat of a looser," grumbled one of the players under a long moustache and I watched him as he gazed on my appearance. "Hmm, five pieces'll be the stake."

Leon moved to my side and leaned over the table "Him be with me, John," he said, his accent suddenly broken and ragged as he spoke with foreign words. The moustached player casually waved the Moor aside and cut the deck.

I played that table in surprisingly easy company with the humans, gazing over my dark glasses and watched life flames blaze from the mortals around me. I guessed my opponent's intent from the curling essence that flowed within the hazy room, and a pile of coins grew in front of me. When morning threatened its coming, the game had long finished, Leon secured the pot in a large obscure fold of his amazing jacket and we left the beaten players.

We walked along cobbled roads leading away from the docks, I caught the first baleful rays of dawn as they came screaming over the horizon and pressed my dark barrier sharply against my fragile sight. Leon sensed my shock and took me by the arm, silently guiding me as he set a fast-paced jog that led us up and into the city's heart. Within minutes we were dwarfed by the grey facade of a tall and looming building.

"My family's trade house," he said and opened a small door that admitted us into a kitchen.

Within the darkened house, the Moor led me through richly decorated corridors and to a quiet inner lounge that sat illuminated only by the fading glow of a small fire, and my new friend gestured for me to sit by the hearth.

"Benedictine?" he asked and crossed the cosy room to a carved wooden cabinet and shelves full of bottles.

I nodded, settling peacefully behind the safety of my glass shield, easy in freedom from the curling madness of day and accepted the drink, to rest and gaze into the smouldering fire.

"And so, Julian, how do you fair this day?" his voice flowed rich in the silence.

I smiled slowly, "Better than I have for centuries."

"Ha," he gave a deep bark. "A vampire who walks in the day, who would ever have credited that?" He shook his head at me and sat back in his chair. "You, sir, are an amazing man."

Within short time, a deep rumble of sleep gave up music into the air, I caught his glass as it slid from the arm of his chair and smiled in good company of the sound. I sat silent, unthinking in relief from sun loved pain and peered a little over the absolute barrier of glass, to be caught in amazement at the difference in the quality of light. The dark blue protection suspended my sight in a cloak of night that banished the day, the partnership of glasses and silk made the ceaseless stroke of sunlight bearable on exposed skin and dampened the reacting dance of my hair.

Elsewhere in the house, the sound of humans following the routine of mortal life; the sound of a bell caught me often, a salesman's spiel, his smooth compliments and tales of other lands, echoed beyond my haven throughout the day. Voices that became familiar as employees of the business, taught me a little of the life of Leon's family, the trade between Briton and China would impress clients the most. The gruelling voyages sailed to fetch the finest cloth in the world would set any female in a breathless titter but no one came into the lounge where I sat with my sleeping companion, sipping Benedictine and waiting patiently for the end of day.

I became good friend to the cloth trader, amused by the contrast between our worlds and yet I took him close into my confidence and immersed myself in his quiet strength, growing over time to feel almost human myself. My godsent velvet and silk provided such an absolute barrier against mortal fire that I lived without noticing the pull of instinct within me. Leon took me freely into his grand house, and I would spend my days there as much as I would the tavern if the dawn caught me out gambling too late to reach the haven of my apartment. My existence was simple and unthinking and as days cycled into months, I carelessly let myself forget even the dreadful journey of my soul.

Chapter 8

I found my place by the gaming table and sat shuffling the deck as the other players came into the room. Leon as usual stood mute by my shoulder watching as my opponents made their way to the game and I smiled slowly as I watched human fires gather above the rim of blue. The room was filling steadily, ale and strong spirits mixing their rancid way into the glowing light of mortal life and as I heard the door open once more, I was accosted by the faint odour of something old and horribly familiar. My head jerked as the scent came into my awareness and I looked up to find the source, raised a hand to my companion and whispered low as I fixed my gaze on a small and insignificant human standing beside the wall.

"Leon," I whispered in his native tongue "There is a stranger by the door," and I raised a hand imperceptibly to indicate his presence. "I feel something from him."

The giant nodded briefly and moved casual from my side. The game began and I played with the loathsome faint smell of death lingering around me, the long fingers of its sickly scent distracted me from the cards I held. But even though I could barely hold my concentration, still I took my opponents with a hunter's skill and as usual a pile of coins began to grow before me. Leon stood beside the stranger speaking low and after some hours moved back to my side.

Leaning close by my ear, his indigo essence curled the tendrils of my white hair and he whispered, "That man is the vassal of one Count Douvélle. The count has learned of your reputation and invites you to join a private game." A flame of hot excitement flowed betraying from his skin, though his words were spoken flatly.

I shifted slightly to observe the mortal whose eyes were fixed to the cards that I held, his countenance was meagre and poor but the scent that he carried interested me more than any guise of dress or demeanour. So laying down a winning hand, I retrieved my night's profit and let Leon and the serf take me from the room.

We walked the streets under the midnight sky, through the cobbled ways and up to a hill that nurtured one corner of the sprawling city. At a large gate the small man pushed aside its ominous black wrought teeth, and beckoned my friend and I to enter the grounds beyond. We strolled along a dark avenue shaded by trees, the grounds behind the wall stretched far up onto the side of the hill and came to the grand house that stood proud and brilliant above the estate. The lights behind the windows were inviting, but I could feel a presence of death and smell the awful scent of fresh blood.

"Be on your guard," Leon spoke softly by my elbow. "I feel uneasy about this place."

His words rose a small laugh from my throat, *So well you should, my friend,* I thought, directing my words onto the veil in his mind and his eyes became flat with unease.

We climbed the grand staircase before its massive arched entranceway, the serf knocked timidly on the solid door and was answered by the gaunt form of a tall mortal, almost as tall as my dark companion, who admitted us to the great hall. I could hear music playing softly from somewhere in the house that caught and echoed within the high dome above, the melancholy refrain lifted my sight upwards and I saw angels flying high on the walls, their wings casting great shadows on the intimate designs of the dome.

"This way," the gaunt servant was waiting to one side of the hall and raised a hand to an open door. A small laughing crowd waited within and fell silent as we entered. Turning to watch our approach, the stylish group paused from their convivial gathering within the rich confines of the gaming room, and all attention turned to a broken ring of men sitting around the deep red velvet of a table. The players' eyes raised from their cards as the hushed party alerted them to our presence and a slim, elegant man rose quickly from his chair.

"Ah, gentlemen, please come to the table, we have been awaiting your arrival," he extended his hand to an empty seat. "I am Count Douvélle, welcome to my home." The count's unusual accent caressed my ear as I slipped into the offered place.

"My name is Jack, and my friend is Leon," I replied, but the count was nodding, a smile lifting the corners of his mouth.

"I know, I have been watching you for some time. This is why I invite you to my game." I could feel something on his words that searched for my thoughts and although I picked the scent of death from its touch, I cast a veil over my mind and feigned ignorance of his spell. His eyes narrowed for a moment as he realised something of my ploy, but he sat back into his seat smiling arrogantly and shuffled the deck.

My host was explaining the rules of the house as I moved to take the glass barrier from my eyes, but I hardly heard what he said as I looked around the room. Among the blazing flames of human fire gathered at the table, the iridescent glow of

150

something old and familiar held fast in my gaze and I knew I had come into the midst of vampire kind. The count himself radiated the eerie glow of the undead, as did the two beautiful youths that flanked his chair and as they passed the table, I counted as many as six of the creatures stalking around the party. I shot a quick glance at Leon and saw that he too gauged the presence of the undead amongst the guests, but his mind betrayed nothing more than suspicion and readiness to fight.

I took the cards as I was dealt them, watching the players carefully, the glow of vampire light reacted very differently to that of the mortal fire, but I could still read its changes and as we played into the night, one by one my opponents retired. The count was an exceptional player, although it was mostly by sheer luck that he won the pot and soon there were only he and I at the table.

"You play with the skill of many years, sir." The count idly toyed with the glass that he held.

I smiled low. "I have had much practice. You yourself are a master of the game, Count," I responded with the nicety required, raising my Benedictine to him but I could feel something deeper behind his compliment.

"Do call me Henrë," he insisted casually leaning forward over his cache, "Jack." I could feel his probing mind once more and reflected it blankly, staring long into his piercing eyes, his presence oozed under an odd dark beauty, alluring me to his spell. "You must stay in my home today and play with me again when evening falls," he said rising from his chair and his two young companions followed suit. "I will see to it that my man will make you comfortable. Unless, of course," and he raised a high arched eyebrow to me, "you have some other business this day?"

False dawn crawled into my mind as he spoke and I could feel the sun behind it, if I stayed in this place I would have to remain until sunset, although with the vampires retired too, I was intrigued to stay. The count led us from the gaming room and into the hall beyond, his lithe walk floating gracefully before Leon and me as we followed through the house. He led us into a comfortable fire-lit living room where tired minstrels were gathering their music from a late night of play and turned to leave.

"I will be back this evening, gentlemen," he waved a flourish of his rich sleeve. "Call on my man should you need anything, and as I felt the first rage of dawn's call, he was gone.

Behind my veil of blue the piercing dance of sunlight was cut absolutely from my vision and I smiled faintly at the caress of heat on my exposed skin.

Leon crossed the room and picked casually at a fruit bowl on the low table before the fire. "Can we speak?" he asked quietly in his native tongue.

I reached out and felt the sleeping presence of vampire kind. "I think so, I would not think the servants speak Moorish."

"I counted eight of them, but there was another party in here," he said around a mouthful of fruit and spat a pit into the fire. "I could smell the foul stench of death on them as I did on you the day we first met. But I suspect their odour is fresh." He mused for a moment and then turned to me, "I do not smell that on you now, my friend."

Yes, I could feel the irresistible pull of blood slowly coiling around my spine, that pull would take me one day when its viperous intent rose beyond my control, and I could see that Leon knew that of me. "I would say this gathering had a double purpose," I replied, taking my thoughts from my awful nature.

He mused quietly over another mouthful and stared into the fire, keeping close counsel on his thoughts and finally spat into the fire. "Well, then, we shall see what is afoot when the sun sleeps tonight, eh, Julian?" He shook his head slowly and collapsed sated in a chair. "Now even though I know you need no sleep, I a mere mortal do," and promptly he was snoring, head back against a high cushion.

I wandered through the echoing rooms of the grand manor house, the faint awareness of being watched following me through long corridors, and innocently I studied the magnificent art and design of the building. High arched domes and decorated ceilings captured the scent of their masters, filling my senses with eerie ghosts, the rich tastes of an eccentric count and a feminine touch which echoed strangely of love beneath the tall spires of a castle in a time gone by. I passed a dark corridor, which reached for me with the gagging stench of a crypt and knew that was the count's private chambers, but the gaunt servant was beside me before I could take a step into the black maw.

"Your friend has arisen and is asking for you," he stated finally and drew me back through the house to the cosy living room where Leon sat stretching and yawning in his chair.

"Food for my companion," I dismissed the servant crossing the room to a vacant chair beside the fire. "I have been watched," I said simply, "but the vampires are still underground." I peered briefly over the top of my shield into the violent storm of sun rays. "It is late afternoon. They will rise soon."

The Moor nodded, "Then the game will be on again. But tell me what game that is, Julian?"

"I cannot guess."

He regarded me for a long moment, "Perhaps they do not know that you are one of their own."

I had not thought that perhaps these creatures did not possess my ability to detect vampire kind, or perhaps my essence was as divorced from them as my ability to withstand the day. "If they do not then I am sure they will try to kill us once the count is bored of the game he plays." Leon grunted roughly at my words. "Perhaps it would be wise to leave while the sun is in the sky," I said softly, knowing the danger he courted.

"Then you must leave with me," he replied blunt.

"Not under the sun." My words fell into the still air and he turned his dark gaze to the blazing hearth.

We sat for the last hours of day, waiting for the setting sun and when I felt the bright rays of its heat touch the horizon, I could feel the vampires stir.

"They wake," I whispered and Leon blinked in acknowledgement. As I took the glasses from my face I could feel the presence of the count standing in the doorway.

"Good evening, Jack," his greeting was smooth but I could feel damned hunger stirring beneath its subtle spell.

I turned, rising from my chair and he was by my side, his eyes betrayed their yearning for my blood and casually I faced him, "Another card game tonight, Henrë?"

"I thought a little dinner would be good to begin," he spoke softly into my ear, his cold breath curling seduction around me.

"Henrë," a lilting voice beckoned from behind the count, "introduce me to our guests."

A smile crossed the count's face as he stepped back to acknowledge the woman, "Of course, my dear. Please, Vivien, I would like you to meet friends Leon and Jack." He held his hand out to his lady and as my eyes met hers, I could feel a roar of old dead pain.

"Niamh," I whispered as she drew before me.

"I'm sorry, monsieur, you have me confused. But I am pleased to meet with your acquaintance all the same." Gracefully she held out a porcelain hand for me to kiss and I took its cold radiance to my lips. Memories of love flowed over my skin in her cool essence and I was held in sweet pain of love for Niamh. "Why, Henrë, your friend is the most charming fellow," she spoke gaily, her accent thick and as beguiling as the count's. "Our guests will be arriving soon and then we shall eat." She smiled at me, her eyes sharp and eager and set on studying my skin intently. As she caught me watching her, she gave a girlish and mock-innocent laugh and floated elegantly from the room.

"So you like my beautiful wife, eh, Jack?" The count had strolled over to the fireplace and stood in its brilliant illumination. "She remind you of someone, perhaps?"

Ghosts and visions danced within my century worn gaze, my lovely Niamh lost and gone forever more. Cold anguish from her spectre stung my dark soul, "Perhaps I will not be such good company this evening," I said turning from the door.

155

"Nonsense, my friend, old memories can have no place in my house," he chose his words carefully. "You can pine tomorrow, Jack, but tonight you can enjoy, come."

I was taken about the arm by his cool touch and led half resisting from the room. We crossed the grand hall and entered the smaller dining hall that I had encountered on my investigations of the day, brightly lit and set for a meal. The chamber had many occupants already, a few of which I judged to be vampire kind but a memory of Niamh's beauty and the presence of mortal fire lulled my instinct for caution. We sat around the long heavy table sipping spirits and I watched the countess in easy conversation as she laughed and chatted gaily to her human companion. The illusive veil of her beauty took me far from the party and deep into my own sorrowful thoughts.

I started suddenly as I felt a light touch on my arm and Leon leaned into my ear. "I feel we are to encounter something very ugly soon," he whispered.

The Moor's low words stirred me from my malaise and my gaze was caught by the count. "Your hospitality has been most exemplary, Henrë, but I feel a game waiting for us," I forced more levity than I felt.

"Ah, but, Jack, the game is already afoot," he spoke softly, coming close to my face.

As if that had been a signal, a high wail split the gentle conversation and the violence of vampire kind erupted at the table. The dark creatures moved as one to fall upon their human victims, holding down the screaming mortals as they feasted upon their living blood. Their feeding was bloody but well organised and as I jumped from my seat, I could see they were well practised at their evil art.

I backed away from the scene, vile in the sight of my beloved Niamh greedily drinking from her prey, the smell and sight of fresh blood churned against my stomach, drawing and revolting me and I flattened to the wall with my giant companion beside me.

"Are you alright. Julian?" he whispered urgently as I reeled against the pain in my guts, his eyes narrow and fixed on the horrific scene before us.

"I do not know," I gasped retching, turning my head from the carnal feast. I could not look at the sight for the revolting hunger it lay blankly in my mind.

"Should we try to leave?" he asked shortly.

But the count had raised his dripping mouth from the corpse by his side and turned dangerously toward us. "Gentlemen, do you like?" His lips parted in a long red smile. "Perhaps you would care to join us, no?" and I watched him flash from his seat to stand before my face, the odour of fresh blood sick against my empty soul.

Leon gasped as his mortal eyes failed to see the quick movements. "Devil!" he whispered.

"You will not leave this place tonight, my beautiful friend," the vampire used a beguiling tone, "but I can offer you eternal life by my side as an alternative." He raised a cool hand to toy lightly with my white hair.

I laughed shortly at his proposal brushing him from his preoccupation, "Eternal life in damnation of the dark, is that all you have to offer? I would rather the sleep of death, but even that you cannot give to me. I have walked a hell greater than you could ever imagine! For lifetimes."

But the count had not heard my careful statement only my savage laugh. He roared fuming away from me, to sit amid the carnage of the feast. "Very well, lovely Jack, is this how you see the end of your life?" He waved a casual hand over the blue corpse beside him.

"Indeed no," I replied, being sure this time that my voice spoke in his mind. "I have seen my end more than once and my beginning. But I would not think my blood will taste too good to you vampire, since it has been stagnant in my body for over a thousand years."

His eyes grew wide as he realised my words were in his head and the room became still. Slowly he shifted on the chair and regarded me closely in the awful silence, "Your name then is not Jack, eh?"

I cast my gaze deep into his immortal eyes, "Best not to speak my name, Count, it could mean death to you." This time it was he who laughed, a thin sound that belied growing caution at my words. "But even so it is mine to take the abominable life that you hold, child of my darkness. You who were brought into being by magic's cruel trickery, twice damned are you who stir my age-old pain."

Fear suddenly sparked in the vampire as he listened to my voice, and slowly he whispered my name like a release under his breath. Instinct erupted in my soul born under months of neglect and I flew at him screaming my fury. I took him back across the table under the force of my charge and crashing through the terrified crowd, I pinned him to the floor.

"Dare you speak of me, foolish one!" He thrashed under my vengeful grasp and with a roar pushed me back. I let the momentum of his charge lift me from the floor and holding him in my grip, raised to hover in the air.

Below, Leon was assaulted by the evil creatures and defended himself in a corner as I struggled weightlessly in the embrace of the count. The vampire worked to part with my iron hold, but I held him fast and laughed, "Vain and stupid creature, you have not the strength to be cursed with my dark gift." I released him with one hand and held it high above his breast. "Now I take what is mine."

I plunged an iron claw into the cavity of his chest, breaking through the fragile bones that protected what lay within and slashing at the flesh, tore the heart from his writhing body. A small cry escaped the count's lips as his eyes flashed wide in the shock of his death and I dropped the corpse to the floor below.

With an ecstatic scream, I held the oozing black heart high before me and my words forced silence into the room. "Be warned, your day of judgement is at hand and I am an avenging angel!" I launched myself into the throng of screaming vampires and madness took me. Thrashing and clawing I killed without discrimination, the bodies of the damned fell lifeless at my touch, their frozen screams dying without defence, until at last I had the fragile pleading form of the count's mate in my hands.

"Please, monsieur, I have done nothing." Her fear brought sharp focus to my sight.

"I have missed you, my love," I whispered, rage draining away in her beautiful eyes, memories of lost love rose to hold me for a moment, confused between time.

"Would you have me love you?" I could see a sudden change in her, my memories fuel to save her wretched life but in that shift I could see now the cunning eyes of Margueritte watching me.

159

I turned away in anguish. "Will I live to eternity with this pain?"

"I will soothe your pain, my love," her dark accent was thick with the seduction of her spell.

"And then?" I gazed on her quickly, the mocking smile of her false promise played on her mouth. My eyes moved to tears, rejecting her hollow trust and rage seized me, my hand moved almost of its own accord, viciously plunging into the breast of the startled vampire and I took her wretched life as well.

In the quiet stillness of new death, Leon shrugged himself free of the corpses around him and walked slowly into the room, I released the dead woman and turned to the uncertain flames of his awe filled essence.

The Moor was watching me fearfully. "Will you kill me?"

"I gave you my word, friend Leon, that you would be safe from me." My gaze was becoming fixed on his vital fire and I felt the hunger for life blood reaching for me. "But I must leave, this night has stirred something old within me."

He nodded, a spark of terror flaring in his mind, "Go then, I will take care of this." Almost before his words ended I was gone from the room, across the great hall and out into the night.

High and far from the grand house I ranged, peering into the shadow at the edge of the sprawling city for the lure of human life, and saw the lonely form of a caravan making its way out into the country. I flew low to the moving carriage, sensing the two humans within and landed lightly on top, matching my stance to the pitch of the roof. Mortal fires reached out to me through the light structure, inflaming my instinct to kill and I ripped the thin covering away to expose the couple within. I reached down and pulled the man up to me, holding him easily with one hand and sank my bite into his muscled neck, puncturing his vein and freeing his life essence to course in a rapture of pain through my soul. Within moments, the fury of my need had drained the body to a dying corpse and I reached back down to complete my awful task. I took the screaming woman by the throat and raised her high into the night above the ruined caravan, fastened my long fangs deep within her slim neck and cut through her cry in my insidious need. Agony of the caress of female fire flowed long on her essence. When the last spasms of her heart grew lax with death, I release the corpse to fall below and hung suspended in the air, writhing in the sweet lucidity of stolen blood. But in that moment an inner vision overcame my senses and I was locked in the awful sight of another life; a flash of bright silk caught my eye and I knew, I had caught the image of a being I had seen before.

In the vision I could feel the terrible crushing force of a silken rope held tight to my throat, my life breaths coming ragged and short from the merciless grip of a noose, I could dimly hear my vain struggle as my legs thrashed hanging in the air. In the last throes of death, the door of the room crashed open and an angel stood in the entry, black dressed and shocked into stillness, his white hair floating gently around his face, and my heart jumped with a deep confusion of emotion and melancholy pain. I saw him rush towards me, lifting up in the air to catch my awful suicide, but I writhed in a last moment of loss and desperation, and died before he could take me from my fate.

A cry of anguish tore from my tortured soul and I fell from the sky, landing heavily with the pain of my vision and I lay weeping beside my lifeless victims. After long moments, the energy of plundered life beguiled my aching heart, I pushed the phantom from my mind and rose to walk slowly back into the city. I would entertain no thoughts as I walked, each time I closed my eyes against a flare of human life, the spectre jumped into my sight and I pushed its awful face from me until I was numb from the effort. I moved through the sprawling community, instinctively following dark streets and by the time false dawn came balefully to stare across the horizon, I found myself on the steps before the grand house of the count.

Quietly I crossed the great hall and came to stand in the doorway of the cosy lounge where I had spent the previous day. Leon sat by the fire, dozing lightly in its warm company, but before I could speak, his dark eyes flicked open and he looked up in sleep confused fear.

"Oh, it is you," he said, his gaze coming to rest on my face. "So, you have returned. I think you will be needing these," and he held up the slim frames of my protection from the sun.

I moved slowly across to the fire, sat in the other chair and took the machine, covering my eyes from the violent storm of sunrise. "And how did you fare, my friend?" My question was as dead as the blank eyes of the corpse in my vision.

A small smile played on his strong dark face, but there was no mirth in its movement. "It seems that the servants here are as glad to see their masters gone as I," he inclined his head to the door. "We took the bodies and entombed them all, three or four to a coffin, in the same hole that the creatures had spent all their days. I had the corridor walled up in the night so now, my terrible friend, it appears that you are the owner of this grand house and all the servants within."

Such wealth held no joy for me in light of its getting and I turned my face from his sight.

"I am leaving today," he said at length, his words even and controlled. "My business requires more stock, so I sail for the orient on the evening tide." I nodded briefly, I had suspected as much. "I have informed my men to care for your needs, should you require the services of my tailors."

"When will you return?"

He shook his head, "That I do not know, Julian. I am not sure I have the stomach for a friendship such as that which I have gained in your company."

I closed my eyes against the pain in his words. "Very well."

Leon stood from his place by the fire and turned to leave, "I have sent word to have your horse brought to the house. Thomas knows of your move here, but nothing more."

I sat for long hours gazing into the fire through the dark barrier of my glasses, hiding from the nightmare of my memories in pain, dreaming lightly of love and a lifetime gone by. I could hear whispers in the empty halls of the great house but their silent questions did not stir me from my position before the fire.

A small cough at the door moved me to glance at the tall gaunt servant I had met on entering this place. "I am George," he said with quiet reverence. "I saw what happened last night, sir." I nodded and he took that as permission to come to my side. "I was most gratified to assist your friend with disposing of the carcasses."

"Then you know what I am?"

"Yes, sir; my old master often used your name to curse his confinement in the dark." I smiled at the irony of his words and he continued, "I would hope that you will take the title that Henrë's demise has left."

"Are you prepared to stay with one who is the father of all this dark evil?"

His look was odd as I gazed into his eyes, "I have seen more compassion within you, sir, in these few days than Henrë could ever know. I feel safer with you than ever with them."

I grunted slightly and turned back to the fire.

"Is there anything you need, sir?"

"Maybe some Benedictine if you have it, and my name is Julian. I would rather you speak to me in that fashion. Do not call me sir."

"Very well."

I was interrupted from my thoughts once more as the servant brought me a bottle and glass, and then I was left to my solitude.

I gauged the passing of days and nights only by the spirits that were brought even before I had finished the last, and the flares of light of the moving sun. Memories clouded my mind and I was left with the sight of eternity spreading before me in its infinite cycle of damnation. I walked the lonely corridors of my new home and indeed, I roamed the streets of the city by night, occasionally in the lofty company of Demon but mostly alone. Often I found myself in the dark back alleys that spanned the harbour district, drowning in memories of earlier days and unreserved peace with my dark and silent friend. I would hesitate in the shadow of a street corner and watch the lights of the small gaming room where I had spent many carefree times with my lamented companion. But I could not enter into their world so lost in torment, I would leave invariably drawn by the scent of the sea. Many nights I found myself standing on the point at the harbour's rocky peer, watching out over the eastern horizon waiting for the dawn. Each time the blazing fingers of the sun's false glow would come to sit within the bowl of fading night, I was driven back to the solitude of the manor's quiet living room.

As time passed I was moved to feed again and did so without passion, seeking out the most wretched of life to sustain my ever-present need, but the liberation of blood brought me no release from pain, thoughts of Leon and his brilliant, accusing eyes would send me into a deep melancholy for days after. I sat in the dark confines of the lounge at Thomas' inn, watching mortal life flame around me as I sipped Benedictine but I had little interest in conversation directed towards me from the curious patrons and eventually refrained even from that contact, preferring the quiet solace of the manor and my chair by the fire.

Occasionally George would sit by me and we talked at great length about the world beyond my peaceful refuge. He showed me the horror of the Inquisition and poverty of mortal life in this age; the awful hardships imposed by greedy kings and bishops, and the steadily growing fear of the plague. I listened to his monologue, prompting only seldom with a question or statement until he, with nothing more to say, released me to my solitary contemplation.

Spectres filled my isolation, consuming me in their whispers, driving reason from my clouded understanding, and when I could see and hear my past before me, I took the path into insanity. Niamh floated upon my sight, giving me secrets of the lives I had seen. The echo of her voice reached in haunting phrases over the horror of my existence until the ghosts of my beginnings congealed, like the fierce rays of the sun, to grasp at my immortal soul. I became a creature, lost and desolate, hiding in the cold comfort of my depression, cowering from the persistent rhythm of passing light and the hideous truth of my eternal walk in the dark, and as time flowed doggedly, my insanity deepened. I listened to the mocking cacophony of madness, howling faces of times gone by hovered before my tortured gaze, giving up twisted secrets and the frail awareness of my inescapable journey in damnation.

"What more do you want from me? What pain must I still endure?" I screamed to their intangible essence, "Leave me demons, I have no strength left for this life." But only the sweet laughter of Niamh's gentle voice greeted my pleas, and that too in time, passed.

What day, or month or year it was I had forgotten, as empty madness kept me company, but one evening as I sat in open thrall of the dying sun, a spectre came before me that had not shown its face for many years. I let the vibrant life of old friendship stir in my sorrow and laughed bitterly, but my voice was broken with pain, "You too, Leon, have you come to haunt me at last?"

"It seems I have been away too long, old friend." The ghost approached me through the writhing haze of sunset and I flinched from the compassion in his eyes and even though I raised my hand against his advance, he crossed to sit beside the fire. "So this is how you spend your days when I'm not here to nursemaid you."

"What do you want?" I snapped hoarse.

"Ah, it's good to see at least a little life in you yet, Julian." My dark ghost laughed low, "Would you have another glass perhaps?"

I did not answer and did not see how a glass appeared in his hand, but soon the terrible spectre was warming a Benedictine quietly beside me, and the sun left its last rays to slip blissfully into the realm of night. With my vision clear of the madness of day I turned to regard my companion. "I have not seen your face for many years, Moor. Do you come to end my judgement?"

"No, friend," he shook his head, a long smile creasing the furrows beside his eyes—crow's feet that had not been part of his countenance and indeed strands of white amongst his long ebony hair—and when he spoke his voice was deep with knowing many years. "I have travelled long thinking of you. I have encountered vampire kind on the farthest shores and learned much from them, before taking their wretched lives away. I have heard tales and descriptions of you, that have you as madman and monster, demon from hell, and yes, these things I have seen in you. But never once in all those tales did I see you as I know you to be, each story a lie passed down from the gypsy Margueritte. So I thought long and hard about you, my friend, and tried to fathom your existence." He leaned forward and anchored me with a midnight gaze, "I know you to be different from those of your kind, Julian, and that is why I came back."

But I would not be lured by this new demon and turned away, "I have no need of your kind, leave me in my sorrow."

"You have been driven mad by too much sun, come out with me and I will see you whole again."

I recoiled instantly from his casual words, go out into the realm of mortals? I had not listened to my instinct to kill in a long time, I could not risk the contact. "No! Go from me ghost," I wailed and closed my eyes against his presence.

"Ha, he thinks me a phantom, by god." A chuckle erupted from deep in his throat, "Many things have I been called in my travels, but never a ghost!" and laughing hugely, he reached over to lay his massive hand on my shoulder, "I am flesh and blood, man. And probably in mortal danger at the moment I would say, to judge by the scent of you, eh?"

My eyes flashed on him, "I have told you..."

The warmth of his hand left caressing flames stirring over velvet as he roughly patted light plume of dust from my shoulder. "Yes, I remember your oath, I do not make light of that, Julian. In fact I see that is one of your greatest virtues." He sat back into his chair with a short laugh, "Indeed in my travels, I had taken it upon myself to promote your virtue and have been slaying vampires at every turn. And, by god, I have enjoyed seeing the end of every vile one of them." Flames of disgusted satisfaction oozed thickly from his vibrant skin and I was allured by his essence, feeling the promise of life blood calling, suddenly urgent within old, coiled hunger.

"I must go," I said, drowning under the raw edge of sudden and dreadful need.

"Yes, so must I. Another reason for my return. My sister's family has been hit by the plague, she has lost her husband, so I have taken her into my house. I must return to her, now." The dark merchant stared at me intently. "She has asked to meet with you if you are able."

I nodded, distracted by his blazing lights and knew I had to leave. "I will meet you there," I said shortly and rose from my chair.

I flew high above the darkened city, unconsciously driven by Leon's words, and found myself in a district whose lights of failing mortal life were betrayed by large white painted crosses, stark on the doors and walls of some houses. I was drawn instantly to the first one of these awful places and burst into a small hovel full of the stench of rot and decay, grey corpses littered the room, maggot infested and rotting where they had died. I saw only two faint glows of human life among the awful scene and was instantly by their side. Blood festered obscenely from the mouth of the more lucid mortal, and his eyes widened in horror as I leaned to taste the flaming essence from his lips. More delicate a touch could never be as he gave up his life blood to my awful desire. I lingered, savouring the pulse of his heart as it beat out his life through diseased and rotting lungs, filling me, searing me with its rapture and hungrily I invited its flow but the taking of one life was not enough and I turned to the other small body of an unconscious child, essence curling slowly from her still form, speaking to me of the pain she had endured. I took the last of her energy and gave her peace in death.

The sweet caressing fire of child life filled my soul with the most vital heat of all mortal kind, even this poor and diseased body enough to quench my hunger for blood. Strength from innocence filled my mind and I turned from the awful stillness of death, the scent of the plague reeking from putrefying flesh, gagging in my throat, chasing me from the stinking hovel and out into the night.

I flew quickly over the city, running from the horror of the plague, back into the company of the living and descended to the bright lights that illuminated the domain of the Moor. As I emerged from my place in the shadows, I saw Leon arriving on horseback and crossed to meet him before the door.

"Ah, Julian," he greeted me with a flat smile and ushered me inside, but I saw that he would not stand too close to my fresh odour of death. "Come and meet my sister Isabella."

We entered the cosy living room that I had known from years earlier and were met by a charming exotic lady, warming her dark and elegant hands by the fire.

"Julian, what a pleasure. My brother has told me many things about you." Her voice was warm and deep, her countenance strong with sibling inheritance, and she lifted the heavy train of her long dress to stroll casually to a wide chair. "Come, sit by me and I will learn truth from fiction, eh?" She patted the chair and threw a piercing gaze to the ageing giant beside me.

Leon chuckled lightly, urging me forward, "I will bring some Benedictine for company," and he left me to sit with the grace of his sister.

We talked of inconsequences and her laugh filled my mind, lifting me back into the humanity that I had forgotten over years of isolation. She told me of the demise of her husband and one of her five children in the days gone by, and took great pride in the virtues of the four that remained. The easy conversation betrayed an old family bond between brother, sister and her progeny, setting them often to bicker and I laughed at their casual banter.

"Ah, you have such a lovely laugh, Julian," she sighed under heavy dark lashes, indigo fire caressing her ebony throat, moving alluringly toward me. "You should try to use it more often. You must have so much sadness in your life."

I flashed a gaze at her sibling. "What would you know of my life?" I asked, a bitter edge in my voice.

"Oh, come now, Julian, you cannot expect my brother to write to me for over fifteen years without finding something of the dilemma that sent him to sea. What do you think finally convinced him to return?" She raised a light hand when Leon began to splutter. "I know you came to it on your own, my brother, but the letters you sent to me were your journal of that time and your conversations to me were the arguments you should have had with Julian himself." She regarded me levelly, "In fact, I construed more from those letters than was written in the words."

"Come to your point, Isabella," Leon shifted cautiously, his gaze apprehensively cast on me.

"I have no point, brother, other than to know that my children and I will be safe in the company of your friend." The pulse at her throat glistened as she spoke and heat flushed through her vibrant flame. "My brother says that you are an honourable man, Julian, I would know that I can trust that, sir." Her midnight eyes challenged me.

"I may be honourable, madam, but I cannot escape what I am." How could this fragile mortal fathom the creature that I was. A great sigh took me and I began to laugh, the tension sparking between brother and sister snapped with the sound and they both fixed me with the same curious stare. "I am not in the habit of keeping company with my prey."

Isabella flushed even darker, holding my sight in her deep flaming aura.

"Ah, this is nonsense, sister. Julian bonded me his oath many years ago." Leon reached for the bottle and refilled our glasses.

"I'm sorry if I offend you, Isabella. But I give you my word, for what little it is worth, you and your children are safe from my realm, at least." My eyes met hers for an eternal moment, and those depths were more exquisite than the infinite heavens.

"Very well," she said after a long heavy silence and rose from my side. "Now I fear, I must retire. I have four growing children to busy me upon the morrow and unlike my brother, I do need to sleep. Thank you, Julian."

She left the room and I sat opposite my old friend, brooding over my glass. Indeed it was like times past, neither one of us had changed much in the years apart and our conversation, what little arose, continued as if it had never ended.

I spent the better part of the next day getting to know the children. They had a sense of me to judge by the fear in the eyes of the youngest, her sisters and brother took agitation from her, but by afternoon I had won their hearts with simple magic and faerie tales, until they accepted my dark countenance and blue mirror eyes. As sunset came on and I removed my protection from the sun's dying rays, I watched Isabella's teenage daughter be taken by her first love. In the moment she saw my uncovered gaze, her face and fire raged a rich, velvet crimson and she fled the room from my presence.

Isabella from her couch, laughed quietly over her stitching as she watched her daughter's retreat, but said nothing and I let the moment fall away. When the children had retired, Leon, Isabella and I sat beside the fire, and chatted in pleasant conversation sipping at Benedictine and laughing over the first love of a young life.

So held the pattern of my life as I lived in the glowing friendship of these simple and honest people, enjoying their open company, resurrecting joy in my cool soul and giving me sweet respite from my eternity alone, but that this life changed from that time in an instant is hard for me to fathom and far more painful for the joy we had shared. One awful evening, late after Isabella had retired, a wail came from the nursery and both Leon and I moved to investigate. Mara, the youngest child, was sitting on the edge of her bed doubled in pain and calling in anguish, her mother came to sit beside her, checked the child where the pain had gripped her and made her spit in her mother's hand.

Isabella's face was pale and her radiant essence withdrew to meagre flames. "The plague," she whispered, tears welling in her stark eyes.

Within hours of the discovery, Isabella and her oldest love-struck daughter, lay beside Mara and we turned the nursery into quarantine. I took the two healthy children to the servants' quarters and had them stay, while Leon and I nursed the diseased family but before the dawn broke on that endless night Leon had too fallen to lie ashen with his sister and I held a vigil of death beside them.

"Julian," Leon whispered against the pain in his gut and coughed thickly. "I realise the wisdom in an act that I thought foolish only weeks ago." He gasped a little with the effort to talk, an engorged welt bulged purple at his throat. "I made changes in my family's title to the business and trade, when I returned to Briton, I was feeling a little, should I say, old," and he gave a small wheezing chuckle. "Since my sister's husband was dead, I needed someone to ward over my sister and her children in the event of such a disaster as this, and my friend, I'm afraid I gave you that honour. I have given you my trade and estate in return that you care for the children that are left," he reached out to grip my arm. "Will you do that for me, Julian?"

"Ah, Leon, you have given me more than you could imagine in our friendship, that alone is enough for me to carry your family with me until eternity." I leaned low into his ear, a frozen tear falling unhindered from my sorrow and I sat beside the failing Moor, watching as the Black Death led him unerringly onto his life's end.

After two awful days, the plague had taken Isabella and her lovely budding daughter far into delirium and she thrashed around, blood and sputum flowing from her wasted body in a long and steady stream. Leon indeed, was in a state not far from her and the smallest child, poor little Mara, had already died. I sat and watched in great fascination, the thick flow of blood oozing from the dying mortals, letting my senses be full, for the first legitimate time, of the vibrant living movement of human essence, and under quarantine, I was left alone with my study. By the morning of the third day in the rancid infirmary, the diseased humans had been reduced to rotting spectres of themselves, their life fires growing faint and low as their mortal essence was taken from them. Leon was humming a sea shanty through the fog of his demise, his raving taking his mind far from the pain of death as I sat by his wasted form, and I talked quietly to him about the days of our old friendship, reminiscing on the life that I could see ending before me.

In the late afternoon, the dark giant came into lucidity for a moment and turned suddenly to look deep into my eyes. "Ah, old friend," he whispered, softly coughing against the pain inside. "After all these years, I should end up dying in this way." His eyes wandered to the still forms of his sister and niece, and subtle tears flowed over his gaze. "I cannot bear to see them in such pain, Julian," and he returned his gaze imploringly to me. "I know you can end their suffering, vampire. I implore you, please, friend, release my sister from her pain."

I recoiled from his fevered words, I had never contemplated taking a life through a deliberate act and the thought repulsed me. "I cannot, Leon, you ask too much."

But pain had gripped him once more and he slipped back into his malaise, ranting and raving over vampires and their shallow promises, recalling old memories in other lands and his younger days of vampire slaying. Each delirious phrase caught deep in my soul, and eventually and in agony, moved me to action. I paced the room furiously, turning at any sound in the quiet nursery, my gaze inevitably falling on the blood that oozed sickly from my charges, and when Isabella began a high death wail, I was instantly by her side.

"Julian, I have so much pain. My children, oh, my beloved children." She blinked at me through the blank haze of her sickness and rent my frozen soul.

I leaned close to her ear, but I could never be sure if she had heard my words. "Isabella, beautiful woman, I will care for your children, I am an honourable man. I will take the pain from you and make it my own." My tears fell like the blood from her mouth. "Do not be afraid, death will be sweet release from this suffering."

Delicately, I kissed the glistening skin of her fever strained throat, my touch caused a soft moan to stir in her and she leaned into me, calling quietly to the spectre of her dead husband. My long fangs pricked through her fragile flesh and deep into the vein of her life blood, a small gasp escaped from her and she gave herself to my touch. The subtle tang of plague washed over me in the flow of her sweet blood, the vile disease dying in the stream as I took its essence into my soul and with a soft sigh her life ended. I sat up and wept for long moments in the intimacy of her death, and when the strange and melancholy wail began in her lovely daughter, I moved to her side and took her pain too. As if it had been a release, the death keen of the young woman stirred a great, heavy sigh from my dark and ailing friend, and his eyes flicked open to gaze upon me.

"I thank you, Julian, you have been a good and honest friend," and with those words falling mercilessly into the still room, the giant Moor died.

I disposed of the bodies myself, not allowing any to enter the miserable room of death. I carried their still and wasted forms out, far from the city and setting them to rest upon a blazing pyre. I watched them burn, the tall pillars of flame reaching heavenward in the dark.

I set the affairs of my newly acquired empire into order, caring for the young boy and girl that had survived the death of their family, as if they were my own but the echoes of ghosts and memories gone forever haunted me through that house, and even to the empty corridors of the manor house. Every day a fresh nightmare came to admonish me of the end of careless life and I retreated from the idyll of an easy existence, pain of loss a constant reminder of the isolation of my eternal journey.

Within weeks I made my mind to leave this place, the ships of the trader's fleet made ready by my order, and I gave strict instructions to the staff in the care and guardianship of Leon's remaining family. So late one evening before the midnight tide, I made my way, carrying a small parcel of new clothes and scant belongings, to the tall merchant ships that would carry me in an epic journey through the world and move my destiny once along the path of my immortal soul.

Chapter 9

We walked through the cool air on the path that
led from the tavern's back stairs, through alleys and
the forest that nestled behind our town, and down to
the jetty. Morag strode along at the front of the
narrow way, her bawdy jokes floating with the sun
through her long golden locks, welling laughter
from all four of us, but Marion's aside before me
caused the laugh to skip lightly between the girls.
When we got to the river, Morag swatted Marion
with her shoe and fighting, they both nearly fell
from the pier.

"Watch y' clothes!" I called, laughing, and shed
my own to dive into the cool depths of the water
below.

"And so are y' going to get yourself a beau
tonight, Julia?" Raehima flashed her dark eyes as
she surfaced beside me in the river.

"Ah," I squealed at her sly tone. "It would only
get in the way of business," I laughed in reply to the
old standing joke.

Raehima shook her head, long droplets of water
cascading from her deep brown locks, showering me
in light and then she was suddenly serious, "But no,
Julia, I see a man in your eyes."

The gypsy girl said she had the *sight* but we
never paid any attention to her witchcraft and I
splashed water at her. "Come out of it, Rae," I
laughed and dipped below the river's face to scrub at
my flaming red hair. When I came up, I found
Raehima had told the girls and they laughed and
joked about the ridiculous prediction.

"So you'll be leaving us then," Morag pouted
slyly.

"And I'll get y' room," Marion called by her side, giving the blonde slut a good pinch.

Morag howled like a cat and launched through the water onto her attacker and they both disappeared below the surface to come up spluttering. Marion bled from a good scratch on her cheek. Rae and I laughed at them.

I splashed around in the water with my sister whores, and as we swam I could feel something had changed in the air. I could almost feel it when we had walked down the track, but now the sensation was quite strong and it tugged on me in the moving stream, like a reminder of old love.

"Come on, Julia," Morag called as the girls moved back to the pier and I followed them, feeling eyes from somewhere.

I could feel the strange presence as we wandered back through the forest, but the others were laughing in the shady light and even Raehima was oblivious to its touch, so I put the unease from my mind. The path broke from the forest edge and into the meagre streets behind the tavern, leading us to the stairs of the inn. We walked along the balcony that ran across the width of the tavern and into the back door that housed the brothel suites.

My bedroom, the largest and grandest room, spoke of my place in the prostitute hierarchy and I hummed merrily as I chose a gown for the markets that night. The deep russet flow of heavy linen caressed my fingers as I chose the rich gown to complement my deep fiery hair, and I dressed and twisted my hair into an elaborate knot. I swirled the long-weighted hem around my feet and danced a small step around the room, laughing in the smooth feeling of my luxurious dress.

Morag poked her head through the door and caught me dancing, "Oh, Julia, you wore that old rag last market day, y' look like a washed-out old canvasback." She shrieked and ducked back as my hand found a tallow lamp to throw at her.

I floated down the stairs, feeling like a goddess as I stopped activity in the tavern proper, and lifted my head regally as I met the girls at the bar. Fredrick and Colin, two of my older and more revolting customers, sat with a crony I had not serviced, leering across their mugs. The stink of unwashed ale oozed from the corner on the pungent wind of their breath.

"Oh, Julia," Colin sneered under a drunken brow. "Y'r so beau'ful, will y' marry me?"

Morag squealed with a high-pitched laugh and flicked the head of her mug at the drunken sod, and he rose with foam sticking to his scruffy chin, yelling abuse at the slight girl.

"Let off her, arseflapper," I jumped to the whore's defence using my position to stare him down and his rage abated. "Go back to y'r drink, Colin." I raised a hand casually to slap his face but he grabbed me and pulled me down to sit struggling on his filthy lap.

"I can pay," he said grabbing my arms and pinning me to him.

"I am going to the market tonight," I spoke with more strength than I felt in his grip. "So why don't y' just go home and shaft y'r loathsome wife." I wriggled and stamped on his foot and he yelled like a wolf under moonlight, releasing me to stand by my friends. I turned my back on the vile man and Marion gave me a drink.

"I can wait," Colin mumbled behind me and I heard him scrape his chair across the floor.

"They're gone," Morag whispered, her sly eyes watching the door of the tavern.

Silence surrounded my friends for a moment and I drained my mug, clearing the tension from my mind. "Look, come, girls, the market and all the youths of the village await us tonight." I smiled to lift their spirits and restore the excitement of our evening of leisure.

At the front door of the tavern, I stopped to look out into the gathering dusk, checking to see that our unwanted patrons had indeed left, and Raehima was at my elbow. "Frightened y'll be had by all three at once?" She cackled unmercifully and I laughed at her bawdy wit.

We descended the wooden steps to the town square that boasted our fine whorehouse right on its verge, and into the gathering lights of the evening market. As the sun left its last rays in the twilight gloom, the stallsmen and minstrels set up their wares and entertainments. The night set in and we strolled around fingering the goods, making light plays against the poor men we met along the way. The old, rehearsed acts of four whores were too great a match for the young travellers that our market would attract. We crossed the square, casually caught by the alluring flow of fabric that shone softly in the light of many torches. As I reached to feel the strange smooth texture of one of the trader's wares, I was caught again by the feeling I had had earlier in the day. I could feel eyes on my hair and I paused in my admiration of the material to look for the source of the touch.

I cast my gaze around the market square, searching the faces of people making merry for the sight that I could feel upon me, and came at last to rest on the dishevelled form of a pale young man, standing at the mouth of the alley beside the tavern. As our eyes met I felt a chill crawl over my skin and I was fixed to the sight of him. It was as though I could see myself in his body—his eyes, his features called to me in recognition of another part of my soul. I could see pain on his face and in an instant he fell from my view.

I dropped the fabric from my hands and turned, heading for where I had seen the youth. My companions called after me and I told them to follow. Making my way through the crowd, I reached the beaten rag of the unconscious boy, laying unassuming in the corner of the market. When he did not wake at my urgent words, I had Marion help me to carry his light frame into the tavern and up to my room.

"What will y' do with him now?" Morag sat on the edge of my bed, stroking his elfin face.

Raehima came upon him, her lustful claws ready to envelop him lest he woke. "Is he not just angelic?"

I shooed them both away, "Be gone harpies, can y' not see he has taken a beating? Get from my room and about your business." I waved my hands at all three, rounding them through the door to slam it behind them.

I took my wash basin and towel to the bed and dipped the soft corner of cloth into cool water, wringing the fabric damp and carefully clearing the dirt from his face. The poor beauty of his features had been marred with splinters from rough wood, and I came close to his translucent skin to tweak them out with my long nails. In his sleep, he stirred a little under my gentle touch but did not wake, and I watched his fluttering eyelids as he rocked in a dream. I cleaned the dirt from his perfect mouth, the rose blush of his lips begged for my kiss as I revealed their elegance. I brushed my lips against his and he stirred in his sleep, reaching up lightly to share the kiss. The caress of his vibrant skin seared into my heart and I felt my breast burn with love. For a long moment, I was caught to watch the rise and fall of his breath, awed at his unearthly beauty. The odour of his water sodden clothes invaded my examination and I moved to take the filthy rags from him, gently taking the ruined fabric from his slender form. Rough bruises blued a ridge across his smooth chest and stomach that spoke of being hit hard, but when I took the trous from his supple legs, my eyes were caught by more evil clusters of splinters that had been forced into his dainty cock and the sac below. I took my ministration to the dirt on his genitals and carefully pulled all of the wicked long fragments from their infected wounds. I mopped blood from around his shaft and saw drying stains, deep between his legs. Wringing the towel out fresh, I went to work to clean away the old blood, his leg jerked under my arm and he groaned. I sat up guiltily and threw the covers over his exposed legs, smiling at my own coy behaviour as I watched him slowly regain consciousness.

"Hello," I said huskily when his fathomless eyes opened on me and I was breathless like a young girl.

His voice was broken with pain when he spoke, but even so it was soft and alluring "Where am I?" he asked.

"Y're in my room. I am Julia," I said shyly coaxing him to speak. He raised to one elbow, wincing as his stomach tensed against the bruises, "Careful now. Y've been hurt, please rest."

"I was in the square," he said blindly and recollection of what had happened before he had passed out, flashed tormented through his eyes. "I remember," he murmured looking around my room. "How did I get here?"

"Marion and I carried y' up the stairs." I picked up the wash water and took it back to the stand, and turned to look at him through the veil of my hair. "Y' can stay as long as y' like, unless y've somewhere else t' go."

The youth shook his head sadly and his sorrow took my heart. "I have no home," he said after a moment and I crossed to sit by him again, took his small hand into mine and urged him to speak of his circumstances. In tears he told me of the death of his family. The brutal rape of his mother and sister squeezed at my heart and I too wept but when he came to the end of his tale and told me of the awful crime that had seen him fall unconscious in the square, I realised in horror that he had been taken by the very men that I had rudely dismissed earlier in the evening. I looked away from him as he spoke and hid my face from the guilt of my crime, in my vanity I had caused him so much suffering. As he fell into silence, I cried for a long moment and then he took my face with one of his slender hands.

"Beautiful Julia, do not weep." Jeremy held my gaze before him and whispered, "I love you so very much."

And I, an ageing whore, queen of my brothel, felt those stirrings too. He leaned forward and kissed my lips gently, the full blossom of his blushing mouth so sweetly taking me on airs of love's pleasures. He held the covers back a little and I lay next to him, and kissed him long and slow as we talked quietly together into the night. He told me a little of his gift and how he had known love in the first instant that he had seen me at the river, and I knew it was his gaze that had reached out to touch me there. I cried again when I realised that I could have saved him, if I had but looked a little harder to find him. He whispered sweetly to ease my sorrow, cradling me in his young arms and I took heart at his strength. I spoke softly of my life in the brothel and warned him that I would have to work my business in this room and, although he said nothing, I could tell that the thought of my profession caused him distress. We fell asleep in each other's arms, our faces close and when morning came, I woke knowing that I had found love.

Jeremy's beautiful white lashes were swept low onto his cheek, but my eyes flicked open in the sunlight that peered in my window and I gently lifted my love's arm to rearrange the shutter and keep the room dim. I changed my creased gown and busied myself in the upstairs kitchen, humming merrily as I prepared a feast for the breaking of my love's fast. I arranged a tray and wandered down into the littered square to steal a deep red bloom from the garden that edged the village well.

By the time I returned to my room, Jeremy was sitting up in the bed stretching against the tension in his bruised muscles and I sat with him on the bed, eating a lover's feast. I took the spoon and watched his lips as he accepted my attention, and I fed him porridge in rapture of his perfect face.

"I will find you some clothes to wear," I said at last, breaking the spell and rose to open the cupboard where I had thrown the forgotten mementoes of my craft. I found some clothes that were close to his slight frame and he slipped into them while I rummaged in the back for some boots that I remembered I had kept.

"These are wonderful, Julia," he said lightly, and I turned with my arm deep in the cabinet to admire his handsome form. My hand reached into the corner and a sharp pain lanced through my palm.

"Ouch!" I gasped and pulled my bleeding hand free of the pool of clothes and held it up against the pain of a deep slice through my flesh.

"Julia!" Jeremy called and was instantly at my side, fishing out one of the light linen shirts and tearing it for a bandage. He strapped my hand with great efficiency, surprising me with the skill for one so young and he shrugged it off as a talent of his other worldly gifts. He reached into the cupboard and retrieved a deadly looking blade, stained with the red of my blood.

"I'd forgotten about that thing," I said with disgust, remembering the foul beast that had left it in my room and, under the wrath of my tongue, had not dared to retrieve it from me.

Jeremy regarded the narrow sword, wiping my blood on the ragged shirt he had torn. "I need a sword," he said, the painful sound of memories stirring in his voice.

"Then take it." I looked away from him as he weighed it in his hand and I lay on the bed as he played, a child with a new toy. I watched him move gracefully around the room, his stance with the blade showed some practice and I laughed as he began to defend me against imagined attackers. My merriment arrested him from his game and he came to me, but I would not have the sword in the bed so he leaned it in the corner of the room. We kissed and whispered for many hours, our bodies pressed close and intimate as we lay together in a tender embrace.

As evening came on, Morag popped her head through my door to see us lying in the bed and laughed. "Look at the love birds," she screeched, casting her words back out into the corridor, and in moments the other two whores had joined her at the door.

I extracted myself with a sigh from Jeremy's lovely embrace and sat on the bed to call the girls in. "You may as well meet these gruesome sluts," I said with a laugh and introduced him to my friends.

"So it seems I get your room anyway," Marion gibed in her blunt way.

"Not likely, gullybum, y'r too ugly." Morag ducked as Marion's fleshy arm moved to cuff her. "Ha, too slow, old woman," and she darted quickly from the room.

Raehima had moved to sit glowering at Jeremy, ready in her viper way, to have him if he offered. "I have seen you," she said, her voice rich with gypsy heritage, and I lowered a warning hand to his leg. Her smile told me she had understood my movement and more, the feelings I had for him glowed in malicious recognition in her eyes. "I see nothing good in this." Her words flowed icily over me and I lowered my gaze from hers.

"Go away, Rae, y'r tricks have no power here," I said lightly patting Jeremy's slender thigh

"I see something wrong in y'r union, Julia," she spoke intensely, catching my hand in her urgency to be heard. "There is a closeness that is dangerous for y' both."

"Raehima, you..."

But Jeremy quelled my comment, "What do you mean?"

The dark whore looked into his eyes, "I see a likeness around y' both, something that I have seen attract spirits and the horrors of their realm before.

187

Please have a care." Her words carried fear and she rose suddenly to leave the room.

I stared after her in puzzlement, "Pay no mind to that one, my love, she has been cursed with this madness as long as I've known her." I turned to Marion for confirmation and she nodded obligingly.

"Certainly so, Jeremy. Now, Julia, will y' be working this night or do we fight over y'r room?" I let her banter carry the sting from Raehima's words and turned to more practical matters.

"Indeed, I will, doxy. Now get out so I can make m'self ready for m' customers."

The last of my friends left and I made about my toilet in preparation for my night's work.

"I will wait downstairs," Jeremy spoke after a long while, his words strained with distaste. I nodded briefly and he too left me to the quiet of my room.

I met up with my sister whores in the tavern downstairs and within a short hour I had solicited an old balding farmer that had seen me at the market. I took him past Jeremy's angry eyes and made for my bedroom. Using the skill of years at my profession, I quickly removed his unwashed clothes and kicked them into a heap on the floor and although he smelled like a cow, I moved to take him on the bed. The jellyfish lay on top of me like a dead weight, his stubby cock hardly big enough to find its way past his rolling paunch, so that I had to grab the offensive member to guide it away from stabbing me continuously in the leg. If he noticed that I lay without moving while he worked out his orgasm, I will never know, but when he was spent, I rolled him off me and rose to rid myself of his sticky seed. He began to mumble something as he reached around his gut to fasten his trous, but I told him shortly to put the money beside the bed and leave. He must have been glad for the reprieve from social platitudes, and fled as soon as he could fumble the coins from his sash.

I knew my reputation would suffer with such abrupt behaviour, but the vision of Jeremy's eyes sat stinging in the darkness of my mind. I imagined his silent judgement and it put me off the game, so I went down into the tavern and sat beside him. He said nothing of my business and neither did I expect him too, instead we sat sipping ale and quietly whispering lover's talk into the small hours of the morning.

The next day, my love was sufficiently recovered from his attack to take small walks through the town, Jeremy commented on how much larger Landsdunne was than the small village that had edged his parents' farm. In glowing sunlight the streets were clean and fresh and an idyll for the wary eyes of my young love. He insisted that he carry the sword, much to my distaste, but considering the trial he had gone through I said nothing, confident that his suspicious fear would one day abate.

I took him down to the river and we sat on the jetty throwing crumbs at the fish that swam in its flowing depths and this became our favourite place. We sat hand in hand over the water, made small and loving conversation for long hours in the glorious new spring sun. The ever-present flow of the stream and gentle winds did more for his recovery than even my generous cooking and within a week of meeting my beautiful young man, I was getting to know him again. His vibrant personality and wit certainly made up for his lack of muscle and pale skin, and I was surprised at the wisdom that came from one so young. Many things he absolved easily within the excuse of vision, though I could tell there was a deeper well than this to him.

As his health improved, so his sleep became fevered at night, his dreams filled at first with the nightmare of his lost family and then the stirring of a dream that came from some other place in time and space. The sound of his screams in the night terrified me and more so when he told me what he had seen and the visions were growing worse.

When we sat in our favourite place by the river's edge he spoke, strained and nervous. "I haven't seen dreams such as these since I was a very young boy," he said and his face was grave as he struggled to hold the image of his vision.

I could feel the thrill of apprehension in his words and I smoothed the frown from his noble brow, "Oh, sweet Jeremy, y' need not think of such things. Be with me and I will ease y'r troubled thoughts."

But he jerked his face from my hand and gazed on me almost stern. "No," he said, "I have pushed these dreams away for too long. I would understand their meaning, I want to know why they plague my sleep."

I sighed and lay my hands mutely in my lap, "Tell me then, what y' have seen."

"I used to dream of flying," he began, staring very seriously into my eyes, "and being free from the shackles of my life, like a premonition of something that I would eventually become. Nameless and void like a vision of time yet to happen, and the dreams I had last night were the same. The same feeling, the same beginning, but, Julia, so much stronger, near somehow and very dangerous." His gaze darkened and I caught a chill from his words, shivering suddenly in the warm air.

"Please, Jeremy..." I whispered and he put his arm around my shoulders.

From the path to the village, the company of my friends came upon us and to my relief, our conversation ended. The girls bathed in the river, ridiculing our love in their own way and my Jeremy joined in to bait them, quite happily giving them back their spite, and when we took to the water, he swam like a salmon and attacked from beneath.

We returned to the inn and as on other nights, Jeremy waited in the tavern for me to finish my work, returning to my room when my customers had left and though he lay down beside me to sleep, there was anger in him.

"Oh, Jeremy," I pleaded, taking his hand in mine, my breath stirring the white tendrils of his hair as they lay on my pillow. "Do not judge me for my profession."

"I will not stop what you do, Julia, but I cannot be with you unless you are mine alone." There was strain in his young face, and his eyes burned guilty of knowing that his plea to be my lover would force me into a terrible choice.

I sighed and rolled away from him, staring as the moon peeped gently through the shuttered window and soon I could hear the slow rhythmic rise and fall of Jeremy's sleep.

Hardly it seemed a moment had passed and my doze was disturbed by a sound in the night. A noise reached into my dreams and dragged me conscious, and I sat up to see my love thrashing about under the covers. I took his shoulder to stir him from the nightmare and fear shot up my arm. I flinched and gasped, and called his name to wake him and his eyes flew suddenly wide. He jumped bolt upright and, with a cry, threw his hands over his face.

"Jeremy... Jeremy, what is it?"

"A beast," he gasped, "a vile creature. A foul thing of hell," and he turned black and stricken eyes to me, "something so evil, so cruel and... Oh, Julia, something that I know is waiting for me."

I took him in my arms and lay his head on my shoulder, whispering sweet lullabies to calm his tender heart and he slept again in the care of my embrace.

When morning came Jeremy woke and his eyes were still dark, his temper was even darker and we began the day with an argument. He stated quite abruptly that his dream had shown him that my profession was evil, its only outcome led to the depraved realm of the beast he had seen, and he would not share my bed again until I took no other man there. His angry words sacked my heart, his fragile nobility condemned the harsh reality of my craft and he reduced me to tears. He shamed me with his purity and in turn, I promised to give up the life for him.

So I went to Sire Johnson, our innkeeper, and told him of my need to leave and he, a ruthless and callous man, would have me pay board on my lodgings and even change rooms with Raehima until we could find a place of our own. I took his cold words back to my love and he endured my fury.

"That evil, money drunk, meat vendor!" I said rounding off the account of my encounter.

"So I see he took it well," Jeremy laughed, his voice suddenly light and free of the pain that had been there when we had argued.

I turned my eyes to him, amazed at his mercurial mood and he took me in his embrace. "I swear I'd kill him if I could," I said quietly. My spite still seethed but my love's reassurances took the sting from my temper.

Jeremy stepped playfully away from me and caught up his sword, brandishing it grandly around the room. "Let me at him, fair one, I will send the dog packing."

I let his graceful movements lull me from my hate and as he approached, I caught him. "So now that I'm a free woman, my beautiful Jeremy, will y' be mine?" My voice was low with need for him.

"Oh, sweet Julia," he whispered, the aching love in the way he spoke my name caused a shiver. "Not cold, my love?"

He held me to him gently and I melted against his embrace, "Not when I'm in your arms."

A knock came at the door and Raehima came into the room struggling under an armful of clothes. "It's about time, I have lost all my bets on how long it would take y' to lose y'r room," she said, throwing her burden onto the bed and turning to my flat gaze. "What, not out yet?" and her dark eyes smiled maliciously.

"Hag," I spat and pulled myself free from Jeremy's arms.

"Now, Julia," Raehima placated mockingly, "Sire Johnson told me it was y'r own choice."

I flicked the hem of my skirt at her and turned to take my belongings to the room she was busily vacating. Though much smaller than the plush room I had been used to, it had a doorway that led straight onto the balcony, and would give us the privacy to come and go as we pleased. Jeremy helped arrange our new room, carefully hanging my clothes, as I carefully laid out my trinkets and he settled his sword in the corner. I wrinkled my nose with distaste when he brought the thing in, but he gave a wry smile, took my hand and led me sweetly to the bed. He laid me gently on the pillows, kissing me tenderly like an angel, glowing in the afternoon light. And so he was paying me affection when Morag knocked on the outside door. I sighed, frustrated, and Jeremy smiled at the interruption, crossing the room to let the sly whore in from the balcony.

"I brought you a feast for your first night in your new home," she teased and entered carrying a large wicker basket. She sat herself quite comfortably on the floor, quite oblivious to the mood she had broken and began to arrange quantities of freshly cooked food before her. Jeremy looked at me and shrugged, and we joined her to eat the meal.

She produced a bottle of ale and we sat chatting until tallow light replaced the light of day. My love's hand found mine and Morag looked longingly at the casual embrace.

"Don't y' have to work tonight, strumpet?" My spite caught her from her gaze.

"Oh, I suppose, eventually," she mocked with innocent eyes.

Jeremy took a long draught of the bottom of his mug and causally began to undress. "Well, I suppose you will not mind that I go to bed then, Morag." His casual ploy caught the young trollop by surprise and she stared wide eyed at his bare chest. He laughed and she flushed a little.

"Oh ho, so now the tale is told," I ribbed her mercilessly, "The doxy loves y', my young prince."

The flush in her cheeks grew brighter and she rose quickly from the floor. "Julia, y're a wicked bitch!" She crossed to the inner door and slammed it as Jeremy burst into laughter.

We finished our ale undressing slowly as we talked in quiet tones, his hands light and loving as he helped me from my gown. I cleared the food from the rug and closed the shutters against the cool night air while Jeremy made his toilette from the balcony. When he came back in I had drawn the covers and was lying invitingly across the pillows.

He stood in the doorway with an odd look in his eyes and took a long moment before entering. "I do not need a whore," he said quietly, lingering by the door.

I felt his words hold me frozen in guilt. "I… I'm never a whore for you, my love."

My plea caught him from his suspicion, he gave a childish shrug and came to my side, "Never mind." He cast off his discomfort easily but I was still taken in the moment.

"No, Jeremy," I put a hand to his shoulder forestall his caress. "I swear to y', I have left that life." I looked deep into his eyes to make sure he would understand me well. "I will be yours alone forever."

He nodded slowly, his young mind grappling with my change of heart and I took him to my bosom on the smooth white linen of our lover's bed. His hands turned from virgin to sensitive beloved as he caressed my body and my touch found each intimate fold and curve on his slim taut flesh. We kissed and our limbs entwined in glorious union. Ah, the pleasure in his sweet kiss, the touch of his skin and the magnificent young member that I eagerly guided to my most intimate embrace. I felt a tide of pleasure launch through my body from our love and as he gave to me his essence, my beloved Jeremy groaned in rapture and I was filled with his tender passion. I lay lost in a long moment of ecstasy looking deep into the soft gaze of love, but as the moment passed, so his eyes changed and he jerked his head suddenly. I followed his attention and saw a pale wraith standing naked in the doorway.

I screamed and brought the glowing figure out of his malaise to cast his gaze on Jeremy, who had already taken from me. My love picked up his sword from its trusted position by the wall and approached the stranger, its point waving in shock at the intrusion.

"Get out, dog!" Jeremy called nervously at the ghostly figure.

But the savage gaze of the stranger never strayed from Jeremy's face. "Do not harm me, mortal, you have neither the wits nor the strength to keep me from taking your life and my need is greater than any of your passions." He spoke quietly, but the words struck terror into my heart and I watched as Jeremy's trembling hand held the blade dangerously close to the spectre's face. In a horrible instant the point of the sword touched, oozing black on the wraith's flesh and I was caught in a frozen moment as his face contorted with rage. Jeremy backed away suddenly but not quick enough as the creature transformed and caught the sword. The hideous figure that the wraith had become held the blade steady in an iron grip and so too my stunned beloved on the end.

"I told you, human, do not provoke the lord of flies," the lipless mouth of the beast dripped as he worked his bristling fangs to speak, his words seeped across the room, crawling in frozen torrents over my soul.

The beast jerked the flat of the slim blade into his claw tipped palm and ran it down the length to the handle, leaving a long black stain on the gleaming metal. A long viper's tongue darted out to scent the blood. He put the reptilian flesh of his hand to his face and breathed deeply, "Ah," he sighed and, with lightning speed, moved the wounded hand. The sword flew across the room and landed in a noisy clatter against the wall. I turned back from my distraction and again the beast had moved. As I watched in horror, suddenly he was on the floor bent crab-like over my motionless lover. His deadly fangs attached hideously onto Jeremy's face and the monster bit through his eye, sucking blood straight from his veins until my love went blue in the tremors of death. In that awful moment, I knew this was the creature that Jeremy had seen in his nightmare and the awful premonition he had felt, had been an echo of the terror of now.

The beast was caught in thrall and I moved quietly off the bed, but my foot caught in the folds of linen and I fell to cower in the corner of the room. The creature turned in a long moment of agony and something akin to recognition came into his eyes. An ancient cold and eternal longing flowed over me in his gaze and the horror of its dark solitary touch made my breath catch in terror.

I began to scream.

As my cry pierced the night, the form of the beast melted suddenly before me and the angelic wraith came once again to take its place. My voice fell into frozen silence as his beauty arrested me. His looks echoed my Jeremy, the strong proud brow and fathomless eyes but this face belonged to a much older being and he too had a look of long recognition in his eyes. I blinked and in that instant he was kneeling before me, his fingers cold on my hair.

"I have killed others like you," he whispered, his voice soft and alluring. His arm darted out and cut a gasp from my throat, seizing me in a grip of iron and I could feel the blood roar in my ears. I was struck immobile by his lightning quick and overpowering will.

He brought his perfect lips close to my neck and suddenly there was the sweetest pain I had ever known. The long draw of his suck seared in ecstasy through my rigid terror, my vision faded and I collapsed against his deadly embrace.

Chapter 10

I stepped onto the pier where I had gazed toward dawn many nights in older solitude. The dark forms of three floating giants dwarfed me, their transparent and billowed sails strained on the midnight wind. Moonlight reflected low across the pregnant flow of the rising tide, wild and bright on the black surface of the ocean depths. The glow of three tall carracks lightly straining at their moorings stood sentinel in the night. As I moved along the pier's stone span, a ship's gang came before me, swaying gently in its uncertain position between land and sea. My legs easily found level standing against the swell as I stepped onto the precarious bridge. I took on the bearing of a sea-dweller that I had learned in my days on the Roman barge and crossed the creaking boards, matching my pitch to the light tide. A frame of light betrayed the presence of the crew down below and I descended to the smoky light of the ship's lower decks.

Hanging lanterns and rum scented smoke greeted me and I climbed easily down the steep ladder to stand before a crowd of rough sailors caught by my intrusion on their ribald party with the local whores. The parody of their writhing essence against the frozen moment in which they were caught brought a smile uncensored to my lips.

"I realize that you marauding crowd are probably impotent without a captain, though I suppose there is a mate among you?" I asked by way of introduction and from the midst of the mortal blaze, a stocky sea dog rose from a chair, ginger head and beard as brilliant as his human fire.

"We've been waitin' on yer, Count Douvélle."
His voice was as rough as the seas he sailed and
loaded with caution. "I'm the first mate, Patrick."

"Then we will be getting under way?" I asked
eyeing the crew, letting my will to be gone fall like a
veil over the room.

"Aye, C'ptain," the first mate called and began to
stir the ship's company into movement. The
nightbirds were sent ashore and runners to the other
ships, and as the out flowing of the ocean's pull took
hold of the carrack's hull, we slipped from the pier
and out into the sea.

The gentle lurch of rolling tides played rhythm to
the rise and fall of the endless horizon and I watched
the passage of my fleet sail out into the trade winds
that would carry us across the world to China. I
stood on deck that night, watching the fading lights
of the coast move to the edge of my view, rolling
waters parted smoothly before the *Isabella*, and the
endless depths of universal fires blazed my path like
an omen from God. Leon had talked of times on this
deck watching those same stars, memories of older
times congealed in the heavenly fires, reminding me
of ancient pain. So my old friend had indeed come
back to haunt me, his spectre joined my beloved
Niamh to haunt my immortal hell. The cold well of
isolation that I carried was fitting on the deck of this
speck in the universe, the infinity of my existence
stretched before me like the beguiling expanse of the
ocean and I let dryad scented winds of anguish carry
me through the night.

As dawn came upon the ocean, I covered my
sensitive eyes from its piercing light, watching the
deep magenta of sunrise until its rays caused enough
discomfort for me to seek shelter in the captain's
cabin. I retired to the deep comfort of dark wood,

rich furnishings and the simple but vibrant tastes that spoke of my old friend. Lounging in the well-worn dark leather chair that sat behind a finely wrought desk, I ran my hands over the smooth wood of its oft used surface, letting the touch give up memories of Leon's years onboard the ship. I reached into the drawers, sorting through the small souvenirs of the life of a Moorish captain at sea, a silk scarf that spoke to me of frivolous times with Chinese ladies and a lock of auburn hair that carried an age-old scent of love. A tiny exquisite carved elephant fashioned in the deepest jade, showed me within its gleaming heart, the remembrance of family love that had kept my friend company for the years of his travels and eventually brought him back to his death. As the sun made its way west and moved to peer in through the starboard window of the chamber, a short knock at the door found me playing with the little frozen elephant and the first mate entered my cabin. The short and stocky mortal crossed the room to a waiting chair in front of the captain's table and I inclined my head for him to sit, as I was sure he had done many times before. He regarded me, measuring his judgement of what he knew from his former master against what was presented for him now.

"I assume Leon spoke of me," I said when the silence grew long.

"Aye, Captain, that he did." The words came low within the dwarfish red head, his beard bristling with the extent of his knowledge of me.

Slowly I nodded, "I thought it so. You know, I could just kill you all and get another crew at the next port."

Even though my voice was light, the mate did not miss the awful meaning of my words and eyed me from deep under his brows, "Leon said you were an honourable man."

I sighed under the spear of his weapon, it was a clever ploy, "Yes, indeed."

"Then so're the crew of this ship, sir. We're quite happy stayin' on as long as none of us goes, well… missing, you catch my meanin', Capt'n," and he cleared his bushy throat.

I watched him for a long moment and a smile came to my lips, "Patrick, you have my word that you will be quite safe from the likes of me. Though I cannot say the waters we shall be sailing will be quite as accommodating."

But my light words of assurance had affected the mate and he visibly relaxed, lounging back comfortably in the chair, a position that befit the character of the cabin. "I wouldn't be worrying about that Capt'n sir, this lot've been sailin' the high seas for years 'n' years. Seen some pretty strange things I might say, even some the likes of y'rself" and he cast a quick and apologetic gaze against the barrier of my glass shield. "Anyway, there be food in the mess at sunset if yer be wantin' the company, sir." He rose then and left my cabin, an air of satisfaction following on his vibrant heat.

I went to the ship's mess that night and sat in the shadows, aware that my presence had interrupted what would normally have been a loud and easy scene. I allowed their inquiring eyes to flicker over me, judging me against second hand gossip, and entertained some cautious questioning from the crew as they gathered in small groups, speaking hushed conversations about my notorious past.

A mandolin began to play as sunlight disappeared from the world and I let it lull my senses in its ode to the sea. Softly a deep voice sang with its refrain, catching the scent of the ocean in the lamplit room. As night drew in, the mandolin moved out on deck with a party of sailors off watch, and I wandered out to my place by the bow, letting the sounds of music lift my soul on winds of the night sky.

"And how is it that one such as you would take to the seas?" I heard the low grumble of the first mate beside me.

I laughed low staring out to the glowing horizon. "The curse of too long a life my friend, to try everything and find it lived out before me. Maybe this life will suit a little better." Though I knew that even in this existence, I would outlive the grand vessel I sailed upon.

The solid mariner puffed shortly under his moustache and stood beside me watching the horizon. He took noisy draws from a tankard and great clouds of alcohol heat transpired from his beard with each heavy breath. The vapours of his essence curled to mix with dancing stars in the distant cosmos and I coaxed the vibrant mortal flames into a writhing jig, demonic in its rhythm and beguiling as I let the energy settle onto my skin.

The night moved through its cycle as we sailed on across the Bay of Biscay and on to Spain. We sailed south with the trade winds, and gradually these seafarers and I came to know each other. The heat of the sun grew greater and I was moved to board up my windows against the constant barrage of its equatorial caress. I vowed to have the room lined with deep silk as soon as we arrived in China.

I spent my time toying with the small piano that Leon had kept in the captain's cabin as a trophy of another love. In the dark confines of the chamber, bent low against the onslaught of the sun's rays, I fathomed the science of music from the instrument's regular keys. I invited the attention of the mandolin player and he shared with me his knowledge of the minstrel's craft. He taught me bright jigs and melancholy ballads, odes and songs aplenty for the love of the sea and I practiced these lovely songs with thoughts of Niamh; how she would have loved to dance to such soft and beautiful music.

In this way I let the voyage pass and the heat and fierce light of the tropical sun too, until we had come to the bottom of the world and the roughest seas known to man. The Cape of Good Hope and the dangerous passage into another ocean came before our small fleet. I braved the sun on deck to watch, squinting as our navigator took us into the raging current. Foam and thrashing waves drove like banshees at the hull and more than once the deck was swamped in our dangerous tilt through the meeting seas. I could hear the faint roaring of orders being shouted roughly over on the *Antoinette*, the vessel so called for the owner of the lock of auburn hair. In endless moments, the ships lurched with their grappling of the violence of the seas, then set their sails again as we were caught in the grip of the new water and turned the prow northward once more.

It was perhaps the third evening after rounding the Cape and I was standing on deck, the ravishing violence of sunset caressing my naked eyes, that a call from the crow's nest caught my attention. The boy had his arm long out to the horizon and, as I peered north of the blazing rays, I could see a black speck making its way across the ocean on our route.

"Well, this looks grim." The first mate appeared by my elbow, called to my side by the cry from above, his tone alerted me and I turned to him.

"What do you make of it, Patrick?" I deferred to his judgement.

"I have seen pirates around these waters before, Capt'n, it'll be the right time of night for 'em too. They come in at twilight when the watch is least reliable."

"Then we must be ready for their advance, eh?" The thought of defending my fleet from invading pirates had an alluring challenge that I was ready to take up.

"Aye, Capt'n!" the mate called rising to the thrill in my voice.

In short time the complement of all ships stood ready with cudgels, daggers and swords, and waited for the approach of the pirate fleet. The flotilla of four giant, many masted galleons loomed ominously out of the dark. I could see the flames of human lights blazing on the decks long before they came along side, and I was appalled at the numbers they had to pit against our small trading fleet.

The high prow of the lead ship came crashing against our port and a flow of pirate men poured over the side, descending ropes thrown down from above, and began the assault. I stood amidships, holding my sword up in defence, a parody of a vampire reduced to kill with the simple tin of mortal man. But even if my weapon was not as effective as claw and fang, my intent was perhaps stronger with the nobility of defending the honour of my ship, and I stood my ground hacking and swinging at the invading hoard. Patrick battled beside me and he showed good Scotch courage, screaming and raving like a Celt, the blood of our enemies sprayed thickly about under his able defence. We had fought our way through many of the pirates, holding our perimeter under the weight of their dying bodies and

I looked up into the heights of the lead ship, casting my gaze for the captain of this pirate venture.

"Oh, ho," I whispered under my breath as my sight came to rest upon an elegant gentleman, dressed in dark buccaneer fashion and exuding the eerie glow I had come to associate with vampire kind. I leaned as close to the mate as I could reach under the blows of my latest attacker and called to him sharply, "I will go up there, you hold these off until I return." I jerked my chin briefly to the deck of the pirate's galleon and moved quickly from his side. I heard him grunt as he moved over to fill the gap and then I was fighting through the press of pirates flowing in the opposite direction. I fought my way to the bulwark and knocked one of the sea dogs over into the water and he fell screaming, to be crushed as the ships crashed together in the rolling ocean. The rope he had left bore my weight and I easily ascended the length of it, up onto the deck high over the melee below. I slipped quickly over the heavy rail that bordered the galleon's edge and was greeted by the sharp point of a blade.

"A valiant climb, noble captain," the deep brown voice of the vampire held a disdainful note as the sword waved dangerously in my face. His lips drew into a lazy smile, "but unfortunately not worth the effort, since you shall die anyway."

His casual arrogance stirred contempt and I slapped the flat of his sword away from me. "I have killed others of your breed," I said quietly, a dangerous spark ran through my words.

"Foolish mortal," he laughed, his rich dark hair shaking with insolence, "you surely do not know the fire you play with."

I regarded him levelly, again vampire kind had missed the evil nature of my immortal essence, "Nor you, vampire."

"So you would challenge me then." His sword came back up to cut at me and I raised my own in defence. His eyes narrowed as he saw the speed of my action and we stood as he reviewed our imminent battle but, with a malicious smile, the pirate captain brought his long blade crashing into mine and our duel began.

I ranged across the high deck of the pirate's galleon working hard against the skill and power of the dark vampire, and after a while I could tell that either one of us would have to make some awful mistake or tire of the duel. The pirate was a good swordsman, many years of practice had made his actions neat and efficient and, although I had never picked up a sword before this night, my ancient and dryad gifted instinct was a good enough substitute for his skill. The captain lunged at me and roared in fury as I stepped lightly from the edge of his sword, his movement was quick but not enough to fool my senses and I turned and watched as he went sprawling into the bulwark. I gave him the grace to right himself and took stock for another barrage, but he dusted his jacket with a brief laugh, "You have some skill, human."

I accepted his compliment, raising my sword before me, "Indeed, sir, I have. I would wager that our fight could continue until dawn."

A small flicker of caution played over his eyes at my carefully chosen words, but his laugh swelled again in arrogance. "Oh, you will die long before the day, mortal, and I will feast on your blood." The vampire lunged forward with the last of his speech and in a lightning rush was on me again, thrusting at me with his sword. I tapped the dangerous point of his blade away as he moved and we continued our duel high above the discordant battle on my ships. We fought for perhaps an hour or more, neither gaining nor losing ground against the other and eventually came to a futile halt in the stalemate.

Leaning heavily on his sword, the pirate captain watched me from under dark brows. "Sir, you have too much skill at sword play to be a simple merchant, join my fleet and I will spare your life."

I laughed low, "Your statement defeats you, sir," and let the mocking words drop frozen directly into his mind.

But the lights that flashed understanding in his eye had lost the quality of the fight and the vampire pirate was struck into a moment of still. "You are not human," he said at length, his gaze fixed to my face.

"No," I sighed.

The captain tossed his sword frustrated to the deck. "Then why the charade? Obviously you cannot die." He threw up his hands in disgust when I shook my head, "Then what are you?"

Dangerously I weighed his words, memories of life flowed across my mind and I said, "If I tell you, you will die."

A bark of laughter came from the vampire's throat, "Ha, touché, sir. If you know of my kind, surely you know that we too are immortal."

"I have seen your kind die many times," I spoke low letting him feel the approach of his death. "Indeed, Margueritte your loathsome mother died by my hand."

Recognition stirred, growing in the pirate's mind, "Then you…"

"Speak my name and you will die, vampire!" I cut him off, my voice menacing, but I could see the knowing of me blaze in fire across his mind. My sword dropped slowly away from my grip, sounding a chaos of release as it struck the wooden floor and I sprang at the pirate with fangs and talons bared. I crashed into him and under my savage attack, he overbalanced and fell sprawling to the deck. He reacted instantly, bringing his arms before himself in defence, but I was much stronger than he and pinned him easily beneath me. "Are there more of your kind here?" I spoke quietly, bringing my face close to him, long fingers of dread reached out through my words as he struggled against my grip, and I picked the faces of each of his insidious fellows from his mind. "Good," I whispered and his eyes told me that he recognised my spell. His face grew pale and hollow and in his eyes dread rose to replace all that had been insolence in him.

The pirate writhed and screamed under my grasp and I laughed, an evil sound, into his fear. My hand raised high above his breast and plunged deep around his heart, breaking bones and severing dead black flesh, and with a roar of instinctive madness, I tore the bleeding heart from his startled body. A false sigh flowed from the lips of the twice dead corpse and I released the body to fall lifeless in a pool of stagnant blood.

I flew over the battle, searching for the glow of vampire light and the faces I had seen in the captain's mind, placing each one in the throng of human flames, and descended to lift the closest abruptly from the crewman he fought. In shock the vampire tried flight to save himself, but my grip was fast and I let the impact of my charge lift him high on a savage claw of rage. Ramming my hand

209

through his fragile chest, I took the heart out through his body to hang, ragged on the black stained lance of my arm. I took each of the other five easily, in the same aerial attack and cast their bodies into the ocean, to be taken by the sirens that called from beneath the waves. When the last had fallen from my grip, I descended to land lightly over the billowing sail that flagged a salute to the battle below.

The bloody noise of the fray lifted on the air and with it the scent of life essence, reminding me insidiously of an instinct that had been hidden by vengeance but now, free of my duty, I chose a victim quickly from the onslaught. Lifted on the searing blaze of mortal battle, I snatched a massive pirate from his stance over one of my crew and raised him thrashing into the night sky. Manoeuvring easily to bring his bulging throat to my lips, I drank deeply from the channel I pierced in his skin. The flow of his blood carried me high amongst the stars, the power of his vibrant sea kissed essence filled my soul in waves of life, the vitality of the seadog fuelled my core against the last diseased life I had taken weeks before. I let the corpse drop from me in surrender of consuming life and hung raptured in the air as the body fell heavily to the *Isabella* below. As heat flowed into my writhing being and the red flow of blood washed my vision clear, I looked down to the wave of terror that had broken out on the ship, and a smile parted my lips as I descended to land high on the stern of the carrack.

The pirates were scattering in the face of their missing officers and my crew made good use of the sudden confusion to push back the invaders' advances. As I touched to the deck, I let my presence be felt on all my besieged ships and slowly the battle ground to a halt.

Although I spoke quietly, my words fell compelling across the whole scene; every eye turned my way. "I am Julian, master of this fleet. Your captain and officers lie dead by my hand. I am taking your vessels, stay or leave as you choose." I held the crowd in my will, stilling the blood lust from their simple minds, absorbing their energy and rendering the horde powerless and still in spellbound confusion.

Amid the pirates' number, my crew let out a roar of triumph and I saw the distinctive blaze of my fire maned mate, working his way through the crowd with a small band of my men. I made them all ranking officers and gave them command of each of the seven ships and they quickly moved out among the confusion, rounding up the pirates like sheep under their leadership and the influence of my spell. I climbed back up to the lead pirate ship where I had killed the vampire captain, cleared the carcass from the rolling deck and watched as it disappeared into the dark waters below.

The creak of a door closing caught my ear and I moved to where the sound had issued. The captain's chamber at the stern of the grand galleon betrayed a presence from cracks of light that peered through weathered boards. I lowered the smooth bar of the door handle and stepped into the warm glow of a lamp lit cabin. I moved into the chamber following curling flames of human essence, toward the grand structure of a brightly veiled post bed. A small gasp greeted me as I reached to pull the silken gauze to one side and revealed three terrified women sitting huddled together, the rich bed covers giving them scant cover from my approach. Their awful pallor and fearful gaze told me that they had been subject to the tender affections of at least the vampire captain. My gaze was drawn to the ooze of fresh wounds on each of their lovely necks, the fragile skin supported the attention of many bites and I sat on the edge of the bed quietly letting my presence fill their frightened minds with calm. Even through their haggard appearance, I could see that the captain had chosen these women for their beauty, though his intent was evil, his taste was impeccable and their rich colour of skin spoke of piracy in many oceans.

"I will not harm you," I said after long moments and watched my words instantly melt their fear.

They all began to talk at once and I was aware that each spoke a different tongue, and found that none had been able to speak to the others since the time of their kidnapping. The range of the vampire's taste impressed me as I learned that these were no ordinary females, but young ladies of great estate in their native homes and heirs to royalty; each one stolen for the ransom they would bring. I sat with them listening to their stories, interpreting when one girl would want to speak to another in my unearthly knowing of the languages that they spoke. I learned of their awful time onboard the pirate ship being used as herd beasts in the larder of the vampires. Fascinated I listened to their tales, the accounts of frequent bloodletting impressed on me an understanding that I had not yet come to in my life.

I did not have to kill my victims.

These girls had been used many times, especially the lovely gaunt Chinese princess whose energies coiled slowest from her tiny form. This beautiful bird held my gaze out of the three, her striking almond eyes held a depth that called Niamh unbidden into my mind and I found myself staring at her, watching intently her small and graceful movements and the vibrant glow of her tawny skin.

As the first rays of morning came over the sky, the flotilla had begun its journey northward again, the swollen ranks setting glorious sails against the reflecting sun. Patrick, who had named himself captain of the *Isabella*, took great advantage of my reputation and converted the pirates into an almost worthy crew within the night. The three beauties in the captain's chamber relaxed enough to sit chatting openly about their lives, until long fingers of the sun touched searing into my sight and I covered my eyes with my blue glass shield. The dark barrier shocked the girls and they all turned from my face in fear, but the lovely Chinese maiden was more curious than her companions, and with defiant grace, she finally looked into my eyes. I explained the machine and my aversion to the sun, and winning their trust with my simple friendship, I vowed to send each of the young beauties back to their homes.

The young Emir princess recovered in quick time from her brutal captivity and well since she had been the last to be napped from her homeland, and I escorted her home on camel back for the fifty-mile journey through shimmering desert sands. I delivered her formally to her anxious father and returned the precious cargo of royal jewels that had been taken in the same raid, and took the longboat back to my fleet loaded with more treasure than the carrack had already stored in its hold. The crew feasted that night on the finest treats and indeed, the gifts we received from the family of the second royal lady as we delivered her safe to her family, was cause for more revelry and set my place as a worthy captain of the trade fleet.

Our journey lengthened and I found my days and nights in the comfort of the arms of my sweet Mai-Lin, I played to her on the small piano I had brought from the *Isabella*, she sang tales of sweet love from her homeland and I grew to know her well. I told her a little of my nature, always shying away from her burning eyes when I spoke of my awful instinct, but gradually I let her become aware of the creature that I was and found solace in her acceptance of me. Even though their two faces were so different, still a vision of Niamh came into her dark eyes so readily when I watched her graceful movements, that the two grew together in my mind and my love for this tiny Chinese princess grew in the careless days of our voyage.

After peaceful weeks of our journey by sea, we came into the grand harbour of the royal port of Hsü-chou, capital of the coast district and home to the royal cousin of the Emperor of China. Standing with Mai-Lin high on the prow of the grand lead carrack, I braved the harsh light of an overcast day and my crew sailed the flotilla smoothly across the gentle waves of the captured sea. I took my beautiful lady down to a longboat that was lowered into the water before the royal pier, and with the other two I had loaded with gifts for the Prince of Zheziang, we made for the shore. Great jade dragons lined the edges of the high stone bank and on the descending steps that led down to the water, rich figures of the royal entourage awaited our arrive with great expectation. Mai-Lin waved, clutching at my arm in excitement, pointing to all of her relatives at once, their names floated into my mind like the flowing tide and we pulled alongside the pier.

A great feast was set in celebration of the rescued princess and I, as honoured guest, was placed at the head of the banquet hall with the royal family. The Prince had insisted I sit beside him and tell him of the adventure of his daughter's rescue and so I recalled the events of the capture of the pirates' ships. I was guilty of the sin of omission on only one subject and I knew that Mai-Lin had picked my deliberate avoidance of that terrible fact. I smiled a little under the compassionate gaze of her infinite eyes.

The evening carried me in the bright colours of exotic entertainment and I was entranced by this striking culture, the lilting refrain of sweet melodies I had heard from the voice of Mai-Lin, played by a lonely *pipa* and sung by the angelic voice of a courtesan. Orchestras of delicate percussion and great writhing plays of dragons dancing to the music that they made, feasted my watering eyes on their vivid barrage of colour, and Mai-Lin sat by my side, speaking low of the custom of each of the entertainments that came before us. For all there was a long and honourable tradition that up-held this civilization, politics and hierarchy infused the royal banquet, the cover of a feast was always set with intrigue. She was called for a moment to speak with her father and I let my attention wander around the feast of human flames before me.

For an instant I saw the clear eyes of an old and wizened man peering intently at me from the shadows of the hall, but before I could question Mai-Lin, he had vanished. I searched the room a little for a glimpse of him again, but when it was clear that he had gone, I excused myself from the prince, curious as to why he had sought my attention and then disappeared.

I wandered out into the quiet hall beyond the noise of the banquet and slowly along its length, cool shadows betrayed no signs of life from within the massive vault. But as I stepped past one of the looming pillars, I was startled by the sudden feeling of a touch dangerously close to my shoulder. "If you move, vampire, you die." The point of a needle pressed at the exposed skin of my neck.

With lightning pace, I brushed my assailant aside and stole his weapon from his hands, and came to face him as he overbalanced and landed painfully on the polished floor.

I laughed lightly at his predicament, "So, mortal, you know of my kind." I casually toyed with the poisoned barb. "I am curious to know how you disguised your essence from me though?"

The old man rose slowly and brushed himself off, smiling briefly as he realized his magic indeed had worked. "I know many such tricks," he said bluntly.

I regarded him, "I will not harm you, old man, that is not why I came to these shores."

He toyed with his long whiskers for a moment, weighing my words. "I am Lao-Tzung, master magician and alchemist to the prince," he introduced himself shortly. "I know of you, I have seen you in many visions."

"Then you will know I speak the truth Lao-Tzung." I smiled as his essence began to seep around the blanket he had spelled over its flame and offered up the small weapon. "And you will know too, master magician, that your weapons have no power over one such as I."

A light sparked in his aged eyes. "I have studied deeply in these matters, vampire, I know more of your realm than you think. This small dose, enough to kill a mortal," and he fingered the poison tipped barb, "would render you immobile and thus I could destroy you."

His words fell into the cool silence between us, "I would welcome death," I sighed and a lure of hope reached into my being.

The old man smiled, "I have seen a great many things, in visions. If you wish, I will share with you what I have learned. Come."

He preceded me, his light step echoing along the vaulted walkway as we crossed the antique Mogul palace and I followed, a light of amused interest sparking from within my cold well of eternity. When we reached a small door set in the smooth stone wall of a corridor, he bade me enter and I stepped into a large apartment. High roofed and pillar edged in the style of this remnant of a vanquished dynasty, it was warmly lit by a small, covered brazier and filled with long tables of the alchemist's art. While the old man took a long taper to the room's illumination I wandered, curiously peering into flasks and bottles that smelled of potions and struck a memory of love and learning in the company of my beloved Niamh. At the end of the long table a heavy scroll sat partly exposed and I was drawn to the characters and symbols that flowed across its surface.

"Do you understand what is written there?" The question flowed across from where Lao-Tzung stood illuminating the last of the room's candles. His breath extinguished the taper and a plume of smoke curled from the flame's end.

I studied the writing for a moment, the graceful brush strokes of his language glowed under the power crafted into their vibrant sigils. In an instant, words formed into patterns of understanding and I could see the intent and meaning behind each line. Niamh came hauntingly beside me as she had done so many times, and taught me once more, love of such a human art.

Lao-Tzung had moved to his seat between the brazier and the table, before I raised my eyes from the dangerous magic I studied.

"You know of the Art." It was statement, not question.

I nodded, "But this is far beyond anything I have learned."

"Yet you know it, do you not?"

Again I nodded and turned back to the scroll.

"I saw our meeting in a vision many years ago and have been prepared for your coming for a great deal of time, *Lord* Vampire." He leaned forward, took what looked like a strange long slender spoon from the table and gestured with it for me to sit in the seat that keep him company by the fire. Lao-Tzung took a taper from the brazier's heart and touched it to the bowl and inhaled slowly, and when he exhaled smoke I was intrigued.

The wizened mage stroked the long ends of his whiskers smiling faintly. "Opium," he said after long moments and held the contraption for my inspection. "Smoked as such, in a pipe, it has abilities to aid meditation or induce an altered state but also it can encourage visions." His voice sounded well-rehearsed and held under tight control, "The study of such things is my Art."

I crossed the warm lit room and sat beside the old alchemist, but refused the pipe, "I have had enough visions in my terrible life, Lao-Tzung, I have no desire to encourage such nightmares."

"Ha," he laughed derisive, "and so you would stay in the dark forever. Are you so foolish?"

His words stung me to examining the visions I had had in ages past and how such sights could have aided me if I had heeded the warnings they held. Indeed, my protection from the violent blaze of the sun was prompted by a vision of another life and the terrible understanding that I had been somewhere in time, with myself. but what of the cost of seeing such things? Their memories tormented my exile in the dark.

"If you know anything of me, Lao-Tzung, you know I am damned to that place forever. None of your tricks and magics can save me from my fate." I turned from him to watch the filigree patterns of brazier light.

The alchemist sighed and took another draw on the pipe, a long curl of smoke floated beyond me. "You are wrong, Julian," he said with self-possessed assurance and drew my gaze. "Perhaps you would have thought to explore my craft eventually on your own, but fate is not your enemy here and such a meeting as we have had is more than just coincidence. I can teach you things that would take you at least my lifetime to learn, simple understanding of the cosmos in which we exist and manipulations of powers in many realms..."

I shook my head wearied by the eager note of mortal hope in his voice.

He fell silent for a moment, and then, "What is it you seek, Julian?"

I cast a glance sharp upon him, "An end to the madness, the hell into which I have been cast!" I threw up a hand in frustration and then retreated brooding, "Peace from the beast that sent me here, a reason at least for my becoming what I am." My voice ended on a trailing whisper and silence fell between us. I stared over coals for long moments. "I learned of the fates of others who have held my soul, I have seen their lives by accident of my birth, yet I know not why I see myself thus. Their wasted ways mark a passage into darkness of one who has sinned even against their soul's own journey, seeking such demonic satisfaction in life that my existence has been baptized in blood.

"How, Lao-Tzung, is it to help that I witness such things as the depravity that created a creature such as I? What can you offer to right such a past?"

"You seek to end your life?" He rose from his chair and walked the length of the table, drawing my gaze as he reached to pick up the barb he had threatened me with earlier. "The poison on this needle is a simple enough recipe and others I can manufacture, I know, can give you power over the beast that holds you prisoner. And who can say, perhaps one day we may discover a way to beat that demon and free you from this existence." He moved slowly back along the table, toying with the needle and as he returned to his seat, the long folds of his rich embroidered robe folded in volumes around him.

I regarded him for a silent moment, the sight of an end to eternity dancing enticing in imagined hope. "Tell me, Lao-Tzung, why you would aid me in this quest. What benefit would you gain by such an ignoble deed?"

He smiled at my cynicism and casually tossed the barb into the brazier. "My vision of you," he said at length, "came when I was a much younger man. I had returned to my home village after a journey that had kept me away for too long, yet when I arrived I was greeted with a sight that made me afraid. The village had been decimated by vampires, my friends and family, dead or, more horribly, missing. I fled to the forest and that night I saw you in a dream. It may have been years ago, but still I remember the vision so vividly." He shook his head slowly lost in thought and then looked to me with wry apology in his eyes, "The next morning I vowed I would find and destroy that father of evil. I was only a young man, full of energy and little sense, but after a fruitless search I met a magician who also had experienced vampire kind and he taught me my craft. He also had in his possession a book, a diary of another who searched in vain for you." Lao-Tzung leaned forward and lifted a small leather wallet that sat suddenly conspicuous and mute beside him on the long table. "Not from this part of the world obviously, yet my mentor often spoke of his search and how it took him to many lands." He handed the tied bundle to me.

The leather was ages worn, smooth and paper thin at its edge, the thong that held it in place, hard and sculptured into a knot. The cover held no inscription, yet within I leafed through the scribings of a monk whose search for the source of vampire kind took him eventually into madness.

"Ahh," I said on reading the last entry. The poor monk had searched for me long and in vain, and I had slept in the clutches of dryads. Tiberias predicted the spawning of my evil children long before I had been tricked into such an act and had sought to find me before it could happen. The last entry was a conviction that if ever others came from me, then surely my death would also be theirs. The significance if this notion was not lost on me and I looked sharp at the ancient alchemist as I closed the book's cover.

"So," he said, "it seems both you and he have a quest in common and I perhaps, have the means to achieve it."

"Yes…" I sighed.

The door latch sounded a warning and my eyes were drawn to see Mai-Lin enter with mock anger in her deep gaze. "The banquet ended hours ago. You were missed," she said crossing the room to warm her hands by the fire, her chiding smile an oblique apology for causing the end of our discussion.

"I think my nephew will understand that I am recruiting my new apprentice, grandniece," the old magician replied fondly. "He knows my time is short."

She gave a graceful laugh and turned to me. "My uncle has been saying that since before I was born." Her eyes shone with family affection. "Still I see you are quickly becoming accustomed to the ways of court, beloved."

"Yes, I see that I have much to learn and my reasons for staying grow more numerous with each passing moment."

Deep in her eyes a spark of hesitant love flamed under the promise of my decision to stay in China and I bathed my cold soul in her essence.

"And yet I wonder if I will not regret my decision in years to come."

"Oh, Julian," she said smoothing velvet plush against my shoulder, "think not of what may happen. We have what is now, my beloved, live for that."

Lao-Tzung laughed. "I trust your relationship with my grandniece will be honourable, Julian," he said and concern rippled beneath the surface of his light words.

I looked from the exquisite eyes of my beautiful princess and faced the magician's half veiled challenge. "Mai-Lin and I have spoken already of how we would be, should I remain once my ships leave. On the voyage here I was unsure and Mai-Lin encouraged me with such wise words as she gives me now. I love her, Lao-Tzung, if such a thing is possible for an immortal being. Already I have asked if she could face a lifetime with one who will not age or even change, if she is prepared to live beside me as I am controlled by a nature too great to control, and not once have I seen her eyes change from their exquisite devotion. And I too am doomed to live in knowing that so soon for me, she will take her mortal love away and her eyes will haunt my eternity, forever.

"Oh, yes, Lao-Tzung, our relationship will be honourable, I can promise you that. And even so, I have already requested a private audience with the prince, to formalise our liaison."

The old alchemist smiled with thinly held relief, "So I will stand by you, Julian, since now I am your mentor, and the wedding will be spectacular."

I married my beautiful Mai-Lin in a day of great ceremony, an event that was recorded by artisans and scribes in paintings and stories that would one day become legend. I was accepted into the royal family and made a Prince of the Ming dynasty of mighty Emperor Chu. The grand affair marked for me a time when I began to control my walk on earth and gain skills and knowledge to end as horrible an existence as a mere pawn of my most reviled nature.

I sent the fleet back to England loaded heavily with vibrant luxuries of the East and exquisite gifts for the remaining progeny of the *Isabella*'s namesake. I watched her billowing sails disappear over the horizon in a frozen eternity of remembrance of times gone, and I remained in the orient's amazing culture to learn intimate secrets of the alchemist's Art.

I spent my days bespectacled by the magician's side, learning of substances and their effect on my physical being and my nights content, for the most part, in love with my beautiful princess. I gained a peace in the ancient stronghold that I had rarely experienced in the company of the living, the soft cool of the palace walls soothed fierce rays of the penetrating sun and the gentle love of Mai-Lin eased my heart. I spent long hours poring over lessons, conducting dangerous experiments in the company of growing camaraderie and under the careful instruction of my devoted allies, I learned much of my existence and a course of action to foil my terrible fate.

I studied the magical texts that Lao-Tzung had as his library and learned much of the turning of the heavens, how such influences as the movement of planets would affect the potency of our alchemical preparations, and even how they effected my malevolent rhythm. At certain times, I discovered that I could be affected by a drug and yet as the heavens turned it would work no longer. As I charted such cycles, I learned an innate defence against my needs and the influence of my dreadful burden. Lao-Tzung showed me a secret to the beast's control of my being, charted times in the heaven's cycle when that demon's influence was at its weakest and the working of a method that would put an end to my eternity.

Years passed and Lao-Tzung died, leaving me the honour of becoming alchemist to the prince and with the quiet company of my beautiful Mai-Lin, I continued my work. I took over the alchemist's apartment and spent my days searching the secrets of the universe and at times it was almost as if the old magician was still by my side.

For the most part, those years spent in mortal company were striking in their peaceful nature, it seemed an age before the extra vibrancy that flowed from Mai-Lin's love failed to satiate my hunger for human essence. When eventually I did leave her company reluctantly to feed, I ranged only as far as I needed to find a victim. Never did I kill a mortal in all that civilised time and never did I seek prey in the same place twice. I learned a subtle magic to bathe my elegant princess in currents of stolen energy and she retained her youthful beauty for many, many years. In our love we outlasted the princes and emperors of the dynasty and we watched the rise and fall of power in China and survived the evolution of this ancient culture in the strength of our love together.

My fleet came and left, their mighty sails changing shape and colour as fashion in Europe dictated, ensuring the wealth of my business in England and the survival of Leon's descendants. The captain would bring word each time of the family that had grown from the two children I had left behind, and it pleased me to know that the line of such a noble family would survive beyond mere memory.

I constructed a mighty chart that could project the movement of the planets and eventually came across the flow of a conjunction that held promise of liberation. I plotted an alignment that could be used to confound the beast within me so that I could take my life away, so that I could be free of this eternity. Mai-Lin had been with me when I reached my answer and she moved away from my side as I stepped back from the table, confident in success.

I tasted the date only short years hence and spoke it several times, knowing that now I could count myself as mortal at last but, as I turned to see Mai-Lin standing silent by the brazier, the smile stilled even before it infected my lips. "What is it, my beloved?" I asked and moved to encircle her in an embrace.

But she said nothing.

It was winter beyond the palace walls and my tiny Chinese princess fell ill. I sat by her side and held her delicate hand and begged her to share with me the burden of what it was that caused her to so quickly fail.

But still she said nothing.

She was as frail as the filigree of an autumn leaf and as cold as the midnight snow, curling with slow and loving flames in the soft folds of our bed, and she knew when death walked into the room to pay his respects. I sat amid the last curls of her aura as she greeted the spectre of the reaper and watched her essence fail through my tears. Briefly, the ghost of the young love I had known touched me and then she, as all who had come before her, was gone.

I had a grand tomb constructed in the royal forest and laid her there myself, braving the frozen bite of snow and sun to weep as the grave was sealed. My love was interred in the bitter earth and I was left once more, to walk in darkness alone.

Chapter 11

The palace walls echoed with carefree laughter and memories of love, and now even the lights of the living had become only insidious reminders of the dead. For all I had a destination and plan that settled my end in time, and even though the years would soon pass, still the emptiness of losing love again settled cold around my empty heart. Each day came with the sun's fiery call and tugged painfully at me. Now that I had lost my most intimate source of nourishment in the loving arms of my lamented princess, I had been cast once more into the terrible need of my nature. I went to the sake houses, trying in vain to find solace from my loneliness, but the flavour of China had died with my beautiful Mai-Lin and soon I knew that I would leave. So I orchestrated the ending of my life in the court of Zhenziang and had my possessions, my precious books and the workings of alchemy, crated and stored for when the trade fleet was due to return. I tried to wait until the spring when I had had word that the merchant ships would arrive, but memories distracted me so greatly that I left on horseback and then by night, and let a journey overland take my forlorn memories away.

I followed a route into Europe that had been vaguely described for me by Lao-Tzung, the passage of the diary that he had given me and the walk of the monk who had died more than a millennium ago. Indeed I found my way even to the memory of my first crazed journey, a ghost who murdered unthinking along an ancient Roman road, and followed the trail eventually into France.

I spent some time in crowded Paris, learning the popinjay ways of wealth in this time and took a conceited laugh to mask sorrow in my heart but a Parisian life became uncomfortable and it mocked the sentence I had to wait until, with heaven's aid, I could end my miserable life. So I made my way back to the shores of England and the growing city that had been a home to me in times past. Memories of my surrogate family now shrouded by distance and ages of man, sat bleak with all my loss of friendship and love, yet I sought to occupy my last days in carefree and ephemeral company with those who I would call my own.

I took passage on an England bound ship from the seaport of Cherbourg and passed the crossing in company with the captain. As with most ocean-going traders, he knew of the Moors' trade empire and we chatted amiably as he entertained me with fine ocean scented Benedictine. And so, when we pulled into the busy harbour of Portsmouth city the following day, I descended the gang and stood on the wharf, reminiscing over the bitter-sweet memories of times long gone.

I watched the unloading vessel for a while, from the protection of a newly constructed barrier, fashionable spectacles I had commissioned in the time I had spent in Paris. The small, sleek glasses fitted closer to my face than the primitive counterpart I had designed originally in an older Portsmouth, and cut light so effectively that daylight hours became quite a civilised encounter. As the sun climbed over its zenith and began its descent to dusk and tired of the distraction of the wharf, I turned up the high collar of my simple silk and velvet coat, and made for the sprawling city heart.

The influence of this new century had evolved Portsmouth into a thriving industry of human life. Cobbled streets were lined more closely with towering buildings that served as housing for the ever-growing population and, even more profound than I had felt it in Paris, mortal heat from the many, many inhabitants reached out to caress me as I passed by. Yet ancient trails echoed of my movements through the city, often lost under the press of new buildings though enough to guide me without faltering on visions of bygone days. I rounded a corner and smiled as the steady form of the trade house came before me. Its grand façade had changed little but for a coat of paint and large glass windows displaying some of the fineries that had evolved out of the last century or more. I crossed the road, amused that I should suddenly hesitate at the thought of such an unheralded homecoming. Yet I assumed that my possessions would have already arrived and my letter of introduction to the family in this time would have prepared them at least a little. Still, I felt the prodigal and almost chided myself for the anticipation that flared irrationally on the heels of what I would want to be such a careless time. As day's last rays of golden summer sun dropped from the rim of the world, I took a futile but steadying breath and lowered the ornate handle of the trade house door.

A bell sounded with my entry, clear into the mute atmosphere of displayed fabrics and when the door closed behind me, sound from the street beyond fell into quiet. I waited, not sure of quite how to proceed, wandering slowly amid the show room and its treasures, knowing though that someone would be summoned by the sound and the etiquette I had learned in France was also the British way of the day. Noise issued from behind the door to the house proper and then it opened, whispering across the carpet.

A tall, dark-skinned gentleman passed through the portal and his indigo essence was cool with a well-rehearsed spiel. "I'm sorry, sir, we are closed for the day."

He wore no wig, even though it was the fashion, but still his own jet hair fell in a mane of ringlets that sat on the shoulder of his jacket. An ornate lace cravat tumbled beneath the ebony locks and his demeanour marked him in the social set. His gaze fell onto my ancient being and a half-formed thought grew in his pitch eyes.

Echoes of lost companionship confused time for an instant. "Leon," I whispered amazed.

He came slowly forward and puzzlement was struck against his naturally veiled mind, still I encouraged him to find a deeper knowing of me and after a heavy silence he came to where I stood. "I know you, sir, do I not?"

I smiled gently at memories of the meetings I had with his family line and took refuge in a simple worldly connection, "I sent a letter with the trade ship, *Isabella*, along with my belongings. I hope it was received."

The dark young man smiled as broad then as his ancestor had often done and enthusiasm touched him. "Count Douvélle! Well, I'll be," he beamed and extended a hand to me. "The whole family have been hedging bets on how long it would be 'til you came."

I laughed at his excitement and let him take my gloved hand to shake.

"My mother, I believe, will be most pleased by your arrival," he said conspiratorially, "and she will now be most assured of herself as psychic. Still, come, you must need refreshment at the end of your journey, and I for one need fortification after such a surprise."

He ushered me with great excitement into the house beyond the shop front and into an inner lounge that I recognised from another time. For all the rich trappings had changed with the fashion, still the hearth blazed a welcome and so too, the open faces of the family socialites, gathered in coincidental anticipation of when I would arrive.

Leon stepped beside me and held an arm out long in introduction. "Mother," his dark brown voice fell among the convivial gathering and whispered mutters scattered amused among the family ranks. "I'd like to introduce Count Julian Douvélle." He gestured at a grand matriarch seated by the grate, obviously from her white complexion, an English import, though none of the pale skinned essence yet tainted the strong indigo aura of the Moorish line. "Lady Elsbeth Taylor, widow of Leon the fourth in the family line of our mutual ancestry..." I raised an amused eyebrow at his pretence of my mortality.

"And I am right in assuming that you are the fifth Leon since the days of our last connection?"

The dark mortal nodded, laughing, and he ushered me toward the hearth. "Our family has grown much since that time, Count. Come meet those whose ties remain linked with the fashion house."

Elsbeth insisted that I speak first and foremost to her, she wanted to know the whys and wherefores of my return from China and I told her how love had died and left me on those shores. She laughed when

I spoke of the depth of my love for Mai-Lin, a cynical mocking of my youthful appearance, but still accepted that as being my reason for coming home. For her own part she told me of her husband, whom she had loved and respected even in his devotion to the sea. While he was captain of the trade fleet, she had cared for and nurtured the fashion house and even when he had been killed by pirates on his only journey to China, she had kept the family empire strong.

When she released me from her demand on my attention, Leon introduced the others of the small party; an older couple, another mixture of cultures and the dark lady bore her carriage with a family pride that I knew well. Of their children and nephews and nieces, they were the fashionable young upper class of the day, rich by connection and peppered with their white friends. More than one of the young men tasted with the familiar essence of my old ally and the dark-skinned ladies caught my eye in memories of Isabella and even her budding daughter. But later in the evening when I had learned as much of the family history as each could give to my thirst for their stories, Leon brought forward a late comer whose beauty transcended time.

"Count, I'd like you to meet my sister, Isabelle."

I sighed and took her extended hand. "Ahh, a pleasure to meet you," and I swept her long fingers up to the merest touch of my cool lips. "I insisted that my belongings be given passage on the ship that bears your name. I hope you are not offended, but I had imagined you and could not think of anything more fitting. And yet here you are, and more beautiful than any of my imaginings."

Colour flushed to her high cheek bones and indigo swirls of feminine life essence blossomed from the flattery, and when she took her hand away she snapped open her fan for air. "Oh, Count Douvélle," she said and her voice rang with dark allure, "I have had such thoughts about the romance of our connection," she laughed. "But never once had I imagined that such a friendship would be renewed in our lifetimes."

"Neither I, dear lady, yet it is good to see that the family has prospered since those older days." I smiled and gestured the others, and an accolade of light chatter and *"Well said, sir"* was passed around the party.

Isabelle told me a little of her history, the children that were responsible for her tardiness in joining the party and her husband who himself was away at sea as he apprenticed himself to the running of the empire. "I must say, sir," she said after retelling in a half jest, her fears of him being taken by pirates as her father had been, "a much wiser choice you made by travelling overland."

"Oh, not so," I laughed, "there are bandits a plenty both by land and sea, my lovely Isabelle, and I have my own share of tales to tell of encounters with that kind."

"And you must," she said, flushing with youthful excitement.

"Yes, indeed you must," Leon came to my elbow with a fresh glass and laid a hand on the velvet of my shoulder. "Yet I have something first to speak of, Count."

"Oh yes, Leon," Isabelle said and her eyes filled with excitement.

I gave the conspirators a smile of puzzlement as they shared a private glance and then Leon turned to me with mock apology, "Your arrival, Count, has been a double surprise."

I raised an eyebrow, "Oh? How so?"

Leon paused as if in thought and Isabelle gave his arm a pat, laughing at his indecision, "Do tell him Leon," she said, "or I will."

He flicked a long lock away from his embroidered collar, "It seems perhaps our ancestors were more men of the world than we would allow in our legends."

"How so?" I said bemused.

The swirls of his essence built in excitement and I took a little of the surfeit to bathe in his mortal heat, he opened his mouth to speak but snapped it shut again as he unconsciously felt my theft.

"Oh, Leon," Isabelle laughed in light frustration unaware of what had passed between us and I looked into her beautiful gaze to avoid the beginning of suspicion. "What my brother tries to say, Count, is that you have a twin in Portsmouth."

I looked back to Leon and he shook his head as if to rid himself of dawning realisation, and caught again Isabelle's infectious excitement. "Yes indeed, Count. I have known a young man for some time, Justin is his name, and so similar a countenance to your own that I wonder now if our families' history was as virtuous as the centuries have told."

I laughed at his supposition, it seemed that time indeed had made a fiction of my years in the company of the family, well perhaps in light of my reason for returning, it was for the best. "So a distant cousin I have, even outside the family," and I winked with the alluded crudity.

Isabelle laughed and shook her fan coltishly before her face, and Leon thumped my shoulder with relief. "I think it would be a novel experience if you were to meet."

"Indeed," I agreed without thought, "I will make for the manor on the morrow to unpack my belongings. Perhaps we could have drinks in the afternoon."

Leon nodded, "If I can find him," he laughed and Isabelle joined in what appeared a familiar family debate.

In the early hours of the morning the small party retired, and only Leon and I were left to share generous glasses of spirits and tales of faraway lands. We sat in armchairs by the dying embers of the hearth and I watched the young dark socialite fall into slumber. A smile parted my lips for memories of another who bore such a semblance to my new ally, one who had kept me company often in such a manner. And yet, as time confused my reckoning, how now was it that these people knew another like me here? Like me perhaps, though quite human from what I could tell. Still his presence made mortal sense of my coming home, gave the innocence of another age a reason for my existence and, frankly, I was intrigued to meet the young man who would be my cousin.

As dawn sent long fingers of light to penetrate the inner walls of the quiet lounge, I rose and left Leon in the company of his sleep. With my glasses mercifully cutting the swirling madness of sunlight, I walked casually through the awakening city and towards its edge. The house I had bought with the blood of immortals, the house of Count Douvélle, my home and my privacy in this age, was where I

235

had requested that my belongings be sent. Leon said he had taken it on himself to undertake the fulfilling of my request for its renaissance. I found easily my way to its estate, following the scented trail of earlier times and the sun was well in the sky as I came before the building's face. The tall dark wooden door was opened by an aged, portly and well-dressed servant, a man chosen by Elsbeth herself, known simply as Henry, who stood in guard at the open portal until I introduced myself.

"Sir," he said as I spoke my name and stepped to one side with a short bow, no apology in his eyes for his initial caution. "Please, come in, and welcome home."

I smiled as he closed the door behind me and looked around at familiar eyes. Painted cherubs flew against the ceiling above the entrance hall and stared down, reminding me of what had once happened to leave me as master of this place. "I take it my things were left in the library?" I asked returning my gaze to the short servant.

He nodded and gestured through the entrance hall. "This way, sir."

"I know," I replied, turning from him to cross the mosaicked floor.

He said nothing but followed beside me and I could hear a half-formed question in his mind. So I stopped as we traversed the patterned centre and turned. "Elsbeth assured me that you were a trustworthy man?" I offered him a question.

The servant nodded brisk with inferred pride and the question in his mind was replaced with a bondsman's honour.

"Good," I said and made for a small open doorway that stood shrouded in the richly furnished wall. "Then know, Henry, that things will be done in this room that you have no interest in. I would ask that you stay out."

I let my will be known on currents of his own energy and he gave a small and hesitant bow.

"I understand your need for privacy, sir," he said, making mortal sense of the spell I had cast, "Lady Elsbeth has chosen me well, sir."

"Set the hearth in the lounge then, I will receive visitors later today."

The servant gave another portly nod and turned about his business, and I entered the library and almost another time. The room still held its shelves of books and austere furnishings, but a new and oddly fresh rack of shelves looked out of place and begging to be used. Long tables that had not been part of its décor minded me of life in the present and I moved among the new furnishings to where the first of my empire gilded crates awaited attention.

Time left me in the privacy of this bridging of ages and as I took out the workings of my craft to fill the room, I could sense the change in the air. Already a presence of the destiny I planned here, flowed like a djinn from the crates. I opened each one, knowing of every detail of my end on earth as it began to play in my mind's eye, ready for the acting. Even so, I did not have long to wait for that time I had predicted, the time that had caused love's demise and as I laid the workings throughout the room, I made the place mine in preparation.

A knock came at the library door and reluctantly I looked away from my work to place the late afternoon sun. I laid down my lingering preparations to attend the realm of the living.

Henry waited obediently in the hall beyond. "Your guests have arrived, sir," he said as I opened the door.

I stepped through and closed it pointedly, flicking a layer of powder from my jet sleeve, an accident with a jar of refined opium that I had inadvertently spilt. "Thank you," I said quietly and crossed to the lounge.

Something stopped me as I came to the door. Something wrenched my soul as I came to rest by the portal. Something familiar held me as I looked into the room.

Leon stood by the hearth already nursing a large glass and though my view was obstructed by the tall chair back, I knew his friend, Justin, sat under his gaze. The dark young gentleman flicked a habitual lock from his collar, saw me and smiled and I, with my glass barrier pushed before my eyes, stepped strangely nervous into the room.

Flames of the kindled fire blossomed from the hearth and touched the naked flesh of my face, feeding my cold being as I approached my guests. Leon stepped aside, his face split with a grin as he alerted his comrade of my arrival. The other sat forward in his chair, straightening his lopsided clothes as he prepared to meet me.

I saw his face.

Even the air in the room stood still under terrible recognition and I was cast into the memory of another time, a vision and memory of things yet to come. Yes, I had a twin in this time and I had seen the end of his life, taken by his own hand. His face was as mine had been before my immortal beginning, his countenance like mine though human and degraded, and in his eyes, awfully, I saw my soul.

"Count," Leon said in wry amusement, "it pleases me to introduce you to a close acquaintance, Mister Justin White."

A smile came almost hesitant upon my cold lips. Being a stark contrast to Leon's dark features, Justin indeed merited his name. Still mortality coloured the society counterfeit with a blood tint and rendered him the sun to my moon, his cast was blonde and mine truly white. And he was young, barely a man at all and by the confusion that suddenly clouded his mind, he had been given the same fateful sense by our meeting.

"Well," I said, sighing long, "I greet you, Mister White. Welcome to my home."

Justin took fright at my voice I could tell, but Leon clapped him on the shoulder affectionately, freeing him to collect his thoughts and spoke instead, "So, Justin, did I not speak the truth?"

The young man took a deep breath and rose with an over enthusiastic smile. "Y… Yes, of course, Leon." His light voice came rough and uncertain, though he raised a hand, quite eager for my touch.

I felt myself yearn for the mortal warmth of his handshake, though I had put on gloves to receive him civilly and his heat flowed over the leather and away.

"I must say, sir," he prattled nervously and his shake was weak, "that this is quite a surprise." He looked into my covered gaze as if burned by even that hidden sight and I too felt the exquisite pain of the contact. I had felt the same when I had crouched over a flame haired woman and the pale frailty of her young lover. Before me now, in this place where soon I would end my life, I had found another step in the fate of my soul: so corrupt, so far from the light that even the laws of reincarnation would be forsaken. What fate had brought about our meeting?

I stepped to the bar and poured a drink, struggling to adjust to the terrible new draw on my soul. "So,

Justin… may I call you Justin?" I queried, observing the young man over my velvet shrouded shoulder. He nodded with a hesitant cough and I continued, "Good. And you must call me Julian. Well, my friend, so it seems that we may have a mutual ancestry," I took refuge in shallow, mortal coincidence, "and Leon's pride in his line, a little more haughty than he has a right to insist."

Leon laughed huge, his pleasure in our similarity untainted by knowing the dreadful truth of our connection. That truth of destiny's journey I would spare my young counterpart as well, if I could, and spare him the future I had seen.

"Yes," Justin said as I came into the circle of chairs before the fire, "Leon has told me a great deal of your story, Julian." His eyes lit in his thin face, tasting of the intimacy of saying my name. "How exciting it must have been to have lived your life in China."

I laughed light, letting such idle chatter mask the disconcerting sensation of my guest. Leon sat beside his young friend and I retreated into my chair, to watch him through blue glass. "I was not born in China, Justin. I have been in Portsmouth before."

"Oh?" the pale youth's voice was shaken with surprise and he turned to his companion, "You had said nothing of that, Leon."

A frown creased the other's dark brow and his Moorish looks were belligerent. "Neither did I know," he said.

I laughed, "It was a long time ago, it would be a wonder if anyone would remember."

Leon leaned forward openly curious, "I find that hard to believe, Julian. You can be no older than I."

I waved his statement away with a wistful sigh, "Still, Leon, I am as interested to know the story of your young friend, and leave the retelling of my life for another time." I lowered my glasses for a moment to place the last writhing currents of daylight and pin the young men with a subtle finger of my will, diverting the conversation to an easier topic.

"There's little to it really," Justin said after a long moment, obedient to my spell. "But needless to say, I've never been further than London, and only because I was born there. I'd never go back though, since it had done nothing but try to kill me." He smiled sadly as memories of his early life flowed through his mind; kept from starving—only just— by a gang of thieves in the slums of London, his mother dead of a slattern's disease before he had reached the age of ten. His eyes cleared and he said, "But Portsmouth has been a friendlier port." He chuckled small and reached to pat Leon's stolid arm. "And I have better friends. And now meeting you, sir, is a rare oddity in a life full of the same."

"To that I agree," said I, raising my glass in a toast. "Gentlemen, I propose that we have struck a friendship of the most unusual kind and ask you to join me in celebration."

"Here, here," said Leon with enthusiasm and drained his glass.

We talked until late in the night. I told them some tales of the sea and of my beloved China that marked both young men often suspicious of my lying about my past. Justin spoke of his life on the streets of Portsmouth, living day by day and expecting nothing better than a short existence as a beggar and pickpocket, until Leon had befriended him and seen to it that he at least had a roof over his head. Leon had convinced his mother to fund the purchase of an apartment that would at least afford the young man a respectable home. Justin spoke of his affection for Leon in even grander terms than I had experienced with the young gentleman's forebear and was caught often to watch the proud dark face of the Moor. Inherited family strength and compassion that I had so valued in my association with his line echoed proud in his eyes, such qualities had grown ever stronger with time.

Later, when the street youth slumbered, snoring in alcohol induced sleep, Leon spoke. "And so, Count, what is your opinion?" His words were almost restrained as if deeper concerns lay behind his conversation.

"A strange event," I said, adding no fuel to his curiosity.

The tall socialite shook his heavy, dark mane and laughed, "There is more to this meeting than mere coincidence then Julian, eh?" When I did not answer he continued, "And much in your being here that you do not tell, is that not so?" and arched an eyebrow.

I sat for a long moment and the fire spat a red ember into the chimney, I watched its spirit dance and weave on the cooler night air. "I have come home to meet my end, Leon."

Shock registered on his dark face and then his eyes narrowed, "Are you ill, sir?"

I laughed at the absurdity and then quietly said, "No, I have not encountered that state for..." and paused to consider my sentence, "too long."

"I do not understand."

"Neither did I expected you too, my friend," I replied and lifted my glass gesturing the unconscious youth. "Still, how strange that your young friend is so alike me and how alike our

242

ancestors' friendship is that which you two have created."

"Yes," Leon gazed with open affection over the sprawled figure. "I doubt he would have survived as long as this had I not sponsored him though, sir, life has been very hard for him."

I nodded. "You are a credit to your ancestry," I said into the rhythmic hush.

He eyed me, suspicious of my words, "Yes, sir." He raised his glass slowly, "And you, Julian, what of the lineage which seems now that you share with Justin?"

"Ha, our connection I believe, goes by far deeper than that, I hope our meeting is not a mistake," and I thought, *or at least, not as ill-fated as my last encounter with a holder of my soul.* But in the back of my mind memory stirred again, the vision of his suicide by hanging, and I took a drink to keep the sight at bay. "But that yet remains to be seen."

Leon leaned over to take my empty glass and caught my naked gaze with his, "Yes, Julian, there is much that you have not told of yourself, I know it." He stood and crossed to the bar, taking a golden bottle of Benedictine from the shelf.

I laughed with forced levity, "You are as forthright as your namesake, my young friend, yet I suspect you will not enjoy such truth, if it ever be told."

Leon returned my glass to me and sat once more beside Justin lost in thought. And when the sun came to force me behind the safety of darkened glass, sounds of his sleep joined in symphony with the pale youth.

I spent the first hours of day light ensconced in the simple task of housekeeping and continued emptying crates, arranging the library to satisfy my plan. My books I settled in their new case and as I took each treasure from the carefully packed crate, I spent time flicking through familiar pages remembering the study I had done in earlier days. Brother Tiberias had penned my least lavish volume, but the small parcel of his diary was my oldest and most valued book. He, who had chased my first days in the dark and had followed a line of thought which I shared and indeed had pursued for years, had become a close and valued advisor and his book's place on my shelf, a guarded secret. I hid it, like another I had kept for love's sake, among the pages of a more inconsequential collection of tales, and spelled it with a veil to avoid any casual observance. So close to my time of destiny, it felt an ill omen should it be idly found, the diary had aided me thus far and would guide me still, I planned, on to my end.

A sound broke the silence and I was caught in the performance of my spell by the opening of the library door, I rushed across the room to halt the intrusion but Justin was half into the room even though I had moved quickly and shock mirrored briefly in his eyes as I came beside him. His long blonde hair had escaped most of its ribbon when he had slept and hung now in forgotten tendrils around his face, but his ocean blue eyes were clear and bright. He had been awake for a while.

"C… Count," he stammered as he focused on my sudden appearance.

I tried to usher him from the room. "I'm sorry, friend Justin, I must not have told you of my retreat."

But he had already seen past me and refused my gentle insistence, craning to see past my dark clad barrier, "Still, an intriguing room, sir."

"Yes," I whispered and let my will drive him more surely into the hall beyond.

"So you are a magician then?" Justin leaned indolent against the wall as I pulled the door to with an audible snap.

I gazed on him through deep blue glass. "I have studied the art of alchemy for many years," I said simply.

A light of fascination sparked in the corner of his eye. "Well, sir. It is no wonder at your appearance then. I had thought of a thousand and one reasons to explain your youthful look when you say you have done so much," and he laughed lightly and shook his head, "and some strange things I had thought of too. But this, I can almost understand."

I smiled, relieved that what I would have considered dangerous to allow, in fact could benefit my friendship with the youth. "So you know of alchemy?" I asked innocently.

Justin nodded enthusiastically and pushed away from the wall, "I've been interested in such things for many a year, Julian..." and again there was a halt in his voice as he tasted my name. "I had lived for a time with an old man who taught me to read and write, he himself had been a magician."

"Had been?"

"Oh, he was old and old things die," the young man said inconsequentially, yet when I lowered my glasses a fraction in the late afternoon light, I watched his essence grow weak.

"Yes," I said quietly. "Still, come, Justin, that time is gone. I too have lost friends and loved ones, but I carry their strengths forever within me and hold that as the legacy of our time together."

He looked at me for a long moment under the watching eyes of painted angels and then, "A romantic notion sir."

I nodded, "But one that holds me steadfast as time moves around me, in my life I have had to do no less."

The youth smiled a little, but his pale lips betrayed a deeper pain and questioning that held his energy low. But he gazed again at the library door, taking his thoughts away from their direction and onto a safer path. "I have seen the workings of a magician before, Julian, and I am respectful of your art. Still I would be intrigued to see the mechanics of your work, sir." His face grew brighter and his essence less morbid.

I pressed my glass barrier back around my eyes and regarded the youth for a long moment. So I had thought to keep the knowing of my existence away from him and keep him from discovering the awful reality of our meeting, perhaps a deceit so close to the truth could keep him ignorant and safe. "You must understand then, Justin, that this is a private room. You must not interfere with anything without my permission."

He nodded but excitement was growing around him, returning the pallor in his skin to a flushed pink. "I may be of low station in life, sir, but I have my honour."

Honesty blazed in his eyes and I smiled at his mercurial emotions, "Then come into the library, Justin," I said, amused, "I would be pleased to show you a little of my art."

Justin walked around the library and peered at the freshly unpacked apparatus of magic and I stood watching him as Lao-Tzung had once watched me.

At the end of the table his eyes were drawn to the library proper and he moved to examine the shelves.

"You are most welcome to borrow the books at your leisure, Justin," I said, coming beside the tomes that were my private addition to the library, "but I ask that you stay away from these shelves, for the books here I use in my work."

He nodded shaggy blonde locks and took to studying the more innocent volumes. "I had a dream last night," he said at length, as if he dreamed now and turned to me almost anxious, "though I have forgotten what happened. I had known when I woke, the reason for my seeking you out here." His fist clenched beneath a jacket cuff. "I know you were a character in it though, Julian..."

"Well, perhaps if you do remember, we can talk about it. I have had some experience in interpreting the meaning of dreams," I smiled, smoothing the way to broach such strange territory.

Justin nodded, "Be that as it may sir, I feel odd in your presence and have done so since we met. I take it you know why?"

I bade him sit near me on the library's leather suite and measured my words before I spoke, "I know that we share a common thread, one that has fashioned our bodies and minds alike. And I know this only for it is my life's work to see into the destiny of my soul and when I look, there you stand looking back." I gave a wry chuckle. "Such coincidence has followed my path from its very beginning, Justin, and I would spare you the experience, though I see fate at work here and wonder at such a trick."

He stared at me for a long moment and his eyes bore though my ancient flesh, deep into my soul and he said, "Then, what is your work, sir, that it causes such feelings within me."

"I have sought to fathom the reason for my being," I said, convincing in my half-truth, "and see if it were not possible to be free of the consequences of what has happened in the path of my soul."

He raised a fair eyebrow. "Why, what has happened to make you study so intently?" and he gestured at the complexity of my equipment.

I laughed almost futilely and leaned forward gesturing with a silk touched hand, and took a breath to fathom what I should say to him. How honest should I be, how much should I show him of his own fate touched path? Certainly I could not tell him of the creature that I was, but should I share the simpler side of destiny with him? Surely that would ease the strange energy that flowed between us, appease his curiosity and perhaps keep him safe.

A knock at the door arrested any answer I would have made, and I smiled at the timely interruption. Breathing a mute sigh of relief, I rose to cross the room, "We will speak again, Justin, and maybe you and I will learn something that will be of aid to both of us."

"I trust you are right, Count," came his reply and I opened the door.

Henry stood patiently waiting in the hall beyond. "Lord Taylor is risen, sir, I have served him breakfast in the lounge."

We rejoined Leon and the young friends shared the platter of food that Henry had judged fitting for breakfast so late in the day. To their inquiries why I did not join their feast, I made a brief excuse that I covered with a subtle spell. Still, as they ate and twilight bade me take my glasses from my eyes, I was drawn to the curling flames of each youth's unique essence. I would have to feed soon and often in such company, if I did not wish to inadvertently reveal my true nature. It seemed an ever stranger game that I played as I waited for death; an immortal planning death, playing at mortality and life with those around him, I wondered where such a game would take me. Well, if nothing more, I would see what I could do to prevent the vision of Justin I had seen, so long ago, a dreadful premonition yet to be played. Lao-Tzung had been adamant that my visions were keys to help me change my future and now it seemed, I was being given the chance to prove him right, and what better subject than my pale and angelic young friend? Yes, I would rather he be spared the truth of our connection, but his life had touched mine and I knew that would bring its own mischief.

We went that night to a tavern that was a favourite of the young men, a cosy inn that could receive the society lord and where Justin was also welcome. They drank with a ribald crowd of mixed heritage, a rougher circle of their friends, and I sipped Benedictine, shrouded quietly in the darkest corner of our booth.

Heavy wood and the scent of ale kept me company, the intoxication of mortal flames and the thoughtlessness of society in this time. I had long enough yet to wait until my life would end and such innocent enjoyment of mortal company seemed a fitting final chapter in the unheralded epic of my unlamented age-old life.

Chapter 12

I couldn't say when it was that summer overtook me, though it could have been even then that my days became brighter and my soul gained a strange lucidity, like waking in a dream. Leon, Justin and I took each other into such a confidence, reminiscent of once upon a carefree time with lovely Mai-Lin, Leon or even my beloved Niamh. Thoughts of ancient love moved me to recall that first vision of my glasses, as I had caught another scene from this future, ages ago in time. And some nights when we were abroad at sunset, that memory would arise and I would watch Justin's elfin form as intently as he watched me.

So went my friendship with the pair and our camaraderie grew strong as we ventured the streets of Portsmouth, three men of the world. We travelled the city seeking pleasure where we could find it and during the day when my nocturnal friends slept off the night before, I prepared and waited. So simple was this life that I could easily have lost my knowing of fate and my terrible damnation. So frantic was my need to enjoy my last days that I could easily have changed my mind, preferring another lifetime with Leon's good company and the disconcerting strength of my feelings for Justin. Rather that than the inevitable date of my death. And perhaps I would have done so, but for a night when winter had begun to taint the air and the company of my friends at our favourite inn had clouded my caution.

We sat as usual in our shadowed booth, Leon and Justin were arm in arm singing their latest rendition of an evolving drinking song, and friends and acquaintances moved around us in friendly company. During the evening ladies came into the inn, none had a look of gentry and yet all held themselves with an almost regal sisterhood. A young and delicate looking blossom came and sat near me as her sisters amused my companions, and she leaned into the velvet of my sleeve to whisper among the writhing tendrils of my hair.

She asked for money in trade for her company, so I slipped a golden coin into the tuck of her bosom. The young jaybird leaned even closer at my touch and flicked the careful long ringlets of her wig away from her naked throat. Aching against desire, I leaned back with her into the heavy cushion of my chair and touched my lips against her mortal heat. The current leaped through me and I opened my mouth.

An exquisite slicing of skin and sinew, and blood flowed intoxicating from the slight prostitute, but I schooled my terrible appetite and stole only a little of her mortal essence. Pulling away from her then, my teeth ached for more, yet I sheathed their deadly points with struggled control.

I felt eyes. I turned and Justin was watching me from where he sat, tankard in hand and pretending to sing with the others but his eyes were on me. I had had my back to him as I took the girl and imagined that I had blocked his view, and yet his eyes held a spark akin to suspicion. Even as I would have forestalled the accusation in his eyes, the blood of the girl was in me, gushing in torrents of mortal heat, down into the empty void of my immortal soul. As had terribly happened to me before, on the heels of the essence of womankind, the room disappeared from my sight and another vision came before me.

Justin… or perhaps not. No, I saw another standing, a savage dagger raised in his hand, staring in horror at something beyond me. Or maybe not beyond; it seemed he stared into my eyes. But the terror that flared from him, I had seen in Justin when we had first met. Perhaps it had been that sensation which confused my judgment of this path of my soul, but now I could tell it was someone I had not encountered before, someone new.

Vision melted into those fearful eyes and the inn came back around me. Leon's booming voice drowned out his fellows as they each tried to out perform the others. Justin still stared at me, but his gaze had become concerned, he was aware that I had changed perception and was left now, shivering in the cold aftermath. The fair mortal moved to break from his company and come to me, but those familiar shaded eyes condemned me too readily. I turned away, rose and fled the booth.

I made from the shallow protection of the inn's stone walls and walked along the length of the outer city street, the moon's full face touched the road with a magic that sunlight would not allow. The street ended in a small park, complete with lovers seated beneath a tree. I walked to the far end away from the terrible draw of their alluring mortal blaze to fathom the vision. I had not had sight of another of my wretched lives for years. In my arrogant assumption of an almost normal existence, I had forgotten the prophetic qualities of feminine essence. The experience left a sour taint in the taste of her blood and the horrible need for more vital fire to cleanse the corruption away. Under such an insidious curse I could not think of the import behind this new damnation and until I fed again I would think of nothing but blood.

I walked under a high pruned tree and stood resting in the shadow of its trunk as I grappled with such a treacherous need.

"Are you alright, Count?" the sound of a youthful voice caught my attention and I turned startled. A young friend of Justin's, bewigged and powdered, stood almost guilty behind me.

"You followed me from the inn," I said, struggling suddenly in the sight of his flaming mortality. "Why?"

The dandy shook his head foolishly and laughed, "Why, sir, you looked a little ill."

I reached a hand into his essence and drew him toward me and under the shadow of the tree. "Yes, my friend, I am ill. Though with your help, I could be well again." I pulled him closer and gazed deep into his eyes. The youth was entranced as I whispered a spell over his effeminate form to dull body and mind. "And in return I will give to you more intimate a lover's kiss than even the memory of this moment."

I took the fop close and menacing, yet he sighed like a woman and lay bemused and fragile in my arms. In an enthralled moment and shrouded in shadows, I stole a tenuous measure of his vital fire.

Long after my cavalier victim had stumbled away from my place in the shadows, reason came slowly and gave up once more, this new face of my eternal journey. In my years of magical study I assumed I had seen as many lifetimes as my soul had held, yet the vision I had seen under the influence of that feminine essence was new. How, when I had experimented successfully with such bridging of the realms, had I missed the existence of another incarnation, and what brought it for me to see now? Another part of my journey, another man fighting against something that was again, myself. Would my fall into the dark never end? To live eternally and know each of those who have come before me to create such a hell spawned fate, and I the one to bear such a final sentence.

Oh, God, I am not strong enough to bear this!

Darkness grew thick beneath the tree's obscure branches and I could feel mist come around me. My clothes fell away and I rose into the form of a cloud.

Sadness, loathing of my path; pain of being the most evil and final of all mankind's horrors. In these eternal chains, I was so destined to see all of Man's journey—the dryads had told me so, and now I saw how true their evil words had been. I remember the pain I had raged as a storm to let anguish come under my control, those spiteful creatures had indeed taught me well. But even as I raged again in the star thrown heavens and released my pain in a bellow of thunder and lightning strike, I found my place once again beneath the tree, of human form and clad in velvet and silk. Thoughts tugged, urging me along my path, thoughts of the time when those stars could aid me end this, my lowest incarnation and I would be free of this life. I regained my form with a thought on the edge of words and my lips seized it and spoke as they condensed into flesh; "Soon."

Although the reality of my vision still weighed heavily upon me, I recovered from the sight sooner perhaps than I had in the past. A sense of knowing that this life was to end came as I stepped from the shadows of the tree and a sense of perverse relief that grew to ease the pain of my burden.

Back at the tavern I moved through the drunken revelry, my young friends had ceased with their demands to hold focus of the room in their ribald songs and I returned to the booth. Justin sat over the table sharing an amused whisper with another and when he moved back to look at me, I noticed the young man who had had the misfortune to be my last victim. When my eyes met his, the popinjay gave a coy wink, yet his mind revealed nothing of our encounter and I smiled that my magic had freed him from such a memory.

But Justin held something in his eyes that stirred deep recognition in me, what it was I could not tell, but his essence when he looked guarded upon me, crackled and flamed with a passion that I had seen between lovers. I stared at him for a long moment, a serving girl came to me with a Benedictine and Justin turned his attention pointedly back to his new friend. Confused, I touched his thoughts, but their ragged jumble gave me no more sense than his wondering of where I had been. There could have been something more hiding under such surface babbling, but the strength of our ties and the insipid working of ale and spirits stung at my touch and I withdrew into the corner of the chair.

The night rolled around to its darkest, Justin left and in the company of the young fop and his eyes, when they met mine, held a look I could not fathom. Leon had long since fallen asleep by the fire and I drained the last of my drink, alone among the shadows.

"Come, Leon," I said and the dishevelled young socialite jerked awake at the sound of his name.

"Wha'…?" he said thickly.

I rose, an eyebrow raised in amusement and took him by the elbow. As we stepped out onto the pavement, I looked to the pitch sky above to determine the arrival of the sun, but clouds obscured the stars now and I knew that they had been attracted by my magic. I half carried the drunkard to his bed and, even before he had finished thanking me, he was asleep on the pillow.

I left the Taylor mansion by a servant entrance much quieter, in the predawn chill, than our arrival had been, and made my way back through the city toward home. As my path wandered by the street where Justin lived, and still in mood to match the hour, I walked by his corner terrace apartment. There was a light framed in his upper window, his bed chamber, and I wonder that he had gone to sleep without thought for the candle. In his drunken state he could too easily burn down his house and himself with it.

The street was deserted, not even a mortal flame penetrated the night here and all was quiet. If I knocked on Justin's door, I knew there would come little of it besides waking the neighbourhood. So I let my will carry me quietly upwards beside the corner wall and flew to his window. The curtains were parted slightly and I peered through their crack to place the stub of a burning candle, with relief I saw it innocently sitting on the stone mantle of the hearth. I would have turned to leave, but movement from across the room caught my attention behind the curtains and I rounded the windowsill to see the tall, posted bed.

I watched, an unintentional voyeur of the scene within and saw Justin, kneeling on all fours, his face toward the door and naked, but for the long silk ribbon that held his hair. The young dandy that he had taken with him from the inn, his shirt billowing full sail from atop his mastlike legs, strained and grunted as he followed the urges of their bestial copulation. I turned shocked from the scene and quickly flew to the roof, up and away from what I had inadvertently witnessed.

In the last moments of night when twilight changed the world, the dandy left the apartment alone and I covered my gaze, to sit on the gable, lost in thought for many hours. I had not realized that Justin so preferred the company of men, his demeanour had not struck me as that of a homosexual. Even so, it was an odd coincidence that he had chosen to consummate the sexual act with the very same fop I had entertained for my own benefit.

I left the roof top when the sun rose blazing overhead, its rays had burned away the clouds that had gathered because of my pain. Without the blessed screen of that moisture laden blanket, my hair thrashed under naked rays of sunlight and its searing caress drove me to seek asylum from the day. I retreated to my home and the relative safety of the library, but even though I surrounded myself with the paraphernalia of my work, I was preoccupied by this new twist in the sharing of our fate. What could it mean to our friendship, should Justin prefer the courtship of men—I had seen him look at me often and now confusion fell like a veil from my understanding. Now, what I had felt from him, the way he had hesitated in saying my name, his looks and lingering touch, all thoughts of him now I could colour with an emotion akin to love. But to love one such as I?

Memory of a vision was called by my tacit question, the image of Justin hanging obscenely by his neck and I, powerless to do ought but watch. Anger sparked in my eyes, and I realized that I had been standing by the small case of my books for hours, light had already left the library in gloom. I sighed and folded my glasses away into a pocket and ran a hand down the spine of a leather-bound work. Among its pages, hidden by my magic was the vampire hunter's journal and my link with a time, so near and yet so dangerously far, that its coming still could be heralded by the young man's death. I turned away from the shelf and gazed into the darkened space, frustrated that I had no knowing of where or when Justin would die. Even now I knew not if I could stop it before it happened, but for certain I knew that his apparent devotion ran much deeper than I had anticipated and felt terrible danger.

I crossed to the bar and poured a drink and then sat beside the table in silence, until beyond in the hallway I could hear a voice raised in anger and Henry struggling in vain to contain the mortal fury. The voices grew nearer and then the library door was thrown wide. A tall rectangle of light from the room beyond filled the doorway, pushing aside the darkness that framed it, and Justin stood imposing and irrational on the boundary.

"I'm most sorry, sir," Henry said into the lashing silence.

"Be that as it may, it seems I have a visitor," I said as light as I was able. "Thank you, Henry, you may leave us now."

The portly manservant bowed quickly and departed from beneath Justin's vengeful gaze and then the youth turned on me, "Why do you sit in the dark, sir?" he asked and his tone was incriminating.

"Justin," I said and rose from the chair, "to what do I owe the pleasure of this visit?" I was as casual as if I never had encountered his predawn activity, and moved to strike a light.

Shadows fled the room as flame took hold of the candle wick and I turned to see Justin, dark eyed and angry, watching me. I crossed to the bar and poured the youth a drink, in his state it could do him little harm and urged him toward a seat. His angry resolve weakened under the influence of my will.

"Friend, why have you come to me this way?" I asked quietly and he took the drink as I offered it.

He downed the alcohol like an elixir to his pain and brought his hand to his brow, "I have had a dream," he said, his breath coming ragged and shallow, then he looked sharp at me, his blonde lashed eyes accusing, "A nightmare!"

I waited for a long moment, letting his quick temper fade once more and then, "I have told you, Justin, I know a little of such things. If you tell me your dream, maybe I can help with its meaning."

"Huh!" he grunted but it held no strength. "I would take to insomnia rather than see it again."

We sat in silence, only the occasional guttering of the candle flame marked a noise in the library. Justin held a delicate hand pressed to his forehead, his gaze purposefully clear of mine and when he spoke, it was a whisper.

"I dreamed a nightmare scene of long ago. You were there, and a woman and a man. But all three I know are as one, how can this be? Each one of them, I see from their eyes, a nightmare of experiencing death by my own hands." He fell silent for a long while, yet even so I was stunned by his vision, a vision we shared by the damnation of our soul. "Julia and Jeremy," he said at length and his words were like vipers that knew how to sting me, "Did you know their names?" A mute tear fell in pain, but he continued before I could reply, "I saw what happened when Jeremy defended the honour of his

259

lady. I saw too what happened to cause their demise, not once, Julian," and his voice took on a frozen edge, "but thrice. Thrice I did endure that dream to see death acted out in the most heinous of ways, to see myself at each point, predator and prey. Interpret this then, sir, I challenge you, and tell me the meaning behind the terror of two innocents and the creature that came, to do such dreadful things."

I stared at him and woe lanced through my cold heart. What could I say to this mirror of myself now he had seen something of our mutual path as intimately as I. The youth had fathomed such a fateful meeting that echoed eternally through the journey of my soul, and the terrible coincidence that condemned me yet again. What could I say?

"Tell me what I saw was only a dream, Julian," his whisper rent my heart and I turned away.

Sudden noise, a cry and he threw his glass to the shadowed wall and it splintered to the floor. "What are you?" he yelled and burst angrily from his seat. When I said nothing he vented his fury by pacing across the cool stone floor and said, "Have you no heart? Do you care so little for me that you would let me think such terrible things of you? You have challenged me since the first time we met, sir. What right do you have to lead me on so?"

I raised a weary, tear-stained eye, "Sit down, Justin."

Again, as when I had first spoken to him, fear leapt abject into his eyes at my words and instantly he obeyed. "What are you?" he whispered.

"I would have spared you such knowing," I sighed, futile in the face of this play of destiny and judged his mood not to be so tolerant of a more innocent tale. "But time and fate have played their own hand in your knowledge of me and so it seems I can do naught but share with you the truth."

He stared at me with those angelic, accusing eyes and so I looked away from him as I spoke. "I am a creature beyond redemption, Justin, and you and I, little more than steps in the path of one eternal soul." I breathed and let him sense the emptiness of my infinite existence, what else could I give to him to make him understand? "I have seen and lived through every injustice, every evil act, every thought and feeling that has blocked light from my heart, and God knows I am lost in darkness. So I search in the hidden realm of magic, that realm that I have been condemned to for eternity, I search for an answer to the riddle that damned my existence, a way to cheat the demon that dwells in my soul. I seek to bring about an end to immortality and rid this world of a plague that should never have come into being."

"And I?" His voice was smaller than the mute candle flame and drew my eyes to gaze on his mortal mirror of my pain.

I looked at his anguish for long moments, "That you have stumbled into the middle of my search is unfortunate, my young friend, and, as I said before, is a fate driven coincidence. I know not what part you hold, but we share that same soul you and I, and have to play the hand fate has dealt. But, Justin, I am no pawn of that fickle mistress and I intend to be free of this deathless state to which I am condemned."

The young man blinked and stared at me, and after long moments said, "How has this happened?"

I laughed bitterly at his ignorance, "This much I have learned from my art, my young friend. Each life I have discovered has been a lesson in hate, a fall from grace; self-mutilation on a cosmic scale. My soul has followed a path into damnation with the passing of each life it has led until, by the horror of my own acts, I came into being."

He said nothing.

"I have seen all this and more, Justin, and I have seen you as well, even you have played your part in the damnation of my immortality."

"What?" he whispered, slack with fear, "What have I done?"

I turned from the sight of his accusing eyes. "You have died in a crime against nature," I replied, afraid to say more.

Silence descended for and age and then he said simply, "I see," and rose from his chair.

"Where are you going?"

He looked at me unsure over an embroidered shoulder. "Home," he said quietly and turned back to the door.

"Can you manage?"

"Yes."

The old year closed and a new one brought with it freezing winds and snow. I took myself away from the company of my young friends, making excuses of trade or estate to cut my contact and even spent some time in Paris, procuring a delicate shipment of fashionable cloth for the trade house in an excuse to stay away. When I did return to Portsmouth, I did so without formality and spent time holed up in my library, working to manufacture substances that would let me complete my dangerous and deadly magic. I went into the city only when the curse of need drove me from my work and found my path often crossing the familiar territory of what had been a carefree and strangely intimate summer. did not seek out Justin's company and neither did he return, and I wondered if our conversation had altered his destiny as I would have wished. Still, if such a change were to come about then it was prudent that I spare him the horror of our connection, I resolved that I would stay away. With a matter of short months until the heavens aligned, I let the world move on without me.

When spring came, I took to walking the streets in the early evening to watch the blossoming of the mortal world. With all in readiness and tested tenfold in my work, I could think of no other pastime that held peace from memories of my ages alone. Portsmouth shone in evening sunshine, clean and refreshed as all life caught the season, flowers and trees filled with leaf and bloom and even mortal faces held a lightness that had been missing in the winter. I walked down familiar streets and inevitably spent a little time after dark, watching the corner terrace where Justin lived and, once or twice from the shadows, I caught a glimpse of him. I could tell nothing of his demeanour since he was drunk each time he passed by and neither did he see me through the haze of alcohol but one night when I rested in the mouth of the alley beside his house, he came to his door clutching something to his breast and entered his domain in violent anger. Piqued at the flaring of his incensed energy I rose, a shadow, to his window and peered in at his rage. With a bottle in one hand and a bundle held close in the other he paced the room and drank, and when he did nothing more I retreated.

I walked down to the harbour district and along ancient streets. So close to the end of my eternity, time meant nothing and memories of gambling in older days flowed carefree on the ocean scented breeze. So the end of my life would cut away such a press of past ages and, I was sure, cut that demon's hold on the lives of all of my incarnations on earth. Soon I would free even my young and angelic friend from the horror that was resident in his soul.

Slowly I made my way back to my home and entered the darkened hallway, without thought for the cherubs and their accusing, painted innocence. Scant weeks now it would be until the stars shone their cage for the beast and I could ingest a poison that would kill me, a thought I held to more and more as darkness of isolation closed in around me.

I put a hand to the library door and knew even then, that the room had been entered by an intruder. The darkness held a vision of Justin caught in a guilty act forever in the aethers and I saw that he had looked through my books. On the shelves and scattered on the floor, books of my craft lay opened and discarded. On the table, amid the mound that cheated my experiment of its order, the leather-bound manuscript that had hidden Tiberias' diary lay ominously exposed and the diary itself was gone.

I sank to a chair, knowing the bundle under Justin's arm for what it was, and sighed under the weight of inevitability. I had assumed the young man would move on, but now I saw his fixation had kept him company even though I had not. Then...

...I could not breathe! What use I had for such a mechanism had always been for a memory of my lost humanity but still, such a sense of foreboding flooded the darkness of the library and I shot from my chair in abject panic. I could not breathe!

I fled from the room and out of the house, throwing the door wide to the night and took quickly to the sky. I flew over the crowded city, uncaring in such a state whether I would be seen by mortal eyes, and came quickly to the roof of Justin's terrace. No gap now formed light at his window and the cover of the curtains so complete that I could not tell if there were light or no and my heart was squeezed once more.

On the road below Leon came beneath my gaze, whistling in innocence as he came to knock on the youth's door. Time passed agonizingly and he knocked again, and when there was still no answer, Leon stepped back to look up at the bedroom window and shouted Justin's name.

I left the roof top and walked from the darkened alley to join him on the corner.

"Julian!" Leon said as his eyes came to rest on my sudden appearance. "What brings you here?"

"Something is wrong," I said urgently and looked up at the building.

His dark lips pressed into a bitter grimace and he reached into a fold of his tunic's skirt to retrieve a bundle of keys, "I would not ordinarily disturb his privacy so," he said sorting one from another, "but, I have a spare key to his door." He shrugged uncomfortable and stepped under the lintel. The door opened with a foreboding and empty click.

I pushed fearfully past the dark socialite and almost flew up the stairs to Justin's domain. On the night table by his bedroom door Tiberias' diary lay open and a large sheet of newly added paper sat on top with horrible finality. The bedroom door was closed as if what happened beyond had been kept private even from the rest of his own life and when I flung the door wide, in terror, I knew why.

Leon gasped beside me.

From the tall trusses of his post bed, a cord made innocently to tie a curtain stretched to its limit under its load. Justin hung at its end, his fair head tipped obscenely over the join, his eyes bulged and body still quivering in its death rigors. Without thought for the mortal standing by me, I rose to catch the energy void corpse.

Holding the body to me, I untied the knot and saw the scene in reality now for the first time. And it was more terrible than any vision that plagued my nightmare existence.

I returned to the floor and slowly laid down the already decaying body and I heard Leon speak as if he stood as far away as the walls would allow. "There is no saving him then?"

What he meant by his words I was unsure, but I knew there was no saving Justin even to the path of his immortal soul. I had seen his death and no matter my conviction at changing that, he had died just as I had known he would. I shook my head and knelt in sorrow over the morbid doll, tears fell unhindered over pity at my unavoidable descent into hell. So another being had once more sealed my fate, what had I expected? Not even I had been given a chance to know the consequences of what had happened in my life before immortality had doomed me forever.

"Oh, Justin," I whispered through unquenchable tears, "never had I meant for this fate to play itself, never had I intended that you fall victim to this terrible destiny. I am so sorry." And silence descended for an ageless moment.

"He left a note," came Leon's deep voice through pain racked torment and the sound of paper being moved on the table beyond the bedroom door, "and it seems, he borrowed a book from your library."

266

I listened to his deep faltering voice as I stared at Justin's lifeless and death ravaged face, yet I hardly heard his monologue as he read the note to me. I shook my head in pain racked guilt. Justin had spent the months of our estrangement in a terrible spiral of self-doubt and my wish to spare him from the reality of our connection, only fuel for this insidious act. *My god, what have I done?*

"I do not think anything could have changed this, Julian, he had a fragile mind."

I dragged my gaze savagely away from the corpse and looked to Leon like one accused, "I could have left the first time I saw him!" I spat.

From beside the doorway, hesitation in his eye, the dark-skinned society lord shrugged a richly embroidered shoulder. "Come, Julian, I too could chastise myself with what I should have done. Though hindsight is a great teacher, sir, it is a poor excuse."

I nodded in futility, "And so another step in my destiny comes to seal my fate."

Panic flushed quickly through his life fire and I saw him sway under the pressure, a vision of my rise to catch Justin flared bleak across the veil of his thoughts. I sighed and turned back to Justin's mortal end, laid and ready to bury before me, it was easier to bear than the awful draw of such living flames on my soul.

"I will see to his burial," Leon's voice rose into the quiet and long fingers of morning sunlight broke across my sight, mocking my eternity in the dark.

I pushed deep tinted protection before my eyes, mercifully cutting even Leon's accusing lights. "Yes, you must send word," I said slowly watching as he resisted an urge to flee, "and when it is done, I too will go."

Relief settled on the young man and mixed feelings of regret chased in readable patterns across his dark chiselled face, but his eyes held ocean deep compassion. "I misjudged many things about you, sir, but at last I think I am beginning to understand."

I nodded and turned from him then and made my silent way from the apartment. Sunlit streets of the city chased darkness away and I found my way home with as little protection as velvet and silk, and my blue barrier against the sun.

With methodical precision I rescued my library and the delicate workings of the experiment which Justin's outburst had destroyed and counted the moments until the alignment of the heavens, short days until all that I had intended would come to be. But it brought me no joy and the morning when a messenger brought word of Justin's funeral, melancholy settled around my heart once more.

I walked through the outskirts of the city and to the graveyard where the Taylor family had been interred, even to a moss ruined plot of those who had been burned after a plague. It was protected now by a wall and when I came by the gate, a shade waited for me. Among the remnants of ages of death, Justin stood as yet untainted in his fashionable shroud and I came before him with tears in my eyes.

"I am pleased that you could attend my funeral, Julian," he whispered and a chill wind touched my soul, "a pity that you couldn't have attended me when I was living, eh?" and his eyes became dark pools of regret.

"I would rather wish that we had never met, Justin, then perhaps you would have been safe from your part in fate's callous game."

But the shade shook his blonde locks and laughed like a breeze. "Are you that naïve, Julian? Your path has been set for many lifetimes, do you think you could change it? You think to cheat fate? Well now, I know of our fate when it is too late to change anything, and I know what steps you will take to end your walk, for end it you will, one day..." His voice trailed back into regret.

I watched the ghost waver for an instant as if memories robbed him of the present, but the sound of a mortal voice raised in single prayer hardened his form. He came beside me, a wind across a glacier, and snaked an arm long to where a group of mourners stood in sombre congregation. I moved under the shelter of a tree and watched as the family gathered to pay their due respect. Leon stood forsaken and Isabelle clutched to his arm, veiled and unmoving in her duty to the dead, but Lady Elsbeth and the others of Justin's connection stood almost bored by the inconvenience of the day.

"They will not miss me," Justin said, his sight fixed steadily on the small group, "but then I won't miss them, except perhaps Leon and Isabelle," and he pointed toward the dark couple, "they were good friends."

I nodded mutely and the priest's monologue filled the silence and, from beside me, the shade stepped out to where his grave beckoned him to rest. On a breath of other worldly air, Justin moved through the company of mourners and Leon shuddered as the ghost touched a delicate hand to his shoulder. And then as the assembled took their dutiful handful of earth, the ghost descended too and disappeared.

I turned to leave then and Leon caught the movement, his dark eyes fell on where I stood and I paused to gaze into his sadness. *Thank you, I thought* and let him catch the refrain, *you have been a good friend and I am grateful that such nobility has blossomed in your line. May your descendants be as wise as you have been, my friend.*

A suspicious light veiled the young Moor's eyes as he heard my words in his mind, though as I turned from him again he nodded and I heard a sad *"Goodbye"* echo faintly in return.

I made my way back to the manor house and the imminence of my own death. I dismissed Henry and thanked him for his dutiful care of my home, his unquestioning obedience and, when he had left, I took to the house entrance with boards and nails. Only days now separated me from the end of my ageless walk on earth and a sense akin to morbid excitement took me as I sat in the company of my little phial of poison. Watching the heavens and waiting for the moment their sanction, I reread Tiberias' diary, Lao-Tzung's notes and all my own study that had led me to this moment. In the seclusion of the library, memories of time past also came to keep me company, visions of those I had loved and lost admonished me to continue with this, my final act on earth. Even so, in the days I waited I could feel the lethargy of the grave come to caress my form and even surprised myself by realizing I had actually fallen into a doze. With less than a week until the heavens aligned, I wondered at such a thing. I had slept before and more time than I care to think of had passed without my knowing. At this time I hardly wanted to succumb to such a state and so I busied myself as well I could to hold sleep at bay.

Evening came and my mood was as devoid as the moonless heavens above, I stood by the library window watching stars come out in the darkening sky. Clouds scudded among those lofty heights, inviting and beckoning flight but I resisted the magic of nature's guiles and toyed instead with the phial of poison I held ready to ingest. The library was prepared.

I had ground incense in measures of a concoction to blur the edge of reality, to dissolve the barrier between me and the stars, and it burned in hellish volumes of smoke across the room. A pattern of candles I set around the floor, a tiny mirror of the moment I waited for. I moved across to sit among my simple magic and *listened* for the workings of the cosmos beyond the room. No more subtle a spell could I have devised, but magic, true magic, was ever a subtle realm. I wove the heat that rose from each flame and sent it to touch with the moving heavens and when the moment came upon me, I knew it. I lifted the phial before my naked gaze and looked deep into the heart of its innocent amber lustre, now was the moment I had waited for, now I would make eternity in hell end. When the stopper came from the bottle, I could almost feel the demon that inhabited my soul and the prison of heaven's workings came steadfast around me in cosmic aid but, even as I watched my hands through flames of candlelight, dread flared with thoughts of that beast, even as I brought the potion to my lips, I trembled. Why?

Laughter echoed beyond me, a silent monologue that caught my attention, *"You think to defeat me? I am your father! You have nothing that I have not given you. You wish to invoke me? Then drink the potion I have supplied."*

I looked to the bottle as if it had become a viper, was what he said the truth?

I steeled myself with reason, he was the prince of lies. I had devised my work even under the guardianship of Lao-Tzung, it would not fail. And yet even as my hand traversed the distance to my lips, the phial slipped dangerously and my resolve, that which had carried me through hundreds of years, that which had withstood every pain and heartache in an immortal life, my one strength, my resolve, faltered.

The bottle fell to the ground in shards and the heavens moved, a sensation like the piercing of flesh pricked one booted foot and I was left horror struck by my failure. Far beyond, laughter began and I was caught immobile by the terror of its touch. My sight failed and before me came the beast.

It snorted and stamped a hoof and yawned to vomit its words over me, "Foolish creature, know this; I am your creator and you, my greatest treasure. I will keep you on this earth, forever!"

I tried to back away from the terror of his voice, but I was still, immovable under his will. The creature laughed foul over me and then all things failed.

The library came into view, sideways and ravaged, I lay sprawled on the ground and everything in the room had been destroyed. Furniture lay in splinters among the rubble of where such force had broken the very walls, no book remained where I had laid them, nay the very shelves themselves had been torn down and pages still floated from the ones that had been destroyed. The fireplace was gutted as if a mighty wind had seared its fuel into nothing—my sun had been extinguished.

A sob rose through my abused lips and I lay for long moments in abject dejection, aware so painfully of my downfall. How had it gone so wrong? I was a coward and a failure and condemned to carry my burden forever.

I was unaware of how long I lay devastated on the floor, but the savage lights of the sun filled my naked gaze with madness and I did not move to cover the sight. It mattered little now that I should lose sanity in the face of the day. More than once I found myself reminiscing over long dead ghosts and in the light of the evening when the sun retreated and reasoning allowed me to know my indelicate prostration on the floor, the air congealed around a spectre, and Niamh came before my face.

"Oh, my love," she whispered and the sound of her voice unleashed tears in my eyes. *"There is hope, beloved, please know that peace does wait for you and the end of this life, if you are wiser than the machinations of the devil in your soul."*

I would have turned away from her alluring promise, such a falsity of hope stung and the revealing of truth laced my eyes in tears but my body was still beyond my control, I had surrendered even as she tempted me to go on.

"Come, my beloved Julian, sleep beyond the bitter living of your life."

She reached a ghostly arm out to me and gratefully I unshackled myself from the leaden bonds of naked human flesh. I was drawn, a mist with a wraith, away from my failure.

Under the library door I drifted and through the silent echoing hall, under eyes that painted, could not see our passing and through the manor house. At a wall, no different in its clothes of plaster and paint, I paused to taste a crack and beyond where a corridor lay hidden through time, I flowed to fill the dank space. Down into the presence of a crypt I floated unthinking, and the dreadful sound of scurrying vermin brought me to a halt. Niamh lit up the space with her unearthly glow and her gaze was as deep as the night sky.

"Sleep now, my beloved," she said and I was once more given flesh, *"and take heart. One day you will find peace, and we will be together again. Take heart and know there is a way..."*

I fell uncaring into centuries of dust and decay, unthinking as the ghost vanished beyond my perception.

Niamh said that there was hope. Yet I could not think to fathom her meaning. She had said that one day I would find peace, but sleep called me and my thoughts dulled.

And she had said we would be together again.

But I was too lost to let such hope stir me.

I lay among the clouds of dust, waiting for the sweet release of sleep to come and in the hours I drifted along its boundary, all memories and ghosts of my life spanned themselves before me. I hardly knew how long such visions held me, but finally darkness overcame my eyes and my spectres vanished too...

And so I slept...

And I dreamed...

Chapter 13

Down and feathers flew choking into the air as I vent my fury on a nursery cushion. My four-year-old brother screamed as I threw his toys crashing into the wall.

"How old do they think I am, *four*?!" I spluttered venomously at the nurse as she endured the tantrum. "I will not say in this house until some fat prick marries me for daddy's money! Who does he think he is, *ordering me* around! How dare they confine me here with just an ugly stupid old woman for company!" I paused fuming with my hand on my brow, hearing for the hundredth time the argument that sparked my fury.

"But, daddy, all the girls are taking Autumn work in Torbay, it's not like I'll be unchaperoned." I used my most beguiling voice, but my father, who had already said no and sat mute behind his voluminous newspaper, had finished listening and would not back down from his tacit finality. I looked imploringly to mother but she sat stricken dumb by her husband's laws.

"I've had enough of this!" I spat, turned hissing on my father and with a claw, reached over the breakfast table and tore the barrier from his grasp. "I am eighteen, for God's sake, I have a right..."

My father rose in anger suddenly, my mother gasping beside him and cut me off in religious fury, "Meena! How dare you profane the Lord's name in this house? You are nothing but a stupid and ignorant child, and you will not speak in that way before your parents. Eighteen years is not long enough for the likes of you to learn enough respect to sit in the company of adults. Your place is in the nursery with your brother, learning at the foot of your nurse and if it takes *another* eighteen years, you will take that time to put a civil tongue in your head. Now get upstairs!" In shaking anger, father's arm shot up, pointing in the direction of the nursery.

But I had inherited the rage of my father and I stood before him shaking equally, and with a measured breath said, "No."

In a flash his hand had snaked out and caught me savagely across my cheek, blood flared behind my eyes and I was thrown to the floor. In the moment of roaring that came with such a cuff, I didn't hear my mother's stifled scream, but as I looked up, her eyes were ashen and feverishly imploring me to surrender. My father had turned from me and was savagely tugging at the hem of his jacket. He cleared his throat several times, habitually soothing his mind, before he reached for his work sachel and kissed my mother's cheek. "Keep your daughter in the nursery today, Ellen, I will deal with her when I get home." Then he strode from the house without a glance back.

Jacob was still crying as I ended the scene in my head, his noise grating on the pain in my face. "For *God's* sake, shut up, brat!" I turned screaming at my little brother who hid in the skirts of his nurse and in venom, caught my foot under the edge of the dolls' house. It launched across the room and a flare of outraged spite blossomed from me. The structure exploded into fragments just before the nurse and in a frozen moment, I saw a shard of the broken wood fly from the floor and lodge itself deep in the eye of my brother Jacob. In horror I saw him fall to the floor, now silent, a small rag staining the carpet red. The pain in my face gave a sympathetic jump as the room fell into silence. Nurse just stared at me grave faced and I stood for a moment and weighed what I had done. My father's son, his favourite and only son, his only chance at immortality, lost in a moment by me. For an instant all things stopped and I was filled with a knowing that I had killed, in my rage I had killed. It didn't matter what or how I had killed but that I was capable of such a feat and I was filled with horror.

My God, the God of my father, would punish me for this. I needed to leave. The nurse started to scream and I fled.

I catapulted down the hallway and burst into my bedroom, my luggage from school still sitting at the foot of my bed. I did reason then, that it was good luck I hadn't planned to move back in for the holidays, ironically it was that luck that had been the beginnings of this. I threw closed the catches of my carpet bag and grabbed my coat, stuffing my feet into boots that I didn't bother to fasten and hastily left the room. By the time I reached the stairs, my mother had already been alerted by the nurse's distress and I heard her scream my brother's name as I flew downward and out of the front door.

In the noisy street before my parents' elegant town house I paused and took stock. Carriage wheels and horses' hooves sparked the cobbles, fine ladies meandered on the path, the sounds of city life floated around me as I fathomed a plan. The most logical thing to do I suppose was just go on to Torbay and meet with my girlfriends, I could lose myself as well there as I could staying in London, so I hailed a taxi carriage and initiated my plan.

"Where to, muss?" asked the cockney driver, helping me to arrange my bag.

In the sweetest tone I could affect, I replied, "The train station, please."

"Off on 'oliday then, is it?" he quizzed conversationally, chucking the horse into a gait.

"Working actually," I replied with less fury than I felt.

The driver threw up his free hand in mock disgust. "Now then, who would send a lovely young lady such as yourself out workin'?" Smiling, he turned to look at me.

Defiantly I threw back my hair revealing the bruise on my cheek. "Me, actually." That silenced him enough so he left me alone for the rest of the journey.

I watched busy London pass by as the taxicab clattered along the streets, not pausing to care or think of the life I was leaving behind, seeing only the pool of my brother's red blood as it pulsed in a crime against God. I knew that running would not hide me from Him, His word was everywhere in modern Victorian England, but I'd rather face God than a man like my father when he learned of the destruction of his dream.

All too quickly I was stirred out of contemplation and the carriage pulled up at the station. I smiled apologetically at the driver as he turned to me and I offered him a pound for his trouble.

"Naw, muss, I figger you'll need that pound a damn sight more 'un me." He waved a finger at the open purse on my lap. "That sixp'nce'll do for 'is feed," and he nodded back at the horse end of the carriage. "I 'ope you find what you're lookin' for." He tipped his hat to me as he helped me down with my carpet bag and then left me standing before the great iron gates that stood like open sentinels at the entrance to Grand Central Station.

I purchased my ticket for Torbay and held it close to my breast as I pushed through the crowded hall, a huge steam blowing monster came hissing to a halt on the platform where I had to be. The press of people around me flowed in a tide that slowly had me move away from the train that was waiting for me. In frustrated panic, I pushed against the throng of milling people and tripping, careened straight into a boy.

"Eh, watch it, luv," he said catching me in soot-stained hands. "Watch y'r step then." I was pushed back to my feet and he disappeared into the crowd.

I was sitting in my seat watching the landscape roll before me, well on the way to the sea before my stomach reminded me of food and in my search for my purse, I was arrested by the memory of the young man I had seen at the station. I had been set up for that fall, my palms turned icy, he had taken all my money. In more calm than I felt, I relaxed back into my seat and let my gaze rest unfocused on the dreary moving landscape. I was lost, I would have to return home but I could not now ask my parents for money to buy a ticket, yet once in Torbay where could I go? For hours I sat with my thoughts chasing each other around and mercifully they finally gave way to a scent of brine and the approach of the small seaside town of Torbay. As the train pulled up at the dingy platform that was the town's link to the railway, I gathered up in a bag too old and threadbare to sell the remainder of my worthless belongings. Vagabond and destitute I made my way out into the cold.

I wandered through the streets of Torbay in the growing twilight chill and eventually found myself sitting on a seaside park bench, shivering and hungry, braving the cold September winds. I would have searched for my school mates, but I knew that none of them would be here for at least a week and we had not yet arranged a meeting place between us. I could not last a week here on my own and without money. I watched the moon come from behind a cloud when at last the gripping winds eased, and as the clouds slowed their pace, the eerie light cast frightening shadows all around me. Twice I jumped at a shape out of the corner of my eye and before long I was ready to seek for some other place to rest.

I made my way back into the centre of the town and wandered behind the closed shops, searching their bins for some scrap decent enough to eat, scanning yards and back streets for a warm corner to sleep in. My search led me at last into a blind alley that led down the side of a butcher's shop. It was dark and looked to me the perfect place to rest, so I stepped quietly from the lit street. I had perhaps taken three or four steps into the darkness when I heard the sound of footsteps come away from the wall. Large, rough hands descended on me and held me immobile and as my eyes became accustomed to the depth of the shadows, I saw the outline of a face near me and then stars as I was knocked out.

When I came too, I was gagged and blindfolded and I could feel my hands and feet tied down onto a bed. My groan brought a man's voice in my ear, the stench of whisky and ale on his breath turned rancid in my stomach.

"I'm glad I found you, my dear," the voice whispered, "I have had something special planned for a very long time, waiting for just the right beautiful young lady to come along." I felt fingers twisting a curl of my hair, and then an awful, quiet laugh, "and here you are. We will play tonight." The laughter began rolling again, only thinly concealing an undercurrent that chilled my heart. I felt the fingers move on my skin and then the blindfold was gone. In the small light of a single candle I saw the hideous face of a man twisted with intoxicated glee. He was perhaps as old as my father and from the cut of his clothes he was probably in much the same position in life, but this man had a vice that my father would never condone and from my position now, I could see why. The ugly man stood away from me and turned to the small table that held the candle and as I turned to watch, I saw a small wooden case bathed in the light. The man reached down and turned purposefully so I could see the large syringe he was busy with.

"Heroin," he explained casually to me as the syringe filled, "have you ever heard of the drug?" I could see a smile play across his lips as he glanced at me under an eyebrow. I nodded imperceptibly, my eyes wide, surely I had heard of this raw and awful drug, even in a girls' school we heard of the terrible addictions of our time. "Good, good," he muttered and holding up the needle, gave it an expert flick. "Well then, it's time to try it, my dear." I gave a muffled cry through my gag as the man descended upon me and, in a painful jab, I could feel the warm liquid sting insidiously into my arm. He came close to my face again, his rancid breath filling me with vomit. "I've given you a nice big dose, my sweet love, soon you won't feel a thing."

I'm not sure if he said anything after that, I could not even be sure if I had heard all of what he said to me then, for the drug took hold and I was caught in the dream. I watched in peace and stillness as the man untied my arms and legs as if I was watching a play and when he tore my dress, I could only see what was happening as a reflection of someone else's life.

When my body lay naked the man returned to his table and I caught the shine of a cut-throat razor as he sharpened it on the strop. In slow motion he waved the razor before my eyes to be sure I would see when he cut me. Like a porcelain fine doll he raised an arm and laid a deep red gash into my wrist trailing the cut ecstatically off like a conductor's baton. I fixed my eyes to the welling blood and remembered Jacob lying on the nursery floor, how much the same the colour was as it trickled onto the bed. I saw him cut my other wrist his face contorting over the wound in an ugly gaze of pleasure and carefully setting the blade down next to my bleeding arm, he unbuckled his trousers. He dipped two careful fingers into the dark red pool beside me on the bed and rubbed the slick fluid onto his naked flesh, his face a contortion of rapture and then, picking up the cut-throat once more, set to work under my body, below my vision. I could feel nothing, but the smile on his face broadened even wider as he sat back to observe his handiwork. Licking his lips and holding the knife in one hand he forced himself onto me, my doll like body felt nothing. He rode me steadily for a while until his pleasure became great and in his throws the blade in his hand came down time and again to slash great open wounds in my body. I felt no pain, no hatred, no bitterness, in fact this illusion of my first sexual encounter played in my mind and I felt an insane stirring of pleasure. If I could have spoken, I might even have encouraged him but, after an aeon, he was spent and lying grotesquely across my bloody form. Now that it was over, I wanted to close my eyes and sleep, but the drug still had me and my lids remained fixed open and I had to see what the dream held next.

The man raised up sharply and I was dimly aware of a door slamming open. Mutely I heard a groan turn to a scream as a dark form burst into the room. The newcomer took my rapist in what looked, from my position on the bed, like a passionate embrace and within seconds the perverted man that had condemned me sank limp to the floor. I struggled to adjust my vision to see my saviour as he moved to sit beside me on the bed, but I was too drugged to see past the hallucination of him, he was the most beautiful man I had ever seen. His hair shimmered, strangely alive, impossibly white and was quite unfashionably long and thick, his eyes were clear as the sky and, even through the blood that I saw staining his mouth, I could see his full lips and teeth that pointed sharp and white against his alabaster face.

I heard him speak from far away and as he spoke, he was crying, '"Mena, I should have known this would be your fate. I should have known that I could never save you."

In an instant I could hear him clearly sobbing as he raised me into a lifeless embrace, I could feel his body against mine and the breath of my life slipping from me and then… no more.

Chapter 14

Come, Julian...

Why do I wake?... Who calls me?...
Come, oh, master of my fragile soul.

...I would rest...
Come see me die....

Hunger.... Age old, savage and merciless...
choking centuries of death...
Come, beautiful ageless one.... {Ahh}.....

I screamed....

Clouds of blanketing dust stirred with my first call of pain and I rose, gagging, to take a useless breath into my tortured lungs. Cold waves of morbid air stirred with long curls of ancient decay, dark of night greeted my eyes as I opened the rusty lids, and sat up to shake the death shroud from my hair. Hunger reached out to me through the vault, searing through my soul in its need, tearing through me as it blossomed into life from my eternity of sleep and I stirred from my rest, drawn by its awful presence. Rising from the deep carpet of death scented dust, I was driven, aching for the sight of human heat, lusting the vibrant life that would see my freezing torment abate in the cold torture of my soul, and I left the lingering age-old scent of the crypt for the world beyond.

I climbed the slick stairs that led from the cellar into the gloom of the corridor above, moving as fast as my anguished form would carry me, to the rough wall that obstructed me from the realm of mortal kind. I came flat against its freezing face and moaned at the impeding barrier, scratching at jagged rocks with frantic claws, gouging into small cracks that had settled there for centuries and disturbed the blocks from their resting place in a shower of craggy stones and debris. I pushed against the loosened rubble, my cold hands urgent in their work, and the wall fell outwards, leaving a dense black maw in its wake. A long sigh flowed from me, greeting cool air as it rushed in from rooms of the cold house beyond the corridor's mouth, and I stepped slowly across the ruined barrier into the fragrant stream of an ash scented breeze. Lifting my head to the odours that ebbed in the old halls of the house, I tasted the young air of this new time. Rich echoes of the presence of mortals beckoned on wings of night and quietly I stalked the long passage, instinctively following its strong spoor. I came within sight of the end of the corridor, lights of mortal fire reflected beguiling from the entry to the great hall, and when I came to stand in the opening, I was caught by the sting of heat on my naked skin. I threw an arm up in defence of the light, squinting through watering eyes toward the source of my torture and saw a trio of human flames huddled close to a small blaze set carelessly before them on the floor. I could smell their foul odour and the stench of ale from my position across the chamber, and the small sparking flames that sent ash into the vault above but the scent of life essence drew me greater than any revulsion of human existence and I flew across the room.

I took the first one quickly from his position by the fire and rose up, in the first agony of my will, to pin him easily against the fading cherubim and their

285

painted eyes, his struggling bemused form a stark contrast to their mocking smiles. I came under him even before he had knowledge of his flight and took his filthy throat to my desperate mouth, tearing away the gasp that rose unwittingly from his stunned lips.

Ah, flow of life essence, roaring torrent of blood, cleaning, pulsing, aching and sweet, the mortal heart pulsed its vital heat into my soul. I moaned low as I drank the corpse dry, ecstatic and thrilling at my first reminder of damnation. I ripped a gore of muscle from the last beat of life fire, released the dead body and spat away the drained flesh to mark my next victim below. I descended with new strength, caught up another before the last had fallen sprawling across the fire and as a scream pierced the quiet heights, I took his essence to quench my age-old hunger. Buoyed by the vital strength that I gained from the second kill, I dropped the lifeless body to add to the growing funeral pyre, and turning my eyes on the screaming form below, I descended lightly before his terrified gaze.

"Please, please I don't want to die!" he wailed as I closed my iron grip around his throat.

I smiled at his filthy rags in derision. "You would keep this miserable existence?" The question oozed my will over his hapless mind and I took him to my lips. He gasped lightly as I put my fangs deep into the life vein, clutching with burning fire to my exposed skin, and I drank deeply of his raw masculine essence and, when too his heart gave up its last rhythm to me, I pushed the corpse onto the growing blaze.

I stood in the glory of the kill and the writhing glow of another human flame caught my eye from the doorway of the library I had known from beyond sleep and I turned to see the retreating glow of life fire disappear into the room. On wings of hell, I flew to stand within the doorway of the ruined room, odour of faeces and the decay of human existence greeted my senses as I stepped over the threshold to see the terrified mortals cowering in the corner where shelves had once sat. The writhing essence of two vital fires flowed beckoning me from their scant hiding place and drawn like a moth, I was on them. I held the heat of both mortals and worked the life from each, methodically taking one and then the other to my deadly kiss. My grip was an anvil to anchor the human flame in my sight, striking horror from their dying bodies. The last of the mortal's essence flowed over my icy core, and I rose with clear headed regard of the scene which greeted me in the dim room.

Cloths that had been dust covers elsewhere in the house many years before were piled in meagre beds around the room, and by the blaze that threw growing light from beyond, I could tell the humans had been here for some time. I hunted around the room for my clothes and glasses, but as the blaze crept towards the doorway, I knew it was a vain hope that I would find my simple protection from the realm of man and I retreated from the library to escape from the growing heat. Hard pressed against the cool wall, I skirted the demanding flames and flew headlong into the solid oak door, taking it clean off its hinges in my wake. The surviving boards that I had nailed against mortal kind flew splintering from the grand entrance. I stood for a moment taking the scent of the writhing city below me, the glow of countless brilliant flames reaching before me as fire took the house behind. Both energies seared painfully against my skin and I moved down to the heavy gate that stood locked against the centuries. I turned and watched the flames easily consume the ancient building into a burning pyre, a beacon of my return to the world of man, and dull memories of a long past friendship stirred in my soul. A groan rose with thoughts of Leon and Isabelle and all those I had known, and I tore my sight from the savage flaming eyes of the manor, fixing my gaze to an age-old trail conjured by memories of my surrogate family.

I flew high above the city, riding the flaming waves of mortal fire, along the route that I could see flowing through houses and streets in an ancient path, cut by a different road, in a town that had evolved with time. As I had half expected, when I descended to a street corner that marked the end of my trail, the trade house had gone and was replaced by a taller wider building with large windows that housed rolls of fabric in ornamental display. Above the grand entrance way a tall arch with a sign which read "Douvélle Fashion House" and I smiled at the good fortune of the business I had once known. I crossed the slick cobbled road, worn smooth with centuries of passing and stood before the entrance, shadowed from the light of an odd, scented streetlamp, urgently knocking on the grand doors. Casting my will into the building, I sensed life within even at this hour of the night, called that human and waited, cowering deep in the shadows of the entry recess away from the eerie light of the street. A dark-haired youth was the answer to my summons, his strong tanned hand pushed open the handle in writhing flames of vibrant life, and he stood before me clad in silk and velvet. Even though I could not bear the heat from his exposed skin, the cool and soothing fabric took the sting from his presence, and I gazed at his steady chest as I spoke to him.

"I need some clothes." My will cast onto him and though my magic ran away, elusive like water, still I felt something stir.

"So it seems, my good man." The young voice was mellow and as dark as the hair that flowed on his collar. "Come inside before a bobby finds you." He reached out his hand to me, but I entered without accepting his searing touch.

The foyer of the building was high and vaulted, rich with simple elegance that reflected an aesthetic if somewhat barren time. A grand stairway led to the levels above, dominating the high space with the air of a satisfied monster. The young man led me from the echoing hall through a small, darkened office and descended stairs to a factory of unusual metal spiders. They sat mute amid webs of shimmering threads but as my companion led me through their silent ranks, a strand floated out from one and I jerked away from its insidious silken allure. I knew my movement had caught his eye.

"They are sewing machines," he said, casually reaching out to catch a thread and the beast remained mute under his touch.

"Indeed," I said realising the mechanism that they were and the creatures demystified before me. "Much more efficient, I am sure."

The young man smiled at my acknowledgement and guided me to long rows of shelves lined with bolts of fabric, and he touched a slender candle to a strange outlet on a wall that popped and lit the corner of the hall. The sudden light shocked me and I blinked against its glow, but he put a glass over the flame and its heat disappeared to leave the eerie incandescence I had seen in the street.

"We have many fabrics and styles, sir. Is there something I can suggest?" The human took a tape to my measurements and I endured his searing touch, my skin shivering in his passing.

"Velvet and silk," I said, my jaw set against his caressing heat.

"Ah, sir, a very good choice. Our establishment has been known for centuries for its quality of fine fabrics," he spoke conversationally as he completed his painful examination of my size and as he stepped from me, I sighed with a half-smile for his casual banter.

"Yes, I know a little of the history of this family," I replied softly.

The tall, elegant human raised an eye at my words. "You know of the Taylors? Are you an historian, sir?"

He fished around in a bin of materials, gathering scraps of the fabrics I had asked for and I mused on his question for a long moment, "In a manner of speaking, I suppose I am."

"Then perhaps you know my father, sir?" he inquired, showing me the samples, and I found the soothing folds of my ancient ally in the world of man. "Julian Taylor." The name sealed a smile on my lips and the young man regarded me suspiciously. "My father is not in the habit of being a laughingstock."

"Indeed, I am sorry if I insulted your line, sir, I was amused over the similarity in our names. I too am Julian." I let my words flow in reassuring waves over the mortal and his brown eyes changed in the style of his ancestry to a mannered gaze.

"For all your circumstances are unusual, sir, I am pleased to meet you. I am Leon." The name called ghosts into my mind and I looked away from that old familiar sense of family.

"I would have simple dress," I changed the subject to cover my sorrowful memories and discussed with him the form of my armour against the beguiling heat of living things. I instructed him on the simple lined suit that I required in a conversation that could almost confuse time. I watched the same eyes peer from two centuries far from each other, and I answered my old friend as I spoke to that young mortal of a modern age.

In short time he had cut the pattern and was skilfully manoeuvring one of the sewing spiders, instructing me, an easy student, in the intricacies of its mechanical heart, and explaining the steam driven means of its automation. I watched the fabric fall together under his touch and within short hours, he handed me finely tailored garments to soothe my flesh from its reach for the heat of mortal things. Fine silk sat cool against my skin, the shirt and underclothing were an instant solace from the lights of man, deep carmine at my throat reflected its cool stability onto my face. The velvet of jacket and trousers fitted close to my body giving me a dark and potent air that held my will around me.

I slipped into leather boots that Leon had retrieved from another part of the factory and sighed in the coherence of my protection of silk. "Thank you, my friend," I whispered looking deep into his eyes.

He regarded me for a long moment and his gaze narrowed. "I know you," he said slowly.

"You are mistaken, sir," I replied formally, looking away.

He would not be deterred so easily, "Are you sure we have not met before?"

I opened my mouth to answer him but false dawn's warning finger pointed at me from the horizon beyond the room and my words caught like ice in my throat. I could not be caught in the madness of sunlight and the lights of mortal kind. "I need a barrier for my eyes," I said quickly, letting him catch my urgency.

"You mean spectacles." His eyes narrowed as he understood my meaning, revealing a greater suspicion. "Yes, I can get you dark lenses that will protect your eyes. Perhaps deepest blue would be the fashion you require, Julian?"

I nodded slowly and he left me again to stare blindly into the growing twilight of the dim factory, the first piercing rays of sunlight drove my arm before my face in protection from its bright pain. Writhing in the agony of daylight, I pushed the cool fabric of silk lined velvet close into my eyes and stood frozen in the scant darkness, defenceless under the gaze of the merciless sun. I had not remembered the stroke of daylight to be so vivid in my sight before.

"Julian?" the young mortal returned to the factory corner. "Are you alright?"

"Do you have the spectacles?" I replied tense, extending my free hand. Feeling cool metal frames come under my touch and forcing my sensitive eyes closed firmly, I exchanged my arm for the transparent barrier of deep glass. "Ah," I sighed, the shield I set before me was deeper and clearer than the last I had worn and fitted hard up to my face, an improved edition of an invention of long ago.

He stared at me for a long moment, a curious expression settling across his noble tan features. Even so his mouth opened as a conjecture drove him to speak, but in that moment a vision of the present came to me, a memory of a dream coming terribly into play and I sensed great urgency in its touch. A life, my own, from somewhere beyond time, calling me, reaching for me from beyond the embrace of the rising sun.

"I need a horse," I said quickly, cutting through the young man's thoughts in the urgency of my need and he regarded me for a long moment.

He shook his dark maned head, censoring words as they rose through his mind, turned quickly to lead me down through the growing daylight of the factory and out to a stable that nestled in the rear of the establishment.

The warm scent of horse flesh assaulted my senses as we stepped into the stall of a tall, well-muscled beast. "This is our fastest animal," Leon said as he pulled blanket and saddle onto the snorting stallion. "He will carry you where you need to go." With quick deft movements he tightened the girth and in keeping with his high spirit, the dark horse groaned in complaint.

I took the reigns as he handed them to me and looked deep into his eyes with gratitude. "I will return."

"I know," he replied and his eyes held a security of his estimation.

My gaze turned from Leon's strong tanned face and up, into the bright morning light. I mounted the horse, setting my heel to his broad flank, and then off to follow a haunting trail that led me towards the sun.

I spurred the stallion into a fast trot through the streets of Portsmouth and in short time had cleared the city cobbles, the buildings and back streets gave way to open country. Winding lanes cut across its green blanket in a stark wound on the landscape and

I urged my mount into a fast gallop. The countryside flew by under sure hooves as I let my trail guide me on wings of its haunting call in my soul, each agonising mile a loud scream of urgency as my mount took the rolling country under his long stride. As my journey lengthened, sweat foamed white against the stallion's dark hide and when his energy began to weaken, I spurred him again, holding his mind fast in my will. He responded with another burst of mane flaring strength and great speed that eventually found the edges of another sprawling city.

Shivering and nervous, I slackened my mount's headlong rush at the city boundary and trotted quickly through the busy streets under the high morning sun, along an unseen path that led me unerring to the source of my urgency. I blessed the foresight of my barrier against human lights as I made my way through the press of mortal lives that flowed unceasing through the city, eventually coming to a fashionable avenue where carriages and ladies meandered in the routine of day. I came before an elegant town house, its door flung wide to the street and even as I stepped down from my mount, I knew I had missed something important in this place. I climbed the shallow steps to the house and, without knocking, entered to hear screaming from the rooms above. The high wail of mourning women moved me to climb the stairs in rapid pace, and I came to stand before the door of a softly lit child's playroom. Two women sat within, crumpled on the floor by the hearth, the bleeding form of a small boy lying in a red pool upon a lap of fine linen, the long shard of a vicious stake thrust obscenely from an eye.

I stepped into the room and the women looked up at my entry. "I can help," I said and moved to the side of the dying child.

"Oh, please, sir, my son..." The woman's ragged voice broke with a sob.

Lowering my glasses a little, I could see the small curl of his life essence ebbing from the still form. "Leave me and I can save him." I looked deep into her eyes and she nodded dumbly, taking the horrified servant to close the door, obedient to my request.

I took the shard that lodged deep into his eye and pulled the offensive piece free of its lodging, casting it obscenely amongst the other ruined pieces in the middle of the room. Blood gouted from the fresh wound and I put my mouth gently over the oozing flow, carefully drawing as much of his remaining essence until I could feel the heart reduce to a faint pulse. The energy of young blood seared into my soul, filling my senses with the amazing purity that came with so young a life and I lifted my mouth from him, holding his face between my hands as I willed the energy tenfold back into his still form. The boy groaned a little under my touch and his shade came to me in the room.

Waif-like and sad the fragile ghost of the child stood before me in the sunlight. "Why did you come, Julian?"

"Enough have died by my hand," I replied quietly and looked from the spectre to the still form of his body. "This time I will make a difference." I held my hand over the vicious wound in the boy's head and willed the eye to be whole again.

"You are too late," the ghost spoke slowly and I looked up to see the shimmering presence disappear in a mist of other realms.

In panic, I held onto the boy and flooded him with power, desperate to prove his ghost wrong, but as I weakened and the child stirred slightly, I knew that I had mistaken the wraith's words. I felt the essence of my quarry move quickly away from the city and strained against the boy's slow recovery. He stirred against my cool touch and began to cry high and thin.

"Lay still for a while, Jacob," I spoke soft in his ear. "I have not done with you yet," and under my will he relaxed with childish obedience.

"It hurts," he said in a small wail.

"Not for long, sweet child," I whispered, willing the tissues of his merciless wound to knit together under my hand, holding the intimate weaving of human flesh sharply in my mind and allowing my magic to flow rich into his small face.

Suddenly the child moved under my touch and laughed a carefree sound as he sat up. "Thank you, Julian," he said in simple innocence.

I put a finger to his lips as he stared at my dark gaze, "Shh, do not speak of me to your family," I cautioned and rose to open the door on his distraught nurse and mother. "Take greater care of your children, madam," I said and stepped away from the entrance.

"Jacob," his mother cried softly in relief as she saw her son standing in the playroom, and she and the nurse rushed to fuss over the boy.

I watched the tender scene, leaning heavily on the wall as the boy's words echoed sick in my memory and waves of hunger flowed over me. The loss of my essence to sustain his life had taken its toll. "He will need to eat soon." My words flowed quietly into the room and the mother lifted her bewildered gaze to my eyes.

"Are you well, sir?" she asked, but her attention was distracted and she looked back to the child.

I turned from the mortals, urgent fear and sick pain flooded my form as I fled down the stair and out into the street beyond. Human life assaulted me on all sides, I knew I would have to feed or risk exposing myself in anguish of my hunger though I would waste precious moments in sustaining my awful need, rather that than losing control. So I turned from the exhausted horse that stood quivering, reined by the long fence, and darted into the dim alley that flanked the end of the building. I raced along the road, scanning for life through the flat glass that cut my knowing of mortal fire, ranging through the grimy reality of the city's back streets, using the darkened alleys to cover my passing from the vision of mortal kind, until I saw a bundle of filthy rags sitting by the meagre paved curb. The stench of his body's long abuse oozed around him as I watched from a shadowed corner, the long rot of a wasting disease and awful complement of ale gave its nauseous scent to my hunger, turning my gut, but the lust of life essence was more than the depravity of humanity and I moved to take the mortal. Caught in the freedom from agony of ancient desire, the guise of my victim's flesh faded from my senses and I thralled in the ecstasy of searing life heat. The human spasmed under my attack, throat rigid in terror, oozing sweet blood thickly into my mouth and rapture in the frozen core of my soul.

I emerged from the side alley of a road lined with the fashionable gaunt buildings of commerce and

297

quickly along the cobbled street, following the faint and lingering spoor of the trail that lured me on. I rushed through the busy street and came upon the maw of a building that I had seen in a dream, its wrought iron gates catching dull in the sunlight, giving the mouth of its opening a sinister feel as I passed through the portal. Close on the aethereal trail that marked my path, I walked into the vaulted foyer of the grand building, sounds of mortals passing through caught in its lofty heights. Small booths with humans inside lined the entry hall and I noticed that my trail had made a brief pause before one of the strange cages. I moved before the wizened man that sat in the comfort of this absurd little office and he blinked over clear, thin rimmed glasses.

"I'm sorry, sir, the train for Torbay has just left." He looked at me with a well-rehearsed apology.

"Is there another?" I fathomed the words of the pinched man against the memory of steaming monsters I had dreamed of.

"Well, yes, but it stops several times on the way and does not arrive till late in the afternoon."

I lowered my glasses and gazed on the mortal. "I will go on this train."

Automatically his hands moved over a machine that spewed a small ticket of paper into his palm and he handed it to me. "The train stops in Guildford, Salisbury, Chard and Teignm'th before Torbay, good day, sir." I let his mind forget our meeting and made my way to the raised platform where my trail ended.

I saw a pause in the aetheric path and a part of the essence was snatched away to vanish in the haze of other ghosts, then the trail moved along the platform unaware of the subtle vampirism. I lingered in the shadow of a great marble pillar and in short time the screech of a mighty steel dragon came billowing great gouts of angry steam into the vault of the station. The beast subsided with an awful hiss beside the platform and mortals flowed like vomit from its windowed side. I waited until the travellers had gone from beside the beast, stepping cautiously through the open entry in its side and I laughed quietly, relieved to find rows of seats sitting mute along the length of the carriage. I sat by a window while the train filled and soon was taking a speeding journey out, across landscape that was different than my memory of the journey to Torbay. I asked the ticket collector when he came and he replied curtly that it was a different route, so I sat for the hours of sunlight to watch landscape and sprawling human life flow by the train as it sped towards the sea.

Dusk was filling the horizon as the train pulled into the meagre terminal and I descended from the carriage to stand on the empty platform with the fresh scent of sea air carrying the essence of my trail off into the night. I removed my glasses, folding them into a clever pocket in my jacket and hurriedly followed the spoor of my quarry through the evening twilight of the small sea bound town. The trail led meandering through the streets and I knew if I followed this path I would be too late. So I abandoned the chase to make for the beach where I had known the trail would lead. I descended steps onto long sands of the tidal flat, searching to pick up the scent again and found it at a bench where two lovers sat kissing in the romance of growing night. The trail was clearer now and I saw it move away from the seaside and back into the town. As I took to the steps a cold wind came over me, I was caught in a vivid memory of abducting hands and the sickening thump of a cudgel, and I reeled against the low stone wall as I saw the unconscious fall of the young girl. Fear gripped me, the awful tragedy of a life about to play out and I had missed the horrific finale. I shook my head briefly, clearing the sight of other eyes from mine and ran like a demon along the fresh trail. I came to a blind alley shrouded in night and walked cautiously down its length, the aura of struggle and movement played in the air and I saw the trail end at a small door cut inconspicuously into the corner of a wall. I flew to the door and forced it, clawing the wooden jam away from the brass lock that barred my way and threw it open wide in rage. Inside the dimly lit room, a filthy rapist knelt over his victim on the bed, her arms bleeding in writhing currents of life that flooded from deep ravines and rendered her hands useless, and he holding his blood-soaked weapon high as her failing aura ebbed toward death.

I reached out quickly and tore him from the girl and held his throat close to my lips, "A fitting fate, wouldn't you say?" I whispered gazing into his frightened eyes, bearing my fangs and slicing deep into his flesh. My bite severed easily through the muscle and I let the flow of his evil essence fill me in vengeful pleasure but, when he fell from me, his life essence gone ready for death, the other human lay in an awful haze and I remembered the syringe and drugs that had haunted the last moments of the young woman's life. I crossed the room and took her bleeding form in my arms but even though I flooded life essence over her, the drug confused her system and she died from the shock.

I held the corpse close to me, the scent of decay rich in the clot of still blood and wept for the life I had seen in my sleep, the useless waste of existence that marked a signpost in the forming of my soul. Why? Why could this awful destiny not be saved even this time? What place did this incarnation play in the scheme of a creator that could move to allow such sorrow? The memory of Justin came into the dead gaze of the mortal in my arms and I heard his lament over the damnation of my destiny ... *Your path has been set for many lifetimes, do you think you could change it? You think to cheat fate?*... and the words echoed long in my mind.

Lifting the fragile corpse from the bed, I walked slowly from the dim and filthy room and rose from the dark alley up into the air above the small sea village. I carried the wasted corpse far over the edge of land and sea, high in the atmosphere where rain gathered cool against my face, down to where I could see the familiar coastline of the city I knew. I descended over Portsmouth into the graveyard, bigger now than I had seen, the awful wraiths of long dead flesh reached out as I flew over their damnation of remembered life, and on to Justin's gravesite, a fitting place for the long sleep of decay. I landed lightly by the grave, the echo of long ago floating around my feet and looked down at the grass covered earth. I commanded the ground to open before me as I stood in the sorrow of eternal life. And when the rift appeared like a well into the heart of earth, I let the body fall softly with my will to share the cold sleep of death with Justin and all those I had known in ancient times. Turning from the closing earth, I walked past the spectres of other nightmares, unconscious of their grasping hands and pleading wails, and left the graveyard to walk through the city far from the harsh memory of what was passed.

I lingered slowly through the dark streets of the outer districts and on into the lamp lit roads where the fashion house sat like a beacon in the night, calling me to rest in living company away from the damnation of my eternal existence. Standing on the street before the grand building, I probed into its depths, feeling the touch of my young ally and within moments a small light popped, illuminating the shop facade and the door that barred the night swung open.

"Julian." A slow smile played across the mortal's tanned face as he greeted me.

I stepped through the doorway and Leon set the ward to with an audible click that echoed through the vaulted foyer. I followed the tall youth to a lounge that sat concealed beneath the imposing staircase, a cosy room hidden from the eyes of humans by the clever design of its cellar like construction.

"My den," Leon said simply and gestured at the room which held little more than a lounge suite, leather bound and well worn. A small hearth blazed its heat beyond the plush carpet and he crossed to a small carved wooden bar. "Can I get you a drink?" he asked casually. His question was perhaps a little too casual, for although the legacy of his ancestry shielded his thoughts from my touch, still the quality of his enquiry betrayed a scarcely held suspicion.

"Benedictine, if you have it," I replied wearily and moved to sit in one of the deep inviting armchairs.

The young man returned from the bar, a large glass in each hand, a strange smile on his tanned lips as he proffered one to me. "This is brandy," he said and his eyes flashed as I took the glass. "A descendant of that older brew. Try it, I'm sure it will suit."

He sat opposite, beside the small hearth, and watched me with pretended nonchalance as I tasted the spirit. Indeed the brandy carried traits of its ancestor, just as this descendant of my ancient friend, but its essence was refined from centuries of its evolution.

Leon's rich voice challenged the crackle of firelight, after the silence had grown long, "You say you know of my family's history?"

I gazed levelly at him. "Somewhat," I replied and yet sought to direct his attention to more innocent a topic, "I'm sorry that I did not return your horse."

My benign statement caught him agape for an instant and then he laughed as his agile mind grappled with such banality. "It is of no matter," he waved a carefree flourish of his free, silk touched hand and leaned forward onto the leather arm of the chair. The fire touched a light into his dark brown eyes and humour sat even beneath the contemplation that dwelled there. "And yet, sir, from what I am beginning to understand, you have as much right to the profits of my family as I do. Am I not correct?"

"Ah ha," I laughed mildly, the challenge had been openly laid!

Still, I said nothing and dawn twilight began its dance before he spoke again. "I have something to show you, Julian," he said, draining the last contents of his glass as he rose and put it on the mantle.

"Oh?" I took out my barrier against the rising sun and followed behind the protection of deep tinted glass.

He led me around to the grand staircase which was crafted as a ceiling to the room where we had spent the last hours of night. Mortals were already coming into the fashion house and nodded to their employer in the formal morning ritual of their mundane existence. Not a few gave me an unusual glance and the younger girls whispered behind curious hands to their fellow workers but Leon held an unapproachable air that forebode any but routine conversation as the staff made their way about their business.

We climbed the heavy staircase that led high and around to the upper floor salon. Its generous carpeted expanse was still shrouded in gloom as sales assistants made their way to open tall velvet curtains and let in the morning sun. My hair lashed out toward each shaft as it was admitted into the building and when Leon turned and gestured to a wall, I was stunned into stillness.

Before me, framed and gilded in almost royal proportions, a painting hung like a mirror. A brass plate, etched with the work's title, *"The Benefactor"*, made a statement of the figure's patronage, and when I looked up I felt a useless breath catch in my throat. I gazed upon the life-size portrait of my dark and bespectacled form and it reached out and beckoned to me alluringly. The white hair that framed my face stood active with its own serpentine energy, the subtle work of brush and paint gave a terribly striking representation of life.

"Painted by Isabelle Taylor, grand matriarch of the Taylor women. A lady of great vision and admired in our family for her compassionate works." Leon's deep voice spoke close to my ear and held me immobile as my attention was commanded by the timeless mirror. "She declared that her great strength had been guided by the family's ancient patron, a Count Julian Douvélle, whose past and indeed future was shrouded in mystery. Still, his humanitarian acts were a model for my family and led Isabelle on to a life of piety and grace." He paused for a moment and turned aside, yet I stood, still entranced by the image of my frozen angelic and unyielding visage. When he continued his words were light, conversational, yet I was alerted then and stung back to myself. "She painted the portrait after he disappeared from the funeral of a young man who...."

"Yes, I know!" I cut him off abruptly, stepping back from his mortal heat and tore my sight away from the awful angel that hung in an eternal moment to taunt my damned existence.

"Then you *are* the Count!" A woman's voice, so alike Leon's yet with the grace of femininity, spoke quietly from beyond and I turned with sharp accusation to the newcomer. Her quiet words stabbed into my damnation and recalled every moment of my eternal walk and when I saw her deep sapphire eyes, there stirred something more.

"Niamh," I whispered, another cold finger of ancient abuse reached and embraced my stagnant heart.

There was a smile on her full lips as she slowly shook her russet fringed face, and Leon hesitantly said, "Count, this is my sister, Isabelle."

I staggered under the burden of memories, a thousand pages of too long a history flashed through my mind and beyond.

"Are you ill, sir?" Isabelle asked and extended a deep red velvet clad arm to assist me.

I recoiled, burnt by the allure of her familiar warmth. My empty heart mocked me in its yearning for her and for the reminder of all my eternity alone.

"No... I... I..." I stammered and fell mute under their gaze.

"Come," Leon urged as more curtains were drawn by inquisitive staff, and gently led me back down and into his den.

I walked hesitantly beside these descendants of my ancient family, slowly in a confusion of time, and when we returned to sit among the security of the well-worn lounge, I was grateful that my dark shield covered the yearning of my gaze. How could fate play such a fickle game? The young fair skinned Isabelle had a look that so dearly matched my beloved Niamh and her eyes…

"… Count?" Leon stood above me, his hand extended with a glass.

"Oh," I accepted the drink and took a long draught to clear bittersweet memories.

Leon sat in his place by the fire, its low embers reflecting in a dull sheen from the black velvet of his attire, and Isabelle sat on the wide couch between us, her eyes and his locked in some family understanding.

"I can't quite fathom it." Leon spoke after long moments and both turned their attention to me.

I sat mute, nursing the glass under the briefly held accusation of their gaze, my mind and heart grappling under a confusion to bring the likeness of one I had loved so long ago, to marry with this innocent of a new age.

The young man shifted slightly in his chair as he accepted my reticence and gestured with his drink, "That painting has been in our family for over four hundred years. There is nothing that I know of that can live so long!" and his statement was a blatant challenge.

But it was Isabelle who rose to my scant defence, "Mister Woo has prolonged his own life through his Art brother."

"Pah," Leon waved her argument aside. "Yet Mister Woo *has* changed Isabelle, he's a veritable prune. The Count here is identical to *'The Benefactor'*." He looked at me with a stern eye, "Come, sir, surely you have an explanation. I am loath to assume you a charlatan..."

"Oh, Leon, I hardly think so," Isabelle broke in and he held up a silencing hand.

"As do I, sister," was his allowance and he inclined his head to her protestation. "I..." he hesitated, his dark eyes narrowed, "I *feel* something too deep to so judge you, sir. In fact, my suspicions lead me altogether in another direction."

"What is it you mean?" Isabelle asked almost aghast and held a white hand delicate to the high velvet collar of her dress.

Leon sat forward, an elbow on the chair arm and both sets of eyes turned expectant on me.

Even on the heels of my own confusion, such family banter finally caused a faint smile to rise on my cold lips. Their ancestors had been so easy in their conversation and even so, those more recent memories stirred me from remembrance of my ancient loss.

"I live under sentence of a curse," I said finally. How could I explain in easy terms the full horror that had been my life?

"A curse? How so?" Isabelle was consumed by curiosity.

I sighed and looked through blank glass into the hearth. Briefly, hardly an explanation at all considering the terror of the truth, I told them of my conception; the evil of my father's powers and how he had been the last and most reviled holder of my pitiful soul. I fell mute at the end of my scant tale

307

and the silence drew long as I sat with feelings of brief guilt over my gross omissions.

A deep rumble from beside the hearth stirred a glance from both Isabelle and me. Then she turned to me with a smile and a whisper, "My brother is well known for his nocturnal habits, Count, perhaps we should leave him to his sleep." When I nodded, she rose with an extended hand and said softly, "Come and take a walk with me and we can continue our conversation."

Isabelle took my arm, a companionable embrace which had my hair stir toward her vital heat and my heart fill with a richness of feeling that I hadn't experienced in so long. She led me out from the fashion house and under the violent light of the sun and though its heat stung like madness on the exposed skin of my face and hands, her company was a welcome distraction. Her beauty and light conversation enamoured me so that I could almost ignore my eternal discomfort.

We walked along busy roads, horses and their carriages clattered the cobbles, elegantly dressed socialites made about their day's business and even an occasional steam driven monster passed by often startling horse and pedestrian alike. This Portsmouth and the one I had left, were not so vastly different, the bones and even some flesh of the city called familiar memories to my mind, yet its face had grown and its fashion changed enough so that I was glad of the guidance of my companion.

Isabelle laughed lightly at my reaction to the steam carriage and I let the musical sound take my brief fright away. "Where have you been, Count, that you have not experienced the miracles of our modern age?" she asked in innocence.

I watched the mechanical beast chug down the cobbled street and pause under a curb-side tree, and I know when I answered that my explanation did not satisfy her. "It was my choice, after Justin's death, not to be in the world." Still she accepted my words and as we began again our casual stroll, I continued, "I would have chosen to stay away from your mortal realm forever if I could. But I have yet to discover a means to remedy my infernal eternity, and what teachers I have found along my journey, have yet to lend competent aid to my quest."

Isabelle stopped beside me at the corner junction of four roads and gazed hesitantly at my flat glasses, "And what is that quest, Count?"

I sighed and knew she already guessed my reply, still I suppose she needed to hear it from me to have her suspicions confirmed. So I said, "I seek to end my life and all the misery that my damnable existence has caused."

She looked away then, and I fancied that there were quick tears in her deep sapphire eyes. She said nothing for a moment and only the violent heat of her emotions caressed the naked flesh of my hand. "A strange quest, sir," she said at last, though she would not look at me as we began to walk along the adjacent road. "I know of ways to prolong life. Indeed, I know of a gentleman whose unusually long-life attests to his skill in his craft. Yet, I find it strange that it should be so hard for you to achieve the opposite." She flashed me an almost accusing glance. "Surely, just a pistol or some other such base machination would resolve your predicament, sir?"

I laughed almost derisive and she took affront, so I raised my free hand to forestall her ire. "Beautiful lady, my eternity is sealed by a fate that allows me no such simple a solution. Still, this gentleman of whom you speak, his craft, I would be interested to know a little more of it."

"Really?" and she seemed almost eager for the diversion of my inquiry.

We walked beyond the bustle of shop lined roads and on into a relatively quieter park. Isabelle sat beside me on a wrought iron bench that waited isolated and cool beneath the spreading arms of a dense shadowed tree.

"Mister Woo," she began in earnest, "is what we call him. Though I must say, I doubt if he has ever really told me his name and he always seems to be amused when anyone calls him by it." She flushed and smiled fondly. "He's a Chinaman you see. It seems appropriate and he never takes umbrage at our familiarity—it has always seemed to me that he holds no other emotion than amusement, I have never seen him angry. Still, I say, we," and she put a delicate hand to her velvet clad breast, "since I am part of a select group chosen by the old man to teach his craft. I should like to say that I am particularly one of his best and most dedicated students," and her blue eyes flashed with pride, "besides his own grandson, of course," she relented with a smile.

"Alchemy," she stated uncategorically. "I've been studying for a little over five years now, and quite a tight group I've been a part of. An amazing teacher, Mister Woo, is, I have learned so many fascinating things. Still the man himself remains somewhat of an enigma in our midst," and her eyes took on a distant quality.

But I had heard enough, "It would please me greatly to meet your Mister Woo," I said after long moments.

Isabelle gazed out across the sunlit park. "Yes, I have always believed in destiny," she said from far away, and then turned to me with a smile. "And so it seems that fate has brought you to me for this very reason, don't you think, Count?" She put a hand over mine and, though concern at the corpse chill of my skin caused a thick eyebrow to raise, she made no move to withdraw her touch.

"Thank you, Isabelle," I whispered and she smiled with newfound understanding.

"There is a great deal that you have not told me, isn't there?" she said and it was a gentle statement of her deeper conviction.

I nodded and took up her hand to brush her mortal warmth against my cold lips. Almost unconsciously I breathed her vital energy and she gasped lightly at the subtle theft. "Yes, Isabelle," my voice was barely audible. "My existence is as great a curse as I have ever encountered, even through my whole unnatural life. I would spare you the pain of even the tale of its telling."

I released her hand and she took it back to warm against its partner and we sat again in silence as her thoughts struggled with my brief magic. Still, she sat close and did not move and her warmth surrounded me like the return of a promise of love.

"Yes," she whispered finally sensing somehow the depths of my thoughts. "I think I have loved you since the first time I saw your portrait," and she turned her deep gaze upon me uncertainly. "Do you think that foolish of me?"

Oh, how my cold heart yearned for her, my arms longed for her embrace, ancient pain of loss rose tears to my ice-cold eyes. "Oh, Isabelle," I sighed and agony cracked my voice. "How can you surely know what it is you say? I have seen the destiny of such feelings play out before me time and again."

311

Indeed I could feel fate's merciless hand holding the threads of this new friendship.

Isabelle would have turned away, my betrayal of her feelings a stark shadow in her gaze. But I commanded her attention with a touch and said, "To love one such as I, dear lady," I shook my head, "even to befriend me carries dangers that I would not wish upon anyone, least of all you."

Sorrow overcame her in the cool silence of our seat beneath the park side tree and when she looked back to me finally, I could see such a strength of resolve as I had encountered once upon a time and the return of an ancestor into my company. "Well then, Count. Let us retain a casual acquaintance and enjoy each moment for naught more than what it is."

I smiled with a regret to match her own and laid a cold hand against her velvet clad arm, "You are a credit to your line, Isabelle, and I am infinitely grateful."

She rose then with a brief sigh and turned, "I am to attend Mister Woo this evening, Count," she said with almost forced levity as I took her proffered arm and she led me back towards the fashion house. "It is probably as well that you come with me to meet him."

I said nothing on our return and she seemed almost relieved when an employee called her attention to business matters. With a brief cold sigh, I entered Leon's den and sat with a large glass of brandy while the youth snored through the day.

In the late afternoon Leon stirred and we spoke of inconsequences as he took a hearty breakfast. He asked me if I had enjoyed the company of his sister and though my scant reply rose a questioning eyebrow, to his credit, he said nothing more and our conversation ranged through little else than the evolution of his clan.

Leon spoke casually of the centuries that had passed while I had slept, he told me of my old family and the young socialites that I had known. The Leon of that age had taken to the sea after the death of Justin, taking up the mantle of his ancient namesake and, after a lifetime as captain of the *"Isabelle"*, he had ended his days with a princess in India. I smiled for the bittersweet memories of how the young Moor had often pressed me into the telling of tales of pirates and sailing and adventure in exotic lands. He talked of Isabelle, how she had inevitable taken over the family empire and wisely invested some of the growing fortune to build a trust for homeless youths. A grand estate set by the boundary of a cold northern city had been added to the family's legacy and had been a passion in her old age. She had ended her days in that estate, writing and painting and establishing in her caring way, the generous compassion of the Taylor clan. Over the centuries, the house had burned to the ground and twice been rebuilt, the last time less than fifty years ago, but true to their ancestry, the Taylors had been clever merchants and the family's investments had seen the wealthy continuance of the flourishing descendants and that matriarch's dream. Even so, the clan had maintained their long tradition of sailing and foreign trade, passing the business down the line as they passed the names of their ancestors through the generations. My name had been added to the ranks of family title in honour of my memory and though my connection had died with the people I had once known, a stark familiarity of my existence still remained in the legends of the descendants.

There had been an account established after I had left that time gone by, funded by the sale of Justin's apartment. It was arranged and could be accessed by none other than the trade house or, oddly enough, my hand. The story went that in the weeks after the funeral, that older Leon had thought to seek me out and found the ruins left by my failed experiment. He had created the unusual trust in the sublime knowing that one day I would return. It had been arranged in such a fashion as to mask its origins and still, none of the family had since questioned the exacting standards by which it was engineered to ensure that I could return to such society, an independent gentleman. The family's empire had often been bolstered by this cornerstone and their grand lifestyle attested to the intelligence and planning of their predecessors. The fortune had grown through the centuries to be a pivot of financial power in these times, as too the fashion house and cloth trade had become an authority boasting a fleet of vessels that had evolved from sail to steam, forging ties in many lands and even in my beloved China. As day's end came on Leon's oration spoke of the deeds of his ancestors, through wars and disease, love and loss, and always against the constant flowing lineage of the family's spirit of adventure. Their empire had grown and evolved greatly through time and to the dramatic changes of this new era, yet always strong with that familiar connection of family pride.

"It was grandfather who brought Mister Woo home from China, wasn't it, Leon?" The sound of Isabelle's husky and feminine voice brought an effective ending to Leon's tale and both he and I were caught by her entry to the room. She stood by the door, a hand held high to adjust the gas wall light, for the fire had fallen dark and shrouded the room in growing night.

Leon laughed and stood in greeting to his sister and I followed in recognition of the formality. "Yes, I do believe it was," he said with a brief, good natured laugh and then cleared his throat. "By god, I'm hoarse. I've done nothing but talk all afternoon."

Isabelle crossed the carpet and gave her brother a sibling smile, though I could see there was still a sadness that touched the depths of her endless sky eyes. "And not given the Count as much as a breath to reply, I'll be bound." She moved between her brother and I, her exquisite black velvet evening dress such a compliment to our company.

"You off out then, sister?" Leon gibed.

Isabelle gave his arm an easy swat. "You know very well that I am brother and," she turned her formal coiffure slightly to include me, "the Count will be accompanying me."

"Oh?" Leon's deep brown eyes gazed quizzically.

"Indeed," she retorted before I could speak. "The Count has asked to meet with him," and she nodded with authority.

"So be it then," Leon laughed and gave us both a small bow. "Hope you know what sort of superstitious rubbish to expect though."

"Oh, Leon!" Isabelle cut him short in a flare of quick temper and mischief sparked in her brother's eyes.

I raised an easy hand. "I have had such encounters before, Leon, and indeed, it was I who requested the meeting."

Leon threw up a dark clad arm and laughed, "I might have known," and left it at that.

With quite regal acceptance, Isabelle took my
arm and we left Leon's den with the sound of his
chuckle following in our wake.

"Don't mind my brother, Count," Isabelle said
conversationally as she retrieved a long dark fur-
lined cape that lay waiting on one of the entry hall's
long lounge chairs. She gave it to me and I held it as
she donned it against the cold night. When she
turned to me again she smiled, but even so I sensed
that the mirth ended at her full lips. "He's well
known in the family for his brand of mischief.
Anyway," and she took my arm, "Mister Woo is
expecting us, I sent a message earlier."

I said nothing but allowed the beautiful lady to
lead me out into the gathering night, glad, no matter
how reserved, of her company and radiant heat.

Under the false glow of streetlights I folded my
glasses away into their pocket and watched the
mortal heat of passers-by as we went. We walked
through the city and out to a district that I had not
encountered, although perhaps at one time it may
have housed a sad and now extinct community of
plague victims, but that was a distant memory, even
for the city and the costume it wore now was more
civilised, even as Isabelle commented, "sub urban."
We rounded a street corner at the end of a long row
of terraced houses and climbed the shallow steps to
a door at the end. Isabelle's knock was answered in
a short time by a young man, oriental in appearance,
though when he spoke his voice was quite English.

"Good evening, Miss Taylor," he said beside the
door and then his eyes came to fall on me. In his
mind I felt a sudden fear jump and a word grow, but
my sense of him was cut suddenly as he cast an iron
shield around his thoughts. His almond eyes

narrowed and his tawny skin lost some of its colour in fright.

Isabelle too saw his unease, but still she replied with civil accord, "Good evening, Gregory. This is Count Douvélle," and she gestured to me easily, "I sent word that I'd be bringing him along tonight. Did you get my message?"

The young man stepped backward, perhaps a little too hastily. "Yes... yes," he stammered and his fright led him uneasily back behind the shallow safety of the door. "Please... please, wait there. I'll just get grandfather," and he shut the door abruptly.

"Oh," Isabelle stood, shocked, staring at the barred way. "How odd. He's never been so rude before."

"Perhaps," I said quietly, "though he has never met one such as I before."

Scant moments later the door opened again and beside the young man now stood a wizened old Chinese mage, berobed and moustached as I had once known another in the land of his heritage.

"Oh, Mister Woo," Isabelle began with apparent relief for his appearance. "Gregory said you had received my note, yet..."

"Who are you?" the old man cut her off and by the odd inflection of his voice, I could tell he spoke Chinese.

I smiled. "I am Julian," I answered in kind and Isabelle stared suddenly at the foreign words.

Mister Woo sniffed reflectively and looked long into my cold gaze. A challenge rose sharp as he spoke again in his native tongue, "Julian is no more than a legend of my homeland and you smell fresh from the kill. Do not fool with me, dark one, I have my own defences."

I sighed and, for the benefit of Isabelle who was beginning to shift uneasily under the clipped conversation, said in English, "I have returned into the company of my surrogate family after," and I paused to find suitable words, "some time. Surely Miss Taylor's reputation can vouch for my integrity."

"Come now, Mister Woo," Isabelle laughed, a little unsure, in my defence. "The Count may have an unusual background, but I assure you, his honour is as steadfast as that of my own family. Come, sir, he is no thief or vagabond and it's not as if he'll bite you," and she laughed again at her own wit.

But Mister Woo still stared at me long and hard, his flat black eyes accusing. "So, you keep the truth from her," he said in Chinese, "Why?"

And I replied in English, "Mister Woo. I have come for naught more than an acquaintance with an alchemist. Surely your own legends speak of my studies in your homeland. Perhaps, sir, I cannot help what I am, but know that I have no desire to harm you. For that I give you my word."

Mister Woo nodded throughout my speech as if taking mental stock against what he knew of my ancient self and finally, after a tense moment of contemplation, he stepped back and nodded for Gregory to open the door. "Very well," he said in English and I saw Isabelle sigh with relief. "I will take you at your word," and admitted us into the house.

"And I am a man of my word, sir. After a life such as mine, it is perhaps the only thing I have that I can truly call my own." My voice echoed strangely down the dark hallway and seemed to be taken by the very building as proof of my bond.

"Interesting," Mister Woo noticed it too and now a smile crept beneath the long corners of his moustache. "Come into my study," he said abruptly, stalking down the corridor to the back of the house, "and Gregory will bring drinks." He stopped and turned suddenly and the young man nearly fell over him. "I am right in assuming that still to be true of you?"

Isabelle laughed short and a little nervous and I said, "It seems you know a great deal about me."

Mister Woo barked a sharp laugh and turned just as suddenly to precede our unusual company through a door at the end of the hallway.

"It is from my own family legends that I have learned the story of Julian and Princess Mai-Lin," Mister Woo said in clipped conversation as he stepped under the lintel into his laboratory. "My ancient grand uncle many times removed was alchemist to the prince of Zien-ziang in those days."

"Ahh, Lao-Tzung, yes," I said, reminiscing absently as I looked around the mutely lit room. Even had the old magician not spoken of his family, I would have guessed the connection, I'm sure. The room so tugged at memories of the laboratory I had inherited in that ancient Mogul palace. A brazier stood to one side glowing with well-tended heat. Long tables supported a chaos of order and experiments that, although in that older time had seemed so random, now I made a mental check of the magic brewing there. Books and scrolls littered both the table and a generous expanse of shelving around the room kept company by bottles, jars and vials of every description, colour and shade, and before a hearth set in the far wall, a mismatched and augmented suite of chairs alleged the company that would come this evening.

As my gaze came back to rest on Mister Woo, his smile echoed in his eyes. "Yes, Lao-Tzung. He was a master magician. I have much of his writings in my library. Come," and he extended a hand to the chairs by the hearth, "sit and talk with me. I'm sure we have much to discuss."

Isabelle took my arm and walked gracefully beside me to sit by the fire, "So you don't doubt him now, Mister Woo?" she mocked.

"Good lady," the alchemist smiled and sat in a chair opposite, that looked as if it had only ever seen to his comfort. "I doubt very much that any but Julian himself would have recognised so easily my ancient ancestor, and from the legends I have learned, there could be none other that could ever have discovered the secrets that he keeps." He turned, a shrewd eye on me, "Am I not correct?"

I laughed and accepted a large glass of brandy from Gregory.

The sound of the outer door diverted our conversation then, much to my relief, and, once I had been introduced to the others of the group, we settled on more general magical topics of discussion.

At the end of the evening when the others had left and it was once again only the four of us sitting by the fire, Mister Woo gestured the door and the departed company. "You have not come to me for such elementary learning, have you, Julian?" he said easily but beneath such blithe words was the wondering of my true intent.

I shook my head slowly, carefully, the warm air in the room fell heavy with silence.

Mister Woo regarded me for a long moment, then, "My ancestor kept a journal that is, on occasion, somewhat difficult to decipher," he said and rose to cross the plush carpet. He caught up an

320

ancient, cracked scroll that tugged at my memory and happier times in love with that lovely Chinese princess and opened it partly across the least cluttered end of a table. "And still I cannot fully understand what was his intent. But here," and he put a gnarled forefinger on the patterns of Chinese glyphs, "he notes the preparation of a formula worked carefully in conjunction with the map of the heavens and the conjuring of a magic that could only have been a time well beyond the date of his death. Indeed, I have never understood the why and wherefore of this notation, yet it is inscribed with the glyph of your name. Is this part of your seeking me out?"

I sighed, "Lao-Tzung and I sought for many years to find a solution to my problem."

Mister Woo glanced suspiciously at me and stalked back across the room to sit again beside the fire. Isabelle shifted uneasily, her eyes turned resolutely away, but I laid a cool hand on her velvet clad arm as I spoke. "My immortality has cost me a great deal, Mister Woo, the price I have paid for the evil that created my unfortunate life. My quest has become simple, if somewhat difficult to achieve and even so, I have yet to find strength enough to complete the task." An image of my ruined experiment rose horribly from a memory beyond sleep and still I wondered that I should ever have the strength to quell the beast in my soul. Mister Woo gazed at me respectful of the pause in my oration but expectant. "Your ancestor was of invaluable help to me, Mister Woo, his alchemical studies and conjurations instructed me to the preparation of a potion that would end my life and our studies of the heavens ultimately gave me a time to carry out my task."

321

"And yet you failed?"

I nodded gravely and even Isabelle turned to catch the affirmative, "That which has imprisoned me in these chains of eternity is most cunning, sir." Mister Woo nodded, a finger twisting absently at one long corner of moustache, and his eyes were calculating, but it was Gregory who spoke then, so similar to his grandfather but brash and eager, "So really, sir, your singular quest has become divided."

"How so?" my attention settled on the young man and his throat bobbed uneasily as he swallowed.

"W... well," he stammered, hardly masking his disquiet at my cold gaze, "as I see it, Count, your em... end would be a simple matter if it were not for your..." and he cleared his throat nervously, "your curse." I nodded and he continued in a rush, eager to finish his thought and have my attention off him. "So, you should first seek to remove the curse, and then..." and he fell silent with a flap of his tawny hand.

I sat for a long moment wondering at the idea, I had not thought my death and the death of the beast to be separate events, yet... "Maybe," I replied, challenging the crackling fire for a voice in the silence. "It is something I had not thought possible."

"Still," said Mister Woo. "My grandson may have a point."

I nodded and a drop of hope fell into the void of my dark heart.

Mister Woo sat easier against his chair, a sharp smile cut into his ancient Chinese countenance, "Come tomorrow night, Count, and we will see what we can discover, eh?"

Isabelle rose beside me, a yawn barely masked behind a polite hand and, amid easier pleasantries than had seen our entry to the house, we left to stroll back to the fashion house.

Leon met us at the door with a gibe for our expedition, but Isabelle was too tired to rise to his bait, bid us a short goodnight and went upstairs to the apartment she used when in the city. Leon led me into his den and we sat in company of the fire and glasses of fine brandy. The young Taylor badgered me with insults and quips for my evening with his sister, but soon ceased when I said nothing in return. My thoughts were filled with wondering at the hope I had so suddenly stumbled upon and the possibilities of what I would have to undertake to accomplish the freedom I sought. Even so, as dawn came and I retreated behind the safety of my glasses, I almost fancied that I could hear the tortured cry of the beast as he realised that now I had found a weapon to fight his insidious control of my destiny.

Late morning and Isabelle came into the den, freshly dressed and coiffured for another day. I hardly noticed that Leon had long since left me to my own musings, they must have spoken in passing. "Leon says that he hasn't been able to get a word out of you all night, Count," she said with shallow torment her in lovely endless eyes. "That would not sit well I'm sure," and she laughed like spring moonlight. "Well, I'm going up to the house today, sir. Leon suggested you may find the library beneficial. We have an interesting collection of books. Perhaps not as extensive as those kept by Mister Woo," she temporised, "yet, it may prove to be a worthwhile diversion."

She took me through the factory to the stables and into a coach drawn by two fine horses, driven by a liveryman so we could sit in privacy within the cabin of the coach. I watched the streets of

Portsmouth fly by our passage and out beyond the city's edge, until we turned along a tree lined avenue that cut through the grounds of the Taylor's family estate. As the coach drew around the circular driveway and before the generous steps of the mansion entrance, an older couple, grey but still strong with the family look, came from within.

"My mother and father," Isabelle said with a smile, "they have been eager to meet you."

And so formal introductions were made and their manner was as stiff as the seats that they sat upon to take morning tea. They spoke in banal pleasantries, noticing yet never so impolite as to speak of my rejection of the repast, and though there was the typical family acceptance of my presence, all too soon the older couple excused themselves to the importance of their own mundane lives.

"They just wanted to make sure of your intentions," Isabelle said with a smile as she led me through the ostentatious house. I recognised many of the treasures still retained as family heirlooms, sculptures, paintings and even furniture, and when we entered the library, I recognised some of the more antiquated volumes preserved through the centuries.

Isabelle was good company for my meander through the library's extensive collection, she spoke little during the day and as I scanned through as many occult teachings as I could find, she became engrossed with one leather bound tome. She sat quietly reading, a picture in the bay window with golden afternoon light warm against her russet hair. My search was, as I almost had expected, fruitless, though a pleasant diversion and the day was ageing to dusk before I moved to join her.

"A good read?" I inquired lightly, yet something about the book she held struck at familiarity in my memory but it was not until I saw stark and growing recognition in her eyes that my suspicion stirred at the volume's origin.

"Very... interesting," she said hesitantly and closed the pages with a snap.

Then I recognised the plain, aged cover. We sat for long moments, confusion rich in the air between us and the sun sent long accusing shafts to stir my hair. When I spoke, it was with resignation, "I had not realised that it had been rescued. Leon must have liberated my library." The accusation that drew across her gaze stirred a mirthless laugh. "Perhaps he should not have."

"You wrote this?"

I shrugged, unmoved to hide the truth from her. Better it be out now, than continue under a lie. "Translated from older works that I found in my travels."

"But there is truth here." She held up the slim volume for emphasis, "You mention Niamh, she was real? Just as..." and she stumbled as thoughts formed into words, "Just as Margueritte was real? Just as," and her voice became a whisper, "Brother Tiberias was real? And you... you..."

"As I have said, Isabelle," I cut her off, unable to bear what she may say next. "I seek to end my existence and the terror it has brought to the world. If you must judge me as the monster that the priest saw, at least remember that."

She rose suddenly, the book falling forgotten from the volume of her skirt, "I... I..." she stammered in confusion and I could see judgements, emotions, fear fly across the stage of her unshielded thoughts. "I need some air," she said vaguely and fled the library.

I watched her retreating form and sat in silence for long moments before I reached and dumbly retrieved my book from the rug. Sunlight left the window and I removed my glasses, and opened the volume at random to read words written in my own hand, that I remembered writing so long ago. Yes, Tiberias had seen me as a monster and indeed such a fate was to be my companion through all of my infernal life. If nothing more, my determination to end such a pitiful existence was strengthened and as twilight left the library in darkness, I left the Taylor house to walk back through the streets of Portsmouth, alone.

I passed by gas lights and the occasional city dweller, the naked flares of their human essence called in yearning to my immortal hunger. I passed a park and, guiltily, set my sights on a lonely mortal that passed furtive beneath the darkened branches of a tree. Silently and without pleasure, I stole some of his vital fire, relieved more than anything else, for the clarity that the energy restored on my senses and left with an uneasy peace that at least, I had hardly harmed the mortal. In comparison with the narrative of brother Tiberias, thankfully, I had grown to be a different creature altogether. Still, Isabelle could not know this truth, and hardly did I expect her to understand. Better perhaps that she live in harsh judgement than be drawn into a worse fate through my friendship.

So resigned I left the park and found my way to the row of terraces where Mister Woo would be awaiting my dark company. But by the corner, silent and shrouded in a dark cloak, Isabelle stood waiting.

"I hardly expected to see you again," I said with quiet humility as I drew up to her.

Her eyes were sapphires in the false light of streetlamps. "I owe you an apology, Count."

I stared at her, stunned, "How so?"

She shook her head so that her long curls caught the light, "I have so often argued with Leon in defence of the Art and against his opinion that it is the product of some superstitious *mumbo jumbo.* Yet here am I, even in the light of my own arrogant assumption of an enlightened mind, falling prey to superstition at the first challenge of my learning."

I laughed feeling tension drain away and relief step up to take its place. "Yet not without cause, dear lady,. I did hold the truth from you."

"Yes," she nodded, "and I see it was merely to forestall such an ignorant judgement as I cast upon you. Hence sir, I most sincerely apologise and, after much thought, I have come to the conclusion that if you accept it as such, my wholehearted aid in your quest would be my freely given penance."

"I assure you I require no such restitution, Isabelle, yet gladly I accept your aid and perhaps, your friendship?" and I laid it, a question before her.

"Yes," she smiled and such a thing beamed in long blooms of her passionate aura, "that would be a very good start."

She took my arm then and we entered the den of the alchemist.

That night, in company with Mister Woo and his grandson, and with Isabelle staunchly by my side, we compared Lao-Tzung's notes and my practical memory of my abortive experiment, volumes of other students of alchemy through the centuries in between, almanacs of magical correspondences and even notes made by the alchemist himself. Indeed it was in the darkest time of morning when we finally bid the Chinese pair goodnight, but though Isabelle was weary on my arm as we made our way back through the city, our conversation was light, good humoured and filled with hope.

How long I spent in that company I could not measure, but that time held a peace for me that often arose lingering memories of older times. I had entered yet again, into intimate contact with the world of mortals, following my ancient road, intertwined with their vibrant energies and found my days and nights, full and rich in my studies.

I allowed myself the luxury of human essence only when Isabelle would comment on my distraction from study, her mortal fire would be unbearable against my skin and would send me flinching from her side. Often I excused myself from even such accepting companions in such an abrupt manner, yet never was I asked to share the details of that awful truth of my nature.

We worked the Art of chemicals and preparations, and studied deeply the movements of the heavens and none of us, it seemed, was more excited by every small success, than the alchemist's grandson. Since Gregory had raised our hypothesis in that first meeting, he took great responsibility for each step we took. Of course, he and Mister Woo argued greatly, Isabelle and I often took a step away from their debate and waited in quiet humour for the oriental fury to subside. But between our small company, a most aethereal potion was brewed—the ingredients procured from the most obscure of sources and distilled in perhaps Mister Woo's most complicated practice. The length of one table was arranged for months, each addition to the process calculated in conjunction with the alignment of the heavens and in the end, to the great amusement of our company, acquired a vial containing no more than three drops of colourless and odourless liquid. Yet, Mister Woo capped the bottle quickly and I had a crawling sense of the potion's power and was strangely relieved when he put it up on a shelf.

"Still," I said with a half laugh, "My reluctance can only attest to the success of its preparation."

Mister Woo gave me a long glance, "Yes, Julian, yet we still have the debate of an alignment of the heavens."

His words caused Gregory to roll his eyes with a groan. A popular argument between grandfather and grandson had the figuring of a time to administer the potion. Gregory, who fancied himself as somewhat knowledgeable regarding astrology, had declared a suitable conjunction not far hence, but Mister Woo had come up with his own date, perhaps a half a century away and both had greatly argued. Gregory insisted upon his time, yet the old alchemist had goaded his descendant saying it was his youth that caused such a rush. I was inclined to agree with Mister Woo, yet when I put forth my opinion, Gregory pointedly said that it was my fear of such a close date that coloured my thinking. So I deferred to them to figure it out for themselves. But far from settling it between them, the argument became decidedly more heated, especially since the potion was made, and eventually I threw up my hands in frustration and told them to send word to me when they could finally agree. Isabelle and I left with a good-natured laugh over their passion.

"You really couldn't ask for greater champions," she laughed as we walked home through the city and a midnight breeze caused her to pull tighter the furred hood of her cape. "If they ever get it sorted out, at least we can settle on a time to finally test our theories."

"I'm still inclined to agree with Mister Woo, even if Gregory says my judgement is prejudiced." She shrugged and we walked on in silence.

I spent the next few days sequestered in Leon's den, happy enough to sit by the hearth with little else to do than drink brandy and watch the fire from behind the safety of my glasses. Yet I was subtly aware of the turning heavens and the ominous approach of Gregory's predicted conjunction. Early in the evening of that fated night, Isabelle broke the silence with mixed excitement, holding a note scrawled in the alchemist's quick script.

"Julian," Isabelle said, holding the note to me. "Mister Woo has relented. Our company is requested tonight."

I gazed at her and unease prevented a reply. Instead I nodded dumbly, cold fingers of inevitability insinuated around my heart and horribly I could almost hear the beast as he laughed at me.

I hardly saw the twilight city pass us by as we walked along its cobbled streets. Indeed, I hardly noticed the walk at all and felt almost that we had just appeared by Mister Woo's front door. Isabelle knocked and true to the alchemist's custom, Gregory admitted us. Still, I felt unease once more as he led us along the hallway and put it down to my own fears even as he spoke.

"Grandfather was called away," Gregory said and preceded us into the work room. Yet the walls took up his words and echoed the sound back oddly mocking. "He said to start without him should the time come and he not yet return."

"Fair enough," Isabelle said lightly, removing her cape.

The room had been tidied considerably since the last time I had been there, the instruments arranged once more on the shelves, the books and scrolls so too arranged and the tables and chairs pushed back to leave a suitable working space in the middle of the floor. Laid within the boundary created by the tables, an incomplete circle of thick rock salt and by it, marked by the same pure white edge, an almost finished equal sided triangle. The geometry needed no explanation, Isabelle and Gregory, and even Mister Woo when he arrived, would stand steadfast in the circle and hold the power of the boundaries set by the salt, while I would wrestle with the power of the beast, conjured into the triangle. I nodded my approval of the preparations and, with an almost unconscious familiarity, we moved to sit by the fire and watch a small hearthside carriage clock as it ticked away the moments until the right time. No one spoke, yet the air became heavy with anticipation and even so, I glanced uneasily at the ominously vacant chair when it became appropriate for us to take our places and Mister Woo had not yet returned.

"It's highly unusual of him," Isabelle followed my gaze and answered my unspoken thought.

"Grandfather insisted that we continue even without him," Gregory shrugged, his back turned as he retrieve the crucible of salt from a shelf.

"Still, I suppose we really don't need him now, we all know our roles," Isabelle said and then turned to me in a brief tender moment. "Oh, Julian, I have become so accustomed to your presence."

Gregory laughed, "Come, Isabelle, he's hardly to kill himself tonight. I doubt Julian shall be leaving us yet."

I smiled fondly at her delicate beauty and knew that she sensed this night to be the end of what friendship we had made, "But soon enough, eh, Isabelle?" I whispered and took her warm hand in mine.

She shivered lightly and looked away but allowed me to lead her to the broken edge of the circle and she stepped through as finally as moving into another room.

Gregory handed me the tiny vial and, once I had assumed my position, completed the salt triangle with a muttered invocation.

The air grew thick, the constellations wheeled, moments ticked by. Gregory retreated to the salt circle and repeated the process of sealing its entrance and, as I sensed the movement of the heavens, Isabelle too added her voice. The space around me felt enclosed, solid within the aetheric triangle, a good sign. I gazed toward the chanting couple and they stared back in turn supporting me. I unstoppered the vial and raised it before my face. Odourless, colourless vapour poured snakelike from the bottle and boiled around me. I could feel its touch on my skin. Yes! Now it was time.

I looked long at the mortals and then back to the potion. This time I felt no such panic as I had when I had, so to speak, bitten off more than I could chew. I raised the vial and swallowed its contents. Three drops were as much as it held and as much as I drank, yet I could feel each drop burn unpleasant into my body.

The workroom door slammed open. I dropped the bottle and looked up to the sudden appearance of Mister Woo. His eyes were filled with rage.

"Grandfather!" I heard Gregory gasp and felt the bonds of my aetheric prison falter.

"No!" I called and all but fell.

I heard Mister Woo speak but his words were drowned out by the voice of the beast and then darkness took me.

"No!" I wailed into this space of hell.

"No!" I screamed, desperate for release.

And yet I knew that while my consciousness was trapped here, so that demon was loose in the realm of man. I was imprisoned in this eternity with no frame of reference to judge time or space. I groaned and crumbled under the weight of another failure and so an echo of laughter came to taunt me.

"Foolish creature," came the voice, from where I could not tell but it was all around me, punishing me for my insolence. "I am the father of evil, not one to be quelled by such petty magic!" His voice boomed a noise to lash at me in this no-place where sound came only by the beast's decree. My spirit was beaten by his ridicule. "Your legacy is the blood of all your descendants and that of all your forefathers. This I have given to you," and the voice was screaming laughter. "You seek to challenge me and yet you have not the strength of even these things. Pitiful creature, you will be mine forever!" and the voice range with eternal damnation.

I cowered away from the noise, yet there was nowhere to hide in this nowhere void of the beast's making, and I felt the pain of my sentence given anew to my immortal soul.

Then…

I was lying awkward on the floor, a naked doll thrown and broken in a useless pile. I could hear breathing and only that. The scent of fire or perhaps something more came over me. I wanted to lie unmoving, forever surrendered to the hopelessness of my fate.

But then I heard a whisper, "Julian." It was Isabelle's voice.

Slowly, resisting and miserably, I opened my eyes and the sight that greeted me rose a futile groan in my throat. Of course, the room had been destroyed. It would have been foolish to assume that a summoning of the beast would result in anything less. The boundaries of my triangular cage had been blown away like so much dry sand and before my tear-filled gaze Isabelle's beautiful countenance, still within her own fragile yet surprisingly secure boundary, had gone grey with fright. I could not see Gregory or Mister Woo among the wreckage and was loath to shift my vision to inquire of them.

"Oh, Isabelle," I whispered and tears found their unresisting way from my eyes. "What have I done?"

I struggled to rise and she gazed then toward where the door had been blasted from its hinges. Against the jamb, the unmoving form of the old alchemist was propped, another lifeless doll.

"Is he...?" I whispered unable to finish the question.

"I don't know," was her reply, ashen and grave.

I looked then for his grandson and saw nothing, "What about Gregory?"

Her sob caught me from my brief examination of the ruined room and she was shaking her head, fierce pain of loss radiating in alluring lights all around her shattered form. "When you... when the beast came," she said through gritted teeth, "he...

he…" and again she faltered and swallowed hard against the memory. I would have spared her the telling of his fate, yet her mind as always, was veiled from me and I had no strength to forestall her woeful account. "He foolishly," she spat, "broke from the circle. He only saw Mister Woo enter, he didn't see what I saw. He was the first thing to draw your… I mean, *its* attention. It… took him… and then burned him like the rest of the room. I don't know how Mister Woo withstood the fury of it. Oh, Julian, I was so terribly afraid."

I would have gone to her but I was naked now and the flames of her vital heat in the aftermath drew on my infernal appetite and it was all I could do to hold my place on the floor.

"I have not studied my Art for all these years to be taken so easily." Mister Woo's voice came rustily from where he still sat, yet the relief of his survival could almost have stirred a smile.

"Oh, Mister Woo," was Isabelle's gasp and she dashed to kneel beside him, "are you injured?"

The old man put a hand to the back of his head and his fingers came away bloody. The bright liquid drew my insidious gaze.

"Nothing that won't heal, my dear lady. Yet I suppose it's too late to remind my grandson of the danger he courted by going against my wishes in this matter," and his smile was rueful and held no amusement.

"Against your wishes?" Isabelle flashed a shocked glance at me. "He said you had relented. We received a note in your own hand."

The old man chuckled, "Well, if nothing more, he was exceptional at upholding a fabrication."

"You mean he lied?" Isabelle was stunned.

I sighed, "Then it is little wonder, the outcome."

Mister Woo nodded, glancing from his blood-stained fingers and out to the remains of his study, "And such a waste."

I looked away from the pair, struggling with the awful rising of need, "I…" I began but stopped. Long grey fingers of dawn's twilight reached through the ashen room and caught panic quickly in my throat.

"What now?" Isabelle still strung high with tension had not missed my sudden anxiety.

"The day comes," I whispered and naked, already felt the pain of light on my skin. "I must have… protection."

And so they were both stirred into movement. But even though I would not go too close to the fire of their vital heat, neither one would come too close to me either.

"Go into the cellar," Mister Woo said stepping out into the hall and gestured a small, pinched door that was nestled under the hallway stairs. He pushed open the door and I fled down the narrow steps.

I heard Isabelle speak even through the door as it was closed again, "I'll get him some more clothes. Will you be alright, Mister Woo?"

The old man's chuckle assured her and soon enough all was quiet.

Daylight came raging over the horizon. I quivered as its ceaseless stroke attacked me even in my shallow, underground prison. It frightened me that I had been reduced to so primitive a circumstance and recalled memories of madness in a shallow cave, oh, so long ago. The fire of the sun's aura bathed me mercilessly and called hunger blatant into my being, until I could feel nothing but my wretched predicament and the terrifying fire of

336

my need for blood. I endured an eternity with my skin crawling under such pain of my hideous fate.

Eventually, I heard the door open, though I could see nothing past the flaming day, and when I heard a voice, I threw my arms out in defence my savage state.

"Julian," Isabelle came down towards me. "Here are some clothes."

"Please…" I cringed and wished that she would never have seen me in such pain, "Please, Isabelle, come no closer, I cannot bear it! Please, just leave the clothes and go home."

She took a breath as if to speak but said nothing and, only when I heard her footsteps ascend the stairs and the door close behind her, did I crawl pathetically, feeling my way along the cold stone floor. Relief flooded through me as I took up the protection of silk lined clothing and deep coloured glasses but still I sat unmoving in the dark cellar, clench toothed at the hunger that raged threatening to consume me. In the early afternoon, Mister Woo came to the door, gingerly peering down into the cellar and inquired of my health. I told him abruptly to ensure he was secreted away when dusk came. The alchemist said nothing but nodded with deep understanding and not a little fear, and left me to my miserable solitude.

Inevitably, dusk came and when the last of the sun's rays took themselves beyond the horizon, hunger blossomed beyond my control. I felt sick in its grip and it had me more savagely than even the moments when I had awoken from sleep. Blinded by demonic need, hardly had I taken the glasses from my eyes then wings of vampire lust drew me into flight. I burst forth from the dank cellar and raged through the empty house, truly a thing of terror. I caught the outer door in explosive flight and fell through splintering wood into the clear and night filled sky. Up I soared, my terrible sight eager for any that betrayed the essence that I craved, my conscience masked so awfully behind hunger as I dropped on two easy victims—a couple making their way through the night.

No noise came from their struggle as my iron grip took them both stunned and up into the star flung heavens. Madness prevented even my awareness that one of the pair was a woman until, filled to the last drop of their mortal fire, I heard devil laughter and clarity of blood let the carcasses fall as I thralled in a vision.

Night came, a hot and dusty place. I stood exhausted at the end of a convict's labour, a meagre cup of tepid water held in my hand. Then horribly, out of the darkening night, my fellows were attacked and scattered amid screams of the terror of vampires. Then I saw the creature itself, Chinese in appearance as was his mortal legacy, but with the deathly pallor of those created by my foolish acts. He landed and made simple conversation with my mortal self, marvelling that I had not fled like my fellows. But somehow, and ironically so, I had a knowing of his kind and stood my ground in foolish arrogance. The creature laughed at me and goaded my human innocence and, with lightning speed, attacked. My mortal self surrendered and as I, a powerless witness, watched, the vampire took this other bearer of my soul as one of his own.

With a cry of rage the vision left me and I flew in blind anguish, off into the night.

I flew high and furious and, when I finally descended, it was beyond the furthest limits of the city out by the ocean where the harbour district ended at a lighthouse. I walked to the end of its stone pier, beyond the ever-moving light and shrouded myself in darkness away from the eyes of mortal kind to stand unmoving, staring out to sea for the rest of the night. Dawn came finally to banish me behind the safety of glass and I turned away from that barren landscape before the first glance of the sun.

I walked slowly through the harbour district, echoes of ancient times still laid familiar paths through streets that had hardly changed even since that bygone era. Thoughtless reflections soon had me by the busy door of the fashion house and, almost guilty, I entered Leon's den.

"Oh!" he was startled from sleep even though I had entered silently and he stared up at me with some confusion. "Count…"

"Have you spoken with your sister?" I inquired without passion.

He nodded. "Briefly," he said and rose to make for the bar. "She said very little but from her appearance I gathered something… unfortunate has occurred."

I almost laughed at the understatement. Still I remained mute and sank into a chair.

"Brandy?" he asked most civilly and handed me a large glass.

"I must leave," I said after what seemed like hours. My mind was empty but for the terror of my vision and the horror I had committed in my foolish ignorance.

"Where will you go?"

I shrugged, futile. Where could I go to be free of my everlasting prison, even to protect the mortals who were ultimately and eternally to be my prey. I doubted there was a safe haven anywhere on the earth.

"Still," Leon held his glass up to emphasis his statement, "there's a fortune in your account that'll keep you no matter what you choose to do."

"Yes, I suppose," I sighed and fell once again into silence.

Later, at sunset, Leon left and Isabelle came briefly into the room. Her face was still ashen, her eyes sunken and dark like she had seen no sleep for fear of the nightmares such recent memories would stir. Her hair was slate grey now, the lustre of its russet silk gone forever, and her carriage beaten and cowed.

"Leon said you were here," she said quietly but did not come to sit by me even as I rose in polite acknowledgement of her feminine company. Though she gave a small smile, now there was so deep a sadness and fear that caught in her eyes and hardly could she hold my gaze as she spoke. "I'm to leave Portsmouth. I'm going to Bolton."

"I see."

She fingered nervously at an envelope and turned to leave before she even remembered that it was in her hand. "Oh, yes," and she walked cautiously across the carpet. "Mister Woo gave this to me earlier when I went to check on him. He asked me to make sure that you got it." She dropped the envelope on the chair beside me and fled from the room. I sat for a long time, unmoving, with the sad realisation that it would be the last time I would see my lovely friend.

When eventually I retrieved the envelope that waited patient and mute beside me, I could feel the subtle pain that lingered from when Isabelle had held it and my hand shook as I unfolded the letter from within. The white page was stark with the contrast of its thickly calligraphed Chinese glyphs, yet the note was as simple as Mister Woo's clipped speech. It read;

Ancient One,

I have written this in the manner of my ancestors to save a good lady should her curiosity be raised—yet I wonder that it is hardly necessary, she is a broken flower in the snow of her winter now! Still, we have spoken and I have convinced her to allow me to accompany her to the north. I would hope that my craft can help to remedy some of the pain she carries. And though it is true that her love for you is as deep as midwinter snow, sir, my strongest advice—if for nothing more than her chance for healing—is for you not to seek out her company!

I, however, believe most avidly that the date I have foreseen is as strong a focus of power as will occur for many centuries, a black night that has me eager to begin again the manufacture of a certain potion. I will forward it to you when it is complete. It is my greatest regret, sir, that has me believe that I can help you no further than this. Indeed, I sincerely doubt that any mortal being could, since on that fateful night, beyond the devastation cast upon our lives, I believe the creature gave a solid clue to the undertaking of his demise. Although I heard little from my position of scan protection, I did hear a ranting of his that had me wonder at its meaning. The demon talked greatly to itself, I assume in conversation with you since it paid little attention to we humans, and said that you would need the power of all that you had created, your legacy to the world, to fight its curse upon you. I have thought about his meaning and see your battle to require the strength of vampire kind to aid you in

banishing your first curse. Perhaps then, Julian, you should seek your own children to assist you when next the stars align. A thought to consider, maybe just the ranting of a frightened old man, yet ...
I will forward a parcel to the fashion house when I have completed my work.
Good luck, sir,
Mister Woo.

I sat looking dumbly at the script, rereading the letter and recognised the lure of hope that Mister Woo would lay before me, but pain kept my heart terribly empty and, even so, I could hear the laughing of the beast within its infinite darkness.

"Brandy?"

The room had gone dark, sunlight had disappeared without my recognition and now, I slowly lowered my glasses to the vivid flames of Leon standing before me.

"Thank you," I whispered and took the glass.

"She's gone then," he said blandly and sat into his own chair, glass in one hand, fire stoke in the other.

"Yes," I replied and watched as he cosied the grate into its own writhing life.

The night grew and receded without conversation and, when morning came and I could hear activity from without, I rose from Leon's silent company and made for the door.

"Julian," he said and stopped me with my hand on the door handle. I turned to his approach, he held a slim book in one hand. "Take this and make use of it." He gave the cheque book to me and briefly explained its working, the way to fill it out and how my signature would seal its account as my own. At the end of his speech he laid a hand upon my velvet clad shoulder in brief and sympathetic camaraderie and then, without another word, he turned away.

I left his den and the fashion house to find my way in this new, harsh and alien land. Without passion or enjoyment, I found myself a modest house, close to the edge of the city and away from my connection with the family. I sent word of my address to Leon so, should a certain parcel be sent to the fashion house, he was to send it on yet attempt no other interaction. Such was my abrupt instruction.

I took a servant to maintain my modest needs and began for myself a diversion of the working of alchemy. I befriended no one then and spoke little, even to my own servant, yet went frequently enough to certain book shops and supply stores to become noted by their proprietors as a regular customer. I spent my days and nights alone with my craft and watched with only brief interest as society evolved around me.

Auto carriages and electricity became the fashion and the world plunged itself into a foolish war over possession of the earth and the miserable suffering of humankind. Convention changed standards around me, altering the pace and fabric of mortal existence, creating a new and very different world on the carcass of centuries gone by. The barrier of distance vanished in the advent of mass communications, a magic of human engineering linking the empires of the world. I watched such technology evolve, a tool that I imagined could unite the world, but which they chose to use in the age-old tactics of war. From by brief contact with this growing world, I discovered the witchery of an industry that used its selective eye to control the thinking of the population at large. I took it as another diversion to procure a daily newspaper and marvelled as such a subtle influence of the country. Each morning I would read the propaganda of nationalism and by that very evening I could feel the shift of the consciousness around me.

So civilisation shifted gear wholeheartedly into this age of motor cars and aeroplanes, and the weight of change paid out its price on the sons and daughters of England. A great depression arose from the days of unionism, the fragile sense of national pride collapsed in the crush of its own pace. Britain struggled to bring itself back from the brink of poverty-stricken disaster and as time passed, the newspapers became full of the movements of another nation.

The sudden threat of Germany and its Third Reich dominated the headlines and the betrayal of a country who had only recently been such good friends to Britain and its high officials. Once again, the country plunged into war and even more hardship, sending its young men off to be devoured by the demands of terrible conflict. I watched the growth of Hitler's army, his special forces and the fanaticism that swept his people and, although I could not come to condone his actions, the strength with which his country rallied to his plans, sparked my curiosity.

Each day reports of the Nazi's progress came with eagerly read newspapers and I could palpably feel the Third Reich as it unified a formidable enemy across the Channel. As the war progressed, I felt an energy stir that I knew could only be from stronger magic than mere mortals could conjure, and had me recall almost unconsciously the notion raised by Mister Woo in his letter to me. For the first time in many years I wondered about the old alchemist and the welfare of the one he had accompanied to that distant city, and perhaps it was coincidence that within days a package arrived addressed to me in the old man's distinctive style.

There was a note that stated simply that he had manufactured a quantity of that magical brew and had included it in the parcel. I retrieved the well stoppered vial and placed it carefully on a shelf next to the potion I had distilled myself. He briefly mentioned the state of his health and that of Isabelle, perhaps only as a courtesy, yet what interested me most was a letter he had included bearing the insignia of Britain's head of government. The note was an official request for the old man's aid in—and the term used was stated as such in parenthesis— "unusual activities" and Mister Woo's surmise was that such a rational government could hardly speak frankly about dealings with the magical realm. Indeed, the letter did interest me as the alchemist had said it might. If such magic as I had felt from the continent had stirred the British government to seek out a known occultist, then perhaps I also would be interested to discover what game was afoot.

Chapter 15

"My Lord, we must leave!" I coughed as a cloud of white dust billowed around the shaking columns. A cross-member had dislodged completely and come crashing to the crystal floor and on breaking, showered us with fine shards. I steered Lord Tehuti from the debris.

As I touched his arm, he turned to look at me, his eyes a blaze of red coals and I swear I could see the Ibis head about him, he was holographic. "I can hold the Temple for now, the worst of the tremors are over. Bring your tools we must go."

I snatched up my tool bag and followed Tehuti from the trembling structure and, as the ground outside subsided in an awesome shrug, so the Temple eased and re-seated itself onto its bed.

"There is nothing left here now, Ma'eh," Tehuti's voice echoed in the eerie after effect of the earthquake, the tone deep and powerful. "We will cross the ocean for safer shores. The island will sink very soon. There is not sufficient power here for me to generate anywhere near enough energy to close this maw in the earth. I see the end of the Suns of Light all around us," he paused, his fair hawk-like face alert his profile soft in the late morning light, "Come." He turned on his heel and marched off down the avenue. I broke into a jog to catch him.

As we neared the pier, I caught sight of my Lord's barge, moored but ready to catch the breeze. "We will sail to the isle of Lemure, you will be safe there." He turned his gaze upon me as we walked and he caught me, in the midst of all the destruction, with a look of complete love. When I looked into his eyes, I saw that he knew me completely and, as a father, his word was law. "Though I am not destined to rest there with you, my young friend, my divine task takes me into more than you have already witnessed. I would rather you be spared such hardship." The sound of sandal on wood replaced his monologue as we came upon the pier.

My Lord jumped onboard, I untethered the barge and within moments we were free of the land. Tehuti was behind me, his face into the wind, working his magic to bring us safely across the sea. I turned to watch the rapidly receding coastline, watching the only land I had known, move toward the horizon. It stirred visions of the golden days on Unal, me a scribe in the house of Tehuti, the bountiful days of sacrifice to the gods and the bliss of being in their realm. The oneness that their gifts had bestowed on all who came into Tehuti's realm, homage of devotion and the blessing of being a Sun of the Light but even that bliss has its cycle, as Tehuti himself knows and, oh, how quickly the pendulum has swung. The decaying rot of the warrior caste and even the indoctrinated waste of the priest caste had infected all of Atlantis with more cunning than even Tehuti himself could gauge. Within five great cycles even the grand Lord's personal family was affected and the gods are only as great as the humans that worship them. My Lord could do no more here. This place had been destined as a stage to the fall of lesser men, an experiment of cruel and callous gods to be swallowed by the earth that once belched it forth. I turned my gaze onto Tehuti's beautiful face and my heart tore in my chest. The millennia of his life as a Lord of Atlantis, so easily ripped from him by the very gods he served. A tear rolled down my cheek, chill in the cool wind, mixing with the sea foam that spattered across my smooth virgin face.

It was days before we sighted the island of Lemure. My Lord had me take to beginning a new work that I was to scribe on twelve tablets of stable emerald that Tehuti had stored on the barge before the island had heaved its death throes. Tehuti had worked long with the lords of Amenti and had intimate knowledge of the mysterious workings of other realms. He had known of the fall of Unal and was powerless to do anything but surrender. He had known of the time this work would begin and in the scribing I performed for him, he changed his name to that of Thoth, addressing all his comments to the children of the land he was destined for. My love for this god-like being grew on our journey across the sea and indeed I knew that I could never again see a god in any other form. I was watching him as he looked out to sea, the sun making its way down to the rim of the world, when Tehuti lifted his head wolf fashion, scenting the air like an odour of heat, his eyes unfocused, not seeing this world.

"The island approaches," he mentioned casually and turned to me. "I have much love for you, Ma'eh and I know you will be safe here. Who knows? Others from Unal may have made it safely here as well." His eyes were soft and sensual as he gazed at me.

"I pledge my life to you, my Lord," was all I could think to say in this moment when I could have begged him to take me with him, to show him of the depth of my love for him, I shamed myself with a promise that would be my undoing.

The island came upon us like a great bear, suddenly oppressive and alive all around us, a series of jungle topped cliffs breaking the momentum of the sea. Thoth changed the course of the barge and after some hours of impressive, rugged coast, the cliffs broke into sandy beaches and lagoons. Lemure seemed much bigger than Unal to me but perhaps that was just innocence.

My Lord brought the barge right up on the beach and lodged the prow skilfully to take advantage of the turning tide. "I will give you a gift of power, Ma'eh, and you will take on a new name just as I have done. I will not let the work of Tehuti die here so readily. You will be Tehuti in this place with all my powers and rights, and your work here will continue as mine will in Khem. I bless you, beloved brother."

Standing before me on the prow of the barge, Thoth took me into an intimate embrace that touched every part of my body. I could feel his face beside me, his powerful shoulders against mine, the warmth and gentle rhythm of his breath and, oh, his body warm and pressed close against me. I felt his hand rise up to my hair as he gently pulled my head back and, with eyes that were aflame with brilliant turquoise, he kissed me. His mouth opened as he pressed his lips to mine, his tongue flicked into my mouth and anchoring me to him, he opened a channel of energy into my body, exploding and illuminating each energy centre until even my groin hummed. When he released me, I staggered back and almost fell overboard but, even in such a brief instant, our paths had already begun to diverge, Thoth once again was calling the tide to take him on.

Mutely, I obeyed his tacit command to jump from the barge and as I stood on the sand he sailed from me without once turning back. I could still feel his radiant presence, his body against me, the smell of his manhood, and tears of loneliness stirred from my eyes as I watched the retreating boat.

I was alone on the edge of the sea, my lord gone. Crying out I waded into the water, but by the time I had come to the edge of the shallow reef that edged the island, Thoth's barge had disappeared into the retreating sun. Defeated and weeping, I returned to the beach and sank into the sand, lying in the cold comfort of my own tears as night fell upon me.

I must have slept where I was on the beach, for in the morning the tide had come as high as my nose where I lay on the sand. The smell of seaweed was everywhere, the calls of gulls as they feasted on breakfast between the tides and then, as though from another realm, the far-off cry of humans beckoned me from my last moments in a dream. I raised my head from the pillow of weed and opened my eyes on a cruel rainbow of piercing light. I covered my gaze and rose slowly to meet the oncoming strangers. They came upon me, calling in joy and excitement, and I, wretched creature, stood covering my eyes against the brilliance of the light that shone from them. Two of the people moved toward me carefully, sensing my distress, and slowly they guided me from the beach. The others fell in behind us and the whole group became a gentle procession of devotees singing and laughing with the joy of the coming of Tehuti to Lemure.

They led me into the forest, my sight cooled by its deep green healing, along a well-worn path that climbed steadily upward, and soon we came into sight of a bare faced cliff. The procession led me to the tiny village nestled at the base of this awe-inspiring tear in the perfection of the jungle, and I was guided on until we came to a halt before two immense stone doors set into the mountain's face.

We attracted attention as we passed until the whole village had stopped and followed us to the doors, and there the first of my saviours reached out and knocked. A ripple of energy snaked through the crowd and passed through me, stinging with the power of their vibrant light and I heard thoughts of welcome for Tehuti echo everywhere.

I flinched, they mistook me for a god by simple tricks of dress and custom. How could I fill such a high position? I could never be a substitute for my Lord Tehuti. I had neither the wisdom nor the power that he commanded. Fear filled me instantly. How could I know that they wouldn't just kill me should they find out my deceit? My mind was reeling but I had no chance to think, the sound of stone on stone cut through my thoughts and the doors swung slowly inwards. The movement of their passage stirred an eddy of dust that tugged on my ragged robe and was sucked into the chamber beyond. My mind was instantly aware of the monumental size of the halls, carved from the very heart of the mountain and I could see the throb of energy pulsating from within. The two smiling villagers gently ushered me forward and I stepped over the threshold.

The light inside the temple was soft and alluring after the harshness I had experienced outside and the nauseating effect that the startling sunshine had caused disappeared within moments. I wandered in a little and then, by some trick in my mind, a vision appeared before me.

The priest had an expression of awe on his face as his perfect eyes blinked in surprise at me. "My Lord Tehuti, I bless this day," and with a grace that held me suspended, he bowed deeply. To my relief he turned from me then and moved to escort me. "Please, come. I must take you to our High Priest," he muttered and walked reverent across the vaulted entry. High arches connected this cavern with the next and as I stepped through the archway, the great hall spread out before me so large that the other side was lost in the cool light. The beautiful priest took me along the wall and into a corridor that led to a closed door and with a discreet knock we entered.

The High Priest was so humbled by my presence that I was soon enjoying a warm bath in the privacy of his own apartment and the close attention of two priests appointed to care for my needs. The old High Priest had given me his rooms since I had asked to rest and, when I told him of Unal and my desire to remain on Lemure, he bustled off to arrange for me a more suitable apartment.

The bath was warm and soft and one young priest scrubbed at my back with soap, soft casual conversation between he and the other who moved quietly about the room ranged back and forth in the awe of my presence among them. Their island had for centuries held trust to the covenant of Tehuti and now I was here to guide them personally through these uncertain times. I listened in growing frustration to their talk. I was neither a god, nor could dedicate my life to ideals of which I was not worthy. I sat back in the water, holding my own counsel and raging against this awful dilemma. How could they mistake me? I was smaller, darker and much younger than my Lord Tehuti, surely, they could see that?

The click of a door brought me from my thoughts, I watched distracted as Otho left his quiet tasks around the chamber and quickly attended his master.

"Is he pleased with you?" The whispering voice of the fat old High Priest floated through to me on an incensed breeze.

"Oh, my Lord Timar, we have been given such a gift in his presence," the young priest whispered and I could almost see a secret smile that passed between them.

"This is good," the old Priest sounded ecstatic. "His arrival augers well for our ritual. We could not have asked for a better blessing."

"His timing is impeccable." There was awe in Otho's voice.

They came to the entrance of the bedchamber just as Ila was helping me from the bath and, standing before a reflection glass, I was struck too dumb to respond to the greeting of the High Priest. In a blinding flash I recognised the gift that my Lord Tehuti had given to me in that instant of giving me his name. My face, my body, my whole physical appearance had become the countenance of Tehuti. I was transformed, I was a god! A flood of relief filled me as I breathed deep and watched my strong chest fill, and the form of the most exquisite of beings stared back at me. No longer the small auburn headed figure of the youth that I was, now I had taken on the very form of my lord: teacher, healer and maker of gods. I gazed along the svelte line of my new body and to my embarrassment and shame, I felt a stir of lust for my own beautiful facade.

Ila came up behind me holding fine silken robes for my attire and smiled, "I would dress you, my Lord, but I can see that you have a need. May I pleasure you before I do?" He reached out and gently caressed my rising erection.

I flinched slightly to see his lusty face, taken back by his proposition. Was this not a sin against the covenant of Tehuti? A priest, a Sun of the Light offering sex, and even more so to Tehuti himself. Was that not a blessed right of the harem?

But when I turned to the High Priest, his eyes gleamed with pleasure and he bowed to me saying, "As Tehuti desires, my Lord."

Perhaps I had mistaken the place of my Master. I know he had spent time on Lemure constructing the massive sun temple with the natives of the island, but that was, oh, so long ago, in the glorious golden days of our mighty nation, when we had still talked with the gods. And now in the fall? How did that bode for Atlantis when a priest could take the place of a prostitute?

Ila's warm hand touched me gently and I was beguiled, his expert touch giving me pleasures I had only dreamed of in my life of scribe. I let him pay me attention, my thoughts floating away like time, and the priest caressed me in religious ecstasy. I was taken to the bed and, treated to such wonders, I cried Tehuti's name in pleasure. When I was spent and lying in the comfort of soft pillows, I watched the fat High Priest eagerly mop up my seed and pour it carefully into a pot.

I raised to one arm and watched him quizzically, and he smiled through rolls of his chin. "We celebrate your sacred festival tonight, my Lord. The power of your holy creation will be a good omen for our people in these changing times."

"And you would use my seed for the blessing?" A bizarre thought grew in my mind of the power I had in this place.

The old man looked away from my gaze, "Yes, my Lord."

I smiled, to be given such pleasures of the flesh and all the exalted powers of my Lord of Unal, I felt that at last I had been blessed with my right as a Sun of the Light. "I would take the task to issue my seed in this ceremony. Surely fresh is more potent than what has been sitting in a chalice for hours."

Timar looked up at me sharply and then a slow smile spread across his hog-like features, "My Lord, you honour us doubly." I turned from him in dismissal and allowed Ila to clothe me in fine robes. I heard the old High Priest rise and leave the room, in the glass I could see his pudgy face retreating, bowing and smiling like a child with sweets.

"Well, my Lord," Otho began as he came upon me, a tray of pots and brushes in his hand. "If you are to be a part of our ceremony, we had better hurry," and I allowed him to paint my face into a mask of my godlike beauty.

I was taken to the great hall, where already crowds of people were milling around in anticipation of the festival. High around the chamber, shafts of light illuminated the gathering as the sun came to add its own power to the rite. Otho led me up to a stone dais where an altar sat before three great carved thrones. I was sat on the middle throne and the High Priest and a plump, berobed and heavily painted woman, who must have been High Priestess, made their way to sit either side of me.

Hardly did I hear the ceremony begin, I had let my attention be taken by the mind noise of the crowd as they thought about the grace of the coming of Tehuti. Where all these people came from was beyond my wonder. Surely there had not been this many villagers around me when I arrived?

"The city is high on the other side of the Island, my Lord," Timar whispered at my elbow when I casually voiced my thoughts to him. "There are many entrances to the temple, and theirs is used only on days of high ceremony."

I nodded and turned to see a small procession making their way down the length of the hall. All noise and movement stopped in reverence as the absurd group made its way to the dais and all eyes turned to watch five priests dressed grandly in ritual robes leading what looked like a masked priest, crawling slowly among them on hands and knees. I turned to Timar with a quizzical look but his eyes were fixed, greedy and expectant, to the advancing procession. A wave of excitement rose in me as I saw his eyes and the muted sound of an animal bleating, made me instantly aware of the significance of the approaching group. In shame I remembered my pledge on the barge and knew that the centre of this ritual would be the blood sacrifice of this animal to me.

The ceremony began around me and I sat unthinking, allowing their measured movements to flow beyond my perception. The animal was lifted gently onto the altar and the assembly responded with cries of worship. Timar and the woman beside me rose as if on cue and, in an impressively theatrical manner, commanded the attention of the whole audience. As the High Priest spoke, plumes of incense began to rise from below the stone altar and as it curled its way around the hall, I could feel a slackness that came with the onset of hallucinogens and a stirring in my groin from the scent of aphrodisiac herbs.

"The seed of the gods will fill our lands bringing surety of bounty in our lives. Our Lord Tehuti has blessed us with his presence. Bow before the god who brings to us… bounty of the heavens, light from Amenti!" Timar bellowed his lines with power that caused the congregation to immediately obey. He turned slightly and beckoned me to him and, in a clever stage ploy, I was standing beside him before his audience had seen me move. The gasps and murmurs from around me were enough to show how well this recipe for ritual worked. "Oh, Lord Tehuti," the old Priest bellowed beside me. "Bless this symbol of the earth with your seed that we too may be blessed."

At this cue, two heavily painted priests came to my sides and made a great show of aiding me to climb the carved stairs up to where the dressed goat stood bleating, blind on the altar. The crowd shifted in growing excitement as I approached the animal, this was indeed what they had been waiting to see. My priests lifted the rich folds of cloth from the goat's back and displayed for me the shaved pink rear of my waiting mount. For all I had never conceived of the idea of giving my phallus into an animal, the sight of its clean inviting hole and the intoxicating aromas around me, lulled me into lustful excitement. How cleverly this rite had been planned, the fabric of my robe designed to part and display my godly erection to the waiting assembly, causing a roar to erupt from them as a confirmation of blessing. I was deafened for a moment as my phallus was adored. Clouds of incense flowed around the dais and the adulation filled me with lust, the allure of an animal made up to be human captured my attention. I took the nanny goat.

Its startled cry caused another eruption in the crowd and ritual energy throbbed in rhythm as I impaled it, oh, what ecstasy! Power fed to me from all around and I worked viciously into the confused beast, my mounting energy as solid as the rock beneath my feet and driving, forcing such violence, that even through my incense haze, I saw blood trickle around my orgasm. Weak with the explosion of semen, I hardly noticed that I had been removed from the animal and now faced the wild congregation as my seed sprayed out and into the crowd. Those who were near enough to catch my seed fell about in zealous pleasure trying to possess any drops that came their way, and even set about each other in a frenzied attempt to gain as much as possible. I laughed and allowed my priests to take my weight as I spent myself. The sound of an animal screaming added insane pleasure to the languid aftermath of bliss. Rolling my eyes, I saw the High Priest and Priestess standing at the head of the now still and prostrate goat, each with a look of sublime rapture etched into their eyes as they cut the throat of the poor creature, draining its blood into a jewel encrusted goblet.

"The life blood of the Gods," Timar shouted over the noise of the crowd and his counterpart held the goblet up high for all to see it, blood stained and dripping. Ceremonially they approached me. "Bless us, my Lord, drink of the fruits of the earth," and I was handed the cup.

In a great show of my godly state, I lifted the goblet and raising the cup to my lips, I took a long warm drink. Perhaps it was the incense, or the euphoria of the rite, but I was caught in the act of the drink, so warm, so rich, I swore I would live like this forever...

…In the furore of that moment I could feel something change, a discordance in the air, or a change in the light I could not quite be sure, but at that moment I could see Tehuti before me, his wrath all around the vaulted hall.

"You have shamed me, Ma'eh, it is your ignorance that brings about the death of this place. These people had lost their way many cycles ago and I sent you to right the balance so Atlantis could be great as she was when man had faith. But you have fallen prey to your own lust. You see not how potent you are, you are blind to devotion and the love of the Light for you, and blind and stumbling in the dark you will remain until you look away from your sins of flesh and find truth once more. I pray for you, Ma'eh, that you can right this evil you have committed against my covenant, all of Atlantis and the very gods themselves. The power that I have given to you, I would take away, but what was done cannot be undone so easily, you have cursed yourself more greatly than even I could amend. The curse of my power will stay with you through time untold. Now see how you have cursed yourself. I leave you to the mercy and the retribution of what your vanity has created." The spectre of his divine form faded quickly from my sight and was replaced by growing darkness and a rumbling so deep that it started in my soul. The cup fell from my hands to land in a silencing crash on the stone floor. None had seen the vision that I had but, as I started to scream, the crowd caught my fear and a short-lived riot was born.

The mountain silenced the congregation quickly, their confusion dead in its birth, for the chamber rippled in a great shuddering earthquake. No one had a chance to react in the speed of the earth's vengeance. The pit of my guts seemed to leap out of my body and I knew the sensation of the island sinking into the ocean. Within moments there was sea water around my feet as I stood on the altar watching in despair as the chamber became my tomb.

No screams of dying humans moved me as I accepted my return to the watery depths of earth's womb. No sensations of body or mind distracted me from my primal knowing of a deep sense of shame; guilt born in the futility of my vanity and the terrible need to take vengeance on all that had led me astray. I would pay for my sin. I would cycle onto earth again, sentenced by the wrongs I had committed against what I had pledged to my Lord and my gods.

Water, cool and terribly comforting rushed all around me, my breath was taken away by the upswell and I was bloated by the terrible pressure of the flood. My eyes bulged and I was knocked faint by the tactless grip of the sea and floated for a moment as the vast temple was consumed. In the frozen instant of a dream of death by drowning and knowing the cycle I had ignorantly begun, I met my first end.

Chapter 16

I took the train to London, amusing myself with a
novel as the engine took the countryside speeding by
and, as we came closer to the city, the carriage filled
with people from other stations along the route. A
young lady sat beside me, the hem of her short skirt
folded purposefully to her stockinged thigh as she
flaunted her comely body in a freedom of dress that
I had not yet become accustomed. When I ignored
her subtle advances in favour of my book, she
leaned her mortal fire close to my face and sighed.

"I've read that one," her throaty voice penetrated
my concentration. "Y'know there's a good picture
on at the theatre like that too."

I turned to her carefully designed features, her
ruby lips a parody of her words. I lay the novel in
my lap and attended her, "I prefer the flights of my
own imagination than the tricks of modern theatre."

A laugh issued from her dusky voice, "Oh, I
know, but Dracula is so much fun when you can see
all the gory details." A look of morbid fascination
came over her painted features.

"I am quite sure, madam, should you see the real
thing you would not be so interested to see the
outcome."

"Gawn, with yer," she shrieked with laughter
slapping my shoulder with casual affection and I
moved my hands lest she try to touch their icy flesh.
"Ooh, I can almost see you in the part, you're
handsome enough to be the Count 'iself." Her voice
dropped low and seductive as she spoke. I laughed
politely and was relieved when the city boundary
broke her line of thought. "Oh, here already, that's
good. Well, thanks for the chat, my stop's next."

She rose and dropped a glove from her lap and as I reached for it, her hand descended on mine and her eyes became suddenly round, "Why, sir, you're so cold."

I flashed my will from behind my dark barrier and moved the foolish mortal like a puppet to the carriage door.

The train stopped twice on the outskirts of the city and came into the central station that I had visited briefly many years before. The echo of my awful trail still hung a ghost amid the busy activity of its grand façade. I descended from the carriage and patted a breast pocket, a reassurance for the security of the small vial that, with my glasses and cheque book, were my only means. A row of taxi cars awaited commuters from the trains and I made my way to the open door at the head of the queue. I gave the driver directions to the address on the letter that I had received from Mister Woo and was chauffeured through the heart of the sprawling city to a neat row of town houses on Downing Street. I knocked on a solid door and was admitted to the house by a stern man who demanded to know my business. I showed him the letter and he ushered me into a well-appointed anteroom where a blond woman sat behind a desk.

"One for his lordship," the doorman threw across the room before closing the door.

The woman looked up at me over horn-rimmed spectacles, "Can I help you, sir?"

I proffered the letter for her inspection and spoke indifferently as she scanned the note, "Mister Woo is a long-time acquaintance of mine. He sent this letter to me in a recent correspondence. I took it upon myself to attend the interview scheduled for him."

She looked up from her bland examination of the letter, "I'll tell Lord Sommerville that you are here," and turned to a switchboard, dismissing my presence.

A portly gentleman came through the leather studded door that stood protected by his secretary's desk. His round cheeks flushed from exertion as he extended a pudgy hand towards me. "Ah, I was wondering if the old Chinaman would answer the summons. A bit demned awkward to ask him to help the allies considering he's no Brit, eh, what?"

I declined the handshake but nodded briefly in accord, "Still, Mister Woo thought I would be a suitable substitute."

He gave me a wary glance for my refusal and the implication of my admission and I could see brief questions flicker across his mind. He showed me into the office from which he had come, puffing greatly as he rounded the large desk. "Good man, good man," he mused and invited me to sit opposite. He dropped the letter to the wide desk before him and sat, fingers steepled over his wide girth and staring blankly at the unassumingly typed sheet. "So you say you're an acquaintance?" he said finally, staring into the glass barrier of my gaze.

"Yes, sir," I replied quietly. "We have worked together in the past."

He raised a bushy eyebrow, "Really? I'm loath to wonder if you could possibly be as, ah… em… knowledgeable as the old boy… mister…?" and he looked expectantly at me.

"I am Count Julian Douvélle," I replied noncommitally.

His pudgy face broke into a broad smile, "Oh, so you're related to the Taylor clan, huh? Might have known it. That family have been his favourites for many a year. Brought him to England, didn't they?" but he did not wait for a reply, "Yes. Know the story well, reason why I called on him when the PM asked for a specialist. Sommerville's were merchants too, y'know. Our families go back, oh, perhaps two or three hundred years." His gaze blanked for a moment and then, shaking his head, he turned his attention back to me, "Anyway, sir. This is not helping the war effort is it, what, what?" and he chuckled over the shaking folds of his stomach, "So you say your expertise are equal to the old rogue, Lord bless him?"

"Indeed."

"Well, we'll see what old Winnie says, eh?" He toggled a switch and spoke into the intercom box, "Kathy, please arrange a meeting with the PM, I would like to introduce him to Count Douvélle within the hour." With a smile he rose and crossed to a bar that sat beside a small hearth. "Can I fix you a drink, Julian? May I call you Julian?"

I accepted a brandy and we sat in conversation until a knock came on a door that led from the back of his office. "Come!" he ordered shortly and a small waif of a clerk came humbly into the room.

"The Prime Minister will see you now, Lord Sommerville. Please come through."

The wizened clerk ushered us through the door into a long passage that ran the back length of the house and into another anteroom where a replica of the blond secretary sat behind another desk. She looked up briefly appraising our company before turning back to her task on a noisy typewriter. Lord Somerville opened the padded door into the Prime Minister's ostentatious rooms and we came before his enormous desk of office, where the balding gentleman sat musing over a paper in his hand. As we entered, he turned from his brooding and looked evenly upon us.

"Winston, I would like you to meet Count Julian Douvélle, an acquaintance of the Chinese gentleman you asked me to contact. I believe he could be an asset to our efforts," the portly lord beamed from his chair.

"So, Count." Shrewd eyes that seemed almost misplaced in such a round face, gazed scrupulous at my barrier of protective glass. "You wish to fight for King and country?"

"Not necessarily." I shook my head. "I have experienced enough of this war than to desire the pursuit of that politic, though I would fight for the freedom of human rights and a resolution to the conflict. I have done as much before, sir, and would do as much again."

The ageing Prime Minister gave a short laugh, "Well said, sir, well said." His gaze slid past me as he thought, then, "Come and take a walk with me, Douvélle, I have a regular appointment in the afternoons which I cannot break." He rose from his chair and raised a casual hand for me to accompany him from the office. He donned a heavy coat in the anteroom, dismissing Lord Somerville to wait for our return and led me into the street and a long motor car that sat waiting by the curb. "I won't keep you long, Count, but this is a good opportunity to talk free of the prying walls of Downing Street."

His creased eyes shone with vibrant intelligence and he spoke to me of the requirements of his government in seeking to end the war between nations that had, until Hitler's madness, been close allies. The motor pulled before a neat town house, and from the front door a young girl emerged to meet us as we stepped from the car.

"You're late Grandfather," she said and kissed him lightly on a cheek.

"I know, my dear, but you know the rigours of running a country," he smiled easily and took her arm. "This is Count Douvélle," he said as the child watched me in suspicion.

I smiled at her and lowered my glasses to gaze upon her dazzling innocent essence and let my voice beguile her easily, "Please call me Julian."

She flushed prettily and turned to prattle at her grandfather until we came to the iron gates of a large park. We wandered its formal paths and came to a playground, sitting to watch the girl as she took to a tall swing.

The Prime Minister's deep grumble caught my attention, "Count Douvélle, I gather your friendship with Mister Woo was on somewhat unusual terms?" He shifted a little uncomfortable as he chose his words carefully and I nodded. "Then I can assume you have some knowledge of the occult arts?"

"Yes," a wry smile flowed from my cold lips. "I have had some experience in that area."

The old balding gent absently watched his granddaughter for a long moment as if struggling with a thought, "Hmph. Good. Well, we need to infiltrate Hitler's secret service. You have heard of the SS?"

I nodded, I had read something of the progress of Germany's efforts in the newspaper.

"He has given high command of the organisation to an old acquaintance of his by the name of Heinrich Himmler, and they have been up to some very strange things in the past few months. I did have a man fairly close to Himmler, until recently he had been reporting to me of the unusual goings on surrounding the hierarchy of the Gestapo. Along with an odd group of closely guarded officers, it appears that they are soliciting aid from other realms." He turned to look directly into my gaze, "I don't hold too much store in the reports myself, but His Majesty has expressed his concern. So I had a letter sent to someone whom I was told would be discreet and could be trusted." His last words fell meaningfully between us.

"I believe I am suited to the task, sir," I said after a long moment.

The Prime Minister nodded slowly, the furrows in his brow deepening as he spoke, "You will be dropped behind the lines, on the outskirts of Berlin. My contact there will organise a cover for you, not as close to Himmler as I would have liked to get you, but these days, as close as I can get you without attracting the wrong kind of attention. You will be given papers that will see you as a new officer at Gestapo headquarters in Berlin. You will be expected to ingratiate yourself the SS hierarchy. I want you in a place of confidence with the leaders, I want to know what's going on. Unfortunately I have no guarantees on your safety since I have no idea of what they are planning in this unusual tactic and, although we can supply you with a radio, you will be alone in enemy territory. Sir, it is a dangerous mission I offer to you, with no guarantee for your safety or success, so I put the risks to you first before I ask if you will accept my request."

The Prime Minister stared inscrutably into my eyes and, when I nodded my consent, he called his granddaughter from her play and we walked back through the sculptured gardens to the motor that had waited on the street.

The Prime Minister delivered me back to Downing Street and the corpulent ageing lord I had first met, and he took me from the Office to a large manor house on the outskirts of London. The pristine building sat amid grand estates, and had been transformed into a station for tactical manoeuvres and surveillance of the full scale war. We sped down the long entranceway and I looked out on a long tract of land that ran the road edge. It could once have been a simple meadow, though now it had been renovated by the armed forces and played host to an airfield. Large hangars and dozens of small planes assembled in regiments along its length and our arrival gained curious glances from the pilots and staff that littered the field. The motor pulled before the grand stone staircase of the whitewashed house and the door was held open by a young, uniformed soldier, playing his part to his country by waiting on the military hierarchy. I was led by my corpulent companion through the main hall of the mansion, into the briefing room that sat beyond and was met by a brigadier standing at the head of the room. As stiff and regimented as the ordered squadron under his command, he saluted as we approached and handed me a thick manila folder.

"I've just been on the blower to the PM," he said by way of a greeting, his leather clad hand extended. I took the folder and handshake, smiling at his bravado, and he said, "He's organised a flyover in a week, a 'reconnaissance trip' over Berlin. All quite innocent," and he gave a broad wink. "Still, by then your cover will be set and you'll be on your way." He nodded to the folder, "Memorise what's in there in the meantime, old chap. You've got the run of the base till you leave. Dinner's at seven, eat well is my suggestion, you never know what much those Nazis'll give you!"

Lord Sommerville left me then and I was shown to a small private room where I sequestered myself to study the dossier.

I was to be a minor sergeant in the Gestapo, my name, Herr Julian Khess. The cover was to place me in the communications room of SS Headquarters in Berlin. Such a subterfuge was one of many that the British army had arranged in their covert operations for such a contingency as the situation in which I had become embroiled. The folder contained papers and passes and a copy of *Mein Kampf,* the Nazi "bible" of obedience to the Third Reich. I was given a uniform and the heavy overcoat that had become a recognisable insignia of the Gestapo and, though I refused the uniform in favour of my traditional velvet and silk, I accepted the coat and its accessories in keeping with my role. At the hour of my departure I gathered up a leather case, which openly carried my few personal effects and, in a secret compartment, the radio that was to be my only connection with my British superiors. I was taken by the brigadier from the manor house and down to the airfield where a squadron of small reconnaissance craft were taking on board their pilots and navigators for the flight to Germany. I was shown to the lead aeroplane and given into the care of the squadron leader.

The small fleet took to the air shaking under the mechanics of their means of flight and I sat in the vehicle's noisy tail end amused at my ironic situation, a hand folded over my case while I casually scanned my copy of *Mein Kampf.*

As we crossed into German territory, the captain called for me to ready myself and I packed my case and checked the security of the small vial that sat hidden in my jacket. The navigator unbuckled from his seat and came aft, retrieving a bulging package from a locker that he tossed to me with a malicious grin.

"Have you ever used a parachute?" he shouted over the rush of cabin pressure and when I shook my head, he looked forward and threw his voice to the pilot, "Hey, Gunner, they're sendin' bloody civilians out now." I accepted his patronising aid to strap into the bulky backpack, listened politely to his spiel on using the 'chute and the intricacies of landing without breaking anything. The pilot called him back to the cockpit as he launched into another grisly example of a failed jump and silently I thanked the Nazis for being so close.

We passed over the outskirts of Berlin once in keeping with the Prime Minister's deception and, as the afternoon sun slipped slowly westward, we turned into its face and back to the drop point over a small village five miles from the sprawling city. I stepped to the open door of the aeroplane with the navigator shouting good advice to me and let the wind take me from the belly of the mechanical bird. Letting myself fall for some distance, I struggled with the straps of the parachute, shedding it mid-air, tucked the large case under an arm and flew downward toward a small village and the car that would be waiting for me. My orders had stated the driver, who was a dedicated Nazi junior and knew nothing of the espionage he would unwittingly accomplice, had been informed that I had come by train to the small village and would rendezvous with him in the local tavern. I flew to the small lights of human civilisation that competed against twilight for their place in the growing night and came to rest by the gloomy back alley of the small inn. I took from my case the heavy leather trench coat that was an undeniable mark of the Gestapo, and made my way onto the cobbled street.

I stepped from gathering shadows and to the side of the large dark car that sat brooding before the tavern. Putting my case casually beside me, I eased into soft leather gloves that had been in the pocket of the coat and the low hat that covered most of my hair. Even though the sun had hidden its face, I kept my dark barrier before my eyes in keeping with the role I was to play.

A young grey clad officer came rushing from the tavern entrance, tucking his shirt and straightening his short uniform jacket as he came to salute me.

"You are late," I said and flicked imaginary dust from my sleeve.

"I'm sorry, Herr Khess, I had not been informed of the time of your arrival."

"No matter, take me to Berlin."

Moving to the car door, I left him to attend to my case and sat within the dark recesses of the leather-bound seat with my hand on the papers I had tucked into a concealed pocket. The driver closed the door and entered his position in the front of the car, driving along a gloomy countryside lane that linked the pleasant village with the country's sprawling capital. Electric light flooded the horizon as we came into the fortified outskirts of Himmler's tactical headquarters in Berlin. Garrisons of grey clad soldiers, many hardly old enough to support the guns they carried and very few as old as my driver, lounged along the sides of the roads until my car passed them in mindless salute. Their young faces were stark against the sandbags and grey walls of the war-torn city.

We came before the morbid exterior of a heavily guarded building and the car pulled across its face, an aid opened my door and escorted me into the heart of the building. A map of Europe dominated the floor of the large tactical hall, minor ranking staff rushed about their duties and I was taken into a small office and an interview with the division Captain.

The office was decadent and morosely gothic, its rich furnishings dark and sombre under the soft glow of electric light and I stood patiently beside a large leather topped desk, waiting for the attention of the uniformed mortal that sat arrogantly reading a page before him.

Finally he looked up to see me standing and shortly commanded me to sit. "You are Franz Khess, yes?" his eyes narrow against my appearance.

I removed my gloves casually, taking on his cool mood, "My name is Julian, your intelligence is mistaken."

He stared hard at me for a moment, then, "Your uniform is not standard issue, Herr Khess." I told him of my skin disorder that could not tolerate the rough-hewn fabric of Gestapo uniforms and his eyes disappeared in the scrutiny of his gaze. "I trust you are not *mischlinge* with such an imperfection?"

"Sir, I can assure you that my talents more than cover my deficit of a delicate constitution," I replied easily letting my explanation calm his suspicions.

"Very well, Sergeant Khess, come with me."

I was shown the routine of the posting that I was to undertake according to the fabrication of my place, and even then began to unfold the design of my own intentions. I kept the captain easily under the influence of a shallow spell, he made no mention of my indolence in my occupation. Any questions or inquiries directed at Herr Khess, I subdued quickly with an easy finger of my will and, even so, as night followed night and I felt the working of dark energies, I reached out with an unmistakable call. In the back of my mind I kept track on the nearing conjunction of the heavens predicted by Mister Woo almost half a century earlier, and with a deep awareness of the power being wrought from nearby, I sent out a spell of mischief to obstruct what I sensed were carefully laid plans. My interference shattered what I guessed had taken the length of the war to build and I could feel a responding touch, infuriated for a moment, yet ultimately intrigued at who or what could so easily control such energy. It did not take long for my magic to prove its own success and soon, on a night when the full moon's face was stolen in eerie moments by ragged clouds, I stood on the rear steps of the barracks, a flame for a moth to find.

A pale woman, with hair as raven as Margueritte's and clad in flowing evening dress descended from the sky above and came to stand before me. Her lips were as deep as blood and eyes flaming and she stared at me in disbelief, "Who are you to break the magic of my circle?"

I smiled, I had forgotten the shortcomings of my children and their inability to recognise my ancient paternity. "I am Julian," I said, softly weaving a beguiling spell over her, "I am pleased to meet you."

"Why have you called me here?" She knew the magic I had cast at her, but even though her expression was arrogant, my will charged her cool aura and she was bewitched.

"I would like to join your group," I replied.

A light rose in her eyes and she looked about to speak, but checked herself and said instead, "Why?"

Ahh, I almost sighed, "I know a way to conjure the Devil."

Her lips parted and the dainty tips of her savage bite flashed into an eager question, "Why would you need my magic?"

"Ah, vampire, I have been walking my road for many centuries, and not until now have I seen a power to raise the beast and control it," I smiled making light of my double meaning, "and what power to command. I have seen since early in the war, the effect of your magic over your country, the energy you play with, it will take this to hold the beast. Take me into your coven and I will perform this rite with you and then we shall see how your war will go."

Thought flashed across her face as she weighed my words, and I let my will be my convincing argument, still her eyes grew puzzled and she spoke vaguely, "I will have to discuss this with my priest."

"Yes, you will," I whispered and she rose into the night.

I took to my post the following day waiting patiently and, late in the afternoon, the commanding officer came fuming into the hall, righteous in urgent need to get his staff organised for an unexpected visit from the Gestapo leader. We were set to absurdly domestic tasks and by the time the sun began its descent into night, the buildings of the headquarters were shining in anticipation of the imminent arrival. An hour after sunset, in the deep twilight, a motorcade of SS military cars came noisily outside the building and I sat at my post with a casual eye on the entrance.

The Captain, who had been waiting anxiously outside, came into the hall eagerly ushering his guests into his domain and the appraisal of his staff. The junior officers snapped to attention and I rose, catching the bespectacled eye of General Himmler. By his side the cool glow of vampire light leaned close to his ear, the woman I had spoken to, smartly dressed in army grey, whispered my name and he nodded. The party disappeared into the Captain's office, I counted six vampires in their number and, as my colleagues resumed their evening tasks, I sat waiting to be called.

They made me wait for perhaps an hour, I could hear the muted conversation between my Captain and the Gestapo General. Himmler's voice was high and nasal and full of Nazi arrogance, almost resistant to my recruitment to his group and little wonder since I would take his place in the coven hierarchy. The Captain though was full of my praises, eager to accommodate such austere company and bolster his standing in Himmler's eyes even though he was quite ignorance of his leader's plans. Eventually, I was called into the office.

Vampire essence filled the dark room, curling cool around the vibrant glow of their human counterpart, dancing in the scent of recent death, alluring and weaving the energy of a subtle spell.

"This is Sergeant Khess," the Captain introduced me as I closed the door and he beckoned me to step before the solid desk.

I nodded briefly to the Gestapo leader, his light eyes narrow in suspicion and then I gazed past him to the woman, casting off easily the group's attempt to catch me in their magic. Himmler's eyes grew wide as he realised the sudden impotence of his gambit and shortly dismissed the Captain.

"Sit," he ordered and I took the chair before the desk. The silence grew thick for a moment as he sat, pinched faced behind steepled fingers, examining me.

I smiled and watched the woman, her eyes were shining and her thoughts full of excitement at the prospect of using my power, *What is your name?* I let my question flow directly onto the veil of her mind and her mouth grew round with surprise.

"Kitty tells me you know of a ritual that may aid our Führer and Fatherland," Himmler spoke at last.

"Yes," I sighed, but it was Kitty that leaned forward from beside her leader and pinned me with her curiosity.

"Who are you?" she asked quietly.

Himmler turned to her savagely, "I thought I told you that I would interview this man!" he snapped. Do not undermine my authority, woman."

She laughed lightly at his aggression and he turned scarlet with rage. "Heinrich, do be quiet," she said and took the fury from his aura so absolutely that he sat back defeated. "I think there is more than we are aware of in the presence of Herr Khess," and she turned back to me. "Why do you seek to join us?"

"I have my own reasons," I replied letting my half-truth convince them, "but suffice it to say, that I would call on the power of the Devil and I have felt energy in your group to withstand his coming. As I told you last night, Kitty, I have walked my path for many centuries and never before have I seen such a bold manipulation of the hidden realms. It will take all your strength and the ages of my magic to control the beast."

Himmler's eyes became shrewd, "You are not mortal?"

I laughed openly, "No, foolish human. I am Julian."

Understanding came suddenly to the woman's angelic face. "But you are nothing more than a myth."

"Then so are you, daughter."

She nodded with a greedy smile, old energies of ancient knowing flooded her cool essence and she gave to the others, who had listened attentively, her understanding of my nature. *I have heard in ancient tales, that he is the most ancient of us, born before all and the oldest to survive.*

I caught her thoughts and smiled, adding nothing of my own to cover her scant knowledge of me, but let her peers be content under an easy spell of seduction and, held by my will, their reserve disappeared.

"Well then, Herr Khess," Himmler's round cheeks bounced into a sly smile. "It seems I must relinquish my position to you. But remember, I am still leader, you are under my command. Do you understand?"

I smiled and inclined my head, barely satisfying his ego and released my will and my spell of blind trust to feed in their minds on the very essence of their own souls. "Then, when do we begin?"

I was taken out to where a small fleet of vehicles waited for Himmler and his entourage, though I would have collected my belongings before leaving.

I could feel the younger vampires stir with blood lust and Kitty ushered me quickly under the pressure of their need. As the cars ranged north and east through Berlin and into the surrounding countryside, I sat with the Gestapo head, Kitty and three of the senior officers and we travelled for perhaps an hour to the outskirts of a small bleak town. An ancient castle stood on a wild hill, stark against the frozen night sky and light from within gave the entrance the blazing maw of a skull. The motorcade passed under the jagged teeth of its wrought iron barrier drawn up in anticipation of our arrival and came to rest in the cold stone refuge of the courtyard. The occasional light globe cast obscure shadows across rough grey walls.

Kitty showed me to my rooms, a private suite furnished in the rich antiquated fashion of the castle and indeed, so worn with time that a sense of permanence promised cool haven from the light of day.

"This is most adequate," I said, smoothing a velvet drape against the deep narrow archer holes, glazed against the ravages of nature.

"Your things will be brought tomorrow," Kitty's voice was breathless and her essence rose as I turned into her gaze.

"I will see to them myself," I replied and fed on her cool fire, encouraging her foolish passion.

Her eyes became confused, "But... but, surely you will sleep with us in the day, Julian?"

I smiled, chill in my soul, "I am not as you are, Kitty, I am much older than that. I need no refuge from the sun," and touched her with a measure of eternity.

"I..." She was cut off by a high keen, echoing from some far-off place in the castle and was caught for a moment by the sound. When it faded away she turned to the door, *Damn, I told them to wait,* the thought flew frustrated across her mind and to me she said in a ploy of indifference, "Come, Julian, I believe dinner is served."

I knew this moment would come, I steeled myself as Kitty led me through dark corridors, and I resisted every step toward the horror that I knew awaited in the company of vampire kind. In the mute glow of electric light, the gaunt essence of many mortals lay littered against the cold walls of a dungeon and Kitty's brothers feasted on the living blood of their unwitting victims. Mindless, revolting hunger consumed the air in the chamber, cold as the underground crypt and as poisonous as the creatures that dined on the failing lights of human life. Kitty moved into the room and joined the feast, but I stood by the entrance and watched the methodical feeding of the vampires. Mercilessly they took the essence of their prey until the mortal bodies grew dull with the loss of blood, then left the victims to recover as best they could. By the scars and bite marks, I could tell these humans had been kept for some time; a well-stocked larder.

"Will you not join us, Julian?" Kitty turned her evil eyes to me, raising her bloody mouth from her feeding.

I smiled, masking my revulsion with a veil of interest. "I have not seen the habits of my children for many years," I replied and she held a hand out in invitation.

I moved across the room and descended upon the subdued light of an unconscious human, taking just a little, enough to antidote the rending lust that was rising within my frozen core and give me control over awful terror that accompanied the reality of my evil creations.

I rose in the strength of fresh blood and I turned to the eyes of Kitty and her brothers watching me. The deep and vibrant eyes of the vampire witch burned under a spell of my being and although her open admiration could so repulse me to want to take her fickle life, I fostered the lie of her feelings and fed that shallow attraction from my will.

By sunrise I had beguiled the group, after that awful moment where I proved myself, Kitty claimed a place by me and even Himmler, though his thoughts were motivated singly by greed of my power, eagerly sought to command my attention.

They showed me the castle's other dungeon space where cold stone had been carved to support the rotunda of a magic circle; the place where they worked with energies that had called to me far across the sea. The sombre grey chamber reeked of the rape of mortal essence and the air itself was tinted with blood, and I could hear the memories of mortal screams that fixed the dungeon as a portal to hell. A smile touched my lips as I examined the room, surely the power that was commanded by the coven was the key to my success.

Kitty stood nervously playing with an errant lock as I meandered the anti-sunwise round and, when she saw my pleasure, she said duskily, "I'm glad you like our temple."

I moved to take her arm and turned with the group to the door. "Yes," I said softly and the chamber took up the sound, "though I am by far more interested to see the rituals that you do than merely the space in which they are performed."

Himmler stepped pompous beside me. "And so you shall," he said, nasal thin and peering up into my ice cool gaze.

The vampires were easy to control. The novelty of my ancient being and the power of my will utterly seduced them and so completely did they give me their trust that I came and went as I pleased. Even when my belongings were brought to the castle, there were no questions asked over my possession of a British radio. Kitty became totally infatuated, spending every moment with me, imagining love in the spell that I wove around her and every day I tested my influence over her energies, until I could feel so complete a trust that she did not once question my command. Himmler, he I chose for even more special a place. As the coven's only mortal component, I paid him attention easily veiled under a spell of flattery. Since I had found the strength of my descendants in the corruption of the vampires, so I sought to invest the mortal corruption of my "father" upon the visage of this human. I had the coven perform a number of rituals with Himmler as the focal point and as they gave up their power under the guise of my simple ego spell, so I worked the calling of that ancient druid's energy into him. Himmler grew in his arrogance and false security, his assumption of my friendship kept him in close company and I tested my manipulation of him and his abominable group by their insidious affection for me.

Time passed too quickly, the wheeling of the heavens stole each day and Mister Woo's conjunction grew awfully close. Himmler carried himself with the bearing of a true magician, power that he knew came from me, and Kitty too had taken on the arrogance of her Margueritte, her ancient mother. I used my powers without scruple, mercilessly dominating the group even though I assured them constantly of their own prowess, yet under my spell they missed my double cross completely. I had them cast a horoscope and though I firmly planted the date of Mister Woo's conjunction deeply in their minds, I let them imagine that they had produced the time of the Devil's greatest hour for themselves. So the date was set and our rite would be enacted to create the turning point of the war. The night when they would loose Satan in the name of their Führer and Fatherland and purge the world of the unworthy.

I sent word to England, easily avoiding detection under the spell I had cast, and my report was taken by the Prime Minister's office with grave acceptance. Indeed they worked much of their strategy with my advice in mind. As the night of the ritual drew nearer, I spoke again to the leaders of Britain's army and was impressed to discover that they had mobilised the entire country in preparation for the full-scale attack that would follow on the next day.

A chill of anticipation rose in me as I waited out the days, strengthening the strands of my spell over the coven until the time was right.

I sat in my room as I heard the vampires rise and move into the temple, readying themselves and each small detail as they waited for the arrival of the leaders. Himmler had left the day before to fill the vampires' requirement of young virgin blood for the rite's so-called finale. I watched flames licking across the hearth, my hearing keen against the sounds that issued from the occupants of the ancient buildings and the countryside beyond. When the Nazi car came up the road that led to the castle, I donned my ritual robe and hid a small vial of magical fluid among its folds and then left the room and made my way quickly to join the night creatures in the chamber below the castle. Kitty came smiling to me and I took her cool hand to stand like Emperor and Queen before the altar in anticipation of Himmler's arrival with the sacrifices.

The screams of terrified women echoed down the stairwell and into the temple long before the party came into the vault and Kitty turned to me with an ironic smile. "What power Heinrich has," she whispered close to my ear, cold mirth in her words and her voice was rich with the same derision as Margueritte had had, long ago, before I had taken her insidious life. "He has certainly managed to secure willing victims."

I quelled her with a gaze, giving a thought to her mind as the mortal flames of life fire descended to the temple floor, *Do not disturb the energies here, Kitty, now is not the time for cynicism.*

The Nazi leader came, dragging two young naked mortal females on long chains to the edge of the circle and bowed before the vision of Kitty and me. Two young vampires took the shackles of the sacrifices and pulled the virgins heavily to cast them prostrate and rendered unconscious in the centre of the temple. The coven arranged themselves in the carefully planned orchestration of our rite and Kitty began the ceremony, opening the circle and drawing the black energies of hell into the vault. Carefully I fuelled each participant with power to complete the energies I had for months prepared in them. As the group performed their well-orchestrated parts, I walked slowly around the cool dungeon and muttered the final invocation of my own spell. The young vampires seemed to grow in the power of every life taken by my insidious children. I called upon each one and the whirling heavens beyond the vault caught up my will and amplified it upon them until I could feel the beast stir under the focus.

A brief moment of panic descended then as I struggled to continue. I think the others must have felt that demon stir for a greedy light flew between them and, when my gaze fell upon their leaders, they too had fully accepted the parts I had manipulated them into. Kitty stood ablaze just like Margueritte, her countenance grown ancient and perverted, and I felt sick at the visage of that cursed one as she looked on with insane anticipation, and each vampire gave their lustful attention to the mortal women chained to the floor, and I too could feel the power of such insanity rise to hold me. Himmler stood, oblivious of the vampires' bloodlust, lost completely in the ego gratification of such power that had been called upon from my ancient father, that druid who had fallen victim to a curse as that which I had carried for much too long. The light in his eye called to mind a vision that I had seen of the madness with which the druid had wielded his power over my mother as he raped her beside that highway, distant in both time and space. Yet, for the sickness which the power of the vampires visited upon me, such a recollection and the similarity of Himmler's new madness was more terrible and indeed, I had to turn away.

"Julian?" It was Kitty, but her voice was not her own and its sudden confusion was a discord in the rite.

I heard demonic laughter.

"No," I almost shouted and turned with a hand raised to forestall her and set my jaw against my own weakness. "Continue!"

The vampires began a chant, their voices oozed with bloodlust that caught me in its power, I could feel the beast rising and its pleasure at being so consciously called forth. I raged in momentary battle, terribly afraid of its coming and then the unconscious forms of the two mortals caught my gaze. I groaned and felt my control weaken. Suddenly I was over one woman and even before I could hold myself in check, I felt the insane pleasure of her life blood in my mouth. I heard a gasp and looked up from the new corpse, some realisation of what their ritual was actually doing flew into Kitty's eyes and she stared at me in quick panic. Feminine, virgin blood coursed through me and I felt consciousness begin to recede.

"No!" I screamed and somehow, almost of its own volition, my hand found its way to the vial that lay hidden in a fold of my ritual robe. With a strain of the last moment of light, I unstoppered the bottle and swallowed its contents. And then...

...a vision of my first life...

A young scribe in a place of much power cared for and employed by a god, and given such a gift as only a god can give. And woe, how he put his own foolish lust and mortal ego above such responsibility as a god would ask of him. Before me then was played out his crime of corruption... and so too his next life—that of my father! Others, Julia, Jeremy, the terrible suicide that had claimed Justin! On and on, lives of corruption and poison, all fuelled by ignorance and the passion of the beast. And finally… a vision of my own self came before me and the satisfaction of the demon who had encouraged my own self condemnation and my awful fall into darkness.

Yet finally, and beaten by such terrible sight, something felt different, something had changed.

I fancied I could hear the beast screaming, crying, wailing…

And then, after an aeon of darkness, all was still…

In the darkness, when all had passed, a light grew until the translucent figure of my beloved Niamh came smiling into the void.

"Julian," she whispered. "Now it is time to begin your journey home. Now is the time to be free of your burden, free from the shackles of past lives, and now truly to live a life of your choosing."

I looked into her fathomless gaze, "And what of our love?" that which was always my heart's desire.

"Ah, my beloved, this too with time will come to pass. Know now, my love, you are free from the beast, and the pull he has given you to take the life of innocents, but not from the nature of your own being. Let the wisdom you have gained in your life protect you, for surely if you invoke him, he will rise again. There is another step to take on that road home and, always and forever more, it is your choice to take such a step. I will be here, eternally watching you, my indestructible flame of human beauty, but this is your path and yours alone to walk. I love you, Julian."

Her eyes shone and her heavenly smile flowed with unquenchable love and I reached out to hold her, but the currents of energy that held me to the circle beyond the void, grew suddenly dim and disturbed. Niamh vanished from my view and then I blinked and was standing once again in the incense filled temple of the vampire coven...

A human scream carried terror around the circle, I looked to see the petrified form of the remaining hysterical virgin, awake and witnessing the awful end of the ritual. Around the circle edge, the shrivelled bodies of the undead stood gaunt and lifeless, drained grey under the strain of my magic, held only to life by the contact of my will. I turned to the figure before me, she that had been the oldest and strongest of the coven, although now she stood like a desiccated corpse, the remnant essence of her life gone.

"And now, my daughter," I spat, almost gleeful at her demise. "See what comes from your blind ignorance, your foolish stumbling in my realm. See what you have called."

A spark lit hot in my gaze and in that instant a blaze took the undead, consuming each form into a burning pyre and drawing curdling screams that echoed the dreadful and symbolic release of my gravest crime, a testament to the passing of the beast. A flaming corpse crumbled and fell into a heap against a wall and caught a heavy drape that supported the Nazi insignia, unnatural fire devoured the fuel and quickly set the temple alight.

The sound of a mortal scream caught me and I moved to where the unfortunate woman lay, still shackled on the floor. Smoke billowed from the growing flames and shrouded the air, I picked up the mortal who kicked and screamed in my grasp and, carrying the struggling form, I dashed through the temple. Up and out of the chamber, I burst into the darkened courtyard of the castle, amid plumes of foul scented smoke and I lay my burden on the smooth cold cobbles. I touched the mind of the woman and she fell into a deep moment of sleep under my will, to heal and forget this night, and return to her home without ever remembering the ordeal she had endured. I took to my room, quickly shedding the ritual robes in favour of my own silk and velvet and, checking only to ensure the position of my barrier from the vital light of the sun, I left the dreadful castle.

Rising high above plumes of black smoke, I flew into the night sky and over the road that led down and exposed from where the ancient building was being cleansed, far from the exorcism of evil performed below its blazing visage, and the lights of a speeding car came below my sight. I dropped to the ground in its path and let my will take the mind of the human driver, bringing the fleeing car and its passenger to a halt before me. A bullet flew past my face, whistling through the writhing tendrils of my hair and I followed the essence of its trail back to the pistol in Himmler's trembling hand. The metal heated by my will erupted into blistering flame and, screaming, he let the weapon fall from the car.

"This day your war ends, General. Remember well what you have witnessed and what you called through your own ignorant desires," I let my quiet words ring through his terrified mind. "And remember always my vow to you—I will find you and kill you if I hear you have uttered my name and cast you into that place of terror as I have with all those who would think to use my dreadful magic. You have not the strength to dabble so arrogantly in my realm. Summon me again and your punishment will be everlasting." I raised a hand and let my finger point an eternal echo in his mind,

"Remember, foolish mortal. Remember this day well and remember always my oath!" and I rose from the roadway, releasing his stupefied driver and flew westward into the night.

Dawn chased on my heels as I fled across the countryside, high against the scattered clouds that filtered the false light of the sun, and I sped my way on into the alluring peace of the night sky. Over forests and plains, following the paths of roads and rivers as they led their way to the sea, a hundred villages and cities gave their scant light forth to my passing, I flew on night's wings to the Channel and freedom in the success of my awful task.

Chapter 17

I made my way along the coast of England, easily crossing primitive defences on both borders of the sea. Scant moonlight followed the rugged edge of my homeland as I travelled back to the city I had known and earthly haven with mortals I had so many times called family. I flew high above the magnificent southern coast to the headland that marked the entrance to Portsmouth and turned from the sea to make my way over the outer districts. The blacked-out roads were no barrier for the blaze of human fire that I followed to the dark inner-city streets and I came to land on the ruin of what had once been the fashion house.

I gazed over the site, a small plume of fresh dust clouded around my feet as I disturbed its resting place, the long arc of a missile's path blazing a terrible memory in the air above the street, whose corner ended at the great pile of debris. I searched the scene for any energy that may betray movement or life at the site in the moment it was destroyed, perhaps caught in the image that had imprinted itself there for eternity. To my relief there were no memories of humans to haunt the remnant of that grand building. I rose quickly and flew out to where the family mansion still sat, worn but not defeated amid summer gardens of its darkened estate and came to rest before the grand entrance. Large crosses of brown paper tape marked the blank windows as I moved across the shallow marble veranda and a click of the door handle arrested my hand as I reached for the bell pull. Large dark eyes came around the door frame, a young woman who had a look of the family likeness beckoned me inside. She peered nervously into the darkness behind me before closing the door.

"Julian," she whispered, her voice low with awe, "It's been so long."

"I have been to the city...." I began but she put a finger to her lips and beckoned me into the quiet of the family's private lounge.

"Come sit by the fire with me, I dare not make any noise out there. Those bombs come from nowhere."

We sat in chairs that huddled around a smoky oil heater, "What has happened to the family?" I asked, eager for news of Isabelle and her eyes became clouded.

"Mother and my grandparents are asleep with the little ones upstairs." She jerked her delicate chin over a shoulder and in her essence I saw tension rise.

"Tell me about Leon and Isabelle," I whispered, seeing melancholy grow in her mind and she weighed my request slowly.

"Did you know that Uncle Leon went to France?" she asked and I nodded. His call to the front line had been my last news of his progress and, indeed, the only letter I had received from the family since long before the war. Colour flushed her cheeks and she took a breath, "Well, he went to see Aunt Isabelle in Bolton while I was there visiting on holiday, and they had an almighty argument. She said she didn't want to lose him to the bloody Germans, but he left any way. They never spoke again.

"Isabelle was heartbroken and sent so many letters. But of course they were returned to the fashion house when they couldn't reach him. I have them all here," and she crossed the room to the library shelves and retrieved a parcel of envelopes tied with a deep red ribbon of silk. "I kept them. I never read them, I thought perhaps he would return one day. Anyway, Leon was commissioned to his post in France—he sent a telegram to Aunt Elizabeth, I put it with the letters—and went to aid the allies over there. Three months ago a German air-raid took out his post and he was killed." Her voice was flat with the memory of her uncle and tears came into her eyes. "But Isabelle, I visited her after the family had been informed of Leon's loss. She was just not suited to those cold northern winds, she got pneumonia within days of the news and never recovered. Oh, Julian, she just gave up hope when she heard of Leon death, she thought she had lost everything." Her words broke in her throat and she wept.

I sat silent under the weight of memory that flooded through Belle's mind, the delicate alabaster of a cold porcelain doll that had once been my beautiful Isabelle, lying still in the cool ivory silk of her last bed then cold earth taking her away from me forever. I hadn't even said goodbye and now she was gone and her brother too. A cold sting came behind my eyes and a tear coursed its way onto my cheek, the ghost of Niamh and vision of Isabelle became one in the memory of all those that I had loved and always had to leave, and frozen isolation took my soul.

"What of the fashion house?" I asked, my words flat and cold as I regained control of my weary heart.

Belle looked at me softly, "It was the very day we heard of Leon's death, Uncle Jules was closing up early. The bomb heard him closing the front door and he hardly got out before it struck. Honestly, Julian, those Nazi weapons, I'd swear they were possessed by the devil himself."

The light of false dawn came onto the edge of my awareness and I was glad to cover my tortured eyes in the cool barrier that covered my heart too but I could not hide completely my sorrow in the sight of my companion, her young beauty too constant a reminder of love, and I turned from her gentle gaze. "You at least, my lovely Belle, need not be afraid of the war now, I have ended the insanity of the Nazi forces."

Her face clouded in confusion, "The war is ended?"

I nodded slowly, "Today will be the end of it. At least now there will be no more blood from this family shed in such human lunacy."

Realisation crept over her mind and her smile shone forth as she jumped out of her chair. "I have to wake the others," and she dashed to the door. "Please, Julian, wait for me to bring them."

I laughed coldly as she left the room. Where would I go if I left this place? Once again the earth had turned and I, an ancient relic of a time long gone, was left to make my way alone through an evolving and increasingly alien world, to yearn for love and life which I knew could never be mine. A vision of Niamh flowed alluring across my memory, the sight of a ghost in the midst of the void. *There is another step to take on that road home. I will be here, eternally watching you. I love you, Julian.* Her words echoed across space and time, giving my ancient pain blind hope in an old promise of love.

The excited family came into the lounge, Taylor infants flocked around my chair, the older grandparents who I had known to be suffragettes and young men of power, now sat leisurely in the comfortable chairs that marked them as heads in the clan hierarchy. I talked to the middle generation who had been babes even after I had left the acquaintance of their parents, yet who carried the family legacy of my knowing with such pride and nobility.

We spoke of Leon's commission and his bravery in the allied effort, his honour in the gravest hour as he helped the French resistance to oust Hitler from their midst. He had been betrayed by a double agent and marked by the SS in both France and England, and that had indeed been the cause of the bomb attack on the family empire. German spies in London had gained information on the business and trade fleet, both had been destroyed on the same day, and although the Nazi agents had been caught, the fashion empire lay in ruins.

It amused me a little to see resolve in the family rise anew from the ashes of disaster. We spoke of the war and hardships they had endured. The family traced their struggle and an era that united the line in an even greater bond than they had known in other times.

Finally they spoke of Isabelle's small funeral in a cold northern graveyard. A tiny church she had found on her tours of the rugged beauty of lands beyond the Pennine Range. It had marked her mind in its ancient design, which used a graveyard for its fourth arm, and the quaint little village of Daisy Hill that boasted such a building of antiquity. She had rejected the family plot in favour of the cool idyll of moss-covered graves and her last days spent convincing young Belle to let her be buried where her heart could find peace, far from the reminder of what she had lost. As the sun reached into the heavens, the family made off to lunch and I was left once again in the company of the young beauty who sparked the memory of her lovely aunt.

"I need to see her," I spoke softly watching Belle's graceful face.

"I know," she replied, flushing under my gaze. "I'll drive you there if you wish."

A smile played with my lips, wary of another new friendship, "I would like that."

Her eyes deepened as her cheeks coloured and she rose from the chair excitedly, "If we leave now we should make it there today."

I let her energy carry me along and assented to her plan, waiting as she excused herself briefly to explain our outing to the family and change for the cooler weather of England's northwest, then from the house and out to a car that lived in a converted stable.

We drove the quiet lanes of England's countryside, as fast as the winding roads would allow the car to move, taking an old route that Belle had not used in months, but her hands were sure at the wheel and the summer landscape turned cool as we sped northwards.

Our conversation was light and scarce on the journey through the ever-changing country, Belle spoke to me of her aunt's struggle with the malady that had sent her north in the years even before her young niece's birth. In the dark days of the war, she gave the Bolton mansion over to the care of wounded soldiers, refitting the entire building as a hospital and moving her rooms into the cellar so she could live near her work. The lovely lady had been a worthy recipient of her esteemed name. My young companion spoke in awe of Isabelle and her achievements. Belle knew legends of earlier days she had learned at the knee of her aunt, the sad romance of a love that could never be. I am sure she would have said more, but often I was taken to brooding on the flowing road as it took me on towards another life and for many hours we travelled in silence.

As sunlight left the horizon and I took my barrier from the mortal lights of the world, we came into a small dark town who were as yet unaware of the end of the war. Belle slowed the car to pass along its dreary streets, our dim headlights attracting the glow of mortal fire behind the veil of darkened windows. We turned around an odd bend that joined into an intersecting road, stopped before the dark visage of a walled church and, as I opened the door, the whisper of a breeze caught my senses. I heard the sound of ages of death.

Belle rounded the car and walked with me as I let us into the church garden, following the short path around the ancient building and into the graveyard. Isabelle waited for me, sitting in sorrow above the fresh stone of her resting place.

The shade saw my approach and floated to the boundary of her burial mound. "I have been waiting for you, Julian, I knew you would come. You never did say goodbye and I couldn't leave without hearing it from you."

Stinging tears welled through the memory of love, binding eternally with thoughts of my beloved Niamh and the loss of my beautiful Chinese princess and all of my centuries alone. *I never told you of my love for you, beautiful Isabelle,* my thoughts flowed to the shade. She turned from me, a chill wind sprang around the grave and caught stirring in my hair.

"After all that happened, how could you say that to me?" Her words echoed harsh on the frozen breeze.

Belle shivered against the cool night oblivious to the ghost. "I've seen enough of this place, Julian, I'll wait for you in the car," and she made her way from the graveyard.

The closing car door shocked a sound into the still and sadly I said, "I could not cause you any more pain than what I have already given you, I wish I could have spared you even that."

"What more is there to pain than that which keeps me here?" the spectre whispered.

"I did not know."

"You have lived so long, Julian," Isabelle came close to me and studied my face intently as she sought to hold the memory in her gaze. "Will you ever find peace?" Her words dropped like frozen tears into a well of eternity.

And then she was gone and the mournful cry of chill night wind took the place of her aethereal voice.

I passed through the graveyard and into the muffled shelter of Belle's car, closing the door hard against the rising wind and she started the engine. "Are you alright, Julian?" she asked quietly as we pulled back onto the street, I nodded and we made for the Taylor estate not five miles away.

The road turned into a long and darkened driveway that led deep into the grounds, and to the door of the converted manor house. A lingering essence of my lovely Isabelle still was caught in the presence of its building. A guard challenged us at the door until he recognised the slight form of my companion and held at ease as we approached.

"Why, Miss Taylor, no one told me you were coming." He eyed me cautiously, "I don't believe I've met your gentleman friend."

"Come on, Tom, haven't you heard? The war is over." Belle stepped up to him and gave him a gentle peck belying an old friendship.

"You're kidding, Belle." The young soldier was astonished.

My companion laughed and poked him squarely in the ribs. "You should listen to the radio more often, Private Jones," and she walked past him to the door, beckoning me to follow.

She led me through clinical corridors, smelling of old blood and disinfectant, and the tang of diseased flesh rose occasionally from the doors along its length. A small back stairwell led down into the building's lower depths and the cellar that had been Isabelle's final home. I pulled the dust covers from furniture as we walked into the darkened lounge, Belle flicked on a light switch and the silk lined room was illuminated, deep and soothing around me.

"She decorated the lounge when she first arrived here and still had hope, it was her wish that we keep the room for you if you ever returned." The young woman crossed the plush deep carpet to an unassuming cabinet that disguised a well-stocked bar and retrieved a dusty bottle. "Would you care for a brandy?"

Belle left the next day after introducing me to the Commanding officer of the army hospital. She would have stayed for me, but I could see in her eyes that she needed to be with her family as news of the allied victory began to sweep Britain so she made me promise to make use of the money I had invested in the family's other enterprises, and left me in the lonely confines of my cellar below the hospital.

I sorted through the letters that Belle had left with me, poignant with sorrow of the woman who had left me in such confused anguish. Isabelle's conversations to her brother so often slipped into reminiscing over the time we had spent together and the pain that ended that idyll washed me in torrents of cold isolation. I let weeks pass consumed by the memories that had led me to this place and eventually took to discovering the estate left for my comfort by the caring intentions of my lovely lost companion.

Isabelle had brought volumes from the library of the family's estate, those that we had studied together in more innocent days. I discovered that many of the books that I had made comment upon and even those I had mentioned only in passing Isabelle had brought here. Even so, I found among the shelves, the slim volume of tales translated by my own hand, a curio of my origins, and tucked into the last sheaf of paper, I found Mister Woo's Bolton address. I debated with myself at great length at the wisdom of seeking out the old alchemist, wondering that he may have succumbed to his great many years. Yet when I did finally go to visit him, he seemed not to have changed at all. His apprentice in this era was a young granddaughter come from China who had a sense of me as Gregory had. Never did I suggest our working together or mention what I had done to succeed in my first quest and neither did Mister Woo or his granddaughter and so our acquaintance, as little as it was, remained guarded. Still, the old alchemist supplied me without question the needs for me to take up the orchestration of my "second" quest and I began careful preparations for the ending of my eternity.

I made from the privacy of my lounge occasionally to secure supplies for the needs of my carefully planned ritual and I watched the country build again around the shell of post-war England. The century turned on its axis, flowing through the changes of the fifth decade, and the country grew at an astonishing rate as the population boomed against the old memories of war. The charges of the veteran's hospital died or returned to their homes, as nature dictated and I was approached by a group to alter the house once again, into the nurturing environment of a maternity home. Of course, I agreed with the conversion, amused that I should finally be living below the fresh sounds of new life and, as easy years passed, I walked the corridors at night gazing at the innocent babies that slept in the nurseries and the feeding mothers that came when they cried.

I spent that time in more freedom than I had ever known in my dark existence. The pull to feed from the living essence of mortal beings receded far from my knowing and, although the vibrant lights of human fire still reminded me of my awful nature, I found final peace away from the insanity of my being.

I even took to writing my memoirs, laying down on paper all the pain I had endured through my ill-fated life, but when I had finished and re-read all I had lived, I threw the blank reminder of my past into the fire and was glad when it was consumed in the roaring blaze. I think it must have been that which was the greatest encouragement in my dedication to the completion of my journey and final ending of my awful eternity. I commissioned Mister Woo to fashion a silver knife, a complex claw like dagger that supported five finger long, razor edged blades. We designed the weapon, debating throughout the night its indestructible construction, a weapon so manufactured to take the fury of what would be my life's final act. Carefully I orchestrated a death so clean as not to cause the stirring of the beast I had imprisoned within my ageless soul and, when I sensed the coming of morning's twilight and my companion's fatigue, I bid the old man good night. As I stepped out into the gathering mist, I could sense the presence of another.

I saw the aura of a vampire at the mouth of the alley turned purposefully toward him and came abreast of his position in the darkness. "It would be wise for you to stay in the shadows, vampire, to cross my path could mean death to you," and I let the full weight of my words be known to him. Yet, there was something deeper in what I felt from the creature beside me and my magic faltered. He stepped carefully before me and I was caught in the sight of him.

A mirror in vampire kind stared defiantly into my eyes. He said, "Greetings, Julian, I am Matthew," and I was shocked into stillness. "Please don't be alarmed, I have waited a long time for this moment."

But twilight moved toward the eastern horizon, warning me of the nearness of dawn. That call must have touched my twin as well, his life was in grave danger now. We were both aware that his gambit was a dangerous one, "You will need to find shelter and soon, Matthew."

"Yes," he replied, futility in his voice.

"Come with me and I will protect you this day."

I turned and rose into the first faint rays of false sunlight, flying urgently toward my home and came to rest by the cellar's outside door. I threw it open and Matthew flew by me, disappearing deep into the very heart of the apartment and, when I barred the door and retreated to the sanctuary of my library, I found him folded into an armchair, still like the dead.

I sat watching him as the hours of sunlight forced my retreat behind the sanity of deep tinted glass. Without the eerie fire of vampire essence, the breathless body was little better than a corpse, only the occasional flicker of an eyelid marked the presence of life in the face of day. I wondered about the coming of this being to me. I felt the same closeness to him as I had to Justin and even little Meena and still I had a recollection, a memory of a vision, that had this holder of my soul taken and recreated by a creature of my own hell spawned curse. Was it just foolishness that had me offer him shelter? I intruded on his dreams once when his eyes betrayed growing consciousness, but only revealed thrill in the coming of night, and so I sat and waited for him to wake.

At sunset he was instantly aware, a waking that was disciplined to perfection.

"So you rise, Matthew, brother of my unfortunate soul," I began conversationally. "I would like to know why and how you found your way to me."

He smiled briefly, a mannerism that plucked at the cords of familiarity in my cold soul and told me the tale of his existence in the dark. My fair likeness spoke of his journey from convict to vampire and he even spoke of a meeting with Isabelle many years after she had left me in Portsmouth and through all the perils of the world to our meeting. "I don't know what has driven me so to find you, Julian, but even fate has played a hand in the circumstances of my coming. And now that I am here, I have a feeling that you could perhaps use my help."

I could not resist volunteering a smile for the energy of the young man. Though I could not deny that, coincidentally, I had met him on the same night as I had made plans for the manufacture of the knife that was to be my end, maybe his presence was necessary to my success. "So, you would help me with something that would be disastrous to you if it fails and deadly if it succeeds?" I would give him fair warning of the danger he courted.

He just nodded his fair head and I could tell that he already had an idea of what I had in mind. "I saw your life through a spirit dream once, Julian. I have known of your need to quell the demon that resides in your heart, and also, I was near the castle where you performed its exorcism. I was caught in the backlash of that rite, I'm aware how dangerous it is to know you."

I set to teaching my counterpart the things he would need to know to be of use in the ritual. It took months to educate Matthew in the art of alchemy, the mixing of chemicals with enough strength to quell my instinct for self-preservation. The formality devised to empower the ritual with the energy of cosmic forces chosen carefully to support my work was difficult to pass on to even the brightest student in that short time and I pushed Matthew's education unmercifully. I introduced him to Mister Woo and he proved to be useful in the creation of the blade I had commissioned from the old man. When the stars moved in harmony with the metal, Matthew helped with its forging. He often spoke of my motivation for this rite but never questioned why I would be so fastidious in my preparations and carried out my will obediently, as if he had a lifetime of experience with me and knew me well. But the closer the ritual became, the more I was aware of another trick of Fate.

I had taken my young counterpart so easily into my heart and his presence filled that cold void as others had done before. Now with the end of my unnatural existence in sight, I had been given a companion that could have walked beside me forever but could I continue forever, even with Matthew beside me? On the evening of what could prove to be my last night, I could not face to be with him when he woke with such a burning question in my mind. So instead, I wandered the corridors of the hospital above my apartment, letting myself be distracted by the cries of new life.

A young woman came into the hospital in the evening, a good auger for the success of what I had planned. Her agony of labour strained her beautiful features under the effort of her second birth. I wasted the hours before the exact alignment I needed, sitting with her young husband in the waiting room of the hospital. We talked of sailing and the ocean, the career in Britain's merchant navy that took him so often from his wife and young son, and as the night moved on with the struggle of birth, I let him see the love that he missed by being away from his family.

I left the young man, when the calm of the half-moon came upon the earth, with no clear answer to my dilemma but, even so, I could see fate's insidious play. In even my friendship with my counterpart, eternity spread out mocking before me. Resigned, I made my way into the incense filled chamber of my cellar temple, I had prepared it carefully during the day and left instructions for Matthew to ready himself for the rite. Descending the stairs into the dim light of candles that had lit his preparation, the fair and beautiful vampire stood robe garbed and holding another, which he offered for me to don but when I looked into his ice cool eyes, I was thrown into confusion over the finality of what we were about to do.

"Matthew, you know tonight will mean both of our ends," I began, but he stopped me with a sad smile.

"Yes, Julian, I have read that volume that you have cherished. Brother Tiberias is fairly sure of the demise of vampire kind. The way to destroy the infestation is to get to the root. You, the father of this evil breed, tricked by fate through centuries, tonight you will end this atrocity. Vampires will be no more and you too will be free of this life."

His words stirred me, preparing me at last for what was to come, his conviction in justice was powerful and called me into action. I let him help me into the black silk robe, and together we took our places before the altar that sat mute and waiting, and on it, the cold dull shine of my carefully constructed dagger. He anointed me with mandrake oil, an elixir prepared from the root of a betony plant that I had grown for the rite. Plumes of hallucinogenic heat swirled in vibrant curls from its touch on my skin and we used that first breach of the world of man to open a sacred space between the realms. Matthew gave me a small vial and I swallowed the contents, affected by drugs both inside and out to hold the influence of the beast in check. I had ensured the prison of that demon with my ritual in Germany but could not guarantee its imprisonment without aid should the rite proceed as I planned. I took up the mantra that we had learned together for this time and focussed on instigating my will over the mild euphoria that came in a side effect to the narcotic. The planets moved across the heavens and over the dark void of my soul and I could feel an almost audible click when the alignment suddenly came into favour of the rite. Matthew stepped aside, eyeing closely the savage ritual blade as he waited for me to enact my one simple, yet vital part of the rite but, suddenly afraid, I hesitated. Memories of my life flashed potently before me, calling me into life and friendship and the lure of what could be...

...Away from my awful decision...

...The haze of the drug that was intended to rid me of my need for self-preservation, only served to confuse me more.

My companion saw my change of heart and wide eyed turned on me, "Julian, you may not get another chance, the time is right. Now!"

But I was afraid of his strength and tried to pull away, "I cannot, I am afraid."

"But you must, my friend. If you and I are ever to find peace, you must take that step now!" He pulled me toward him and took me in an awful embrace, "Forgive me, Julian, it is the only way."

Grey are the veils of life between life.
Life is gone.
Niamh is with me.
Love takes my hand and smiles.
Gone now are the visions of memories and centuries of pain.

Soft mist moves me along with my lovely Niamh, she carries me on sweet sounds of heaven's music through this world of half formed shadows.

"See this?" she asks, her eyes moving to show me something hiding under the veil.

"No."

Her hand comes to my lips and she puts her finger to my mouth, "Shh, don't tell."

Her touch moves something in me and all my memories have gone, only Niamh and the warmth of love found anew and the echo of her sweet voice saying, "One day, my love, you will see, we will be together until the end of time."

Birth. Pain. Life again.

Grey gives way to painful light striking hard on eyes unused to the cold light of the world.

Life?

I cry. Oh, God, not again!

Epilogue

I woke with the setting sun and opened my slate blue eyes to the dim light of candles. The alcove where I lay was shrouded and still. I tasted the atmosphere as I rose to sit on the edge of the bed, the apartment was quiet. Only the scent of candle wax and incense touched the air; Julian was absent.

On the dressing chair opposite lay a neatly folded pile of cloth and ominously a note lay on the table behind. I smiled, but the smile was laced with sadness, Julian had moved the chair so I would see it immediately when I woke and so I had been tacitly given my first instruction. I donned the black garment and as I shrugged into the silk folds, it took on life and became a ceremonial robe, weighed already with the gravity of what would unfold as the night passed. The note was written in Julian's usual graceful style and read almost conversationally, though I knew that the intention had been anything but light when the note was written.

Matthew,

Forgive me if my instructions are blunt, you know quite well the importance of our planning on this night. If you feel any stirring to feed please do so before you robe. (But I had fed to gluttony the night before, quite knowing the danger of appetite in the coming ritual and so now, gratefully, I felt no such need.) *I have arranged the temple and set the mundane elements of the circle, the knife you will see I have cleansed and laid on the altar. Please attend to the incense and candles, and meditate in the fashion we have studied. I will return when the hour is upon us.*

Thank you, my friend,
J

I raised eyes from the contemplation of Julian's words and caught a reflection in the dressing mirror. In typical Victorian style, even the sleeping alcove of the small cellar apartment still reflected the refinement of the lady who had dwelled here and created it as the last home of Julian. The ancient vampire had altered nothing when he came to the northern English mansion many years before. The scent of Isabelle still lingered to haunt the silk lined vault. Heavy, set in sombre wood the long mirror reflected my dark robe and the beacon of light hair that sat atop my solid black form. My face was pale, almost a farce of the beauty of my friend. We looked alike enough to be called brothers but that was not the case. Whereas I had features which I considered adequate, Julian was an angel. The same proud brow and noble line of nose but as different as unfashioned clay and fine china. I turned away from my musing. *Let's not get caught up in irrelevant things tonight*, I thought and my dull blue eyes hardened as I set my mind completely to my simple, vital task.

I parted the curtain divide that split the sleeping alcove from the main room, the heavy velvet drape whispered over the carpet as I pushed it aside, stepped though and up to the edge of a clearly defined circle of salt. The salt threw a barrier up from the floor, invisible and intangible but filled with power as solid as a wall, its only entrance I had been told, would be opposite the stairs, the southeastern edge. I ringed the salt boundary, from which all the furniture had been pushed back and entered the sanctuary where the line was thinnest. The air was palpably heavier within the boundary, magic already glowing strangely about the manufactured space. I came before the altar, the few simple tools that lay on it glowed with the same intensity and the knife, when my eyes finally came to rest on its many blades and cold dark hue, glinted back with an almost conscious malevolence. Fearful enough it was to just look at, though the months of preparation and even the making of the blade itself were steeped in such a strength of will that I felt the anticipation of death whenever I held it.

I reached over the carmine altar cloth and scooped a spoonful of incense grains into the crucible and a plume of smoke billowed into the air. Sitting cross legged before the altar, I focused on the rising smoke, let my mind become as blank as I could manage and waited.

Time was endless, the candles burned, occasionally I rose to fuel the crucible and flick an eye to the length of the burning wicks and keep my task in hand and, when the stars far above turned to the coming of the junction that we had waited for, the upper door opened and closed quietly, and I rose to see Julian descend the stairs. Dressed in black velvet and touched at collar and cuff by the deep red protection he used as a defence from the sun, the vampire lord came face to face with my younger likeness. I held out the robe that had been placed by the circle edge as Julian stepped before me, his ice blue eyes were unreadable and his face unfathomable.

"Matthew, you know tonight will mean both of our ends," Julian's soft voice flowed rich into the room and struck at the cords of friendship in my heart.

In an awkward moment it seemed my mentor was attempting an apologetic explanation, but that was something I could not bear to hear now we were faced at last with the finale to all our work so I cut abruptly through Julian's thoughts and said with as much strength as I could muster, "Yes, Julian, I have read that volume that you have cherished. Brother Tiberias is fairly sure of the demise of vampire kind. The way to destroy the infestation is to get to the root. You, the father of this evil breed, tricked by fate through centuries, tonight you will end this atrocity. Vampires will be no more and you too will be free of this life." And I hoped that the false bravado of my speech would be enough to encourage success in this, our final hour.

A moment passed in silence, each a reflection of the other as we stood in symmetry before the altar and even more so when Julian clothed himself in the robe and became an almost perfect mirror. I felt a sudden rush of anticipation, the time was so nearly right and we would begin the ritual. And it would end, how?

Out of silence our voices began the simple focussing chant that Julian had decided would best attune our energies to the wheeling of the stars and with an almost visible change in the air around the temple, we began the rite.

Taking up a small bottle, I uncapped it and strong vapours flowed to mingle with the scent of incense. I dipped a finger into the swirling fluid and, although I had steeled myself for the sensation, the power of the hallucinogen crawled numbingly up my arm. I reached out and touched first the forehead of my mirror, my mentor, the one that I had taken an immortal lifetime to find and aid. Now was the time I had been coming to since the moment of my turning.

The simple anointing was planned to have an enormous impact on Julian, designed as a breach of his immortal curse, to take sensation from his undead flesh for long enough to perform the short and deadly rite. Julian had caged the devil that held residence in his soul—the very devil that caused the fall of all of his incarnations—and held it tenuously away from its influence over this, his lowest and most demonic lifetime. And now Julian planned to end the abomination that he had unwittingly aided, end his age-old life and rid the world forever of the evil of his unclean heart. With humility and the dreadful knowledge of the aim of the ceremony I knelt, chanting, and completed my task.

I stood, recapped the bottle and gratefully wiped the oil from my fingers, the stuff was insidious and I wondered how the ancient vampire was being affected. Taking up a small vial, I turned to see Julian, cool and flaming and somehow indistinct, a subtle haze about him rising to congeal in an aethereal cloud above. My eyes were drawn up to the cloud and a feeling of something ominous touched the base of my spine. Still I passed the deadly liquid to him and he drank the potion with ritual finality. I stepped back and next to the altar and the knife caught at my sleeve as I brushed across its many bladed end. I mused over its glinting malevolence for a moment as the ancient vampire struggled with the ingesting of the drugs.

Now it was Julian's turn, for him we had planned this simple part, and when it was done, we planned, there would be nothing left to do, no more, the end.

I raised my eyes expectantly and was caught by the immaterial cloud that had grown above Julian. My chant nearly faltered, the haze swirled and formed taking on its own substance. The sensation in my spine grew to a raging current and I was deathly afraid. A face began to grow in the mist, still Julian had not moved. Now I could see that our time was running out, the beast was struggling in the aether, struggling to form and regain control and still Julian stood unmoving.

"Julian, you may not get another chance, the time is right. Now!" I called urgently, my voice an unwelcomed break in the flowing rhythm of the chant, and the sound echoed awfully up to the forming image. I reached a hand out to urge Julian toward the knife and in the back of my mind, echoing words dissolved into soundless laughter.

Julian hesitated and pulled away. "I cannot, I am afraid," he whispered, suddenly cowed and confused.

Panic gripped me, the beast took on more life with each passing moment. "But you must, my friend!" I said and my voice resounded into the air. "If you and I are ever to find peace you must take that step now!"

Then the beast was real and staring eagerly upon the scene, its lipless mouth drawn into a hideous smile and drool dripped venomously into the air. I dragged my eyes away from the solidifying apparition and they fell upon the knife on the altar. I reached out a hand and took it up almost unconsciously, my only thought now was to finish what we had begun. For if we did not then surely the beast would be upon us and all that we had planned would end in failure.

I stepped forward so we were together and took Julian into a close embrace, rather to keep him from pulling away than anything else, for my mind had lost all sense of our work, and was shocked numb from the horror growing above. "Forgive me, Julian, it is the only way!" I called and raised the dagger. A shriek echoed around the temple, its source was not of the real world and a scaled claw reached from out of the cloud to grasp at my upraised arm. I closed my eyes on the horror and whispered a mindless prayer, then plunged the dagger down through brittle bone and into where I knew it would take the ancient vampire's heart away.

The shriek grew loud, growing and multiplying into savage laughter. Julian's body fell limp against me and then slumped into a pillow of black cloth on the floor. The knife fell after him and I stepped back from the growing furore.

The black robe lay mute and empty as laughter rang out around me. This was wrong, not what we had planned. I was still alive, even though the father of my breed had died. Tiberias had been wrong! For all the signs had proven to us that the race of vampire kind would end with the end of its ancient maker, we had been terribly, terribly wrong!

The sound was deafening, I clamped my hands futilely to my ears but the laughter was inside my head as well, and its power lay me cringing and weak on the floor. Then an instant of utter silence tortured, my hearing strained in agony and cold blood trickled down each cheek.

"Vampire," the word came from nowhere, yet it invaded every pore in my being. "How fortunate that you are here to maintain the legacy that I have bestowed."

I cried out in pain, words wrenched from my lips before my aching mind could hold them, "What do you mean?"

"Ahh," he sighed and the sound echoed cold around the room, "I have carried you through lifetimes, foolish one. I have guided you to become my most treasured possession. Your eternal damnation is my nourishment, each of your frail incarnations brings you ever closer to me." His awful voice rose into a tornado and lashed at the air with its fury. "And now you take your own life once more. I cannot be cheated by the impotent machinations of your small magic, I am Lord of Darkness and indeed nothing you can devise is a match for the powers that I command. It is by my influence alone, the incarnations that you have lived. My glory the fearful darkness into which you have fallen and I delight in your misfortune. But see, foolish one, what will become of you when you invoke the depths of my power over you! Watch as I corrupt you beyond even the petty lifetimes that you have known and recreate you, an eternal abomination, my cherished son!"

With each word I cringed, condemned on the floor, each syllable uttered took my soul unerring into the coldest depths of hell and for the first and most desolate time, I understood the pain that Julian had carried for all those years. My heart turned into stone and my eyes became endless wells of lost light. A scaly claw reached out once again and the beast advanced upon me, fetid and dripping, his foul mouth open and greedy, and I screamed as I was devoured.